Ageless Love

ABOUT THE AUTHORS

BRENDA KNIGHT GRAHAM grew up in the foothills of the Blue Ridge Mountains in northeast Georgia and now lives with her family in the farming district of southwest Georgia. Though her life is centered around her husband's busy veterinary practice and the many activities of her two children, Brenda finds time to play folk harmonica and to speak to civic groups and children's classes. She also enjoys making jams and jellies from homegrown fruits. She is an active member in her church.

SANDY DENGLER and her husband didn't know what they were starting when they purchased a model kit of the clipper Cutty Sark. Over a dozen ship models now sit about their home in Ashford, Washington, and their two daughters—one, a marine biologist; the other, a sailing enthusiast—have come to share their parents' pleasure for things nautical. Sandy's zeal for history, geography, and the sea is tempered by a strong tendency toward seasickness. Ships are romantic so long as they are firmly attached to a dock!

JANE PEART is a native of North Carolina and deeply rooted in her beloved Southland. She is a prolific writer and has published widely. Her current series include "The Brides of Montclair," "Westward Dreams," and "American Quilts." Jane resides with her husband in Fortuna, California. They are the parents of two grown daughters who share their enthusiasm for the arts.

Historical
Romance
COLLECTION

Ageless
Love

VOLUME 2

Juliana of Clover Hill
Brenda Knight Graham

The Song of the Nereids
Sandy Dengler

Ransomed Bride
Jane Peart

ZondervanPublishingHouse
Grand Rapids, Michigan

A Division of HarperCollins*Publishers*

Ageless Love Volume 2
Copyright © 1996 by ZondervanPublishingHouse

Juliana of Clover Hill
Copyright © 1984 by Brenda Knight Graham

The Song of the Nereids
Copyright © 1984 by Sandy Dengler

Ransomed Bride
Copyright © 1985 by Jane Peart

Requests for information should be addressed to:
⚒ ZondervanPublishingHouse
Grand Rapids, Michigan 49530

ISBN: 0-310-20956-0

This edition printed on acid-free paper and meets the American National Standards Institute Z39.48 standard.

Printed in the United States of America

96 97 98 99 00 01 02 /❖ DH/ 10 9 8 7 6 5 4 3 2 1

Juliana of Clover Hill

Brenda Knight Graham

This book is lovingly dedicated
to the memory of
my father
F. S. Knight

ACKNOWLEDGMENTS

I hesitate to make any written acknowledgments for fear I will leave someone out, but I hesitate even more to make no acknowledgments when certain ones have helped so much to make this book possible.

My husband, Charles Graham, must be at the head of this list because of his all-round patience, encouragement, and enthusiasm. My mother, Eula Gibbs Knight, was my main source of information. She never once exclaimed, "You already asked me that!" or "Can't you just leave me alone!" I would like to say a special thanks, too, to my children, William and Julie, for their understanding.

Burns Gibbs, the late Hugh Gibbs, and Emma Berrong gave invaluable help contributing to the background information. Hamilton Gibbs kindly allowed me free range on Clover Hill which he now owns. Stanley Knight, Pat Peck and Jackie Eastham gave me much constructive criticism. Revonda and Marcus Barwick saved my sanity by arranging a secluded spot where I could type, uninterrupted by the telephone.

Helping me with a background reading list were Barbara Williams and her daughter Linda Kay of Cairo's Roddenbery Memorial Library. I appreciate also the help of Virginia Tyre of The Northeast Georgia Regional Library in Clarkesville, Georgia and Darrell Terrell of Kent State University.

Lastly, I must say thanks to my friend Ruth Davis who took over another assignment so that I could be free to spend time on *Juliana*.

CHAPTER 1

JULIANA COULD TELL BY THE tracks in the mud, even
before she pulled open the mailbox door, that the
mail carrier had finally come. Since he'd started
driving a car instead of his faithful horse, one could
never be sure when he would arrive. Henry, Juliana's
farmer brother, wanted a tractor, but not a car. Even
now in 1919, when so many people owned cars that
they were demanding the roads be improved so they
wouldn't have to dart around treacherous wagon ruts,
Henry still said he preferred his horse Maude with
her sensitive response to his every word. Juliana
smiled as she stepped across the ribby track. She
would rather have Maude, too; she didn't make
nearly as much noise.

As she pulled out the mail, being careful to keep it
secure in the roll of Papa's paper so nothing would fall
in the mud, she could hear again as if she weren't half
a mile away now, Mamma saying, "Juliana, why *must*

7

you go for the mail now before dinner? What are you expecting?''

What, indeed, was she expecting? How could she explain that she had no earthly idea—that she was just expecting Something to Happen. At fifteen her whole body ached with awareness—the songs of wood thrush, warbler, and mockingbird, the stirring of a warm breeze that dipped up under her wide hat and brushed her hot cheeks, the crackling of seed pods exploding in the August heat along the roadside, the steamy green smell of last night's rain evaporating from dogwood, pine, and rich acres of corn. Sometimes she wished intensely to know what she was expecting, what was out there beyond hoeing corn, feeding chickens, churning, scrubbing floors on Saturday, and going to church on Sunday. At other times it simply didn't matter; knowing there *was* Something was enough.

Juliana skillfully avoided all the mud puddles, though her eyes seemed wholly occupied with studying each piece of mail. She hefted a letter from Richard's wife Frances to Mamma—a stiff thick letter. Perhaps it had a picture of Baby Jack in it. Of her three nieces and nephews, Baby Jack was the youngest and nearest, living in Clarkesville where her brother Richard was a banker. There was a post card from Brother in his own scratchy handwriting. His name was Calvin, but everyone, including Mamma, called him Brother. He liked his church in Nacoochee and was looking forward to teaching as well as preaching when school began in the fall. His wife Winnie and the two children were fine.

She stopped to look at the next one addressed to Mrs. Grange Neal. Why, oh, why had Grange married Molly? She might not be so dull and boring if she weren't always sick, but she was always sick. That's why she was spending the summer at Clover Hill while Grange worked in Atlanta. Mamma had said if Papa were still here, he would want them all to care for Grange's sick wife. Anyway, Mama herself would never turn down an opportunity to help someone. In the case of Molly, Juliana couldn't help wishing sometimes that Mamma wasn't so soft-hearted.

It was not that she was jealous of Molly, for, after all, Grange was much too old for Juliana to consider romantically. He must be at least twenty-five by now! No, it was just that Grange was a special friend of the whole family, and it was disappointing to see him tied to someone so unimaginative. Oh, Grange wasn't sorry for himself. One would never know he was unhappy by the way he joked and teased, but she knew he must be.

Her lips curved up in a gentle smile in the shadow of her hat as she remembered the first present Grange had given her: blue hair ribbons to wear for her first day of school in Cornelia. "To match your eyes," he'd said, giving her hair a teasing jerk. She looked at her hair now where it had fallen forward down over her calico dress, and she pushed the blond masses back over her shoulder with one hand as she walked on.

She rubbed her finger back and forth over Papa's name on the paper, thinking how strange that Papa was not here anymore, that the Atlanta Constitution still came to L. B. Hamilton, though he was over in

9

Level Grove Cemetery. It seemed so unfair that the essence of Papa was gone—his commanding voice, the rough hands that ran the sawmill and brought Mamma the first clump of violets in the spring, his lively interest in all that was happening in the world—while the house he had built and the dairy and the fields he had plowed were still here.

While thousands were dying as victims of the war or flu, Papa died with an ulcerated stomach. He kept on working at the farm, optimistically expecting good news from Europe, until a short week before he died. Then, in October, with the churches and schools officially closed as the flu epidemic took its toll, he was buried in the cemetery. Mamma said she believed Papa knew that Henry came home safely without being sent to Europe and that Papa was alive in heaven, not in the cemetery.

Juliana glanced ahead at the shafts of sunshine falling through the trees, glancing off the puddles in the road, shifting between leafy shadows in front of her—lively, reaching, *touching* sunshine. Was Papa still somewhere? She could say she believed with Mamma, but down deep inside she wasn't at all sure.

The war itself had been no worse than the flu epidemic, which had taken one from nearly every family in their small church. She still shuddered at the memory of seeing Sister so sick, of the small children whom Mamma bathed and prepared for burial, of the day when even Mamma herself had become deathly ill. There had been times when she and her next older brother Byron had not known whether anyone else in the family would survive. They had worked side by side at Clover Hill, even hauling hay all one night to keep the rain from spoiling it. There had been no Christmas that year. Only she and Byron were well enough to do anything, and they had baked a cake. But because of the sugar rationing, it had to be made with honey. There weren't enough eggs or butter, either, because of all they were required to turn in for government use. It took every shred of imagination to make that cake palatable.

Maybe it was because of the dread and horror of last year that this year was so full of life until her fingertips even tingled with excitement over absolutely nothing. The prospect of school in September was challenging, yet she felt she could never be happier than when she was roaming the woods and pastures of Clover Hill. To find a tiger lily blooming in an opening between the pines, like a queen in her throne room, was a big event. But there was something much, much bigger coming somehow—and soon—even though the mail held no hint of what it might be.

Hearing Byron call her name, she suddenly remembered Mamma was waiting dinner for her. Like a deer newly aware of curious onlookers invading its private world, she sped along the winding woods road, arriving at the porch steps out of breath, her cheeks pink with heat and exertion.

Molly was rocking on the porch, just barely pushing her thick body enough to make the straw-bottomed rocker squeak. She hardly even blinked as Juliana dropped Grange's letter in her lap.

"Come now, dinner is ready. Whatever took you so long?" asked Sister as Juliana hung her hat on a nail by the door. Sister, whose real name was Emily, understood many things, but she couldn't understand anyone's being late for dinner unless the cows were out or the barn was on fire.

"Just—looking," answered Juliana.

"Well, it's most upsetting. There was Byron supposed to be cleaning the barn, but reading a book instead, and Henry taking his own long time coming in from the field. At least we should only have to wait on the men. There's no excuse for you. . . ."

"Now, now, Sister," said Mamma. "We're all here, except—Molly," she directed her voice through the screen door. "Please come to dinner, Molly. You can read your letter afterwards. It'll keep."

Mamma calmly eased herself into her chair, letting out a little sigh of relief for the chance to rest a minute. Then, seeing Sister impatiently pacing, she smiled and motioned her to sit down, too. "No use fuming, Sister," she said, the tiny wrinkles crinkling around her eyes.

Juliana ran some water into the wash bowl in the kitchen and bathed her face, delighting in the coolness of the well water. She knew she had plenty of time to wash up while Molly lumbered to the table. But Sister called out in exasperation. "Juliana! Do come on! You're going to spend half your life primping and preening."

"Oh, leave her alone," said Henry, already seated in Papa's chair at the table. "Sister, you're so insistent that women should be allowed to vote, but you're not being fair to the women in your own household."

Sister's only answer was a quick glance as she

tucked a stray strand of hair behind her ear and bit her lip.

"Come now, everyone," said Mamma. "Help Molly with her chair, Byron."

Whether it was Byron's face peering solemnly over the top of Molly's head, or the way Molly grabbed a biscuit the instant she was seated as if they might all disappear, or whether the tension-filled atmosphere demanded release, when Juliana caught Sister's eye, the two of them seemed to explode with laughter, all ill will forgotten between them.

It had always been so during mealtime at Clover Hill: either Sister and Byron, or Sister and Juliana, or all three going into spasms of giggling. There had been times when Papa had even sent them outside until they could gain control. Not that he was against laughing, but he did not feel the place for hysterics was at the dinner table. Even now it was the memory of Papa's stern blue gaze that caused the girls to choke down their giggles as Henry bowed his head over his gripped brown hands and said grace.

Henry had come back from his stint in the army sobered, thin, and white from a long siege of the dreaded flu. He had tackled the farm work courageously as Papa had trained him to do. Juliana, the faithful water girl, had come upon him muttering to the horses. She knew then he had wanted to go out west, that he had even been bitterly disappointed when the flu kept him from being shipped to Europe. She knew that he shared her love of Clover Hill, yet felt imprisoned by it.

Since eighth grade he had stayed home to work the

farm rather than go to school with the others. Whether it was because he was exceptionally adept with tools and horses, or because the other boys were exceptionally good at their books, it was hard to say. Anyway, he'd always said one of them had to stay at home and work. Fair or not, Henry was chosen. Mamma had pled for him at times, but it had done no good. As determined as Papa was that the others stay in school and learn every bit they could, he was just as determined that Henry should be the farmer. "There has to be one in every family," he said. "Take away the farm, and how will the nation eat?"

Clover Hill House, set among a stand of oaks, was shaped like an ell instead of being square as most farmhouses were. Juliana was glad it was different. Actually the house had somehow grown with the family, as Burns Hamilton could spare lumber from his mill and time from his farming and thinking up new inventions. The first little two-room house was on the property when Burns came to take over the farm from his father. Instead of building onto it, he had built another two-room house beside the first.

Finally, one summer, he had connected them with two more rooms in the middle. Mamma was in Commerce at that time, nursing Byron after an appendectomy. Juliana remembered how Papa and the boys had worked from dawn till dark to finish the rooms before Mamma came home. He was so proud to show her the new addition he almost snapped his suspenders.

Each room, except the kitchen, had been used at one time as a bedroom. The house was adequate, if not spacious, for raising six children. Mamma had hooked rugs, crocheted and tatted bedspreads and chair throws—beautiful things that could have graced the governor's mansion. She had always been proud of the hardwood floors, standing back after a weekly scrubbing to admire them and say, "Thank God for pretty windows and floors." It didn't matter that the level of the three sets of floors didn't quite meet. That gave the house character. Though she must have been exasperated at times with Papa's zeal for creating inventions that somehow never made it to the patent office, Mamma always displayed only pride in being married to the man who was the first to grow winter grass in Habersham County, Georgia.

After dinner Henry stayed at the table reading the *Constitution,* now and then commenting on the news. Mamma read her letter and card out loud to them, while Molly labored over her own letter. Juliana squirmed, wishing she could grab it and find out quickly what Grange had said. Just as she and Sister were beginning to stack the heavy white plates, Molly commented as if it were everyday news, "Grange wants Byron to go with us over to Clarkesville for Sunday dinner."

"Sunday dinner?" asked Mamma, suddenly curious.

"With Mr. Kirk and his old maid aunt.

"Don't you think *spinster* sounds better, Molly? Anyway, who is Mr. Kirk?"

"You don't know?" Molly raised her eyebrows in as much surprise as she ever showed.

"No," said Mamma.

"He's an artist." Molly reached for another biscuit

15

and leaned back to eat it, spilling crumbs in her lap.

"What kind of artist?" asked Mamma.

Molly finished the biscuit and dusted crumbs onto the floor before she answered. "A proud one." She said, "Every girl in Atlanta would like to marry him, but I never saw what they liked about him. He may be good-looking and tall, but he is—well, he's stuck up."

"I think Mamma meant what kind of pictures does he paint," smiled Sister, threatening to burst into giggles again.

"Oh—that. He does pictures of mountains, waterfalls, trees. Grange seems to think Byron would like to see them."

"Grange has always been so thoughtful. Well, Byron, what do you think?" asked Mamma.

Byron seemed even younger than his seventeen years when he looked up from studying his fork as if he'd never seen it before. "I appreciate the invitation, but I couldn't go—that is, not unless Juliana goes, too," he stumbled.

"But I—" began Juliana, then stopped as she recognized her brother's pleading look. The two of them had always shared personal problems, and she realized it was Byron's innate shyness that was behind the invitation, not his overwhelming desire for her to meet the artist, too. "I would like to go," she said, watching Molly's face for her reaction. She looked at Juliana quickly, a look of wariness in her eyes, as if a hidden thought had been discovered and exposed.

"Only Byron was invited," said Molly bluntly.

"That's true. So only Byron will go," said

Mamma, standing up and pushing her chair to the table. "Grange knows Byron is very interested in poetry and art."

"But I am, too," said Juliana impulsively, and then blushed as Mamma gave her a hard look. She hadn't meant to beg. She was only trying to help Byron out.

"I don't think either of you needs to go," said Henry, laying his paper down and pushing his chair back. "Neither one of you ought to miss church."

"But, Henry, you said yourself we depend too much on ritual," said Sister. "This would be an opportunity for Byron to broaden his horizons."

"If Byron has already decided to be a minister, then he need not consider the arts."

"Henry, how very narrow-minded of you!" said Sister, her face reddening.

"I didn't make the decision—he did," said Henry, taking his hat from its nail as he started out the door.

"You know that's not what I mean!"

Henry grinned, shrugged his shoulders, and walked out. "Oh, that boy!" exclaimed Sister, twisting a tea cloth in her hands until Mamma calmly took it from her and smoothed it out on the table.

From Wednesday until Friday the subject of visiting the artist was discussed and rediscussed until Juliana had developed a great interest in seeing him for herself, not just on Byron's account. She was very curious about this Mr. Kirk for whom, Molly said, girls primped for hours, only to have him pay them no heed at all. "A proud man," Molly kept saying. "Talented, but, oh so proud!"

On Friday Grange came, and, in only a few minutes

17

punctuated with explosions of his deep laughter, he had convinced Mamma that both the young people should make the trip. "I've met Foster's Aunt De and I'm quite sure she won't mind having Juliana along."

"But isn't there a phone? Couldn't we call and ask?"

Grange threw back his head and laughed heartily. "A phone? Foster Kirk with a phone! It would be preposterous. Mamma Hamilton, you don't seem to understand. Foster Kirk is a real artist and one I predict will become famous nationwide one day. But like other artists he only welcomes intrusion when he asks for it. A telephone! Never!"

"But what is he really like, Grange?"

"Oh, you have nothing to worry about concerning his character."

"But you said he was like other artists, and—well, I've heard so much . . ."

"Foster Kirk has been called stuck-up because he won't even accept a social drink."

"Grange, if you don't mind my asking," said Henry, "just how did you meet this man? I know you like art and music, but . . ."

"I met him in a men's Sunday school class. He and I had the reputation for being—what shall I say?— troublemakers. Because we asked too many questions, probably. Actually, I think Mr. Keller, our teacher, really welcomed our—discussions. Otherwise, Foster would have certainly found another class."

"In other words, you argued," said Henry, an amused smile playing on his lips.

"Some would call it that. We called it questioning

18

before belief. I will say this about Foster," said Grange, stretching out his lanky legs and clasping his hands behind his head. "Foster has a much harder head than I, yet a keen sensitivity to go along with it. He would no more accept a statement without challenging its truth than he would attempt to capture on his canvas something he had not seen. Truth is the guiding force of his life."

Juliana, her chin cupped in her hands, listened with interest, her eyes fastened on Grange's face. She was eager to glean every bit of information she could about this stranger she was soon to meet.

From under half-closed eyelids, Molly was watching Juliana.

CHAPTER 2

MOLLY'S EYES LOOKED somber, Juliana thought, as they started out that Sunday morning. For one beginning a rare outing, she didn't look very happy, even though she had Grange at her side.

Henry complained as he drove them in the surrey to meet the train. "Shouldn't be traveling on Sunday. Could have picked some other day if you had to go on such a jaunt." But just the same he lifted his hat as they boarded the train, a sign of grudging good will.

Byron and Juliana sat together in the train, across the aisle from Grange and Molly. The car was full of people going to Tallulah Falls for the day. At least that's where Juliana assumed they were going in their pretty straw hats with their picnic baskets at their feet. It was a popular place with Atlanta people in the summer. If they had been going to Clarkesville to stay in one of the hotels or to Tiger to spend the summer in one of the quaint little mountain cottages, they would have their suitcases with them. Tallulah Falls drew hundreds of people just to spend a few hours viewing the spectacular gorge that some, who had seen both, said was prettier than the Grand Canyon.

Clarkesville had two fine hotels, one of which Clover Hill had supplied with milk back when it had been a thriving dairy instead of an all-around farm as it was now, with apples as its main cash crop. Juliana remembered riding with Richard to deliver milk once when she was quite small. The only other time she had been to Clarkesville was when Papa had brought the whole family to the "A and M School" to see a farm exhibit. It had been an all-day excursion with the most significant memory for Juliana being the model of a farm with tiny horses, little houses and barn, wagons, even detailed miniature plows and bales of hay. Papa had spent all his time looking at a tractor and then had talked all the way home about what it could do.

"We won't go into Clarkesville," said Grange, leaning across the aisle to speak to Byron. "We stop at Hill's Crossing on the other side of town. It's a stone's throw from the back of Foster Kirk's place."

"How far is it now?" asked Juliana.

Grange looked out the window, then pulled his watch out of his pocket. "I'd say maybe seven minutes—depending on how long we're held up at the Clarkesville station."

"That close?" asked Byron.

Grange laughed and slapped Byron on the arm. "Now, Byron, loosen up, old boy. Foster Kirk is just a plain guy. He'll expect no fancy talk."

21

"What about talk of any kind?" whispered Byron to Juliana.

"Maybe we could just forget to get off and go on to Tallulah Falls for the day," said Juliana wistfully, picking at the eyelet ruffle on a puffed sleeve of her blue gingham dress. She knew as well as Byron that they must be nice to Grange's friends, but nothing would have pleased them more than to be allowed to go on to Tallulah.

The stop in Clarkesville was not long enough and shortly Grange was getting up, helping Molly out of her seat, and saying cheerfully, "Come on, troops, this is it."

In a sudden panic Juliana wondered why she had ever agreed to accompany Byron. Byron could have just stayed at home if he were too shy to visit without her. Suppose she really wasn't welcome? How utterly embarrassing it would be!

As they went down the steps, Byron pushing her ahead of him—not solely from gentlemanly behavior—she caught a glimpse of the man who must be Foster Kirk. He was squeezing Grange's hand and smiling at Molly. She had time to notice that he was tall and dressed in neat khakis.

Then, as Grange said something to him, Mr. Kirk glanced up at her. For a moment her heart seemed to stop completely. She lost awareness of the conductor's hand under her elbow, of the buzzing crowd of passengers, of Grange and Molly looking up at her quizzically, of Byron crushing the brim of his hat in his hands behind her. Foster Kirk's eyes held hers for an eternal moment—laughing, serious, questioning eyes.

22

She could not look away. If it were possible for someone to scowl and smile at the same time, he was doing
it, and his dark mustache twitched just slightly. Why
did it seem as if she'd seen him before, and as if he
were teasing her about it?

Then, like frozen characters come back to life,
everyone was real again. Pink and flustered, Juliana
lowered her eyes under her blue straw hat and watched
her own feet carefully as she stepped to the ground.

As the train puffed away, Foster Kirk directed them
to a small path through a field of broom sedge. "It will
be cool when we reach the shade of the trees," he
assured them, observing how Molly was already
panting.

"I do hope you don't mind our bringing Juliana
along," said Molly between puffs. "She so wanted to
come. I didn't think it was a good idea, but . . ."

"It was a very good idea," said Mr. Kirk. "My
aunt will be delighted. She has an enormous meal
prepared."

He spoke so positively that Molly could say no
more. Byron nudged Juliana's arm and grinned at her.
"Poor Molly," he whispered in mock sadness.

It was cooler in the woods as Mr. Kirk had promised, and the brother and sister bringing up the rear of
the little parade took time to observe everything—a
vireo's nest hung like a tiny hammock between twigs
of a dogwood tree, an array of bright orange flowers
that reminded Juliana of mounds of grated carrot when
Mamma was making carrot pudding, small huckleberry bushes with a stray berry or two still clinging
to them, and all along the trail, tall pines under which

stretched a thick carpet of brown needles.

"My mother named the place Pinedale," Mr. Kirk was saying. "Though this isn't part of the original homestead, it's very like it. Many, many pines. And here is where I'd like to build a home someday," he said, stopping and directing their attention with a wave of his hand to an opening in the timber on top of a hill. One could see mountains in two different directions. Juliana spied a tiny maple with protective stakes around it.

"It's about time you let us rest," gasped Molly, hanging on Grange's arm. "You and your long legs will have us all exhausted."

Mr. Kirk didn't even seem to notice Molly. "From here you can see Trey Mountain to the northwest and Yonah to the west. I've been keeping the trees trimmed so these views would stay open. I think it's almost as important what you can see from a house as what the house is like itself. But there is good clay here, too, with underlying rock—a solid foundation."

"You sound as if you have plans," said Grange.

"I always have plans," said Mr. Kirk with a laugh. "Not that they always work out."

"It truly is beautiful," breathed Byron, and Juliana knew he was finally glad he'd come. Her own lips parted in pleasure at the view of the distant blue mountains speared by nearby pine. The blue was like no other blue she had ever seen. Not like robins' eggs or the bluest of asters or forget-me-nots. Not even like the sky.

"Well, come now," said Mr. Kirk briskly, starting down the hill. "The two little houses you'll see in a minute are part of the original homestead. The smaller one was built in 1888 by my father, and the other one later, as he needed to divide his own growing family from his in-laws. I use the little one now for my studio, and Aunt De keeps the cottage going.''

"Foster, did you ever tell us what happened to your mother?'' asked Molly.

Juliana was suddenly aware of the muffled sound of their footsteps on the pine needles, and of the clear distinct call of a mourning dove. Ahead of her she saw Mr. Kirk's hands clenched together behind him. After a bit he replied, his words clipped, "My mother died of tuberculosis when I was thirteen.''

"And your father?''

"Molly—really, dear,'' began Grange.

"It's all right, Grange. My father and sister live in Chicago.''

"But wouldn't that be a good place for an artist to live, too?''

Again there was a pause. Molly's labored breathing sounded like the horses after they'd plowed Long Bottom all morning. Juliana wished she would just breathe and stop giving her third-degree examination, although she herself listened closely for the answer.

"It would be a good place to live, I suppose, if that were where one wanted to live. I lived there while I attended the art institute. But for me there could never be any place but Pinedale. And I could spend the rest of my days here and barely scratch the surface of all the subjects there are to paint.''

As they came in sight of the quaint gray buildings, nestled in a valley not much bigger than the houses themselves, Juliana had another seizure of panic. Now she must meet the aunt who was not expecting her and might well resent her presence at the dinner table. There was smoke rising from the chimney of the larger house where they would be eating. She prayed fervently that there would not be fried chicken or anything messy. She could see herself with an awkward piece of chicken in her lap and the laughing eyes of this inquisitive artist fixed on her.

Miss Delia Sweet was tall, angular, her lips thinly pressed into a polite smile, her hand hard and cool as she shook Juliana's sweaty one. Juliana could not be at all sure she didn't mind the extra guest, even though there certainly was plenty to eat.

But there was no fried chicken. Instead, there was beef roast sliced so thin you could almost see through it—if it weren't drowned in the most delicious brown gravy Juliana had ever tasted. There were potatoes cooked in a white sauce, and green beans that were a pretty color, but didn't taste like Mamma's, which she simmered for hours with a chunk of hog jowl.

Everything was served on thin china bordered with a delicate wreath of flowers, nothing like the thick practical dishes at Clover Hill. But Juliana noticed, too, the many chips on the edges and the tiny dark cracks sprayed out in all directions like granny faces.

However, there was one very distasteful dish. When Molly passed Juliana a bowl containing something brown and slimy-looking, she took only a tiny portion. Miss Sweet noticed her doubtful expression and exclaimed, ''The child has never eaten mushrooms! Come now, take more than that.'' She reached across

Byron to spoon more onto her plate. It was all Juliana could do to eat the slick slices that reminded her of garden slugs cut into bite-sized pieces. Byron whispered to her once that he would eat them, that they were really good, but she felt Miss Sweet's eyes on her and, oddly, she was determined to eat those mushrooms, no matter what.

As she ate she felt a cat rub against her legs, then another and another. Her curiosity finally got the best of her and she looked under the table, counting quickly four—no, five—cats. She wanted very much to ask how many cats belonged to this household, but everyone was involved in a conversation about Woodrow Wilson's dreams for the League of Nations. Even Byron was talking now. All that reading he'd done was paying off, and he was sounding every bit as informed as the older men. Juliana swelled with pride and couldn't wait to tell Mamma that Byron had done just fine.

"Foster, I just can't understand your animosity toward Wilson and the League," said Grange. "I know you want peace as much as anyone."

"Peace, yes! True peace, though, not a lid over a boiling cauldron. I agree, it sounds perfect—the League of Nations, I mean. Heads of state meeting, agreeing, and working out all their differences over a table, then policing each others' actions. But I just don't believe it will work. Wilson is trying to create a peace that can't be realized until the Lord returns."

"Well, I'm all for it, and I hope Congress approves the United States' joining. We'll soon know, I guess, for they're considering it right now."

Foster scoffed as he laid his napkin down untidily by his plate and turned fully toward Grange, a sharp intensity in his face. "We'll just be jumping into an on-going squabble if we join. It's unrealistic and stupid!"

Byron blinked in surprise, then said hesitantly, "But, sir, don't you think we must make every effort to avoid another war?"

"I think," said Foster, emphasizing his words with sharp stabs of his fork, "I think the disagreements evolving from the League could very well *cause* another war."

All this time Juliana had been trying to finish her mushrooms, and now, having finally swallowed the last slick blob, began to apply herself to a small, dainty dish of peaches and cream. She thought everyone else was absorbed in Wilson and the League and started visibly when Foster exclaimed, "Aunt De! She liked our mushrooms! Here, have some more, Juliana. They're quite good for you. Pinedale grows an abundance of several kinds. These are boleta."

"You mean—" Her hand shook as she laid the serving spoon down. "You picked these—here on your place?"

"Of course. Oh, don't worry," he said with a sudden laugh as he realized her concern. "They're not poisonous. I know how to be sure about that. I break a piece off and, if it turns blue, it's poisonous. Or I test it with my tongue. If it's bitter at all, we know not to use it. This is a very good little mushroom. Since the weather has been warm and rainy, they've popped up all over the woods."

28

That time she could not eat all the mushrooms, and she felt Aunt De's watchful gaze on her.

"Clean your plate, Juliana!" said Molly in a loud whisper, but as she turned pale at the thought, Miss Sweet said casually, "Oh, don't worry her. I'll add it to Beppo's dish. That dog will eat anything."

Though she was relieved, Juliana felt thoroughly ridiculed for her finicky stomach, and very provoked with Mr. Foster Kirk for the way he kept looking at her even when he was talking to someone else.

After dinner Mr. Kirk showed them his paintings in the studio. Juliana stood perfectly still in front of one, arrested by the mood of the mountain scene. How had he achieved that magnificant blue, the very blue of the mountains? It made her soul throb, which was the only way she knew to describe it to Mamma later. Here was that familiar ache in her when she saw something so beautiful that it seemed she should do something about it.

While the others were discussing the paintings, Juliana looked around the small room. It was orderly, but not immaculate. It seemed natural to find two or three apple cores in the window sill, and bark scattered from an armful of firewood stacked behind the small heater. There was something very comfortable about the overflowing bookshelves and stacks of *National Geographics* on the floor. A blue-and-white porcelain washbowl and pitcher with matching soap dish had been placed on a low marble-topped stand. Again, millions of tiny cracks declared them heirlooms. There was the smell of soap mingled with old ashes, rich pine splinters, and a musty damp cushion smell as if maybe the doors had been left open all night. She glanced into the next room where she could see a desk and the quilted corner of a bed.

"Juliana!" spoke Molly so sharply that she jumped. "Don't stare so. Don't you know it's terribly impolite?"

"I'm—I'm sorry," said Juliana in humiliation. She lowered her eyes and hoped everyone would ignore her, but she felt herself being observed and her cheeks stained hotly crimson.

"She was just interested," said Grange quietly.

"One can show interest without being rude," snapped Molly.

"It really is quite all right," said Mr. Kirk. "I'd like to know what the lady thinks of what she sees."

Juliana was touched by his kindness. He had called her a lady after Molly's humiliating remark. But what *did* she think? What could she say? Everyone was so quiet. Why didn't someone else say something? Then, gratefully, she felt the furry, friendly rub of a kitten at her ankle, and she bent and scooped up a ball of gray that purred against her neck.

"I think your paintings are real," she said, looking at Mr. Kirk confidently. "They're beautiful and they're real, not like pictures at all, more like —poetry."

"Well done, Juliana!" exclaimed Grange, impulsively squeezing her shoulders.

"But how did you ever get that shade of blue?" asked Juliana, emboldened by the kitten's purr and Grange's encouraging hug.

Mr. Kirk looked from her to Grange to Molly, then stepped to his easel and picked up a bit of chalk.

Rubbing it between his thumb and finger, he said, "Just dust really, as all the colors are. Of course I have to mix colors to get the particular effect I'm after. And have you ever noticed how the blue of the mountains is different at different times of the day or year?" He paused as if he expected her to answer, then plunged on. "Somehow one has to be able to see more colors in the subject than usually meets the naked eye. For instance, blues are purplish, pinkish, greenish, cobalt. But I am telling you more than you want to know, I suppose. Here, would you like to feel the medium I use?"

Byron and Juliana each felt the dusty chalk and, at Mr. Kirk's insistence, made small timid strokes on one corner of the sandpaper pinned to the easel.

"Now I'll have your marks in my next picture," said Foster Kirk, and his smile relieved the gauntness of his face and erased momentarily the scowl that lurked around his brow.

"Come now, folks, let's sit on the porch at the cottage," said Miss Sweet. "It's cooler and more comfortable there."

The porch was a wonderful place, shaded by a big persimmon tree whose branches were loaded with ripening fruit. Grange tried his best to get Juliana to try one, but Juliana assured him she knew about persimmons—that she, like a possum, knew when they were best for eating. Mr. Kirk had taken Byron to see his rock collection and returned to the porch just in time to see Juliana playfully hitting Grange with a green persimmon. "I see we've been missing all the fun," he said to Byron.

"You see what you're missing by not having children?" asked Grange, twisting a lock of Juliana's hair around one finger. You really should consider marriage, Foster."

"Yes, indeed, there are any number of ladies desiring to get to know you," said Molly primly.

"None that could put up with his sour ways," declared Miss Sweet, stroking a yellow cat in her lap, the gentleness in her fingers defying the severity of her tight hairdo and her sharp nose.

"That's my loyal aunt for you," said Mr. Kirk with a chuckle, propping one foot up on the stone wall. "Tell me again, Grange, how was it you became such a part of this family—the Hamiltons, is it?"

Grange gave Juliana a gentle shove and sat down beside her in the swing. "I was running away from home and from Georgia Tech," he said, tossing the green persimmon back and forth from hand to hand. "By chance, or by eternal plan, I visited a small Presbyterian church in Cornelia where these wonderful people spied me quickly as a lonesome stranger and took me in. They fed me, worked me, and helped me put the pieces of my life together. Ever since, I have been pestered by this ornery child who, being the youngest of the six, is quite a spoiled brat."

Grange rumpled the back of Juliana's hair as he spoke, causing Juliana to respond with some spirit, even to the point of slapping at his face, but he caught her hand before it made contact and held it tightly.

"I think it's time we started back to meet the train if we don't want to get left," said Molly, frowning at Grange significantly.

32

"So it is now," said Grange, looking at the angle of the sun as it laid bars across the board floor. He stood and stretched. "Well, it's been wonderful, old chap. You must have dinner with us when you're back in Atlanta. A most delicious meal you prepared, Miss Sweet," he said to that lady who dusted cat hairs from her hands before shaking his own. "It was Yankee cooking at its best," he said gallantly.

"Yankee, indeed! We're as southern as you are, Grange Neal!" .

They were starting up the path when Juliana suddenly remembered her hat. "I'll get it for you," said Mr. Kirk and, before Molly had lumbered up the steep terrace, he was back, spinning the hat around on one finger, the blue ribbons shimmering in the sunlight.

"Thank you," said Juliana, smiling up at him, then quickly tying the ribbons under her chin, glad for the shield against the sun—and his searching eyes. Why was it her arms prickled with as much excitement as when she found the first trillium of spring? As she walked on she told herself that when she was alone she would have to try to figure out why it seemed as if she'd seen Mr. Kirk before.

Much later, as Henry drove them home from the train station, clucking affectionately to Maude, Juliana asked curiously, "Grange, how old is Mr. Kirk?"

Grange turned toward her and spoke sharply, all the laughter gone from his eyes. "And why, may I ask, should Foster Kirk's age matter to you?"

CHAPTER 3

CLOVER HILL HAD SOME absolutely magical spots—at least it had always seemed so to Juliana. One she had outgrown now was a tulip tree that leaned far out over Long Bottom Field. Though it shaded the corn, Papa had managed to leave it every year when he cut trees, clearing more new ground. He never really explained why he left it, but secretly they both knew it was so she could continue to climb its smooth gray trunk and perch with her dolls up over the field to watch the men at their work.

Another place she and Byron had always enjoyed was what they playfully called the Potomac River. It was really a bubbling creek that spilled over wide rocks, or around them and under them. There were delightful, splashy little rapids and falls. Often while Papa and Henry were letting their dinner settle, lying back with hats over their faces by the nearby Cold Springs, Juliana and Byron put on their own historical pageants, complete with Mount Vernon, the Capitol, plenty of loud muskets shot by Whigs and Tories, and wonderful victory speeches. That was a place Juliana no longer visited. It would be so lonesome without their childish bang-bangs and shouts of victory, and without the security of Papa's heavy breathing under his hat.

The place called Indian Hill was much nearer the orchard and home. She still liked to walk there when she could slip away from the house. She and Byron had found many a piece of broken pottery there, and it was a good place to look for arrowheads—and wild tiger lilies and wood violets. The woods stopped at the edge of the clover-sweetened pasture on one side, and on another side the hill dropped off steeply toward the little Jenkins Brook where the enchanting Lorna Doone Slide rushed merrily toward Mud Creek and the Chattahoochee River.

Lorna Doone was the heroine in one of Juliana's favorite love stories. She had met her lover at a beautiful falls, a romantic trysting place. The falls at Clover Hill might not be anything like the one in the book, but the children had agreed on the name. With its mossy slide, its boulders to turn the active waters white, and its quiet dark places near the banks—it had to be every bit as beautiful.

And that was, of all favorite places, Juliana's most favorite. She had come here all her life with her problems and her heartaches, as well as to chase crawfish or watch leafboats battle the rapids. There was something about watching the water that calmed her always and helped her sort out her feelings, just as watching a fire in winter might do.

Juliana sat now just below the slide on a grassy bank, dangling her feet in the cool water. She had washed the dishes and then scooted out. It was Sunday, and there would be no more work to do today. Here in the spotty shade, she had dared to remove her hat and fling her hair back over her shoulders. She had taken much ribbing from her family, particularly Byron and Sister, about being so protective of her white skin. But she stubbornly refused to let them change her, and never hoed or went on errands without her hat. Now sweaty ringlets stuck to her face and neck, and she blew a stray wisp out of her eyes.

It had been two weeks since the trip to Foster Kirk's Pinedale, but Juliana had by no means stopped thinking about it. She remembered the friendly little houses in the valley, Miss Sweet and her many cats, and most of all Mr. Foster Kirk. She didn't know why, but she simply couldn't forget him, her mind wheeling back to him like a needle on a compass always pointing north. She had decided she could not have seen him before, yet sometimes his face would swim before her, and the eyes would tease her with a mischievous twinkle. At other times the image in her mind would look so very lonesome with that heavy scowl that she'd wonder again, *Maybe I have seen him somewhere.*

She picked up a mossy oak twig and, breaking it into bits, threw the pieces idly into the stream. At first she wasn't paying any attention to where the bits of stick drifted, but then it became of absorbing interest to see whether they could get past a protruding root in one place, a boulder in another, a fallen limb farther down. She threw a piece into the water, then ran barefoot along the bank, watching its progress. Funny, she thought, how those bits of debris might fight their way miles and miles to the sea. There would be many forces trying to hinder them, but the persistent force of the water moving forward would eventually carry them to the Big Water, unless they washed up somewhere along the creek bank.

She walked back toward the slide, gazing up at the tall trees on Indian Hill, trees that still lived and grew while Papa lay dead in Level Grove Cemetery. Eternity was so impossible to comprehend. She knew what the Bible said, knew Mamma believed it, knew Papa had believed it. But did she? If only she could, then what would it matter what happened, whether the Something she expected—half exultantly, half fearfully—was really good or not? If she could only understand death, she could live without fear.

A breeze lifted her hair and tickled the tiny hairs on her arms. The sound of the wind was whispery and talkative in the trees. She felt an intimacy with the sky, the water, and the trees as she always had, except that now there was a dissatisfaction deep within her, too. Knowing that God was Creator of all and cared about her daily sorrows and happiness had been enough for her until last year. Then she had seen death come to old—and young. Alice Wheeler, flu, age 9; Luke Taylor, flu, age 13; Mike Walker, killed in action, age 19; Andria Adams died giving birth, age 17; Papa died after surgery, age 56. She had mourned the death of these, and she had mourned also the loss of her happy knowledge that one would die only when one was covered with wrinkles as Grandmother had been. Since last year there had been a gnawing inside her to know that God's eternal life was for her, too.

Slowly she put on her shoes, taking meticulous care with the tiny buttons, then tied the ribbons of her hat under her chin.

"I wonder what Mr. Foster Kirk thinks," she said to herself as she walked up the worn wagon road toward the farmhouse. But then, of course, she would never even see him again, much less find out what he thought about eternity.

If she hadn't been in such deep thought, she would have noticed sooner the long brown object lying across one wagon rut. As it was, she saw it just as she was about to place one neat foot right on top of it. She stumbled backwards when she recognized the design of a three-foot copperhead snake. She stood back, her heart racing with the sudden awareness of danger, then laughed shakily. "The poor thing's dead as a doornail," she said with relief.

She studied the coppery-and-beige pattern of interlocking diamonds, leaning forward to touch gingerly the smooth body, then recoiled as it suddenly twitched. The head was quite thoroughly smashed, and there were even wounds along the long body. But it had not been dead long, or it wouldn't be writhing still, and it most certainly had not been in the road when she came down earlier. She stood with hands on hips looking around toward the orchard, the barn, and back toward Indian Hill and its growing shadows. Who had put the dead snake there for her to find? It was an old trick that her brothers and cousins had pulled many times, but she thought by now Byron and

Henry would know she wasn't so easily frightened. Besides, someone had done a very untidy job of killing.

"I could have done better myself," she declared out loud as she stepped over the snake and started to walk on.

But she stopped abruptly when she saw a pair of blue tattered overall legs.

Tilting her head back and back, she looked up into the huge loose-jawed face of Blake Davis. Blake was the middle son of Mrs. Davis, who had the farm next to Clover Hill. Since Mr. Davis had died of flu, it had been harder for Mrs. Davis to keep her retarded son at home. But Juliana was no more afraid of him than she was of snakes—just awed sometimes.

"Blake Davis! You killed this poor snake and tried to scare me with it!" she said, wagging an accusing finger at him, but her lips curled in a smile. "Well, I'll show you how scared I am!"

Turning, she picked up the snake by the tail and started after Blake who paled and stumbled back, holding his hands defensively in front of him. "No, Juliana, no!" he whined.

"All right. But don't you do that anymore, Blake. It's—it's—well, it's just not nice." When his eyes clouded and his head drooped in shame, she said kindly, "Come on to the house and get some teacakes. I'll bet you're hungry."

When she arrived at the house, Blake Davis was plodding along behind her.

"I told you, Mamma," said Henry, leaning his chair back until he was propped against the porch wall. "I told you our Judy would be here soon, bringing something hungry along with her. I just didn't know it would be as big as Blake Davis!"

Juliana slapped Henry's knee affectionately as she went by, pleased at his use of her childhood nickname.

The next day's mail brought a letter for Juliana from Grange Neal. Since he had taken Molly home, it was understandable that Mamma might have a bread-and-butter letter, thanking her for the summer's nursing. Although Juliana had often felt most put upon when she had to walk with slow, lumbering Molly or struggle through a dull game of checkers with her, she knew it was not she who should be receiving this letter. Still, Grange had always written her since she was a little bit of a girl, that is, until he had gotten married. She opened it carefully, as was her custom with any letter, so it would be neat to keep along with her others.

There were two letters in the envelope. She paused in the road, deciding which to read first, and choosing the one that was folded so oddly. It was a short letter, but it took a minute just to get it unfolded. Then it was checkered with creases. A puzzled look turned to pinkness on her cheeks as she read.

Dear Grange,

It was good to have you over at Pinedale the other day. I hope you'll do it again soon. I'll be here for a few months working on some paintings I've been commissioned to do. Aunt De is glad to have me around, I think, though she won't admit it. But Beppo does. By the way, I realized after you left that my dog Beppo had hidden the

40

whole time. He walked with me to meet you, then I didn't see him again until nightfall.

Grange, do you think I might gain the privilege of painting that darned little scrap of nothing you brought with you? Perhaps her brother could come with her? If the portrait is any good, I would give it to her for the experience of painting it. As you know, I've been looking for just such a subject.

See what you can do, and I'll be most grateful.

Yours,
Foster

"A darned little scrap of nothing?" Is that what he thought of her? After calling her a lady and making her feel so important, as if what she thought really mattered, then he had the audacity to call her such a thing!

"Well, he'll wait a hundred years before he gets a portrait of *me!*" she said with a disdainful sniff as she walked quickly along, whipping the letter against her skirt as if to reprimand its author.

Suddenly she remembered there was another letter in Grange's envelope, and she leaned against an oak tree to read it.

Dear Juliana,

You'll soon be back in school and I wish you the very best. Last year was probably the hardest year of your life, my dear, and you need not fear that it will be repeated. You see, I can tell that inside that pretty head of yours there's a lot of puzzling going on. I would help if I could. But I know that you must find the answers to life's questions for yourself.

Please don't let this letter from Foster be a worry to you. I started just to throw it away, but it didn't seem fair to you or to him, so I didn't. It would be a good picture, I'm sure, though he is not a portrait artist. Still, how could it help being good with you as the subject? But beware—if you decide to do it—and be very business-like and cool with him. Foster Kirk is a good man, but very strange.

If you do decide to have your picture done (and I personally hope you don't), then let me know and I'll set up the time for you. Be sure someone goes with you.

Love,
Grange

He had almost thrown the letter away! Well, it was a good thing he hadn't. She at least deserved the right to say no. And she knew she'd have to say no. Mamma would never allow it. She opened the oddly folded letter again. Grange had said Foster Kirk was a good man, but strange. What was wrong with that? As she remembered Foster Kirk's expressive eyes—lonesome one minute, teasing the next—she could not imagine herself ever being businesslike and cool with him. And how old was the man, anyway? Grange had never said. She thought maybe he was twenty-five, yet she wasn't sure how long it would take an artist to become well known enough to be commissioned to do paintings. He must be quite successful.

When Juliana presented the idea to Henry, he was incensed that Grange would have thought for a minute they would let Juliana pose for an artist.

"He should have sent *me* the letter," he said, slapping the table with his half-read *Constitution,* and causing his fork to rattle on his clean-sopped plate. "I would have known what to do with it. Burn it!"

42

"Henry! The man only wants to paint her portrait," scolded Sister.

"As successful as he sounds, he can certainly find another model. Didn't Molly say the girls flocked around him?"

"Yes, but there would be none quite like Juliana. Just think of the honor."

"He doesn't have to use Juliana!" he blustered. Then he dropped his voice, "He probably has—other things in mind."

"Like what, Henry?" asked Juliana curiously.

Henry gave her a sour look, then looked significantly at Mamma. "Just—things," he mumbled and, with no further comment, he rose and stomped out of the house, letting the door close loudly just as he seemed to be closing the subject.

Byron looked up from his book. "Mamma, you needn't worry about Mr. Kirk. He's really quite old. I imagine he's at least forty."

"Oh, he couldn't be *that* old!" exclaimed Juliana.

"And besides, that aunt of his—Miss Sweet? She's anything but sweet. Rest assured, even if he wanted to—he couldn't."

"Wanted to *what?*" asked Juliana impatiently.

Byron looked at her, shook his head, and walked out, tucking his book under his arm. Just before he closed the door, he said over his shoulder, "He's a very good artist, Mamma. You'd probably have to pay $100 to get a picture like that any other way."

The teakettle simmered on the back of the stove, sending a drift of steam up against the warming closet where it formed tiny, hot beads. A kitten rolled on the floor, chasing a ball of yarn which had strayed from Mamma's work basket by the hearth. Out on the porch, a metal dipper rattled rhythmically against the wall as the wind stirred by.

"Oh, dear me," said Mamma after studying her broken, stained nails for a long time. "I do wish sometimes that both of you were quite ugly," she said, and then broke into a shaky laugh.

Juliana knew better than to press Mamma to explain what mysterious "things" Foster Kirk could possibly be planning. She would bombard Sister with questions that night after they blew out their light. Sister answered questions better in the dark, she'd found out. And Sister knew quite a bit because she was five years older and had already taught school for a year.

Mamma stood up and pushed her chair snugly against the table. She reached up and repinned a stray lock of hair that had escaped from the bun at the back of her head. Then, as she carefully stacked the plates, she asked, "Do you want to have your portrait done, Juliana?"

Juliana felt a shock of consternation that Mamma would actually ask her opinion on a matter of such importance. "I don't know. I guess so," she answered slowly.

"I'll talk to Henry some more. Maybe he'll change his mind," said Mamma firmly, adding, as if she were not changing the subject, "You clean the kitchen while Sister and I get back out to the washing. We've still got the overalls to scrub."

Henry could not be said to change his mind. He argued stubbornly that the photograph of Juliana which he'd taken to boot camp with him was as pretty a picture as they needed, that Foster Kirk was up to no good, that forty wasn't too old for romantic inclinations. Then with a grunt, he said, "This is just what we could expect from letting Byron and Juliana go off on a Sunday like that."

But after corresponding with Grange and Mr. Kirk, Mamma decided to let Juliana go to Pineland for as many sittings as it took to complete the portrait. Henry would just have to fuss.

The first Saturday Sister went with her, laughingly telling Mamma as they left that if Juliana were put in a trance and placed in an enchanted castle, she would wave her wand and help her escape by a gossamer thread ladder, and would spirit her back home. Juliana was anything but comforted.

CHAPTER 4

THE THREE-MILE BUGGY RIDE to Cornelia, the wait for the train, and the ride on the Tallulah Falls Railway to Hill's Crossing were not long enough for Juliana, who began to panic as the train slowed down to let the girls out. What would she say? How would she sit? How would she introduce Sister properly?

As it turned out, there was a confusing commotion just as they got off the train so that the introduction seemed to take care of itself. A huge black-and-tan German shepherd dog was chasing a pure white, smartly trimmed poodle along the road, down into the brambles, back again, between legs or whatever else impeded the race. Even before the train left with the conductor hanging out the door to watch as long as he could, Juliana could hear a shrill scream above the din of the dogs' barks and Mr. Kirk's thunderous commands to Beppo, the German shepherd.

When the train was gone, a stylish young lady in a

long-waisted lavender dress came dashing across the tracks, her face quite red, her brown ringlets tossing.

"If you have let your dog hurt my Serena, I shall never, never forgive you," she screamed.

At that moment the poodle came out of the bushes, ears flopping, pink tongue hanging, and ran blindly into Juliana's legs. Juliana had been awaiting her chance and now swooped the little dog into her arms, causing Beppo to put on brakes suddenly and bark as he danced around her.

"Beppo!" said Foster once again, and, whether he was more forceful that time, or whether Beppo just finally heard him, the dog did pause in his dancing and barking long enough for Mr. Kirk to get a firm grip on his collar.

"Give me my dog at once!" exclaimed the young woman, and Juliana handed it over, commenting as she did so that, except for a few extra burrs and stick-tights, the little dog was all right.

"And how should you know?" demanded Serena's mistress, hiding her face in the burry fur.

"Let me introduce you to my visitors, Maureen," said Mr. Kirk calmly as if nothing was amiss and they had all just arrived at this lonely country crossing for a friendly chat. "This is Miss Emily Hamilton and Miss Juliana Hamilton from Cornelia." That was when Juliana realized that she needn't worry any more about the introduction. Somehow Mr. Kirk and Sister had gotten themselves introduced.

"And what would you be doing so far from home?" inquired Maureen, stroking her pet and pouting prettily.

"I've come for . . ." began Juliana.

"They've come to see my studio," interrupted Mr. Kirk.

"I thought Miss Sweet said Juliana Hamilton had already been to see your studio. You are Juliana Hamilton, aren't you?"

"Yes, Maureen, she is, but she's brought her sister this time. Now—if you'll excuse us, please."

"Certainly. And I'll also send you the bill if Serena has to have stitches," she retorted. "I do wish you would teach your dog better manners."

"Perhaps if I knew them myself, I could," he said, touching his hat by way of farewell.

Beppo ran back and forth through the woods as they walked to the cottage, his tail wagging as if he'd done a great thing.

"You have quite a fiery dog, haven't you?" asked Sister conversationally.

"It helps to have one that commands respect. I feel safe leaving Aunt De with Beppo to keep watch."

Juliana was wondering how Aunt De could need anyone to keep watch over her, when that lady came walking toward them across the cottage lawn. She was gracious, but cool, her eyes taking in every detail of the girls' attire.

"You must be quite tired," she said to Sister. "Come in, and we'll refresh ourselves before Foster starts the sitting. I do say, Foster, don't you think you've chosen the wrong one for your painting? This one has a much more interesting face."

"Aunt De, will you just serve refreshments and stay out of my art, please."

"Oh, I'll do that. Only while I'm about it, I must say that you're missing something by not doing Maureen Logan's portrait. Now *there's* a face."

"Aunt De!"

"All right, all right! Just never mind an old aunt without a dab of sense."

Juliana drank gratefully from a glass of fresh-squeezed grape juice as she stroked a cat that had jumped into her lap the minute she sat down. "How many cats do you have?" she asked, for today there seemed even more than before. Everywhere she looked she saw the sleek creatures stalking past an open door, stretching and bathing themselves, or staring back at her with golden eyes.

"Right now I have only ten. I gave away most of a litter not long ago. Usually I keep at least a dozen."

"My, and you keep them fed so nicely," observed Sister, setting her glass down and picking up a furry bundle.

"Yes, they like their mice."

"Oh, they're good catchers?"

"Yes, indeed! They catch them and I cut up the mice for them. With my dressmaker shears."

Juliana paled and clapped a hand over her mouth, while Sister stifled a giggle. A solemn Aunt De observed them both with hawk-eyed interest.

"Aunt De, will you cut out your gory stories," remonstrated Mr. Kirk. "Come, Miss Juliana, it's time for us to get to work if we're to get anything done before your train is back."

Sister, being obedient to Mamma and Henry, followed behind Juliana and Mr. Kirk as they walked across to the studio. She entertained herself for some time by looking at all the paintings, but she soon became bored listening to Mr. Kirk tell Juliana over and over to sit up straight, be still, hold her hands thus and so. When she walked back out into the sunshine, she found Aunt De not far away, pulling weeds from around a lilac bush.

"My dear," said Miss Sweet calmly, "perhaps he will do your portrait next. Yours is the face he needs."

"I do most assuredly hope not," said Sister with spirit. "I could never be patient enough."

Juliana's back ached from sitting so straight, her nose itched, and she had a violent urge to cross her legs. Sitting for a traveling photographer, who hid under a black cloth after threatening certain doom on anyone who moved, was nothing compared with this. She was not at all sure she could stand it. Yet she wanted very much to please this tall, stern artist whose rare smiles were well worth the wait. She didn't know why it mattered so much to her, but it did.

"Miss Juliana, you are so stiff and unnatural," said Foster, stepping away from the easel and coming toward her.

"Of course I am. You told me to sit exactly so, and I'm not used to staying still for so long. If you could only let me read a book, maybe . . ."

"A book? You like to read?" The tension in his jaw relaxed. "Let's try that then. *David Copperfield? Swiss Family Robinson? Hound of the Baskervilles? Jane Eyre!* Have you read *Jane Eyre?*" All the time he was pulling books out of the overstuffed case and looking to her for approval. She had been crossing and recrossing her legs in great freedom, but now folded her hands as he turned his full attention toward her.

"I'd like to read that one, please. It was one of my grandmother's favorites, I remember."

As he stood beside her to hand her the book, she was intensely aware of his size, his strength. But when she looked up, what she saw in his face puzzled her—a look of wistfulness? Surely this man could have anything he wanted, couldn't he? She wondered again at his age and was even more determined to find out.

He smiled as he handed her the book. "Do you think now, Miss Hamilton, that you can sit up fairly straight, read without putting your nose in the book —and perhaps be still?"

"I can be as still as one of your waterfalls, sir," she said primly, and he laughed as he returned to his easel.

As she began to read, she wondered why it was that in so little time she felt she knew Mr. Kirk better than her older brothers, Calvin and Richard. Of course *they* treated her like a baby and *he* treated her like a lady—most of the time. That was the difference. But he was every bit as old as they, maybe even older.

On the way home she learned Foster's age. Sister said that Miss Sweet had told her he was two years old when they moved there in 1888, and it didn't take much math to figure out that he was thirty-two or thirty-three now, depending on his birthday. He *was* old then! But he didn't seem old. That wistful look on his lean face came to her hauntingly during the next week as she drew water from the well, picked August apples, or stood patiently being fitted for her new school dress.

CHAPTER 5

WHEN IT CAME TIME for the next sitting, there was no one available to go with Juliana. Byron and Henry were both picking apples and had a crew of paid apple pickers coming to help. Sister needed to do some research in the library in preparation for the new school term. And no one even considered that Mamma might go. Clover Hill simply couldn't operate without Mamma at the hub.

"She'll just have to stay home," said Henry flatly as he pushed away from the breakfast table. "We can hardly spare *her* from the work, much less anyone else. And she doesn't need to go, anyway."

But Mamma was determined to have a portrait of her youngest daughter painted by this artist whom by now she had found featured in back issues of the *Constitution*. He had a serious face and looked as if he would be both honest and thorough. She prided herself on being a good character analyst and felt only the slightest misgivings as she sent Juliana off to Pineland by herself. After all, the man was Grange's friend, and Sister had assured her that Miss Sweet and her cats would be all the chaperones needed.

Foster Kirk paced back and forth waiting for the train, Beppo following his every step. It seemed impossible after all these years that the girl of his dreams had actually materialized. Yet she had come with all the spontaneity, graciousness, natural beauty, and depth of feeling that he could ever have longed for in a companion. The instant his exuberance swelled, the impossibility of any future relationship clamped around him like a vise. For this girl who had appeared to be at least eighteen was, in fact, barely fifteen—just a child. He had not believed Grange at first, felt sure Grange was throwing him off so he could have Juliana for himself, for it seemed quite likely that Molly was not long for this world.

After that first sitting, Foster knew Grange was right. The innocent curve of her cheek, the complete honesty in her eyes, her childish inability to sit still for even five minutes—all confirmed Grange's word, no matter what the motive had been in telling him. Foster's conviction that there would never be a lady in his life as precious as Juliana left him both joyful and despondent. Joyful because, even if he could never have her, it was wonderful to know she actually existed. Painfully, sorrowfully despondent, because he knew there was no way he could ever have her for his wife, and it would be unfair ever to let her know how she affected him.

Beppo growled deep in his throat and Foster sniffed heavy perfume even before Maureen came into view, her dog in her arms. She stopped suddenly and exclaimed, "Foster Kirk! Don't tell me you're meeting those girls again!"

"You guessed right, Maureen. And how is your summer going?"

"Most fearfully boring, I'm afraid," she said, coming very close, the poodle whining and shaking in her arms as Beppo's ears pricked and his tongue lolled to one side in anticipation of action.

"Boring? In this wonderful country with so many untold mysteries to explore?"

"Now, Foster, don't tell me you don't miss the clamor and excitement of the city. Mother thought I just must spend this summer in the country with Aunt Jill, but I can hardly wait to get back. Won't you be going back soon? I thought you had an exhibit this fall. We shall be sure to be there if you do—Mother and I. She thinks you're just about the best artist this side of Turner."

"Thank your mother for me, will you?" he responded smoothly, sidestepping her question.

One might almost have imagined that he snapped his fingers ever so quietly behind his back. For some reason, anyway, Beppo lost patience suddenly and began barking ferociously around the skirts of Maureen who clutched her pet in panic.

"Better go, I think, before Serena gets hurt," yelled Foster as he grabbed Beppo's collar. He managed to tip his hat politely as Maureen left, a decided pout on her lips.

Maureen was as disgusting to him as all the other painted girls he seemed destined to attract. There was absolutely nothing to her. She would agree to anything that seemed good for the moment. She was undependable, flighty as a feather, and interested only in her silly dog, her shopping sprees and, eventually, in marrying a man with money. But he knew, too, that at twenty-five, Maureen was the "proper" age for him.

His heart beat faster as the train puffed to a stop, and he and Beppo watched the steps expectantly. When he saw her he wondered briefly if one could have a heart attack from beholding too much beauty. There was the slender perfect waist, the sweet rounded figure above it, the intelligent, eager face clothed in a complexion of untouched peaches and cream, the wide blue eyes looking for him, locking with his momentarily, then dropping in that mysteriously lovely way of hers.

When he realized Emily had not come, he went through an inner turmoil, knowing that he had been utterly trusted by the Hamilton family and wondering if he really were trustworthy.

"I'm glad you wore the blue gingham again, Miss Hamilton," he said as they walked along. "It's just the right blue for my picture."

"I didn't know how artists worked," she said, picking an aster as she passed and twirling it like a tiny pinwheel. "I thought it would be frightful if you had gotten to a certain point with blue gingham, then had to switch over to green dotted swiss."

His delighted laugh seemed to fill the woods, ricocheting off the trees. "That would be dreadful."

he said in mock horror. "Actually, though, my memory is pretty good and I'm not *wholly* dependent on what I see at the moment."

"Oh, then you may not really need me any more. Perhaps you have me memorized," she said, a teasing smile playing on her lips as she looked up at him questioningly.

"I'm afraid you don't understand," he said. "The dress is only complementary to the picture and may not in the end be very important. I'm studying your face, and the blue gingham helps to bring out the color of your eyes."

"And you haven't memorized my face? It isn't very big, you know. I've learned poems much longer than my face."

His laughter again burst forth, and Beppo ran back toward them along the path to see what was pleasing his master so much. Foster patted his head and stroked his ears before he answered in a voice first choked with mirth, then growing more and more serious. "A face—like yours—could be studied for a thousand years and never completely memorized, because it changes from moment to moment. I can only hope to capture the moment that seems the most like you."

"That sounds quite difficult to me," she said, contemplating his words with a frown. "Capturing a moment, I mean."

They walked in silence for a ways, going over the top of the hill where Foster had shown them he wanted to build a house, starting down the other side between young hemlocks and tall pines. Juliana gripped a handful of her skirt, then she turned to regard this man whom she had come to respect, wondering whether to open her private world to him. Somehow she felt he might be able to help her as no one else could. Finally she spoke.

"You talked of capturing moments. Do you—what do you think about eternity?"

He looked at her sharply, aware that this was no trivial question. "That's a big one," he admitted softly. "My thoughts on eternity go back to the things my mother taught me. Father was a preacher, but Mother showed me what it meant to love. She died when I was thirteen, and that's when I had to come to grips with what I myself believed."

"That's the way it's been with me," she said, busily pulling pieces of pine bark from a tree where they'd paused. "Papa died last year along with a lot of other people I knew. I've realized I can't go on living on someone else's faith. I need my own."

"But don't get bogged down expecting some fantastic revelation," he said gently. "Just as your face cannot be memorized in a thousand years, God's ways can never be totally understood. I don't accept things very well," he said, his back to her now, flexing a muscle in his jaw, "so I don't feel I have life figured out by any means. But I do feel assured God is in control of eternity—whatever it holds—and, though I may buck and storm, in the end I'm glad He's in charge."

"And you're not afraid to die?"

"Everyone's afraid to die, I guess. No one knows just what it will be like and that scares us. But there's no need to ruin the heaven on this side and the other side of the bridge of death worrying about whether the planks will hold."

"You must be a poet, using figures of speech like that."

"And you must be a good English student to understand figures of speech."

"Who said I understood?" she asked saucily. Then her voice grew more serious as she walked, idly scattering bits of bark along the trail. "I suppose if the planks were to break and the bridge fall down—don't you think God would give us wings then?"

"I do. Whatever death is like, God will be there." He answered so positively, so certainly, that she looked up at him, her face reflecting the relief that flooded her.

"You—you have helped me so much," she said. "Thank you."

"The truth is," he said slowly, watching her profile as he spoke, "that you helped yourself. I was only here. And to me," he added, "knowing how to live this life is much more imminent than what the next one holds."

They said no more as they continued down across the cottage lawn, and soon they were busy in their separate worlds—Foster painting, Juliana reading. Yet there was a togetherness, a peaceful oneness. She felt contented and secure in a way she could not begin to explain. And she was immeasurably grateful that he had not laughed at her concerns, but had taken them to heart as if they were his own.

She stole a glance at his face, visible above the back of the easel. His heavy brows were furrowed in deep concentration, his mouth set in a firm line. *Even when he is grim, he is so very handsome,* she thought and then wondered why he'd never married. Perhaps someone had broken his heart and that was why his eyes harbored such sadness at times.

She dropped her eyelids quickly as he looked up, and spoke sharply, "Be still, Juliana!" She could not know that the roughness of his manner concealed the overwhelming tenderness he felt for her at that moment.

CHAPTER 6

JULIANA LOOKED FORWARD each week to reading the next installment of *Jane Eyre*. Jane was the orphan girl who served as governess to a small child in a mysterious old house and fell in love with the child's father, a widower twice Jane's age. Juliana was so completely absorbed in the bitter-sweet story that she sometimes forgot and swung her foot back and forth or rested her chin on a curved forefinger, but a peremptory throat-clearing by the artist would remind her of her pose.

Always she dreaded seeing Miss Delia. That lady seemed to bore holes right through her, which let her self-confidence run out until she felt flat and plain. Several times Maureen Logan was there visiting Miss Sweet, and then it was even worse. Juliana had the distinct feeling that she was being compared to the elegant Miss Logan and was coming out on the short end every time. Secretly she wished Mr. Kirk would just do Maureen's face and forget about hers, but she dared not bring up the subject. Part of her rebelled at the thought of the triumph in Maureen's eyes should Mr. Kirk decide to follow her suggestion. She honestly didn't think Mr. Kirk would mind too much one way or the other. Didn't he just want the experience of painting a portrait? But then he could have asked Maureen to start with if he had wanted to.

Ever since Juliana had learned Mr. Kirk's age, she'd tried to think of him only as a big brother or an older friend like Grange, but none of the roles had fit him just right. The man was disturbing—a person who could not and would not be ignored. He seemed to want her to understand him, yet he was so different from anyone she'd ever met. And, she decided, he actually *enjoyed* being odd. For instance, he declared once while pounding one fist into the other palm, that he would take anyone to court who was caught hunting on his well-posted land. "Hunting, as a sport, is abominable," he said with dark eyes flashing. She wondered what he would think of her brothers' occasional coon and 'possum hunts, but never got up the courage to ask.

Since their talk about eternity, they had had many more conversations along the wooded pathway from Hill's Crossing, had looked together at the tiny eggs in a vireo's nest, had discussed the differences in pine trees so that now she recognized white pines, red pines, jack pines, and tall, straight short-leafed yellow pines. He showed her a bed of maidenhair fern, ferns that grew out from a center like a head of hair, and he let her smell the broken pieces of a sweet fern.

They were standing on Hilltop, looking at the distant blue dips of Trey Mountain. He had explained to her that there were actually three peaks on the mountain, thus the name 'Trey,' but that from this side only two could be seen.

"You love your place, don't you, Mr. Kirk?" she asked.

"It has always been my dream to enlarge it and make it a sanctuary for wild animals. And . . ." He paused, thrust his hands in his pockets, and studied the mountain peaks.

"And what?" she prompted.

"I want to raise a family here . . . have children to roam the woods."

"That would be wonderful!" she exclaimed. "You will do it, Mr. Kirk! I know you will!" she said, touching his sleeve impulsively.

He turned toward her and she wanted to cry out at the look of pain in his eyes.

"Is something—wrong?" she stammered.

"Yes, but nothing you can help," he replied in such a clipped way that she kept silent as they walked on.

Juliana was to see the hurt in his face once again that same day. He had painted for some time while she read. Sensing a change, she looked up from her book to see Mr. Kirk standing back, head cocked, hands on hips, studying first the picture, then her.

"When are you going to let me see, Mr. Kirk?" she asked brightly, closing her book.

"Not before you stop calling me Mr. Kirk and use my given name instead. I'm really quite tired of formality."

She blushed peony-red and dropped her eyes until all he could see was the top of her blond head. "But, M—Mr. Kirk," she stammered, "It would be unmannerly for me to call you by your first name. After all, we—that is, I . . . the difference in our ages, you know," she finished miserably.

"What about Grange?" he asked in a tight voice. "He's almost as old as I am, and you call him by his first name."

She looked up in confusion. "But Grange is different . . ." she tried to explain, but paused when she saw the wistful sadness fall across his face like a curtain.

"I see. Sorry," he said.

Even Miss Sweet chided him for being rude that day as he rushed Juliana up the path. "Don't hurry the child so," she called out. "Her legs aren't half as long as yours."

Foster Kirk barely spoke as they waited for the train. Then he said with an attempt at cheerfulness, "I'll let you see the portrait next week. It will be your last sitting."

She should be glad that there was only one more sitting, she thought as she rode home. It had not been easy sitting so still for an hour, and she knew she needed to help at Clover Hill. Henry had not been gracious, but at least he had allowed the sittings, and now it would be over. Life could go back to normal. She would have more time for her homework, too. Now that October was here the teachers seemed to take joy in loading her with assignments, and she liked to do everything with meticulous thoroughness. Now she would not be disturbed any more by visions of Foster Kirk.

But she felt strangely dismal at the thought rather than relieved. Shifting in her seat she stared out at the passing scenery, trying to rid herself of an aching emptiness she could not explain.

That night as she tried to sleep, Juliana's mind turned again to Foster Kirk. She knew she could never forget the things he had taught her about God and life and beauty. She smiled to herself in the moonlit room as she considered how she would describe Mr. Kirk to her children one day: "He was a tall man—dark, stern, friendly and laughing one minute—sad the next." He would be quite famous by then, and she would tell them how once he had talked to her as if she were very important, and had held her hand helping her down from the train. Picturing him with his dog there at the crossing, she was suddenly stabbed by the memory of pain in his eyes.

He wanted her to call him Foster. Why should it matter so much? For some reason, though, it did. She reached out and traced a moonlit shape of window-pane, distorted by the heavy folds of the quilt. Why would it be disrespectful if she called him by his first name? It would be their last time together. And, if it would bring the sunshine to his eyes, it would be well worth the effort. Having reached a decision, she dropped quickly off to sleep.

She practiced saying his name the day before the sitting as she sat by the talking waters of Lorna Doone Slide. As she practiced over and over, it began to sound more and more natural. "Hello, Foster." "Did you have a good week, Foster?"

"Juliana, what on earth are you doing?" asked Byron, flopping down beside her.

"How dare you creep up on me like that?" she snapped.

"But I didn't. I just walked up and you were talking away, so you didn't hear me. What were you talking about, anyway?"

She heaved an inner sigh of relief. "Just silly stuff," she said. "You wouldn't be interested." She quickly changed the subject. "Remember how we used to catch spring lizards and make pots from the brook clay?"

"Not in cold October water, though. And back then you would have told me if you were mooning about somebody." He would not be diverted. "It's Foster Kirk, isn't it?"

"Byron! I was not mooning."

"What, then?"

"None of your business."

"I think it is. You're my sister, a rascally one, but pretty precious all the same. I don't want you to be hurt."

"And I won't be," she said stoutly.

"When will the picture be finished?"

"Tomorrow."

"Good, then maybe we can get back to normal around here. I've been missing you."

"Missing me! How could you miss anyone, as wrapped up in your books as you are? You even take a book to milk the cows!"

"Thought maybe the cows could do with a little education," he said with a grin.

Juliana intended to greet Foster by name as soon as she arrived, but it didn't work that way. He was very abrupt and businesslike, and talked more to Beppo on their walk than to her. As a matter of fact, she had to take several quick, running steps to catch up to his determined stride.

She read quickly that day, trying to finish *Jane Eyre* before she had to leave for the last time. Everything was still except for the purring of two or three cats, and the chattering of birds outside. When Mr. Kirk groaned, Juliana jumped visibly, then rose from her chair with a gasp as he snatched the painting off the easel and threw it down on the window seat.

"What's wrong?" she asked, marking her place in the book with her finger.

"Everything!" he said in utter exasperation. "I can't get the feeling . . . the mobility . . . even the color is wrong."

"But I've been still, Really, I have! Was I that bad a subject?"

"No, no! It's not you. It's my own lack of ability to capture—your pensiveness and expectancy."

"Mr. Kirk, it's only a picture. Please don't be upset," she said, laying the book down and stepping toward him.

"Only a picture?" he echoed, looking out the window. "No picture in which an artist invests himself is 'only' a picture . . . this one in particular."

Juliana felt rebuked. She knew nothing about art except what he had taught her, but did he have to make her feel so ignorant? What did he mean by "This one in particular"? Could it be because he had not painted a portrait before? That must be it. This was his first.

"You will do better with the next one," she soothed.

"The next one?"

"Yes. Why don't you ask Maureen to sit for you next? With her dog? Maureen's hair has much more color than mine." Her voice raced to keep pace with her growing idea. "And she would be quite pretty if you would let her smile for you."

She could not understand his total silence. She knew only that he was very upset, judging from the muscles in his neck that were working like ropes, and his hands, fisted hard in his pockets. Quietly she slipped up behind him and looked around the bulk of him at the painting which lay face up on the window seat. She was shocked when she saw it. Though a pretty picture, the woman in it didn't look anything like her. Why, after all that talk about getting the color of her eyes right, had he painted her profile with her eyelids almost closed, as if she were sleepy? No wonder he was upset! It really was not a good likeness at all. But she must think of some way to console him.

Shyly she touched his arm and said softly, "I think it's quite good—Foster."

She never knew how it happened, but the next moment his arms were around her, one big hand crushing her head against his chest. He held her that way for a time, and she wasn't sure whether it was her heart or his beating so loudly—only that she wanted to stay there forever with his cheek against her hair.

"Juliana?" he whispered, turning her face up to his.

She saw warmth and joy in his eyes, felt the tenderness of his hands cupping her face. The ecstasy tingling through her whole body made her aware of life in a way she had never experienced before. Was this the Something Big she had known was going to happen? She felt delightfully secure in the strength of Foster's embrace. But an alarm went off in her head just as he leaned toward her, his mouth just inches from hers. She began to push with both hands against his chest, and he let go so suddenly he had to catch her hand to keep her from falling. He dropped it quickly and turned back toward the window.

"I'm sorry, Juliana—" His voice was strangely choked. "Will you forgive me?"

"Yes, of course I'll forgive you. But you mustn't do that ever again," she warned, frowning darkly. Her brother Henry would have been proud of her, for she sounded quite severe and very grown-up. "And now I must be going. Shall I take the painting with me?"

"No! That is—I wanted to put it in a frame and I thought perhaps I could bring it to you. Next Saturday?" She would not look into his eyes, though she felt them demanding her attention.

"I don't know," she faltered. "My brothers will not like it, particularly Henry."

"Juliana, what I did was very wrong, but you said you forgave me. Only a few minutes ago—wouldn't you have agreed to let me come?"

She considered the truth of his implication, and nodded slightly.

"Well, then, if you truly forgave me, we can start over. . . . We can be friends again, can't we?"

After a long moment, she changed the subject in tacit acknowledgment of his plea. "Are you sure you know how to find Clover Hill?"

"Yes, certainly. Grange has told me so much about it. Come now, we must go and meet your train. Here—take the book. I know you didn't finish it. I'll pick it up next week."

If Miss Sweet noticed that Juliana's hair was slightly mussed and her color high, she didn't mention it. But as the two started up the hill, she called out to Foster to stop by Maureen's house before he came back and get a recipe she'd been promised. "Don't forget now!" she called peremptorily, and Juliana looked back to see her standing, arms folded across her breast, her long skirt rippling with the insistent circling of a cat. A hot prickling of rebellion added itself to the confusion in Juliana's mind. What right had Miss Sweet to decide to whom her nephew should pay his attentions?

CHAPTER 7

JULIANA DID NOT TELL anyone, even Sister, what had happened to her. But she had to explain why she still did not have the painting.

"That man is trying to poison our family!" exclaimed Henry when he heard Foster was coming. "He will bring nothing but trouble."

"Henry, that's not fair," said Mamma, smoothing a quilt square in her ample lap. "You've never met the man, and neither have I. I think it's time we did."

"I tell you he's after Juliana—and the only way he's going to get her is over my dead body!"

Juliana sat quietly in a corner, her hair curtaining her face, the light from the fire glinting on her needles as she knitted a cap for Calvin's little boy, Peter. She wished desperately that she had never left Clover Hill that Sunday morning. Yet at the same time she could not imagine not knowing Foster Kirk. Why, he had become part of the fiber of her thinking. He had helped her to see, and hear, and feel everything more clearly, to be sharply aware of shadow effects, leaf markings, bird calls. Yes, and he had helped her to face the future confidently. Now, though, she wondered if he would be anywhere at all in that future.

She simply could not forget his taking her in his arms, his hand on her head holding her hard against him. And if she couldn't forget, then she knew she couldn't be to him just what she'd been before that episode in the studio. Neither of them could ever be quite the same again. She blushed in the firelight as she wondered what it would have been like if he had really kissed her. She had finished reading *Jane Eyre,* and she reckoned that Foster Kirk was much younger than the hero in the story. But it was only in a book, she reminded herself, that a girl could be happily married to a man twice her age.

"Juliana, I wonder that you can see one stitch in that dark corner," said Mamma, breaking into her thoughts. "Come over here by the lamp light." As Juliana pulled her chair closer, Mamma admired the neat, even stitches she was making. "You've really improved on your knitting, haven't you? Remember how you begged to make sweaters for the soldiers during the war?"

"Yes," she laughed, struggling to emerge from her daydream, "And you would only let me knit cotton washcloths—square, thick things. I wonder if the soldiers ever really used them."

Mamma smiled at her from across the table. "Of course they did."

"But I never got any notes the way you did."

"Wasn't that exciting, Mamma?" interjected Sister. "Getting thank-you notes from the boys who wore your sweaters? The Red Cross did a wonderful thing involving American women in helping to keep the Allied army warm."

"It was a good thing," agreed Mamma. "The poor boys had few enough comforts during that awful time."

"Now you're about to get morbid," said Henry gruffly, adjusting a log in the fire and letting the poker clang back against its corner resting place. He straightened, stretched, then started toward the door. "I'll go see if Maude and the other horses are all right before I turn in," he said.

"Henry and his horses!" said Sister with a little laugh, closing up the book she'd been studying. "I'll bet he wouldn't be so huffy if it were feedbags we'd been knitting!"

Everyone seemed surprised when Calvin, Winnie, and the children rattled up to the door after dark on Friday night. Then, as Juliana was unbuttoning little Peter's coat, she overheard Henry say to Calvin in a low voice, "Glad you could make it, old boy. Just felt we all needed to be here."

"What about Richard?"

"He couldn't be away from the bank tomorrow. Anyway, he's too hot-tempered. It's better this way."

Juliana could barely remember Brother's graduating from high school. In her memory he had always been a man, a stern extra father who seemed able to read her inmost thoughts. Henry talked hard and was very

72

sparing with his affection, but she knew Henry really cared. Somehow she had never been sure about Brother.

Rebellion festered inside her now. So they expected trouble, did they? It was all Juliana could do to act for the rest of the evening like the same carefree girl of a week ago, to be caught up in playing jacks with Margo or taking Peter on piggy-back rides. How she wished she could be that child again, but a door had been opened, and she had walked into a wider place with more possibilities for hurt and happiness. And part of the hurt was in not being trusted. What did they think she would do?

On Saturday morning there was so much activity that Juliana scarcely had time to remember that this was the day Foster Kirk was coming. There were chickens to be caught for Mamma to kill and dress for Sunday dinner, turnip greens to be picked and washed tediously leaf by leaf, scrubbing, dusting, shining, and all the time the babies wanting her to play with them. They, like everyone else, apparently considered her still a child.

When she dusted her borrowed copy of *Jane Eyre* in the room she shared with Sister, she suddenly recalled the significance of the day. She took pains to brush her hair some extra strokes, take off her apron, and volunteer to do the mending so she could keep vigil on the front porch.

By midafternoon Juliana had grown weary of sewing on buttons, patching tears, and sewing up rips, and Margo was begging her to climb a tree with her when the distant throb of a machine caught their attention. Since very few autos passed Clover Hill, she was tempted to grab Margo's hand and run to see. She was glad she hadn't as the roar came closer and closer and she realized the vehicle was not just passing by. She barely had time to stack her work neatly and smooth the wrinkles in her dress when the car stopped in front of the house and Mr. Kirk unfolded himself from it. He took the steps in two strides, then stood in front of her, hat in hand.

"How do you do?" she said politely. "I didn't know you had a car."

"I borrowed it from a friend. . . . You have company," he said, kneeling to meet Margo face-to-face.

"I'm not company," said Margo stoutly. *"You are."*

"This is my brother's little girl," explained Juliana.

"And we live in Nacoochee," said Margo who was anything but shy. "We came all the way down here yesterday, because Daddy said . . ."

Juliana put a hand over Margo's mouth just as Mamma and Sister, hearing their voices, came out on the porch. Mamma looked at Juliana, expecting a proper introduction. But Juliana became suddenly tongue-tied, so Sister did the honors. Mamma invited Foster into the front room.

The front room was both living room and bedroom. Mamma kept her prettiest spread on that bed. It was one she had crocheted with fine white thread in a delicate flower pattern. At the windows were thin white curtains, pulled back with tatted ties. Over the narrow mantle hung a photograph of the whole Hamilton family, including Grandmother and Papa, and around the room were other pictures: a framed *Saturday Eve-*

ning Post cover, a print of a broken farm wagon with a hatless farmer trying to take a wheel off.

The freshly-lit fire cast flickering reflections in the polished floor, the shiny Edison phonograph, and the backs of Grandmother's Duncan Phyfe chairs. The fire was mainly for looks as it wasn't really cold, but Juliana was grateful for its added cheer. Though the room was filled with happy memories of Christmasses past, more recently it had held the strange chill of an open coffin with Papa's profile in the shadows. She wished they could have sat today in the dining room around the big table, the everyday warm family gathering place. But Mamma wouldn't have thought it a proper place to receive a first-time guest.

Juliana was fascinated by the easy flow of conversation between Mamma, Mr. Kirk, and Sister. They were talking about some of the new electrical gadgets on the market. Mr. Kirk had seen a vacuum cleaner demonstrated in a store in Atlanta and was impressed with its capabilities.

"I don't think you'd have much need of it here," he said, glancing around the neat, shining room, "but some folks would find it quite handy. The nice thing about it is it doesn't stir up the dust."

"You've convinced me, Mr. Kirk," said Mamma, with an unaccustomed twinkle in her eye, "that if I ever have electricity, I'll want a vacuum cleaner the very first thing—well, the first thing after an iron. How marvelous—not to have to heat and reheat those heavy irons, but to have one evenly heated, light instrument. I don't suppose you have seen one of those at work?"

"Actually, my landlady in Atlanta uses one." He chuckled and leaned forward. "She confided in me that she thought ironing would be like play with her new iron, but she had to admit it was still hard work."

"It's unbelievable, isn't it, that this time last year one could hardly buy the bare necessities, and now folks are getting all those luxuries," said Sister.

"Yes, but I'm afraid it won't last." Mr. Kirk was suddenly serious. "After this rush there is likely to be a depression."

"You really think so?" asked Mamma anxiously. "Henry said the same thing. By the way, where is Henry? I thought they were coming. Juliana, run fetch your brothers, please, and when you come back, you may bring the refreshments out from the kitchen."

Juliana left obediently, but her pride was damaged. What was Mr. Kirk to think—that she was a servant or something? But what did it matter what he thought? She had to take herself to task over her own inconsistency. One minute she wanted to be far away from the sound of Foster's deep resonant voice; the next, she was fuming for being banished from his presence.

The refreshments were not served after all. Juliana met her brothers coming in and, as they washed up, she began to prepare a tray. "Don't bother with that," said Brother, drying his hands.

"But Mamma said . . ."

"Never mind. We won't need it."

Winnie came in from her walk with Margo in time to hear Brother's curt remark.

"Do you really think you must?" she asked quietly at his elbow.

"Yes. There's no doubt it must be done."

"Well, do be quiet about it and don't wake Peter from his nap."

Byron shifted his feet in obvious misery and hung behind the other two as they literally stomped into the front room. Juliana thought she would never ever forget the rude way Brother demanded to see the portrait, how he made it clear there were to be no more calls, and how Henry offered to pay for the portrait that they not be beholden to Mr. Kirk. She stayed outside the door, ashamed to be in the same room with them. She heard Mamma murmuring something about how beautiful the picture was, and Henry saying, "But, you see, Mamma. He's painted her as a woman instead of our little girl."

She couldn't see Mr. Kirk, but she could imagine his dark expression, heavy brows drawn together, as he said, "There will soon come a time, gentlemen, when you will have to recognize that your sister is no longer a child."

Juliana heard a quick movement and then the squeak of the door leading onto the porch. "Please leave, sir," said Brother icily, "and I suggest that you never darken these doors again. We may be simple country folk, but we're not dumb to the wiles of the world, and we will not be taken in."

Juliana shrank farther into the shadows as she heard Mr. Kirk's footsteps on the porch. There was a bewildering silence, and she wondered if he would just leave without saying anything more. She couldn't blame him if he never wanted to think of the Hamilton family again after being treated so for making a friendly visit. Or was it just a friendly visit? His next words, spoken with steely determination, caused her to tremble.

"You have something against artists, I perceive. I came here intending to be open and honest, and I will leave the same way. Rest assured, Mr. Hamilton, you have not heard the last from me."

During the next two weeks, Juliana was aware of Foster Kirk's various attempts to persuade the Hamiltons that he would only visit as a friend until she was older and could make her own decisions. He wrote letters which were masterpieces of reasoning. He made every excuse for dropping by: buying apples, coming to collect the book he'd loaned Juliana, making sketches of Clover Hill House, but time after time he was told to leave, and never allowed even a glimpse of Juliana. Mamma might have weakened and invited him in, but she didn't dare make matters worse than they already were.

Foster startled her one day by walking up into the yard, whistling, no horse or auto anywhere in sight.

"You surely did not walk from Clarkesville?" she asked, astonished to see him on foot.

"Certainly. It's only ten or eleven miles. Just enough to get one well warmed up."

"Look, Mr. Kirk, I believe you're an honest man and I respect you. But you're being most unfair to all of us, particularly Juliana. It's quite obvious to me that, whether you will admit it or not, you are . . ."

"In love with your daughter," he finished for her,

leaning back against a porch pillar since she has not invited him to sit.

She looked at him, wide-eyed. "Then you do admit it. Mr. Kirk, don't you realize how impossible it is? Why, Juliana's room is still lined with dolls she hasn't had the heart to give away. In school she has normal friendly relationships with the other children— including boyfriends who do such mischievous things as dip locks of her hair in their inkwells or drop spiders down her neck. Leave her alone, please, and let her grow."

"That's exactly what I intend to do. Only I want to continue to be her friend and when the time comes. . ."

"Mr. Kirk, you don't understand! The time will never come when she is the right age for you. Can't you accept that? Go look for a lady in Atlanta, a mature lady suitable for an artist of your renown. And— please—leave our Juliana alone!" There were tears in Mrs. Hamilton's voice, and Foster Kirk turned away from her, gripping the squared edge of the porch pillar.

"I agree with you. It *is* impossible," he said at last. "But there is a thing called hope, too, and I cannot give up. All these lonely years I've known that, however tempting it might have been to choose a companion because she was attractive and available, I must wait for the one who would really be a mate in the truest sense—a companion of the mind and soul. As impossible as it must seem to you who are her mother, Juliana *is* that companion, and I will wait as long as I must. If I am not to see her in the meantime, then you must tell me when I may see her again.''

Mrs. Hamilton sat down hard in a wicker rocker, and the fast rhythmic squeaks of the chair spoke of her agitation.

''When Juliana is eighteen, you may come to call on her again,'' she said heavily.

A cool wind rattled the metal dipper that hung near the well. A chicken cackled, proclaiming a fresh egg. Mr. Kirk turned slowly to look into Mrs. Hamilton's face, then put his hat on, and walked away without another word. She watched him disappear along the wooded road and still sat, a corner of her apron twisted hard around one finger.

''But I don't want to leave Clover Hill,'' said Juliana tearfully. ''You said he would not be back.''

''Yes. But the hope he spoke of—it's very strong. I just want to be sure. Your brother will be kind to you, Juliana. He loves you and wants only the best for you.''

''I imagine he'll be the best teacher you'll ever have,'' said Byron, trying to be encouraging.

''But I'll be so far from home.''

''It will only be for the rest of the school year. Nacoochee is a beautiful valley. We lived there once when you were just a baby, before we moved back here to take over the farm. You'll love the place.''

''May I please wait until after Thanksgiving?'' asked Juliana, her eyes like dark pools.

Mamma bit her lip, walked to the window and looked out at the gray sky, then turned. ''No, you must go on Saturday. Brother will come to get you. It's the only way," she said, and Juliana knew it would be useless to argue.

CHAPTER 8

NACOOCHEE WAS TWENTY MILES away, a hard half-day's journey by surrey. It might just as well have been a hundred as far as Juliana was concerned, for she could not go home at all for weeks, and at Christmas only for a short holiday.

She longed to hear warm sprays of milk hissing into a metal bucket, and to smell the cows eating their hay. She wanted to see the icicles formed around the edges of Lorna Doone Slide, to scatter cracked corn for the chickens in the evenings, to see the sun set behind the oaks over toward the Davises, and to ride to school with a hot apple tart warming her mittened hands. She wanted to see Henry's new dog Spring, a collie cross who just showed up there one day and refused to leave. Henry had written her about Spring and how she followed him everywhere he went. She didn't know that Henry had sat for hours with his farm record books open in front of him, wondering how he could tell her that he missed her intensely.

Brother's position as Latin teacher at Nacoochee School brought him a very small salary, but his house, a two-story hard by the school campus was provided. He also was pastor of a tiny church. One could see the quaint steeple and hear the bell ring from far up the hillside on Brother's front porch. The hill rose steeply, thickly wooded above Brother's house, and across the valley one could see the sister ridge with spruce and pine spearing the sky. Far beyond, sometimes draped in clouds, was Yonah Mountain.

It was a beautiful valley, as Mamma had said, with rich pastureland surrounding an old sacred Indian mound with a tiny gazebo on its flat top. Juliana, always interested in history, in how other people had lived and died, now showed no interest in the Indian mound or in anything else. But she went dutifully to class, did what she was told to do around the house, and entertained Margo for hours on end, playing dolls with her, having tea parties, sewing up tiny bonnets and aprons. Winnie told Brother one day that Juliana seemed every bit as much of a child as Margo, and she herself could not see what all the problem was about. That a grown man like Mr. Kirk could want a little slip of a girl for a bride was simply unthinkable.

"You heard him yourself, Winnie," Brother reminded her. "But here lately I've noticed Juliana withdrawing more and more. I'm afraid she'll never be the same again. I wish she'd never met that man!"

Juliana heard the exchange between Brother and Winnie as she came down the stairs. She wanted to scream that it wasn't Foster Kirk who was making her withdraw; it was being so far from Clover Hill. If only they would let her go home! As she gripped the smooth stair rail and bit thoughtfully on her lower lip, she suddenly realized that perhaps if she could show them she was quite happy, they would consider her cured and let her go. Surely by now Mr. Foster Kirk had forgotten all about her and would not bother them any more.

She began to will herself to take notice of things around her—the fields of winter beige meeting spruce-clothed slopes that yielded to a blue sky, the roar of the Chattahoochee River in the near distance, and the mysterious Indian mound. All this time she'd been going to school, she had scarcely noticed the people around her. Now she realized that the inevitable cliques had formed and left no room for her, for when she spoke to the girls in the hallway between classes, they looked startled, answered politely, and then turned away. She never had been without a friend before. Her heart became heavier still. Yet she had made up her mind to be happy, so she plunged more deeply into her studies, finding there a challenge that excited her.

She asked to go for a walk one brittle blue afternoon when the wind was moaning like ghost cries in the trees. For once Winnie refused to let Margo walk with her, whether because of the cold wind, or because of a rare perception of Juliana's need for some time to herself. She hushed the child's cries with a teacake, and said to Juliana, "Wrap up good or you'll be sick, and be a dear and pick up some flour at the mill—just half a peck."

It was a long walk and Juliana was grateful for it. She missed so much her solitary tramps in the woods, not just for the chance to find interesting things, but to be alone, to think and consider. Margo was her one bright joy, for she felt needed and loved by her, but today it was good to be alone.

This path to the mill took her up a long straight stretch of road to the river, then along the river a ways and across it. She paused on the bridge and looked down at the water flowing forever and forever on. Something caught in her chest. It was that feeling again such as she had not felt in a long time—that feeling of Something Big about to happen. The water gave it to her—the water rushing along, eager to get wherever it was going, just following the path laid out for it, never knowing what was around the bend. Somehow it reminded her of Foster and his paintings.

She had asked him one day why it was that every painting gave her the feeling of needing to turn the page to see what was next, even though there was no page to turn. His face had lit up with pleasure, and he had explained enthusiastically how that was his very intention. "By using bends in trails, streams, roads, I like to lead a person to wonder what is beyond. Because, you see, there is always a beyond."

Always a beyond, she thought as she watched the water. Always a challenge ahead—mountains, valleys, steep winding trails, tough tests. And always God, too, around every bend. Always He was there. She shook herself and pulled her coat closely around her, noticing for the first time a swinging footbridge not far down the river. Why had she never seen it before? Obviously, it was well used, for the trail leading to it was quite beaten. As she hurried on toward the mill, she promised herself that when she came back she'd cross the footbridge.

Not far up the other side of the river was the mill —waterwheel splashing, rugged gray boards dark under a huge, protective spruce. Juliana stopped again and sucked in her breath at the beauty of the falls, the mill, the waterwheel, the spruce. Since Winnie had very little storage space and bought her flour and meal in small amounts, Juliana had seen these familiar sights often. But today seemed like the first time, as if she'd finally awakened from a restless sleep.

Inside the mill Juliana studied the intricate entanglements of dust webs in the corners of the room while the miller was filling her bag. She sniffed appreciatively at the dusty grain smell that reminded her so much of corn-shucking days at Clover Hill. And she wrote her name in the flour dust of a rough board table.

"Want that I put yer bag in a paper, Miss, so's not to spile yer nice dress?" yelled the miller over the roar of the river and flipping rhythm of the waterwheel.

"Yes, thanks," she nodded and felt a wave of warm gratitude for the little gray-headed man whose eyes seemed pale and washed-out from looking at so much flour.

She walked around the foot of the mill before lifting her eyes to the powerful waterfall crashing from its battlements, stamping its feet into the unyielding rocks below. Holding the flour under one arm, she started back to Brother's. She'd forgotten her mittens, but coming over with only an empty sack to tuck under her arm, it had been a simple thing to keep her hands snug in her coat pockets. Now one hand or the other had to haul the flour. She changed hands frequently, but still each one in turn ached, then numbed in the cold.

As she approached the swinging bridge, she walked slower and slower. Could she walk it? Did she dare? Many others before her had managed it. Yet the bridge was long, and there was only a rope on one side to hold to. She looked both ways to see if anyone were in sight. Seeing no one, she stepped onto the planking and giggled softly as she walked, balancing herself with the sack of flour. It was the next best thing to walking on air. The trick, she realized, was to step lightly and rhythmically so as not to bounce herself off into the water.

She stopped in the middle to watch the water tumbling underneath, splashing wildly white around the rocks, flecks of foam riding out to the banks. There, where the water pooled in places behind boulders, she could see the dark shapes of fish darting around. " 'Out of the hills of Habersham, down the valleys of Hall, I hurry amain to reach the plain, run the rapid and leap the fall,' " she quoted happily, knowing that Sidney Lanier must have felt such joy.

She had not worried that anyone would hear her because the wonderful chuckling of the river would cover her voice. But it also covered the sound of approaching footsteps, so that she was completely unprepared for the sudden swinging of the bridge. She had just leaned over slightly to watch the water flow under the bridge and now gave a startled cry. In gaining her balance by grabbing the hand rope, the sack of flour slid out of the miller's protective paper and landed with a plop in the stream.

"Sorry to startle you!" shouted a boy with an amazing profusion of black hair, and with blue eyes that said quite plainly he wasn't sorry at all—had, in fact, *intended* to startle her.

"How dare you, Jason?" she demanded. "Look what you've done! Winnie will think I've been terribly careless."

"Well? You were. Don't you know better than to lean over a swinging bridge? You could have fallen in yourself."

"And if I had?"

"I would have rescued you, of course, and then you couldn't go on ignoring me the way you have. Here, come on off this thing before we both fall." He tried to take her hand, but she stuck one in a pocket and held firmly to the rope with the other.

"I haven't been ignoring you," she said as they stopped on firm land.

"Me and everyone else, too. What are you—stuck-up or something? Just because your brother's a teacher doesn't give you the right to act so high and mighty."

She gulped in dismay. Had she seemed so? No one ever before had accused her of being stuck-up.

"I'm sorry, Jason. It's just that I've been so homesick."

"Well, everyone goes through that. But at least you're with your brother. Some of us don't see our families all year. So come on now and we'll get you some more flour. I have a quarter just burning a hole in my pocket.''

"Oh, but you mustn't do that. I'll explain to Winnie. I'm not afraid of her.''

"Who said you were? It's my fault, and I don't mind at all shouldering the blame. Actually, it was worth it every bit to see the sparks fly from your eyes. I always knew you'd be beautiful if someone could just make you mad.''

She laughed out loud at his boldness and was surprised at a surge of happiness inside. Hadn't she just a short while ago felt as if Something was about to happen? Maybe Jason was at least part of it. She hoped he would be her friend.

She learned on the walk back home that, like her, Jason was interested in Indian lore. He had a collection of arrowheads at home, he said, and was intrigued when she told him about the pottery pieces she'd found on her Indian Hill. When he left her at the back door with a big wink and a ''See you tomorrow,'' she smiled in return. Winnie was surprised to hear her humming a tune as she came into the kitchen.

Juliana saw a lot of Jason after that, though almost always the two of them were part of a small group, not alone together. Brother was obviously pleased that Juliana was interested in someone her own age. He posted a letter to Mamma, assuring her that she needn't worry any more about Juliana and Foster.

One afternoon Jason got up a group to walk to the Indian mound. Juliana took Margo along, for the little girl's heart was going to be crushed if she were left behind. Juliana had told her many Indian stories like the one about the Cherokee named Sequoyah who made up an alphabet for his people, and now reminded Margo to be quiet and listen so that maybe they'd learn something about the mound. First, they walked all the way around the bottom of it, Juliana in much awe of the size of it. It hadn't looked nearly so big at a distance.

"Wonder how many bones are in this thing," said Jason, poking a stick into a steep side.

"Oh, don't do that, Jason!" exclaimed a girl named Amy in horror. "This is a sacred place. Why, it may even be the place where Nacoochee and Sautee are buried."

"Well, they wouldn't be buried together," Jason declared, poking again.

"Why not? Who were they?" asked Juliana.

"You don't know about Nacoochee and Sautee? You must be a foreigner, a lowlander," said Jason, his eyes twinkling.

"So then—tell me who they were."

"Well, you know Yonah Mountain there," he said with a wave of his hand. "You can't see it from this angle, but at the top is a steep cliff on one side."

She nodded and clearly remembered viewing the mountain with Foster Kirk from his hilltop. He had said something about its being a lonely mountain apart from the others—like himself.

"Well, the story goes—" began one of the other boys, tossing a rock to see if he could make it go over the little gazebo.

"Wait, I'm telling this story," interrupted Jason. "What happened is this: Sautee, an Indian brave, fell in love with Nacoochee, a princess from another tribe. Of course they could only see each other on the sly. But one day they were caught, and Sautee was taken to the top of Yonah right up on the edge of that cliff and thrown off. Nacoochee was being held between two strong braves. But just as Sautee was hurled over the cliff, she broke away with a scream, and, running to the edge, jumped off after him.''

"That's true love," sighed one of the girls.

"No, that's true stupidity," said Jason. "Just because one died didn't mean the other had to. What a waste!"

"Oh, Jason! For one who can tell such a good story, you are quite insensitive," replied the girl.

"And you don't think they're buried here?" asked Juliana.

"Would it make sense that the chief who had Yonah killed would then allow him to be buried with his daughter?"

Juliana considered, head cocked, chin resting on a curved forefinger.

"Yes, I think it would make sense," she said. "To an Indian, that is. Death changed everything. What was unforgivable in life was sweet and sentimental in view of the dark unknown."

The sun was behind the ridge now, shining like a red-gold border through the fringe of trees on top. A biting wind swooped down the valley, prodding the young people back toward the school. Jason gave Margo a ride and left Juliana to walk slightly apart from the others, hunching her shoulders against the cold.

She realized suddenly that everyone was staring at her, including Jason. But he quickly changed the mood by laughing at Juliana and breaking into a hard trot, with Margo's delighted peals piercing the chill air.

CHAPTER 9

IT HAD SNOWED SEVERAL times, but the light snows had stuck for only a few minutes. Juliana was as excited as Margo the day they awakened to find a thick blanket of white covering every twig and tree, and they bundled up and went out before breakfast, giggling at the crunching squeak of their shoes in the snow.

"See the rabbit tracks! And look, Margo, deer tracks! Oh, do be quiet, and maybe we will see a deer."

"How do you know who made these tracks?" whispered the little girl.

"I—just know. Because they're the shape of a deer's feet."

On the wooded slope above the house, Juliana turned to admire the scene. Hemlocks dropped graceful white-trimmed skirts; tree limbs were frosted with tiny ridges of snow, and back down the path of their sliding footprints stood the house and the school, black patches of roof showing here and there. Across on the next ridge, dark tree trunks and tips of spruce and pine peered out from the whiteness. The spire of the little church pointed up through snow-laden branches. In the stillness there was the occasional muffled snapping of a twig as snow weighted it to breaking point.

When Margo tugged at her hand, Juliana's eyes followed the child's pointed finger. A deer was observing them, large, luminous eyes wondering, black-tipped nose alert. Suddenly it spun around and was gone, a flash of white tail disappearing among the trees.

"That was a deer?" breathed Margo.

"That was a deer."

It was hard to concentrate in classes that day, for gazing out the windows. But particularly in Latin, where Brother was teacher, Juliana struggled to keep her mind on the subject. Brother had been very strict and had given her more work than anyone else, yet still she managed to keep a 93 average, and she had no intention of letting it slip. Her pride was at stake. She wanted to prove to him that she could do anything he assigned her.

When school was dismissed that afternoon, the path that wound by the boys' dormitory and on to Brother's house was black and wet with melted snow, but there was still plenty piled high on either side. Juliana and Jason walked ahead of a group of boys, Jason gallantly carrying Juliana's books for her. Intent on each other, the two didn't notice any unusual activity behind them until it was too late. Suddenly snowballs were pelting them, and shouts of glee rang out through the trees.

"Quick! Behind a bush!" ordered Jason. What followed was a battle Custer himself would have been proud of. As fast as Juliana made snowballs, Jason threw them. Ducking down behind the bush and scraping snow together as fast as she could, Juliana got only a few sprays of snow in her hair from the enemy fire. But during a lull, when Juliana lifted her head to peer over the top of the bush, a firm snowball connected with her face. She'd thought her nose and cheeks were completely numb, but realized with a sting that they were not.

"If you'll call a truce," she told Jason, rubbing her cheek, "I'll go get Winnie to fix us all some cocoa."

"Good deal. Hey, fellas! Juliana's inviting us for hot cocoa. Come on and behave yourselves, or Mr. Hamilton will put us all on probation."

Mr. Hamilton actually helped to prepare the cocoa. It took every little saucepan Winnie had to make enough of the steaming brew, and they had to take turns drinking because there weren't enough cups to go around. That seemed to make it all the more fun. When Juliana saw Brother hand Jason a cup and then laugh as he almost slid down on a puddle of melted snow, she felt a special warmth in her chest. Brother was not all stern authority. He just had a big dose of protectiveness where she was concerned, without as much of Henry's humor to go along with it.

As the snow melted, the waters of the Chattahoochee rose until there was no murmur and chuckle, only a loud roar. Juliana had developed a habit of visiting the river often. It was the next best

95

thing to watching the water splash down her beloved Lorna Doone Slide. But heavy rains came to add to the snow melt until the whole valley was flooded. Even the Indian mound was almost covered. All that showed above the water was the little gazebo, and Juliana couldn't help wondering if Indians' bones might come floating to the top.

For two or three days the mailman could not make his rounds, but school went on as usual, for the small building was situated high on the hill and only the few commuting students had to be absent.

"If this weather doesn't break soon," said Winnie one day, "we're all going to go stir-crazy. Juliana, take Margo with you to see if the mailman got through today. You'll have to carry her across the bad places, but that won't hurt you, will it?"

Juliana thought she heard a touch of sarcasm in Winnie's voice. The implication that she had done little enough to earn her winter's lodging stung. She wanted to snap back that being there was not her idea and she didn't like it any better than Winnie, but she bit her lip and said only, "Come on, Margo, let's get buttoned up."

When she saw fresh hoof prints at the mailbox, Juliana pulled the door open in excitement. Maybe she would have a letter. Sometimes Byron wrote her; often Mamma did, and she had even heard several times from Grange.

"Let me see, let me see," demanded Margo beside her as Juliana sorted through the mail with awkward mittened fingers.

There was a letter to her from Mamma, mailed almost a week ago, several to Brother from different places, and one to Winnie from her mother; that would make her feel better. But she caught her breath at the sight of a small square envelope with the unmistakable handwriting of Foster Kirk. Margo was still demanding to see, but she heard her as from a distance. What could Foster have to say to her? How could he justify writing to her after all that had been said? A twist of anger burned through her as she studied the Atlanta postmark. Because of Foster Kirk she had been driven from her home, and now when things were beginning to improve between her and Brother, here was trouble again. Perhaps she could just hide the letter. But already Margo was standing on tiptoes to see, and her sharp eyes could not fail to notice the unusual script. Besides, that wasn't honest.

"I'm sorry, Margo, for being so pokey. Here, you hold the mail. Hold it with both hands, so it won't slide out and get all wet and muddy."

What could Foster be saying to her? He'd promised not to write or call until she was eighteen. Perhaps he was just letting her know how his exhibit had gone. She'd wanted very much to hear, but Grange had not mentioned it, and she didn't dare ask. Or he might be telling her he was getting married. In her imagination, the girls in Atlanta, decked out in their finery, were fantastically beautiful. Or what if something bad had happened? It was tempting to take the letter from Margo even now, and bribe her not to tell anyone about it. But as she glanced up, she saw Winnie looking out from the living room window with Peter in her arms. There was no use.

Juliana talked to Winnie about the letter, hoping that she would tell her to go ahead and read it. But Winnie didn't. "That's between you and your brother," she said adamantly. "I'm not getting into it."

Brother's forehead furrowed in a frown when he saw the letter. He gritted his teeth and started to tear it right down the middle.

"No, Brother, no!" pleaded Juliana. "You mustn't destroy it."

"And why not?"

"Because—well, surely he deserves to know that I received it. We must at least let him know it got here—or—or he'll send another."

"You'd like that, wouldn't you? And the next time you might read it."

"I could have read it this time—if I'd wanted to," said Juliana with painful evenness.

Brother looked at her bowed head and said remorsefully, "I suppose you could. Just the same, we can send the scoundrel the torn letter. I think that may be all he'll understand."

"No!" said Juliana with astonishing firmness, lifting her head, damp trickles shining on her cheeks. "Please, Brother, just write him a note yourself and tell him you didn't let me read it. Send it back the way it is. I wouldn't like it at all for him to get it back all torn up—as if I had done it in anger."

"I see. I was afraid of that." He turned the envelope around and around in his hands, walking toward the fire with it, then stopped and turned to Juliana again. "All right, I'll write a note. But if it happens again . . ."

98

"It won't happen again," she said quite positively, knowing that no one in the whole world could predict what Foster Kirk might do next.

Juliana was delighted when the Chattahoochee was back to normal. She took Margo with her to the mill and they stopped on the bridge to watch the water.

"Hear the water laughing?" asked Juliana.

"No, it's crying," said Margo.

"Depends on how you listen," said Juliana. "I'll drop in this weed, and we'll run around and watch it come out."

Margo clapped her hands when she saw the weed float by on the other side.

"I want to go over that bridge," she said, pointing to the swinging bridge.

"No, no, you might fall in. It swings you as you walk."

"You've walked on it?"

"Sure she has," said a deep voice, and there was Jason grinning and doffing a straw hat.

"Jason, did you follow us?" demanded Juliana.

"I just happened to be coming this way."

"To get flour? You bake bread in the dormitory?"

"No. As a matter of fact, a certain person I know has taught me to love this noisy old river, and I was coming to see it."

"That must be Judy," said Margo in surprise. "No one could love this river more than she does."

"Judy? Juliana? Maybe it was she, now that you mention it."

"Jason, you know it's against the school rules for

girls and boys to meet alone like this."

His eyebrows shot up. "Alone? We're not alone. Margo's here. You're somebody, aren't you, Margo?" he asked, trying to curl a strand of straight blond hair around one finger.

"I sure am. I weigh as much as a sack of meal, a big one. My mamma said so." said Margo, pulling her hair free.

"See?" Jason winked at Juliana and put a hand under one elbow, but she jerked away.

"What's gotten into you, Juliana?"

"Nothing. Come on and we'll get Winnie's flour. Don't you think it looks like rain?"

"No. That's just a wind cloud."

"Are you sure?" asked Juliana.

"Do I make mistakes?"

"Only occasionally," said Juliana with a laugh and a toss of her head.

They were almost back to Brother's house when the rain did come, roaring over the top of the ridge like a giant walking waterfall. They could smell it coming, and started running, Jason carrying Margo, Juliana carrying the flour. They pelted to the back door, laughing, out of breath, and drenched to the bone.

Winnie invited Jason to come in and, on Margo's request, they made popcorn.

"I hope you come lots of times," Margo told Jason, cuddling up to him on the window seat.

"I hope I can, too," said Jason, glancing at Juliana who made no response, but daintily nibbled a single kernel of popcorn.

Spring came to the Nacoochee Valley, and Juliana began to long for home in an urgent, painful way. Henry would be getting the fields ready for planting, talking long and patiently to his horses. Mamma would be planting her garden, and taking the mattresses out to sun. She could so well picture Sister and Byron starting out of a morning behind Maude, dear old Maude with the white blaze down her nose. She longed to be there, too.

The trilliums would be gone by now. The red and white clover would be blooming in the pastures, pink thistle brushes along the fences, and in the woods by a mossy tree she might find a clump of purple violets or Johnny-jump-ups.

When Brother did finally take them all home for a weekend, Juliana ran all over Clover Hill in jubilation. She stood on top of Indian Hill and hugged a big oak tree, laying her soft cheek against the rough, bumpy bark. She petted a new calf in the pasture and Henry said with his easy chuckle that no one but Juliana could get past a mamma cow to pet her young so easily. She sat on the porch steps, hugging and playing with Henry's new dog, Spring. And she devoured slice after slice of bread spread with rich yellow butter.

No one mentioned Foster Kirk at all. Finally, just before they left on Sunday afternoon, Juliana asked Byron about him as casually as she could. She and Byron had walked down to Lorna Doone Slide and spent a happy time talking about mutual friends. As casual as her question was, Byron still jerked his head up and looked at her with a sudden cloud disturbing his sunny face.

"Juliana, I know you liked Mr. Kirk. I did, too. I'm sorry he had to be unreasonable and expect to be able to court you. It just means we can't be friends with him, that's all."

"I only asked if you knew how he was—and his Aunt De and Beppo."

She could see Byron swallow, his big Adam's apple bobbing up and down. "I—I haven't seen him in a long time now," he faltered.

"He came to the house—*again?*"

"Yes, several times. He kept wanting your address, but Mamma wouldn't give it to him and finally one day—well *I* gave it to him."

"*You,* Byron?"

"Yes. He said he wanted to write to tell you good-by—that he was going to Florida."

"To Florida? Aunt De, too?"

"I think so. Although—he may be married by now. Grange said he saw him in Atlanta with a girl who lived next to Pinedale last summer."

Maureen. It would have to be Maureen Logan. With her brown hair and green eyes and her quick pouty temper. She knew with a dismal certainty that Maureen would be a terrible wife for Foster Kirk and that there was absolutely nothing she could do about it.

"Judy, I thought—what about Jason? Brother said you were liking him a lot."

"Why, of course I am," said Juliana, giving her long hair a toss over her shoulder. "But I don't think I'll miss him half as much when I leave Nacoochee as I've missed all of you at Clover Hill. I just belong at home. When I hear the roar of the river at night, I picture it with its grays and whites, its splashes and quiet places behind rocks. But then I think about Lorna Doone Slide."

"I know. I'll miss it, too, when I'm in college in North Carolina."

"You're not leaving this year?" Her voice was taut with sudden anxiety.

"No. Of course not. We have one more year to be in school together."

"Good! One more year to be children. Come on, Byron, I'll race you to the barn. Brother will be ready to leave by now."

CHAPTER 10

THAT SUMMER AT Clover Hill was marvelous beyond compare. Mamma's summer Sunday breakfasts were like banquets. She still cooked the way Papa liked, and it didn't matter to her if she had to get up before dawn to get it accomplished. Along with fried chicken (they ate the bony pieces for breakfast; saved the good pieces for dinner), there were sliced tomatoes, biscuits and gravy, fluffy scrambled eggs, and fried corn finely cut off the cob. Sunday dinner, except for the chicken, was prepared on Saturday. But Sunday breakfast was prepared straight from the garden to stove to table, steaming and unbearably enticing to anyone who might still be in bed. It was like a celebration every week.

Henry had bought a tractor. Mamma said he'd almost worn his farm record book out, figuring and refiguring all year, and scrimping along so that he could pay cash for the tractor even before the crops came in. He taught Juliana how to drive it, which she did fairly well, as long as she was in forward gear. Henry finally told her after some weeks that she might as well leave reverse alone before she landed down in the creek. Byron and Sister both teased her about the parasol she tied to herself to protect her complexion while she plowed, but she quietly commented that they could have freckles if they wanted them.

She kept expecting a letter from Jason. After all, he had asked for her address and told her he'd never forget her. Maybe she hadn't always been as kind to him as she should, but it was because she was so confused. Now that she wasn't seeing him anymore, she realized she cared a great deal about him. She wrote several letters to him, but of course wouldn't think of mailing one until she heard from him.

Brother accepted a call to be minister of a church in Linden, North Carolina, and in August he and Winnie bought an auto and moved. Margo hung onto Juliana's neck and sobbed, "Let me live with Judy! Let me live with Judy!" She was still crying at the back window, blond hair framing a red teary face as the car eased down around the bend and out of sight.

"It'll take 'em two days to get there," said Henry, rubbing his chin thoughtfully as he stared down the now empty road. "Brother thinks the road from here to Macoochee is bad, but I hear there are holes big enough to swim in between here and Asheville. And you'd do well to get stuck only two or three times."

"Oh, dear! Those poor children," sighed Mamma, wiping her nose.

Grange and Molly came once during the summer for

a weekend. Molly seemed much better and could get around so well that it seemed Grange never walked anywhere, even to Cold Spring and Ghost Den Ridge, that she was not right beside him. Somehow, Grange seemed more serious than before. He didn't tease Juliana as he always had since she was small enough to sit on his knee. It seemed that, if he talked to her at all, he cut his eyes toward Molly to see how she was taking it.

"Grange is one hen-pecked man," observed Henry after they left. "Doesn't the Bible say something about the misery of a man with a warring wife? You can count on it, Mamma, *this* son of yours is going to remain single all his days."

"I won't hold you to that, Henry," said Mamma. "Seems as if men tend to say things like that not long before they get married."

Richard planned his vacation from the bank in Clarkesville so that he could spend a week helping with the corn harvest at Clover Hill.

"Some life," commented Richard at the table one day. "Take a vacation to slave in the sun. We should have gone to Florida as our Clarkesville artist friend did. If he can afford to move to Florida when he has land debts stacked up to his chin, then I certainly can."

"Who are you talking about, Richard?" asked Mamma, laying down her fork.

"Foster Kirk. You asked me about him once, didn't you? Very upright guy, I'm sure, but I wouldn't want his debts. Somehow he always pays on his notes on schedule. Never once has he been late. But there's something fishy about a man laying up debts like that and moving to another state."

Juliana kept her head bowed over her plate, eating much more vigorously than her hunger demanded so that no one would notice she was interested in the topic of conversation. She wished Richard would say whether Foster took his family to Florida, but he never did. Somehow she felt very depressed thinking of the little gray houses with no smoke at the cottage chimney, no open door to the studio, no cats sunning on the porch and steps, no Delia Sweet in her sharp hairdo—and no Foster whistling, laughing, painting. And what was he doing in Florida, anyway? Maybe that's where Maureen wanted to live. Florida would suit her surely—a far-off romantic place. She could easily picture Maureen posing in one of those glamorous swimsuits from Rich's of Atlanta. She could see, too, Maureen's white poodle Serena running madly from a barking Beppo.

In the meantime the conversation had turned to Henry's tractor. Foster Kirk was only mentioned again in passing. Henry said, while stabbing the air with his fork for emphasis, that he would only buy things for which he could pay cash, whereupon Richard chuckled and said the banks would be in bad shape if everyone felt that way.

Later in the afternoon Juliana found a wild tiger lily in the woods above Mud Creek. She had taken the boys some water where they were plowing in Long Bottom and was walking back over Chestnut Hill instead of along the rocky, rutted road. She knelt beside the flower, looking closely at its orange petals sprinkled with spots like large flecks of black pepper. It was fascinating to study, but she wouldn't think of picking it, for then it couldn't reseed and there might never be any more. But on the way back to the house, she picked a handful of Indian pinks. There were always plenty of those.

All too soon the lazy days of summer passed. No more dangling her feet in the cool waters of Jenkins Branch, or hunting arrowheads on Indian Hill, or exploring Ghost Den Ridge with Byron on a Sunday afternoon, or sitting on the porch breaking beans. It was over, and it was time to go to school, but in Cornelia this time.

On the first day of school Henry found Maude dead in the barn when he went to hitch her to the buggy. Sister said Maude must have been tired of carrying them to school for so many years, and just decided she wouldn't go another time. It was the first time Juliana had seen Henry cry. He told Sister to take Black and Gray, and later that day, after he'd dug a deep grave and dragged Maude to it with the tractor, he walked to town and bought a new horse named John. Mamma told Juliana that she'd found Henry leaning on his shovel handle, sobbing by Maude's grave. "Henry couldn't come home for Papa's funeral," she said, "and, strange as it may seem, I think he was mourning Papa as well as Maude. You know, Maude was a special favorite of Papa's."

The cost of the new horse came close to wiping out the profit from the summer's crops. And John was a horse of a different caliber, not known for his obedience. He made the young people late to school many times because he would simply stop in the middle of the road and refuse to move. Henry could get him to do anything, but that was Henry, not Byron or Sister who drove to school each day.

In fact, Henry really seemed to prefer horses to people, anyway. On a winter evening, as Juliana and Byron sat at the table munching apples and studying Latin and poetry, Henry suddenly threw down his paper and stalked out the door. When he returned an hour or so later, Mamma asked where he'd been. "Down at the barn listening to the horses eat," he'd say. "Can't stand to listen to Byron and Judy chomping on apples."

Juliana's best friend Stella, who had at one time lived next to Clover Hill, but now lived in town, told her she hadn't really missed much the year before. The highlights of the school year had been Margie Whidden's Christmas party, where Buddy Crane had broken his nose running into a door facing while playing Blindman's Bluff, and the school play in which Miss Shannon, the language teacher, ended up playing Juliet because Elizabeth Miller became mysteriously ill at the last minute.

"I think it was because Spike Henderson was Romeo," she confided. "Now that you're back, maybe Spike won't win all the spelling bees. It has been so boring. And now I want to hear all about what happened. Why did you go off to school like that?" Stella's face was full of anticipation for the story she'd been longing to hear.

But Juliana disappointed her. All she would say was that Mamma wanted her to go live with Brother for a while, that Nacoochee was a beautiful place (Did she know that Nacoochee meant "Evening Star"?), and that she'd learned a new Indian legend, walked a swinging bridge, and had a boyfriend named Jason. Stella had heard rumors about the artist in Clarkesville, and tried to pry something out of Juliana. But best friend or not, Stella could not be trusted with the intricacies of that relationship with Foster Kirk. All Juliana would ever admit was that he was a friend of the family and that he had painted her portrait which she showed her awed friend when she came to visit. "I wish an artist would do my portrait," Stella said dreamily.

A little later when the girls sat down to a cup of tea, Stella leaned forward eagerly, ready to hear about Jason.

"Is he very handsome? Does he like the outdoors? Did he ask you to marry him?"

Juliana laughed so that she jostled tea out of her cup and onto Mamma's lace tablecloth. "Stella Adams! I don't plan to marry anyone for at least ten years!" she exclaimed.

"But did he ask you?"

"No. Not exactly."

"Oh, how terribly romantic. I do wish I were pretty and smart like you, and someone would ask me."

"Stella, I told you he *didn't* ask me. And you *are* pretty and smart. Why, with those enchanting curls in front of your ears, you look just like a model."

"Do I *really?*"

Mamma, hearing the girls' chatter, sighed happily. It was so good to have Juliana home to stay.

Juliana soon found it was no small thing to compete against Spike Henderson who had moved the year before from Roanoke, Virginia, and already considered himself at the top of his class. Even when she beat him in algebra competitions and essay contests, Juliana knew that it was a very close thing, and she couldn't help feeling sorry for him as she watched the frustration grow in his sober, never-smiling face. All the same, she had no intention of doing any less than her best.

Juliana enrolled in an elocution class with Byron. Sister also wanted her to take piano again, but Juliana stubbornly refused, remembering the wretched hours of practicing years before. In elocution she and Byron memorized many poems, as well as writing and delivering speeches. They practiced on old stubborn John, the horse, as well as Sister, who were forced to listen to long recitations on the road back and forth to school.

One day on the way home Byron became more enthusiastic than usual as he recited "Recessional" by Rudyard Kipling. He stood in the buggy and waved his arms in emphasis to trees as they passed, exactly as if the trees were grand ladies and gentlemen in a lecture hall. Juliana and Sister both developed the silly giggles over Byron's stern formality, but Sister, being a teacher with a serious image to protect, tried to be sedate when she saw a buggy approaching. She commanded Byron to sit down, then when he wouldn't, she tried to pull him down with one hand. But he was in a playful mood and was thoroughly enjoying himself, forgetful of all his shyness.

As the approaching buggy rattled closer and closer, Sister was able to recognize an old German peddler who had been to the house many times. She sighed with relief, glad that it was not the minister or, worse still, the school principal, and she prepared to give Kurt a friendly nod. But John was very tired of all this nonsense, the wobbling of the buggy as Byron balanced like an inexperienced politician, the awkward handling of the reins, and, above all, the outrageous recitation in full voice. John took matters under his own control as, with a sudden lurch, he plunged forward at full speed.

Byron barely escaped falling out the back as Juliana hung onto him, her books and papers falling to the floor or scattering to the winds. Sister was pulling back on the reins as hard as she could, but to no avail. John's ears were turned back, his neck arched defiantly, as he galloped on. Kurt, the peddler, turned a startled white face toward them just before his own horse, a rib-showing, dull-haired black, broke into his own sudden gallop, spilling some bottles and boxes out the back.

All three young people were holding their sides in helpless laughter when John finally stopped with a loud snort in front of the barn door.

"We didn't hurt John." Byron was defensive when Henry accused him of mistreating the animal. "We were only reciting poetry. I can't help it if he's a temperamental creature."

"Ought to have better sense than to torture him like that," said Henry sourly, giving John an affectionate slap and allowing the horse to rub his head up and down on his shirt, smearing it with sweaty grime.

"I wonder if the poor peddler retrieved his little bottles and boxes," said Juliana, trying to straighten out the crimped edges of her Latin book.

"We would have helped him if we could have stopped John," said Sister. "Henry, you know the German peddler who's been here several times? Mamma's bought vanilla from him before."

"So that's who drove up awhile back," said Henry, leading John into the barn. "I heard the chickens making a big to-do, and Spring ran up there barking. But by the time I got there, there was nothing but buggy tracks left. Well, I won't worry about missing him. I didn't want any vanilla or tonic, although the poor cuss could use some business, I'm sure. A lot of people around here are suspicious of him because he's German. They're still trying to keep the war alive, I guess."

"Funny. I didn't see Mamma at all when we came by," said Byron. "I know she must have been startled. Or has she gone somewhere?"

"Gone to the Davises," answered Henry. "Mrs. Davis's daughter Laura is having her baby, I reckon. Blake came to get Mamma."

"Good old Blake," said Juliana. "I wonder what will ever become of him. I wish . . ."

"I know," said Sister. "you always thought he could have learned to read and write if someone had known how to teach him. Wonder what made him the way he is, anyway. I hope Laura's baby is all right."

"Oh, you girls! Always worrying about things you can do nothing about. Now get out of my way, and let

113

me soothe this poor horse. You could do well to worry about *him* now and then.''

"Henry, you are impossible!" exclaimed Sister over her shoulder as the girls left the barn. Byron stayed behind to appease his brother.

As they approached the house, Juliana paused in the path. "You know, Sister, I haven't seen the Davises very much since I've been back home. I guess I've been too busy. And Blake hasn't teased me lately. I think—let's walk over there. Want to?"

"I'd like to. I haven't seen Laura since she moved to Demorest. But I'd better start supper. Mamma may not be home for a long time. You know how slow these—things—can be. Let me take your books, and *you* go."

The Davises' house was small and unpainted, with lots of room under the house for chickens to take dust baths. Juliana remembered with a shudder the time when she and some other children had been playing hide-and-seek, and she had hidden behind one of the pillars under the house. She'd been so quiet and had thought no one had any idea where she was when, suddenly, hands covered her eyes from behind and clamped tight. In the sudden darkness she'd panicked and screamed, then heard the sniveling, snickering sound that only Blake could make.

Now she could see that old broken chairs, a lawn-mower, and other things had been packed under the house. The low-slanting sun rays made grotesque shadows of handles, rungs, and wheels. As her steps crunched in the fresh, fallen leaves a dog ran down from the porch barking, and immediately Blake's bulky body appeared at the door, his face breaking into smiles at sight of Juliana. She received his hug as she always had when they were children.

"How is Laura, Blake?"

"She's bad. Babies are bad."

"Oh, no, not the babies themselves! Just the pain. I'm sure Laura will be all right. Just think, Blake, you'll be an uncle!" She laughed over her shoulder at him as she stepped into the house. Roger and Ben Davis rose to greet her, obviously pleased to have a fresh face and voice to break the monotony. Mamma, hearing her voice, stepped out of the bedroom where Laura lay. Her hair was falling from the pins, and her cheeks sagged.

"Juliana, I'm glad you're here. You need to cook some supper for these folks. Maybe the boys can show you where things are in the kitchen. You can make some bread and gravy or a stew or something. But be sure and keep the kettle of water hot."

"But, Mamma, I—"

"Yes, you can do it, Juliana," she said firmly. "Boys, see to it she finds what she needs. I think—it won't be long now." She turned quickly as there was a wrenching scream from the bedroom.

Blake clapped his hands over his ears and closed his eyes tightly almost as if he were the one in pain.

Juliana's heart thudded against her ribs, and she licked her lips that had suddenly gone dry. "All right," she said, trying to sound steady and controlled, "show me where your skillet is, and where you keep your eggs."

Juliana gained more and more confidence as she

moved about the kitchen—straining the evening milk, breaking eggs in a bowl, and turning thick slices of bacon as they sputtered in the skillet. *What would Jason think of me preparing supper all by myself for three grown men?* she wondered. *Or Foster?* She paused in her vigorous stirring of eggs. *Foster. Where is he now? Is Maureen kind to him?* She gave a little scream as big arms closed around her from behind.

"Blake Davis, you almost made me spill this bowl of eggs. Now don't do that!" She squirmed to extricate herself from his hold, but found she was quite powerless. "Roger! Ben! Make Blake let me go so I can finish your supper!" she commanded sternly.

Blake suddenly dropped his arms, and her shoulders sagged in relief.

"Don't you like me any more, Miss Juliana?" he asked in a hurt tone.

"Of course I do. That's why I'm making supper for you," she said briskly. "Now sit down like a good boy and wait till I call you."

The boys were eating when the baby was born, a fine healthy baby girl. "It's a shame Laura's husband was out west when his first child was born," said Mamma as she and Juliana walked home in the moonlight.

"Why is he out west?"

"Seeking better things. People are becoming more and more dissatisfied living the way they always have. I declare, it looks as if they would realize how good things are at home without roaming so far away. But then, it's really not a new urge—to wander, I mean.

Your papa had it, too. He would have moved to south Georgia in a minute if his deal had worked out."

"Mamma, you're tired and you're getting out of breath. Better just walk and not talk, don't you think? The stars are out and the moonlight is so pretty—like a peaceful blessing on our trees and the roof of our house. A beautiful night for a baby to be born."

"Yes. A fine baby, too," said Mamma. Then, lowering her voice, she added sadly, "I hope she's not like Blake."

Juliana looked behind her with a sudden nameless fear. She was glad when they were again safe at Clover Hill.

Just before Thanksgiving the Davises had a corn shucking. That was when Henry met Martha Brady and began dressing up and riding off in the buggy behind John for long rides on Saturday afternoons. And that's when Juliana began really to fear Blake Davis, for whom she'd felt only sympathy all her life. The boy had never been quite right and had never gone to school, but everyone considered him harmless, just a pitiful nitwit who was good for nothing but slopping pigs and killing chickens.

At the corn shucking Juliana noticed Blake watching her every move, and his eyes didn't stay on her hands shucking corn or on her face, either. He kept looking disturbingly at a point in between, until she looked several times to see if her sweater had popped a button or if she'd spilled some of Mrs. Davis's barbecue sauce down her front.

Blake handled his sister's tiny baby with tender

care, his big hands making a cradle for the little one as he hauled her around to all the shuckers, bragging on her beauty. Stella, shucking next to Juliana, nudged her with an elbow after Blake had moved on. "I'm glad I'm living in town," she said. "That boy scares me. It's his eyes."

The two girls entered into the shucking contest with spirit and, though neither of them won in the girls' division, they certainly made it tough for Martha Brady. Juliana had seen Henry talking to the dark-haired girl early in the day and was glad her lonely brother was enjoying a little well-deserved diversion. But as things had progressed, Juliana had become almost jealous, for Henry had not noticed her as he usually did. After the final corn shucking contest, as she and Stella stood by the wide barn door, Henry ambled by and pulled a lock of Juliana's hair, a familiar gesture, accompanied by a one-sided grin. Things hand't changed after all.

After the corn shucking Juliana could not feel comfortable when she saw Blake Davis, even at a distance. She didn't trust the wandering look in his eyes.

One evening she was hurrying toward home, having studied late at Stella's. She'd promised to be home before dark, and now the shadows were long and the blackness of night crept in toward the road. When she heard the clip-clop of horses' hooves, she glanced over her shoulder, and, seeing Mrs. Davis and Blake, she walked even faster. But the buggy slowed as it came up behind her, and Blake jumped down, his big red face not far from hers as he announced, "We take you home, Miss Juliana."

Involuntarily she sprang back from him, and stammered, "I-I-I'm in a hurry."

"So let us give you a ride, dear," said Mrs. Davis pleasantly, and Blake grinned at her, his eyes traveling swiftly down her brown coat to her stockinged ankles and back up again.

"No—no, thank you," she said and, with her throat tight with unnamed fear, she turned and walked on again, leaving Blake looking after her. Soon the buggy passed her again, and for Mrs. Davis's sake, she lifted one hand in a little wave, but she would not look up.

"You little goose," Mamma said to Juliana when she heard about it. "To tell our good neighbor you were in too big a hurry for a ride!"

She didn't know how to explain to Mamma how she felt about Blake. To Mamma he was still the helpless child who played silly tricks. And maybe he was. Maybe, thought Juliana, he was as harmless as ever.

CHAPTER 11

WHEN BYRON GRADUATED at the top of his class in June, no one was more delighted than Juliana. She swelled with pride until she felt like bursting as he gave his speech, which was an oration that did credit to the long hours and miles of recitation. She smiled to herself, remembering how Byron had once been so shy he wouldn't even go to Foster Kirk's without her, and now he was speaking boldly before a crowd and planning to go off to Davidson College in North Carolina in the fall.

The family wasn't really surprised that Byron was valedictorian.

"After all," said Henry grumpily, "anybody who drives a tractor with a book in one hand should be voratorian—or whatever you call it."

"Has a girl ever been valedictorian?" Juliana asked as she and Sister washed the supper dishes.

Sister looked at her quickly, her face alert, her eyes

searching her younger sister's carefully curtained expression. She squeezed out the dishrag and walked over to the stove where she began to wipe the white enamel on the warming closet doors.

"Of course there have." She paused significantly. "And there will be again."

Juliana never understood what happened to the summer after Byron's graduation. Maybe it was knowing that he would soon be leaving that made the green-gold days fly by so quickly, though she longed to hug each one tightly to her heart. They did so many things for the last time—picked apples in the orchard, took long strolls on Indian Hill, raced to see who could find the largest number of brown thrashers' nests, and, of course, made one last tearful visit to Lorna Doone Slide.

When the day came to see Byron off to college, Juliana thought her heart would break. She knew a precious part of her girlhood had ended. The falling leaves echoed her loss, until suddenly it was winter, with only her schoolwork and an occasional letter from Byron to remind her that she must move resolutely ahead, following all the bends in the road.

On a cold, windy day in December, Sister and Juliana started toward the stable in town where John stayed while they were in school. Juliana was looking forward to telling Sister all that Miss Shannon had told her recently about the scholarship being offered by an elderly gentleman in the community. She shifted her books to the other arm and dug in her coat pocket for two apple cores she'd saved for John. But John was in a bad mood. He refused Juliana's treat, slung his head when they tried to harness him, even bared his teeth at Sister.

When he planted himself solidly with back hooves in the stall door, Juliana thought they must give up, but Sister sent her up in the loft to try to drop the harness over his head. John tossed his head violently and the harness fell into a pile of fresh manure. The girls shivered and surveyed the situation. They would have to go past John's kicking heels in order to retrieve the harness. When Juliana said, "Let's just walk," Sister didn't argue.

The road had not thawed all day and now purple shadows fell across white patches in the crusty red ruts. The girls' legs felt wooden up to their knees, and they stumbled over frozen clods of clay. Their fingers ached in permanent curved positions around their books, the woolen mittens affording little relief from the penetrating cold. But even with the wind grabbing their words and threatening to freeze their very teeth, Juliana was eager to tell Sister about the scholarship.

"Miss Shannon thinks I have a chance for it, even though Spike Henderson has an edge on me right now."

"And the scholarship would pay your tuition for a whole year? At what college?"

"Any one I choose. Oh, Sister, you know I won't get it! And I don't want to go away from home again anyway. But it's so exciting to try—just to see if I can do it!"

"Of course you can do it!" exclaimed Sister, hugging her books tighter for warmth, and walking faster. "Since I'm going to North Carolina to teach next year, you could go to Flora McDonald in Red Springs. It's a good college for girls. We could get together at Brother's for the holidays, you and Byron and me. Wouldn't that be fun!''

"But then Mamma and Henry . . .''

"They could come, too. They could ride up on the train."

Juliana pulled her scarf across her nose for a minute's reprieve from the biting wind. She knew she couldn't leave Clover Hill again, couldn't bear to go through that terrible homesickness, but—a scholarship that she could earn herself! She had the application with her and would fill it out that night. She had already looked it over, and the only thing that worried her now was what to write on the line that asked what career she planned to pursue.

The girls scooped out the mail as they went by the box, but didn't stop to see to whom the letters were addressed. Mamma met them on the porch, pulling them in, and closing the door against the wind. The creases between her eyes were deep as she listened to John's latest escapade. At the same time she settled them in chairs in front of the open oven door, and set a pan of warm water on a stool between them for their icy hands. Juliana sniffed appreciatively at the warm smell of fresh bread, then felt a trickle run from her thawing nose. Mamma pulled a handkerchief out of her bosom and handed it to her.

"You girls will catch your death this way," she fussed. "Papa would have already had you boarding for the winter in Cornelia, but it's so lonesome here without you."

"Oh, we're all right, Mamma!" said Juliana. "We don't want to go and board again, do we, Sister? Why don't you see what's in the mail?"

There was a letter from Grange which Mamma read to them. It was filled with the usual hilarious descriptions of people at work, but there was a note of concern, too. "I know you always take in anyone who needs a night's rest, because that's how I got to know you myself. But these times can be dangerous, and I wish you would be careful. The Ku Klux Klan has been reorganized, and they're threatening anyone who even helps a German or Jew." He barely mentioned Molly—only to say that she was not very well and maybe spring would perk her up.

"Poor Grange," sighed Mamma, folding the letter, "I'm afraid Molly will never be well."

"And what about the Ku Klux Klan, Mamma?" asked Sister.

Juliana noticed the deep valleys running from Mamma's nose down by her mouth. "I can't believe they'd bother us, but we must be alert, and we *must not* be out after dark," she said, creasing Grange's letter between her fingers.

There were heavy footsteps on the porch, and a rush of cold air as Henry let himself in. He came directly to the stove, holding his fingers over the heat, and stamping his feet to bring them back to life. Juliana looked up at his face, lined already with wind and sun wrinkles and so red now, his lips chapped and cracked.

"I'll make you some coffee, Henry," she said, getting to her feet.

He turned blue eyes on her, then on Sister who had slid her feet into the oven and was blissfully soaking up the heat. "Where's John?" he asked.

"We couldn't get him hitched up," said Juliana. "We tried and tried, but it was so cold we finally gave up."

Henry looked first astonished, then angry, and finally bewildered as he stood there warming himself, glancing out the window at the trees blowing in the wind. It would soon be dark, and threatened to be one of the coldest nights of the year.

"I'm sorry, Henry," said Juliana helplessly.

"We'll walk in the morning," said Sister, "and by tomorrow afternoon John will be glad to come home."

Henry didn't answer. He just jammed his stocking hat back down over his ears, turned the collar up on his old army coat, and went out the door, closing it firmly behind him.

"Supper will be ready soon!" Mamma called after him, but only the wind answered.

"He's going to walk to town and get him!" exclaimed Juliana, watching from a window.

"I told him we'd get him tomorrow!" said Sister. "John would be all right in that stable."

"But he didn't have supper, did he?" asked Mamma. "And you know Henry. He won't eat himself unless his horses are cared for first. I just hope . . . but I know Henry will be fine."

They knew she was thinking of the Ku Klux Klan.

Mamma swished her hand around in the washtub of hominy. It was the third washing. Maybe one more would take out the bitterness of the oak ash, and she would be through. All day since right after breakfast, she'd cooked the shelled corn until it was the color of wheat, each kernel puffy and tender. Now for an hour she'd been washing it, standing by the wash bench out back. Every now and then she found a bad kernel she had missed in her pre-cooking scrutiny, and she threw it to a clutch of chickens that milled around her expectantly.

Scooping the last of the corn into a clean tub of water, she straightened up, wiped her chapped hands on her apron, and rubbed a place in the small of her back. She looked toward the west at the setting sun, outlining a tree full of early starlings that looked like French knots embroidered against the sky. Then she looked anxiously toward the driveway. It was time Juliana was home. This business of staying in town to study with Stella had gotten to be too much of a habit lately. The child was studying herself to death and to what end? She couldn't get that scholarship, and even if she did, what good would it do her to have one year of college when she couldn't have any more? There was no money to keep her there.

She bent toward her work again. Henry had studied and figured late into the night over his farm record book, and she guessed he was wanting to get married and build a house. But there wasn't any cash available for him or for Juliana, and no prospects of any. Besides, what would Juliana do with a college education? The girl had a headful of dreams that she guarded as carefully as a miner would his gold nuggets. Mamma smiled to herself and said out loud, "If that waterfall could talk, maybe I'd learn what's going on in my little girl's head."

She glanced up again, feeling the chill as the sun's rays disappeared completely. "Where is that child?" she wondered, and she couldn't help thinking about her own encounter recently with the Ku Klux Klan.

She'd been on her way home from nursing the little Davis grandbaby who had the croup. It was already dark when she started home, and she'd given old John the reins and let her mind shift into restful neutral, though she was jostled hither and fro on the rough road.

Suddenly without warning she was surrounded by the horsemen in their white capes and black hoods, all silent, all holding lanterns. She tightened the reins and was glad John just stopped and didn't snort and rear.

"Just what do you want?" she demanded, surprised that her voice didn't shake.

At first no one had answered. She remembered her arms prickling, how frightened she'd been of their silence, their ominous masked silence.

Then one had come forward, and, stopping directly in front of her, his lantern blinding her, he'd spoken. "We know you've been harboring foreigners on your farm."

At first she couldn't think what foreigner they could mean, then she'd laughed in relief, "Oh, you must mean that poor old German peddler. You can't possibly care if I buy vanilla from a man who's trying to make a living, and maybe give him a bite to eat and a place to sleep. *You* would want the same under similar circumstances." There had been that awful silence again. Then she'd felt anger surging inside of her, and it hadn't mattered what she said. "There are potholes in this road that need to be fixed, and all you can do is get out in the dark and plague people who are trying to live peaceably. If you want to do something, why don't you fix this road?"

There was a menacing growl from the Klan figures which moved in to envelope her. Then the spokesman held up one hand and the low rumbling stopped abruptly.

"Madam!" he said. "It shall be done!"

She'd sat there, stunned, watching them ride off, the shadows of their capes and masks thrown up against the blackness of the woods in the lantern light.

Now she wondered if those men were out tonight, with Juliana alone and on foot along the road. She knew Juliana was more afraid of Blake Davis than she was of the Klan, but surely that fear was unfounded. All the Hamiltons had cared for Blake since he was in diapers, and he'd always been so lovable and kind. Still, Juliana was not one to complain, and *she* felt there was something to fear. Mamma decided that when Juliana got home, she would tell her she just must not study at Stella's unless she were going to spend the night.

Juliana herself was not particularly concerned as she started home from Stella's house. She knew she had stayed too late again, but she'd gotten so much done. Stella was as interested in her winning the scholarship as she was. In fact, she would have given up before now if it hadn't been for Stella and Sister—and Miss Shannon. Miss Shannon had told her only today that she felt Juliana had some special contribution to make to the world and that she would do all she could to help her. Thinking of it now, Juliana did a little skip in the road and lightly hummed a tune.

A rabbit hopped into the road in front of her, and she stopped to watch it sitting there, a snug hump of fur with perky, pricked ears. A twig snapped, and the bunny jumped on across the road. As Juliana started on, she thought she heard footsteps in the woods beside the road. But when she stopped, she heard nothing and decided it was her imagination. Realizing how dark it had gotten, and that Mamma would be worried, she hurried along.

A scurry of dry leaves blew into the road like so many biddies following a mother hen. At the same moment Juliana heard someone cough. It could only be a cough. There was no other sound it could be. Her heart hammered in her chest, and her knees felt suddenly weak as she looked behind her and realized what a long, lonely stretch of road it was. There wasn't a glimmer of light from a house or cottage anywhere in sight, only the dusky road, and the dark woods shouldering close. Licking dry lips, she started on, willing herself to think about the scholarship and thus forget her fear until she was safely home.

She was totally unprepared to defend herself against the big shape that suddenly extricated itself from the dark anonymity of the woods and engulfed her in arms that were like a steel trap. The hard corners of her books dug into her soft flesh and, with terror, she heard Blake Davis's voice shrilling in exultation, "I got you! I got you now, Miss Juliana!"

The more she struggled, the harder he held her until she could barely breathe. His hot breath was close and heavy with the nauseating smell of onions. In desperation she drew back one foot and kicked his shin as hard as she could. He let out a yowl and let go of her. Her books still hugged to her chest, she started running, but for all her speed he was right there, his big hands grasping her arms, pulling her against him. "I will not let you go, Juliana. You're mine," he cooed. "I've waited, oh so long, and you won't leave me now. I'll take you where no one will ever find you and we'll be happy. Just you and me."

It was dark now. She couldn't see his face, even if she dared to look up. But she must think of something to say that would change his mind. How could she bribe him? *Oh, God, help me,* she prayed, *Help me be calm like Mamma with the KKK's. Help me think of something wise to say.*

"If you'll take me home, Blake, I'll fix you a wonderful big supper," Juliana said in the soothing tone his mother used with him. She felt him thinking about it. He loved to eat. "Maybe some sausage and eggs —and—and—hot biscuits with butter," she continued. He was very quiet, his breathing heavy and horrible, but otherwise quiet. He just stood there, holding her in a frozen vise.

Then suddenly he thrust her from him, his hands gripping bruisingly into her arms.

"You think you can bribe me," he snarled. "Don't try that, Juliana. Don't try it!"

He shook her then and she dropped her books and began to beat against him with her fists. But his grip on her arms was so hard that it did no good, and he laughed cruelly.

"I've been waiting for this and you're not getting away from me anymore," he said.

Neither of them noticed the sound of a car engine until it was bearing down just beyond the turn. Blake tried then to jump the ditch with her and get out of sight, but she struggled and kicked and managed to hold her ground. Car lights flooded them, illuminating the grim tableau. A motor roared and the car stopped within a foot of them, but Blake hung on still, his breathing hard and fast.

"They can't make me let you go. They can't make me!" he was saying over and over, even as a fist connected abruptly with the side of his chin.

"Juliana, get in the car!" yelled Foster Kirk as he dealt Blake another blow, this time knocking him into the ditch.

Juliana stood by the car, but would not get in. She shuddered at the grunts and groans of the men and the sickening thuds of flesh on flesh. It looked as if Blake had given up and was just letting Mr. Kirk pound him mercilessly.

"Don't hurt him!" she cried out. "He—he—didn't know what he was doing!"

But no sooner were the words out of her mouth than she saw Foster lift big Blake by his overalls and hurl him across the ditch. Foster leapt after him and grabbed hold of him as if he wanted to pick him up just to beat him down again.

Juliana screamed, "Don't hurt him!" and was relieved when Foster reluctantly turned away from the shadowy heap.

As Foster strode back into the full lights of the car, she saw the ugly gash over one eyebrow and blood running from his nose. But he stopped anything she might have said by snapping, "I said get in!"

"But—we can't just leave him there."

"What do you suggest we do—take him to your house?"

"No, but he lives nearby . . ."

"He'll get home. He isn't out for long. Now get in before I pick you up and put you in!"

Seeing her shaking uncontrollably, he pulled off his coat and placed it around her, his strong hands gentle as he adjusted it to her shoulders. It was a leather coat and smelled just like him, rugged and woodsy. She pulled it close around her, and as they bumped along, stole a glance at his face. It was too dark to see anything but the barest outline of his jutting chin. Even so, she could feel his anger like a live force between them. It terrified her at the same time that it comforted her in a way she couldn't understand.

"He—he's a nitwit," she blurted out now by way of explanation. "He's never hurt anybody before."

A muscle worked in his jaw, and, after a moment, he said, "I could have killed him. When I saw him attacking you, it unleashed every ounce of anger in me. You were one plucky firebrand, though," he added with a chuckle as he turned into Clover Hill.

A flood of relief swept over her—he didn't blame her! Suddenly the full impact of the shame and fear hit her and she began to cry, pressing her knuckles hard against her mouth.

"Are you all right, Juliana? Did he hurt you?" asked Foster, slowing the car. His voice was so instantly tender that her tears flowed faster.

"It's just—just that—I've lost all my books," she stammered, knowing full well that wasn't why she was crying.

"You were just getting home from school?" he asked in a shocked tone.

"I was studying at my friend Stella's."

After a minute's silence he said between his teeth, "Don't worry, I'll get the books for you. But why in the name of thunder would you have to study so late?"

They were parked now in front of the house. She looked helplessly at his dark profile and could not answer. Then Mamma and Henry were running out with Sister right behind them. Juliana slid out of the coat and was fumbling to open the door when Foster, who had come around the car with Spring leaping and barking around his feet, flung the door open for her and reached in to help her out. Unaccountably she refused his hand and stood by herself.

"What's this?" demanded Henry harshly, recognizing Foster Kirk and seeing Juliana looking scared and rumpled.

"I found Juliana—" began Foster, then looked down at her drooping head. "I'll let her tell you," he said in a tightly controlled voice. "And I hope you'll realize she shouldn't be out so late. I hate to think what might have happened if I hadn't come along."

"Now just a minute, sir," said Henry, stepping forward belligerently.

"That's all right, I'm leaving," said Foster, turning on his heel. "But, remember, I'm not the real enemy," he flung over his shoulder. He raced his motor, turned the car around, and rocked off down the driveway, leaving them in total darkness.

"Juliana?" asked Mamma, an arm around her trembling shoulders. "The Ku Klux Klan?"

"No, Mamma. Blake Davis."

The next morning Juliana found her books stacked in the porch chair by the front door. She didn't know when he had put them there, but she was sure Foster had left them. Where was he today? And why had he been on Mud Creek Road last night? He had not explained, and now she was unlikely to see him again.

Mrs. Davis came over in the afternoon and sat at the dining table, weeping into a cup of strong coffee. "Don't tell on my poor Blake," she begged over and over, with Mamma assuring her all the time that she wouldn't. "I don't know what made him do it. He's not like that. You know yourself, Mrs. Hamilton, he's gentle as a kitten. If it'd been anyone else but you folk, I wouldn't believe it. I'd think it was a trick. But the bruises on Juliana's poor white arms—and her word, too, that I've always trusted. Oh, if only Mr. Davis hadn't left me. How can I bear this all alone?"

"You're not alone. That's what Christian friends are for," said Mamma, standing behind the distraught woman, gently massaging her shoulders. "We would have come last night, but you said Blake was home and you were busy treating his wounds. By the way, he is all right, isn't he? I suppose he walked home?"

"No." Mrs. Davis shuddered in a spasm of fresh sobs. *"He* brought him—that man—the same one who beat him up."

"Foster Kirk?" asked Mamma in surprise, looking quickly at Juliana whose blond head jerked up from her book.

"Yes, him. I begged him not to tell, but he never promised. Just brought my boy in and got him on the bed. He asked if he could help, and when I said no, he left. My boy may go to jail . . ." she wailed.

"He will not!" declared Juliana. "I won't testify against him."

For weeks they expected any day to have a visit from the sheriff, but no one ever came. Juliana kept her bruises well covered with long sleeves, and when the lesions were only pale green, she looked at them and wondered if the whole ordeal had only been a terrible nightmare. She had written to Foster Kirk and begged him not to tell anyone about Blake, assuring him that Mrs. Davis and her other sons were watching him closely now and would keep him out of trouble. But she never had an answer from him. It was as if he'd never been back, as if she'd imagined it all. Finally she stopped watching all the cars in town as if she might see him and settled back into her rigid study schedule, working even harder to make up for lost time, but making sure she never stayed late at Stella's except to spend the night.

One day Mamma found the portrait of Juliana hidden behind the phonograph. Upon questioning Henry and learning that he had done it, she chided him soundly.

"I don't want to be reminded of that man," grumbled Henry. "I wish he'd stay in Florida and mind his own business."

"Henry, I'm surprised at you! You know Juliana could have been seriously injured if Foster hadn't rescued her."

Henry grunted something under his breath and strode out of the house, on his way to the barn to talk to the horses.

CHAPTER 12

ON JUNE 1 THERE WAS a general buzz of excitement in all the rooms at Cornelia High, but particularly in the room where the seniors awaited the news from a panel of teachers as to who would be valedictorian and salutatorian, and this year, even more interesting, who would be the recipient of the Walter K. Durden Scholarship. The teachers had been closeted in the principal's office across the hall for more than an hour now.

"It must be the decision about the scholarship that's taking so long," said Stella nervously, glancing at Juliana's pale face with the flushed spots of excitement on her cheeks.

"They just want to make us sweat," said Spike Henderson, pacing with agitation in the hot room. He talked so confidently yet he was nervous, too, thought Juliana, or he wouldn't be walking back and forth so. Poor Spike, he really wanted that scholarship and he would probably put it to better use than she. She al-

137

most wished she could remove her application, but it was too late now. And anyway she really wanted to go to college, to go on learning.

Juliana's supporters clustered around her. She wished they would leave her alone, but she didn't want to hurt their feelings. She was glad when a spitball fight erupted, for she managed to stay in her desk and not get involved. That way she could think what she might do next, now that school was over.

Whether she won or not, she felt she had made a good showing. If Spike did win, he certainly hadn't had it easy. The competition had been keen. All those late nights by the kerosene lamps, the many afternoons that she'd carried her books with her to study by Jenkins Branch, the tests, the spelling bees, the drills in French—all of it was worth it, no matter what.

Once she'd thought she would be a teacher like Sister, but now she wasn't sure. She just knew she still wanted to learn. There was more knowledge than she'd even scratched, and she wasn't ready to stop now. And somewhere there was a special task for her. She had not been born just to be, but to do.

She started in her seat as someone shouted, "Here they come! Into your desks!" Instantly the tension was back. Her hands were sticky and her heart thumped hard. No matter how she might rationalize, she wanted to be the top student, and she wanted that scholarship. There would have been no fun in trying so hard if there hadn't been that hope.

The principal, whose thin hair was graying, was a little on the plump side. On this afternoon, as he stood before the miraculously quiet seniors, he mopped the sweat from his face with a handkerchief, then stuck it in his pocket so he could hold a half-sheet of paper with both hands. He cleared his throat, folded and unfolded the paper, and finally, over the drumming of a bee trying to get out the top of one of the tall windows, he began to speak.

"We're proud of all our seniors at Cornelia High," (one or two in the back ducked their heads) "and we wish you well as you go out into the world. For some of our students, this is a particularly rewarding time. But I hope for all of you it is a time of fulfillment." ("When is he going to stop stammering around?" whispered Stella beside Juliana.) "I know you're all anxious to hear who the two students are." (Everyone leaned forward in breathless expectancy.) "The reason it's taken so long is that our two top students are only a fraction of a point apart in their scores, and we wanted to be quite positive we had it right." He folded and refolded the paper. "According to the scores as they stand, I pronounce the valedictorian of the class of 1922—Miss Juliana Hamilton!"

The room exploded into cheers, but the principal held up a hand to quiet them. "There is more," he said. "We have a fine young man—(did he emphasize the word man?)—Spike Henderson is salutatorian." Cheers again, particularly from the male students. Then everyone fell silent and the whole room barely breathed, waiting for the final announcement.

The principal cleared his throat and wiped his face again. "This year our faculty has had the added responsibility of choosing, not only the top student, but the student with the highest average along with the most practical ambitions for using his or her talents. It is with pleasure that I offer the Walter K. Durden Scholarship to Spike Henderson!''

Sister was ecstatic on the way home. "You really are valedictorian. So what if you lost the scholarship? You really didn't want it, anyway. Being valedictorian was your goal, and you've made it! Won't Mamma be surprised! I'm so glad I took extra pains with your white graduation dress. All Mamma's pretty lace will be seen by everyone, and you'll look just like a queen.''

"Sister! Please hush! We should have *both* been valedictorian, you know. I was only a fraction of a point ahead of Spike. He probably knows more math than I do.''

"But you were ahead, and it's only right you should have the honor. Just think—my own little sister, a winner! I sure am going to miss you next year,'' said Sister in a burst of affection.

"You miss *me?* You're the one who's leaving. Why, you'll be so busy up there in North Carolina making all those children toe a straight line, you won't have time to think about us. But I—I don't know what I'll be doing.''

"Take the class I'm leaving at Cornelia Elementary, Juliana. You would be so good. And they said today they still hadn't gotten anyone.''

"I don't know. I guess right now I'll concentrate on writing my speech.''

The auditorium was packed on graduation night. There were banks of mountain laurel in the front, and, down the aisle, a profusion of rose petals strewn by little girls in frilly dresses.

The heat was smothery, and a flick-flick could be heard all over the auditorium as everyone fanned their programs to stir the humid air. Juliana was about to maul hers to shreds as she waited for her turn to speak. She didn't hear Spike's speech nor the principal's. Strangely, it was Henry she was thinking about. He was there tonight with his girl friend Martha.

Just a few months ago he had declared he would never marry, but then Martha had come along, and though no public plans had been made, they all knew what Henry had in mind. But that was not what was uppermost in *her* thoughts now. It was the fact that Henry should have had a chance to graduate as she was doing. He should not have had to stay home all these years running the farm while the rest of them went to school. Few people realized how much Henry minded not having an education—but she knew. She had heard him talking to Maude, to Black and Gray, and more recently to stubborn old John. He told them everything, and she had heard him when he didn't know she was anywhere near. Why should it be that someone always had to sacrifice that others might have blessings?

She looked down at her carefully written speech, smudged now on the edges from her sweaty hands. There was one thing for sure. She wanted this speech to make Henry proud, and she wanted him and the rest of the family, and all her teachers, to know that she didn't take this privilege for granted, that she knew sacrifices had been made. Oh, she wouldn't embarrass

Henry. But he would know what she meant. She had practiced this speech so many times by Lorna Doone Slide that she had memorized it, word for word. But all of a sudden her throat tightened, and she wasn't sure she'd even be able to read it, much less recite it from memory.

When the time came she walked to the platform and, as Mamma had advised, stopped to take a deep breath before she began. That was when she saw him. Way in the back, on the very back row in fact, a head taller than those around him, sat Foster Kirk. Even from that distance she could see his scowling smile, and her knees turned to jelly beneath her. She had not seen him since that terrible night last winter. The blood rushed to her face at the very thought of that awful night, and she averted her gaze from his compelling look to seek out the row where her own family sat: Mamma and Henry with his Martha; Byron, just barely home from college; Brother, Winnie, and little Margo; Richard and Frances, with wigglesome Jack in her lap; Sister, and Grange who had come up alone, leaving a neighbor with Molly who was sick in bed. She was steadied by the comfortable familiarity of their faces.

Finally, she found her voice and began to speak, carefully avoiding looking anywhere near the back row. She didn't know how she got through. She felt she was reading woodenly instead of speaking with animation as she'd wanted to do. All the fine quotations so diligently gathered, and the resounding challenges to her fellow students, seemed somehow inappropriate and lame. When she finished, she started to leave the platform as quickly as possible, her face burning, but the principal took hold of her arm and stayed her, signing for her to look at the audience. Tears stung her eyes as she saw that, not only was everyone clapping, but they were all standing. As she looked, a movement in the back caught her eye. It was Foster Kirk striding out the door.

The day after graduation a package came to Juliana —a very puzzling package. She studied it all the way back from the mailbox, turning it over and over, gently rattling it, reading and rereading the postmark and the return address. If it were from Foster Kirk, and the handwriting was most definitely his, and if it were mailed in Cocoa Beach, Florida which the postmark plainly indicated, then who was it that she'd seen at graduation? It couldn't have been Foster Kirk. He wouldn't have mailed a package and then come himself, would he?

She sat down on the porch and fingered the firm, neat knot of twine in the middle of the hand-sized package. If he were keeping his promise not to see her for three years, or until her eighteenth birthday, he would have had to mail the package, no matter where he was. She wouldn't be eighteen until August 10. But how did she know he wasn't married? Perhaps he had just happened to be on her road last winter. After all, he was a businessman and an artist. He could have any number of reasons for being on that road. And she really had no reason to think he had more than a casual interest in her now. When she accepted that, she knew that it couldn't matter if she opened the package. He was simply being courteous and kind toward an old acquaintance, that was all.

She had not told anyone about seeing Foster the night before. It seemed unnecessary to cause any more trouble. Grange had left that morning on the early train and, if he'd known his old friend was around, he'd never mentioned it.

As she played with the knot on the package, she looked down to see that the string was loosening; the brown wrapping paper coming undone at one end. Without stopping to think, she unwrapped the little box and opened it up.

She didn't think she had ever seen anything so beautiful, unless it was violets in the spring, as the dainty necklace of tiny lavender seashells on a fine string, done quite professionally with a jeweler's catch for fastening it on. At first she just looked at it, then gently she began to finger the rounded shape of each shell and to trace with a fingernail the thread-sized lines on the back of each one. When she lifted it out from its velvet cushion, she saw a note underneath: "Wishing you all that you hope for. Always, Foster."

She was trying to fasten the necklace around her neck when she heard a firm step behind her. The screen opened, and Brother cleared his throat as he stood over her.

"From Foster Kirk?" he asked with a hardness in his voice, reaching out as if he would jerk the necklace away from her.

"Yes," she said, her hand closing around it protectively.

He stood there looking down at her in such a way that she felt his impatience and exasperation, though she would not look into his eyes. When he walked around to ease himself into a chair beside her, he let out a sigh that was almost a groan.

"Juliana, I thought that was all behind us. It is unbelievable that the man is still trying to contact you."

"Why? Couldn't love be that strong?"

"Of course. Yes. But for such a child?"

"I'm almost eighteen. I'm graduated, remember?"

"And he is twice as old as you, too! Marriage is a partnership—not a father-daughter relationship."

"He never seemed like a father to me."

"I suppose the war and hardship caused you to grow up quicker. But it didn't actually make you any older chronologically. If you were married to a man Foster's age, who would your friends be?"

"Brother, you can read this note. It doesn't sound serious. He is probably already married to—someone else. After all, we were friends, and it couldn't hurt for him to send me this small gift, could it? Look at the shells. Aren't they beautiful? I think he probably picked them up from the beach himself." She could imagine Foster Kirk bending his tall frame to pick up the pea-size shells, shells that would be lost in the big brown roughness of his hand.

There was a rattle of silver and dishes inside as Sister and Mamma put dinner on the table. Beside the porch steps a hummingbird hovered around a red lily. Far away a bobwhite called and after a minute another one answered from nearby, its call clear and distinct above the other little buzzing, sizzling sounds of summer.

"Juliana, I've been thinking. Mamma says you

really wanted that scholarship. You're a very good student, and it's quite a shame for you to stop now. I could tell from your speech that you've given a lot of serious thought to what God wants you to do with your life. There's an excellent college for girls in Red Springs, North Carolina, about an hour's train ride from Linden. If Henry and Richard can help some, we can send you to college."

"But—no!—it would cost too much!" she exclaimed.

"We can do it—somehow. Think about it." He rose and stretched as Sister called them to dinner.

At first she had wanted the scholarship so much and worked hard for it, was disappointed when she didn't get it, but then had really been relieved that she was to stay at home. Now here was Brother offering to send her to college when she knew very well there wasn't enough money.

The questions tumbled and turned in her head until Sister said one morning that sleeping with Juliana anymore was like sleeping with a rooting pig. She went to her favorite places, but even the waters of Lorna Doone Slide could not calm the churning inside her. How could she leave Clover Hill again? And what about Henry? If she left, that would mean he was the only one left to stay with Mamma. What would that do to his plans with Martha? And what if—just if—Foster Kirk wasn't married and he came back, and she wasn't even here?

One day as she walked toward the house from the orchard she heard voices in the barn as she came close, and dropped in to see what was going on.

"Who's here?" she called from the door.

"Me and the musk," said Henry's voice from back in a stall. "Don't come too close. I'm cleaning up."

She climbed the boards of a half-wall and perched there watching him wield the big shovel, filling a wooden wheelbarrow with horse droppings.

"So—Mamma says you might be going off again."

"Might."

"Good idea. A smart girl like you shouldn't be stuck in Habersham County, feeding chickens and weaning little calves."

"Habersham County's the best place in the whole world," she said.

"Think so? Can't tell until you try the rest of the world."

"*I* can."

"Oh, I see. Extra powers of perception. Well, I always knew you were made of special stuff. I guess that proves it."

"Henry . . ."

He stopped and leaned on the handle of the shovel, pulling out a dingy rag to mop the sweat out of his eyes. Then he looked up at her expectantly.

"Do you want me to go?" she asked.

He came to her, reached up and ran a rough, grimy finger down the curve of her cheek. "In a manner of speaking, no. I'll miss you like the dickens. Realistically, yes. What have I worked for all these years—to see you graduate from high school and then be like anybody else?"

"But, Henry, what about you? I know the apples

147

didn't sell all that well last year, and—well, Brother said . . ."

He shuffled his feet and thumped the big blade of the shovel against the floor several times, chopping up wads of dry dung. "The thing about me is—don't worry an inch or a pinch, either. I'm doing quite well for myself. Couldn't be better, in fact. There are always ways of managing, and I can't think of anything better to invest in than you."

"What about—you and Martha?" she asked, prying a splinter up on a rough board with her fingernail.

"Now you're getting into personal business, gal, which I'm not ready to relate. Just don't worry about me. Make your decision independent of me completely. Now you better run. You're keeping me from my work."

As she walked out she heard him resume his cheery whistle, and the rhythmic click, slide, thump of the shovel began again.

CHAPTER 13

IT WAS A SUNDAY in July. The heat assaulted them from every direction—from the dusty road, from the high clay road banks, from the quiet trees that looked deceptively cool in their sylvan setting. Even the wind was hot on their cheeks as the Hamiltons rode home from church. Juliana fanned herself with a Sunday school book with one hand and held onto her parasol with the other. She was very conscious of the shell necklace around her throat, the lavender strand just dipping down over the neckline of her white dress. Mamma had finally said she could keep it, and had let her write a thank-you note to Foster, though Brother had frowned on it and Henry had grunted that it was a good thing she was going off to school.

"I do feel in my bones that something is wrong at Clover Hill," said Mamma as they jogged along.

"Now, Mamma, you've said that three times.

You'll *make* something happen if you keep it up," said Sister.

"Watch this," said Henry. "Watch Black cross this bridge. See? He never fails to step over that board we put in to replace the one he broke years ago. He can't tell by the newness which is which, because they're all weathered the same now. He's one smart horse."

"I think Henry's going to be a bachelor and spend his days communing with his horses and listening to them eat," said Byron.

"Didn't you see him sitting to one side with Martha at the watermelon cutting last night?" asked Sister.

"Oh, yes, but I remember also that he's never going to marry, because warring wives are a curse on any house."

Henry clucked to the horses and said nothing.

"I do believe something is definitely wrong at home," said Mamma, as if she hadn't heard any of the other conversation.

"Now, Mamma," began Byron, as they came around the bend in sight of the Clover Hill road. "But, wait," he said then, leaning forward in the surrey, "whose cows are those in the road?"

"I knew it!" said Mamma. "Our cows are out. And don't they always get out on Sunday?"

They changed into old clothes, sniffed at the tantalizing smells coming from the kitchen, and reluctantly went to round up the cows, leaving Mamma to finish up the dinner. It was two hours later, even with the help of Blake and his brothers, before they got the livestock all back in the pasture.

"It's too hot to pack them in the barn," said Henry,

scratching his head. "They'll smother each other. You girls are going to have to watch them and keep them together while Byron and I check the fence and get it mended."

The boys disappeared and all was stickily still. The cows shifted uneasily, grazing and mooing by turns. Finally they grouped themselves under a wide spreading oak not far from the barn.

"I'll go bring us a drink of water," volunteered Juliana, and Sister quickly agreed.

Juliana's legs stung from briar scratches, and she was so hot that her face felt as if it were on fire. She saw that she had ripped the hem of her calico dress on one side and that she was covered with stick-tights. She walked up the steps, already relishing the feel of the cool well water going down her throat, when she heard a motor slow at their mailbox. It must be someone coming to see Martha and her family who lived in Grandmother's house, but just in case, she stepped quickly inside the door.

"Juliana, is that you?" called Mamma from the front room. Then, in consternation, "Juliana! We've got company. Oh, dear, I was so tired I've lain down here because it seemed like the coolest place. I don't even have my dress on. You do something with them till I get ready."

Juliana glanced again at her dress, hastily picked some stick-tights off, and tried to turn the hem back up where it would stay just for a few minutes. Maybe it was the minister. He had seen her already in all kinds of garb, even once in peach-peeling clothes. But when she peered out a window, she gasped in dismay. Foster Kirk was opening a car door for Miss Delia Sweet.

There was nothing to do but greet them graciously, standing at the top of the steps with her hands behind her back. At least they didn't have to see her dirty hands. She avoided looking into Foster Kirk's eyes.

"Let's sit here on the porch where it's not quite so hot," she invited. "Mamma will be out soon."

"I hope we didn't disturb an afternoon rest," said Miss Sweet, letting her eyes travel all the way from Juliana's moist face to her thick, clumsy shoes.

"How have you been?" asked Foster, not giving her time to respond to Miss Sweet's comment.

"We are all very well, thank you. How are Beppo and the cats?"

"Beppo is glad to be home again. He enjoyed the beach, but the weather is too hot for him there."

"Then are you back at Pinedale—to stay?"

"For a while, anyway."

"He'll probably send me packing down to Florida soon to keep an eye on that land while he settles in back here," said Miss Sweet, fanning herself with her own little folding fan decorated with pink roses. "He has this notion to have a house full of children some day and thinks he must invest heavily in land to pay for raising them. I do think he could have chosen some investment less clumsy to move around—like diamonds. But of course I quite like Florida. If it were up to me, he'd raise his family there in the clean salt spray."

Juliana was trying to think how she could tactfully ask whom Foster was marrying when she heard Sister shouting from below the barn. Her memory goaded her to action. Poor Sister down there thirsting in the hot sun all this time! She hurried into the kitchen and drew a jar of water, then ran back across the porch, turning toward the visitors from halfway down the steps to say in confusion, "Excuse me, please!"

She saw Foster's eyes twinkle in amusement. As she started quickly across the yard, she heard him talking low to Miss Sweet, probably making fun of her appearance and strange behavior. Just as she turned the corner of the house, she saw the cows ambling toward her, cropping along, eating Mamma's lilies, two of them heading back toward the garden. Sister had come in sight around the barn, with her dress tucked up for running, but let it fall suddenly when she saw Foster Kirk coming up beside Juliana.

"Here," said Juliana to Foster, without taking her eyes from the two cows. "Hold this water. I'll head them off this way, Sister. You keep them from running toward the field."

She tried to block them neatly. But in the manner of the willful beasts they are, they broke around her, bellowing and flicking their tails. Then, settling back into a determined gait, they headed straight for the garden, generous milk bags swinging.

Juliana circled around and had at last aimed them in the right direction, though they were making a meal off the bean vines at the same time, when there was a thunderous pounding of hooves to her left. She looked up to see six cows bolting from in front of the house with Foster right behind them, shouting and waving his arms, water sloshing from the jar still clutched in his hand.

Juliana could not imagine one not knowing that cows must not be run—guided, prodded, encircled, pushed, and shoved—but never run. Now they were all out of control, galloping wildly, trampling the garden mercilessly, even running into the woods toward the hog pen.

Juliana planted herself in front of Foster who was still waving the jar of water and shouting. "Foster Kirk!" she yelled, her hands on her hips. "We're trying to make the cows go toward the barn not everywhere else. Take this whip and leave the jar of water. I'll teach you how to drive cows."

Thirty minutes later they had the cows herded back into the pasture just as Byron and Henry walked up, shaking their heads.

"We haven't found a single place they could have gotten out," Byron said.

"You went too far," said Sister. "Here—right next to the gate. Looks for all the world as if someone had cut the wires. I saw the cows come through, only it was the last ones I saw, not the first, unfortunately."

"Why weren't you watching as I told you to?" asked Henry, his brow heavily furrowed as he examined the wires.

"I thought they were safe, and I went to sleep. Juliana had gone to get us a drink of water."

Foster Kirk broke into laughter and they all turned to look at him in amazement. "So that was what the water was for!" he said. "I just couldn't imagine why you used water to chase cows!"

"And just what are *you* doing here?" demanded Henry, not cracking a smile.

"He's come to visit us all," said Juliana, stamping a small foot. "And you don't have to be rude about it."

"I think it's time we ate dinner," said Byron. "I starved several hours ago and now I feel as if I'm dying all over again. Come on, Henry, let's fix this hole while the girls put dinner on. Say, do you really think someone cut the wires?"

"It's quite obvious they did. Only thing is—who?"

"The Ku Klux Klan?" asked Sister.

"The Ku Klux Klan!" said Foster, stepping forward, every trace of laughter gone from his lean face. "If you really think . . . I've a job with the *Atlanta Constitution,* and they're trying to expose these sorry rascals and bring them to justice."

"We don't need help from Atlanta to manage our affairs," said Henry, his eyes blazing. "I don't know who cut the wires, but they've got to be fixed, and then—well, I suppose since you're here, you might as well eat with us."

Foster's face went pale and he gripped the top of the fencepost, then let his hand drop to his side. "I accept the invitation. And as to outside managing of your affairs, I couldn't agree with you more. That's why I'm a Republican. However, we're both in favor of the law being observed, I believe . . ."

"Juliana," said Sister, tugging at her arm. "Let's put dinner on."

To Juliana's relief, the three men were chatting amiably as they walked up the porch steps a short time later. Apparently no one was worrying any more about who cut the fence, and she kept her own ideas to herself. Poor Blake had gotten into quite enough trouble already.

The conversation around the table was lively. Juliana, who had quickly cleaned up and slipped back into her white dress with the strand of shells at her throat, found it quite fascinating to watch Foster Kirk's face as it changed from a scowl of concentration to a relaxed laugh, his dark eyes lighting with interest as he conversed. Whenever he looked her way, she dropped her eyes quickly, and hoped no one noticed that her heart seemed to beat up in her throat, making the shells pulsate. Why had she never noticed before that he had an intriguing space between his front teeth?

After dinner the men went out to look at Foster's car. It was his own, it seemed, an Essex he'd driven back from Cocoa Beach. It had all the newest features—doors that opened toward the front instead of suicide doors, an automatic starter, and, according to Foster, it was a champion for climbing hills, sturdy with a lot of pick-up. What Juliana saw was a smart black carriage with see-through window curtains. She wondered if Maureen had already had a ride in it.

"Miss Sweet, did you take all those cats to Florida?" Sister was asking.

"Oh, yes, and brought back more than I took. It was a bit of a hard trip, though. To be as messy as he is around the house, Foster is religiously particular about that car. You would think that someone who never thinks to throw away his apple cores could tolerate a few well-mannered cats in his car. He says he won't take them back again so, if I go, I'll have to get someone to care for them."

"Cutting up the mice and all?"

"Certainly. Only the Lord can help the person who mistreats one of my cats."

"That sounds rather severe," said Mamma.

"Perhaps so, but people can take care of themselves, while the little creatures are dependent on us."

"I can't help feeling sorry for the poor little mice," murmured Juliana.

Miss Sweet turned sharply toward her. "Don't you know that mice were created for the consumption of cats, child?" Juliana could see Foster walking toward them, but Miss Sweet's back was to him, and she kept talking. "Foster has this odd notion of marrying. Well, I've already told him it must be understood that my cats were in the family first, and if his *wife*," here she bent a significant glare on Juliana, "if his *wife* doesn't like them, it's just too bad."

"Yes, and I tell her priorities are not always formed that simply." Miss Sweet gave a slight start at the sound of Foster's deep voice right at her elbow, and looked up to see his jaw set firmly. "I'm not a man of fancy speeches, nor did I intend to make my mission here a secret to you. I didn't mean to be so abrupt, either. But now that my aunt has brought the subject up for the second time today, I think I had better explain. I have come seeking Juliana as my wife."

It seemed as if the whole house gasped. Juliana longed to fade into the woodwork as she saw the storms gathering on her brothers' faces, saw them take

157

threatening steps toward Foster. But Foster raised his hand firmly and continued to talk.

"I know she will not be eighteen until August 10, but surely you can allow me to start calling these few short weeks ahead of time. If it had not been for the glimpse of her on her graduation night, I would never have been able to wait this long, I'm afraid. If you only knew how hard these three years have been. Aunt De does, to an extent, and can verify that I've worked hard, clearing Florida wilderness land on Cape Canaveral, accumulating investments for taking care of a wife and raising a family."

Miss Sweet grunted disapprovingly.

Henry faced him squarely now, his fists clenching and unclenching at his sides. "We don't doubt your ability to take care of her. To be plain, Mr. Kirk, you're just not right for her. You're in the wrong generation. My sister has other plans that do not include you. I must ask you now, knowing your intentions, to leave."

There was a gasp from Miss Sweet who attempted to rise from her chair.

"Not so fast," said Mamma, coming to stand between the two men who were glaring at each other as if a fist fight might erupt at any moment. They stuffed their hands in their pockets as Mamma turned to Foster. "Juliana has decided to go to college at Flora McDonald in Red Springs, North Carolina." Juliana swallowed hard as she saw Foster, even with his deep Florida tan, turn pale. "She will be leaving in September and will be gone until June. She wants to continue her education, and I think, surely, you wouldn't want to interfere, being an educated man yourself. However, we did promise that you could call on Juliana after three years, and you have kept your end of the promise—almost, anyway—and we'll keep ours, provided . . ." She stepped back at that point and looked firmly at Juliana. ". . . provided it's all right with Juliana. That means you could visit her until she leaves, and if she changes her mind and decides to marry, then we'll have to go along with it."

"Mamma! No! Juliana *cannot* change her mind!" exploded Henry, pounding one fist into the other hand.

"Henry, when a girl is eighteen she has certain rights. I might say I don't think she will change her mind, but Foster can try within reasonable limits. So it's up to Juliana."

Everyone was quiet, waiting to hear from Juliana —so quiet that all she could hear was the shallow panting of Spring lying at her feet. Everyone was waiting for her to speak. It was far worse than making the speech at graduation, and what she wanted to do more than anything was to run.

"Juliana?" prodded Foster Kirk gently.

"But—Maureen," she stammered.

"Maureen who?"

"I—I mean I thought you were going to marry her."

"Marry Maureen? I have never once thought of marrying anyone else since first I saw you that Sunday afternoon."

"Oh," she said, and fidgeted with the shells at her neck.

"That was where we went wrong," grumbled

Henry just under his breath, "letting those kids go gallivanting on a Sunday."

"If you ask me," said Miss Sweet, "and, of course nobody did or we wouldn't even be here, but it seems to me if the child is going to wear the necklace we made, then she could at least accept a few well-intended calls."

Foster glowered at his aunt and went to Juliana, dropping on one knee beside her.

"Juliana, I don't want you to do anything you don't want to do. All I'm asking is a chance. If I can't make you return my love—then I won't pester you anymore. But I do warn you, I don't give up easily. May I visit you for the rest of the summer?" His eyes were demanding, his big, brown hand on the arm of her chair flexing nervously.

"Yes," she said quietly. "But I am going to college. No one is going to change my mind about that."

CHAPTER 14

FOSTER CAME TWICE a week, and sometimes more often. At first he only stayed for an hour or two, and the visit was very proper, with Juliana seating him in the front room and serving him his favorite drink—cool buttermilk. But as time went by Foster persuaded Mamma to let them go on walks together—to the falls, to Indian Hill, or all the way back past Ghost Den Ridge to Cold Spring. He listened, enchanted, as Juliana told him stories of the Ridge, and he could be as quiet as she when they knelt to peer by turns into the cavelike nest of a Carolina wren. Mamma said Foster must have been homesick for family living for years the way he so jubilantly took part in even their simplest forms of entertainment—listening to records or playing dominoes.

Henry, who himself was visiting Martha often these days, seemed to have softened toward Foster and enjoyed talking to him.

"He is a person of overwhelming honesty," he said. "And he knows a lot about land, just not much about farming." He grinned at the memory of Sister's description of Foster's cattle-driving ability.

Byron was not happy about his sister's being with Foster so much. But since he was sure that once she got off to college she would be attracted to someone her own age, he made no serious attempts to discourage her. No one knew just what Sister was thinking about the situation. The most she would say was, "Let her make up her own mind. It's her decision."

Once when Grange and Molly were visiting, they took Juliana and Mamma to see Foster Kirk at Pinedale. It certainly was not Grange's idea. It was the last place he wanted to take Juliana, and he said so. He told Mamma over and over that she needed to put a stop to this romance, that it had gone quite far enough. But Mamma only answered with such comments as, "She could do worse, you know," or "Age isn't everything, Grange."

When Grange offered to take them riding and Juliana suggested they go to Pinedale, Grange came close to exploding. "Do you really think I'm going to take you right into the lion's den?" he asked.

"He is kind of like a lion, isn't he?" said Juliana with a smile and a toss of her hair.

"Don't be saucy with me, young lady! You know what I'm talking about."

"Yes, I know. You introduced me to Foster yourself. He was one of your best friends, and now you're not being very loyal."

"I would never have introduced you if I'd known it

would come to this. He *was* my best friend, but you were my friend first. Now, listen, Juliana, be reasonable . . .''

''Don't ask a woman to be reasonable, Grange,'' said Molly, fanning herself slowly. ''Go ahead and take her. Don't you know that denying her will make her run right to him?''

''It will not make any difference either way!'' said Juliana, her cheeks very pink. ''You can do whatever you want to do. It will not make any difference.''

It was odd—approaching Pinedale by the road instead of walking in from the train. The little gray houses looked the same as before, though, with maybe a little more ivy creeping up the porch pillars of the cottage.

As they walked up the narrow path, Juliana looked from side to side taking in all the dear, familiar sights and smells. Foster had been telling her that he regularly got up at four in the morning to work outside and only went back to the house to paint after the sun was up. She could see now the results of his labors. Foster had planted mountain hemlocks near the turn-around and an ivy bush by the path near the studio. Foster called it a laurel, but she had always known it as ivy. The lawn was neatly trimmed, but the woods crowded in around the edges. Even so, she could see at a glance that work had been going on, for there was a fallen tree cut into lengths, and out toward the moss-grown graves of Foster's mother and grandmother, the path had been carefully trimmed.

They were almost to the cottage steps before Beppo suddenly discovered them, dashing toward them, his teeth bared. Molly screamed and hid behind Grange, but Juliana held out her hand and said, "Quiet, boy," whereupon there was a creak of the studio floor, and Foster emerged, a look of astonished pleasure on his rugged face.

Foster was dressed in khakis that looked as if they might have just barely survived the war, and his face and neck were blackened with a healthy stubble of beard. But he spent no time in apologizing for his appearance.

"Aunt De is visiting the neighbors," he explained as he seated them. "She's teaching someone to sew, I think. So—tell me, Grange, how are things in the big city? At the church? And have you seen the Colvins lately?"

"Just a minute now. You're shooting questions too fast to answer. If you're so interested, why don't you come back down and join us?"

"Unfortunately I am going to have to come down this fall for a short time. I have an exhibit scheduled in October. But I won't be gone a minute longer than I have to."

"I can see why you wouldn't want to leave," said Mamma. "This is such a peaceful, beautiful place."

"I'm glad you like it—and—well, let me get you all some cool grape juice. I picked the grapes this morning from the vine there at the edge of the lawn, and Aunt De squeezed them and put the juice in the spring. Walk with me, Juliana?"

The pathway was shaded nearly all the way by oaks and hemlock and sweetgum. Thick carpets of myrtle and fern stretched beneath the trees, and along the path bloomed Indian pinks and brown-eyed Susans. They paused at the top of the damp, mossy stone steps which led down to the rock-walled spring. Juliana played self-consciously with a glossy leaf of a large rhododendron bush, tracing the heavy veins on the pale underside.

"It is precious to me that you've come, little one. It's been a long, long time since you were here." Foster's hands were behind his back where he could keep them in control.

"I know. I wanted very much to see it again, so when Grange offered to take us riding, I asked to come here."

"You like it here then?" he asked eagerly, taking a step nearer.

"Oh, very much. Wouldn't anyone?" she asked, lifting wondering blue eyes.

"Not everyone. Some would, in the name of progress, cover every available space with cities and towns, ignoring the need for nature's cycles, the need for standing trees, tiny mosses and lichens, little mushrooms, squirrels, birds. By the way," he said, setting one foot on a large stone and leaning forward on his knee, "I'd like to show you the brooks and streams here at Pinedale. Some haven't been named yet, and I'd like to see what you would name them. You have a wonderful imagination."

"What makes you think so?"

His heart raced at the flash of sudden delight in her eyes.

"Do you think I didn't even listen to your graduation speech or that I haven't noticed your charming observations about the world around you? Besides wanting you to name the streams, I'd just like you to see them, because—well, because I know you love to watch flowing water."

"Oh, yes, I do! And—Foster, your place is so beautifully—well, natural. I do hope it will never be spoiled." She looked up into lofty treetops as she spoke.

"It won't be if I have anything to do with it. I'll admit—it's partly selfishness on my part. I love it as it is—untouched, pure—so I don't want it changed and will fight to keep it this way. But it's more than that. Years from now people many miles from here will benefit from this bit of forestland, absorbing the rains and holding them, providing oxygen. And it will be a place where man can view nature as God created it—without a clutter of concrete. And—there could be many children who would call this place home and love it as you love your Clover Hill."

She listened with great concentration as he talked. But when he mentioned children, her eyelids fell. "What painting are you working on now?" she asked quickly, to cover her embarrassment.

"I'm doing one called 'Woodlands.' For some reason I'm having trouble concentrating, though. I think you know why. By the way, though the picture I did of you wasn't very good, do you suppose I could borrow it back for a while? So many times I've wished I had begged to keep it, poor as it was, if it was all I could have of you."

"Mamma might let you borrow it back. It belongs to her, but if you talk just right, she'd let you have it

. . . and now don't you think we'd better get the grape juice?''

"Oh, Juliana . . . always the one for finishing conversations neatly, closing things up.''

A shadow fell across her face. "Did I say something wrong?''

"Not at all. It's just always time to go, it seems. We only get started talking, and it's time to go.'' He reached out and lifted her chin with one finger. "But don't worry. I never want you to have to worry, little one,'' he said, and came so close she was sure he was going to kiss her. His eyes were full of tenderness, and her whole body seemed to be reaching out to him, though she was standing very still. Suddenly he dropped his hand and walked quickly down the steps where she heard a slosh and pattering drip as he plucked a glass jar from the cool water and started back with it.

When Foster and Juliana got back to the cottage porch, they found the rest of the group sitting very quietly watching a house wren feeding her young in a nest at the top of a pillar.

"The little bird doesn't mind our being here at all apparently,'' said Mamma, accepting a glass of grape juice from Foster.

"No. I think after learning to live with all Aunt De's cats, the birds are quite fearless—to a point, anyway.'' He placed the glass jug on the low wall and then sat down on the wall himself near Juliana's chair. "That's a favorite home for the little wrens. I'd like to think it's the very same couple that lived there last year and the year before. But without marking their wings, I can't tell for sure.''

"They're such cute little brown birds," said Juliana softly.

Mamma laughed gently. "Juliana has always been completely fascinated by little things."

"Especially little things that were models of big things," said Grange. "Remember the set of tiny furniture Byron made you? Do you still have it?"

Juliana shook her head. "I gave it to Margo."

"This is good juice, Foster," said Molly, finding an opening in the conversation. "It's almost as cool as if it had been in our refrigerator."

"Your refrigerator?" inquired Mamma in surprise. "Why, you two didn't tell us you'd gotten yourselves a refrigerator."

"We just did," said Grange. "Two weeks ago. It's the newest on the market."

"I hope you don't die of asphyxiation from the carbon dioxide," said Foster, standing to refill the empty glasses.

"No, no, Foster, they've discovered a new coolant now. Call it Freon. It's quite safe."

"And so much more pleasant than having to buy big blocks of ice all the time," said Molly, rocking herself gently in the swing.

"Well, you must be doing quite well for yourself, old chap," said Foster. "Your job's agreeing with you and your pocketbook."

"Not bad, if I do say so," said Grange with a grin. Juliana thought to herself that Grange seemed to have forgotten his animosity toward Foster, and she was glad.

All too soon the afternoon shadows lengthened, and

it was time to go. Foster walked with them down to the car. At one point he managed a walk with Mamma a little apart from the others and, bending his head so as to speak quietly, he asked her if he might borrow the painting of Juliana. She had been holding to his arm as he helped her down a difficult step, and now she stopped, looking up at him with widened eyes.

"If it's all right with Juliana," she said finally.

He nodded. "She said to speak to you about it and you might let me have it if I asked just right. I'm afraid at times I'm lacking sorely in the social graces. I want the picture and so I'm asking for it straight out."

"You may certainly borrow it then. I appreciate your honesty more than you can know."

Foster came to Juliana's eighteenth birthday dinner. He brought her a novel, *Ivanhoe,* by Sir Walter Scott. On the flyleaf he had written: "No matter how things turn out, I will always love you."

She considered that sentiment as she sat with her back to a tree one day. Did she love him or was it just *his* love drawing her to him? And, now that she thought about it, did he love her or was she just a part of his big dream of preserving nature and raising a big family? Because if he didn't love her for herself, there was no sense in continuing to think about him. These were things she had to know.

She told him shyly one day about her desire to help someone, to do something special. She was grateful to him for listening with such interest, but in the end she knew he didn't really understand.

"Wouldn't a dozen of your own children be mission

field enough for you?" he asked quite seriously.

"A dozen?"

"Well, give or take a few."

"Foster Kirk, you are too ambitious!" she declared.

They talked about poetry, art, kittens, and kings. She showed him the field, "Judy's Little Acre," where one year she'd grown sixty bushels of corn, becoming the champion grower of the Boys' Corn Club. Sometimes he brought his sketch pad, and they sat beside a large tree or by Lorna Doone Slide, talking about colors—how the light and shadow changed the shades of blue and green—about the shapes of the forest, the pillars of pine, and the circular sun patterns falling through the chaos of windblown leaves.

"The Lord has given examples all around us of the impossible made possible, of confusion changed to order, and of beauty from ugliness," he said one day. "Take that old rotten log there with ferns and moss taking it over. It's a perfect example of something stark and black becoming, not just covered by, but part of something beautiful."

Juliana had been watching Foster as he spoke, his hands gesturing expressively. "And so death becomes life," she breathed softly, and answered his gaze steadily when he turned.

Foster tried to persuade her to go to school in Atlanta, if she must go to school somewhere. That way he could at least see her. But she would never even consider it.

"Juliana, you are so stubborn!" he said one day at summer's end, standing up and walking the floor, his

170

hands fisted in his pockets. "Why must you be so stubborn? If only I could make you see that learning can go on without college, that you could have all the books you wanted. College sterilizes a person. You'll be educated all right, just the way the professors want you—every student coming off the graduation line like peas out of a pod, all just alike."

"You lay little value to individuality in that case," said Juliana, sparks flying as she rose to face him. "If I'm different in the first place, won't I react differently? Don't you think I have any control over myself? Isn't it really that you think I'm not deeply intelligent enough for further education? Isn't that really the issue?"

"How can you say that? I've told you over and over . . ." He paused in front of a window, his back to her, and took several deep breaths before he turned around. Then he began again, "It's your spontaneity, your spark, your wonderful positive attitude of anticipating what may happen next. I'm afraid you'll lose that in institutional learning."

She laid a hand on his arm. "Foster, I have to go. Maybe when I come back, I'll be the wife you need."

"You're the wife I need right now."

"No, I'm not. Because, you see, I don't know whether I love you or not." She was looking him right in the eyes as she spoke, and she saw him flinch as if she'd stabbed him. Then his shoulders sagged.

"When are you leaving?" he sighed.

"Tomorrow."

"Then I won't see you again?"

"Not for a while."

171

He picked up his hat, turned to look at her one more time, then walked out. She stood leaning against the side of the door, watching him go and aching with longing to love him the way he wanted her to.

Henry took Juliana and Byron to meet the train in Cornelia. Mamma had not gone to see Sister off the week before and chose to tell the two youngest good-by at home, also. "It's easier that way," she said brightly, adjusting a bow on Juliana's dress as if she were a small girl again.

"Now, Mamma, don't you cry or I'll start," said Juliana, stamping a foot on the porch floor where they stood waiting for Henry to bring the buggy around.

"I'll try, honey. But, you see, you're my last one. And—I guess I'm afraid you'll never be my same little Juliana again."

"I haven't been your *little* Juliana for a long time, Mamma. But I'll always be your big Juliana, who loves you very much. Now write often. Here's Henry—"

Foster, as well as Mamma, feared the changes that might come to Juliana in the months she was away. Would she grow away from him completely and learn to love someone else? The night before she was to leave, he walked the floor of his little studio, unable to sleep.

"Should I give up? Can I give up?" he moaned aloud as he stood at the window where he could look up to the dark tossing of treetops against the lighter sky. Those trees grew above the grave of his mother whose companionship he had missed so much all these years. There had never been anyone to take her place. And if he lost Juliana, there would never be anyone to fill her place, either. The lonesomeness would be even worse now that he had known what it was like to be near her, to commune with her on subjects of the soul, mind, and heart. And, yes, she would never be the same again. She was leaving, and the true Juliana—the one who had become as much a part of him as his own breath—might never return.

As soon as the first dawn light showed, Foster took his axe and went to the woods where he began cutting small deformed striplings, laying them in a central pile for chopping into firewood. The chips flew, and time after time he heaved good-sized poles onto his shoulders, almost relishing in the harsh rubbing weight of the wood.

When it was light enough he went in, washed his face, and tried to paint. But he felt as if he were fighting with the canvas, as if the symmetry of nature had turned to hard angles, as if colors actually were flat and there was no sunshine in the green of summer trees or the blue of distant mountains—or the memory of golden hair and gentian eyes that said so much, yet kept a secret always. Finally he threw down a piece of chalk, looked at his watch, and walked briskly to his car. Aunt De called after him, wanting to know where he was going, but all he said was that he would be back.

Juliana was having a very hard time keeping the tears back as she and Byron waited on the platform, their suitcases by their feet. She had thought it wouldn't be so bad since she was going to make the trip with Byron. But she had told Mamma good-by—and Clover Hill—and now it was almost time to tell Henry good-by. She couldn't help wondering why she had gotten herself into this. Hadn't she said once—many times—that she would never leave Clover Hill? And yet she was doing so of her own free will. Of course Brother and the rest of the family had encouraged her, but no one had said she had to go. It was her own decision, just as she had reminded Foster very heatedly one day when he accused her of doing whatever her brothers told her to.

"I hear it coming," said Henry. "I'll help you get on, Judy. Now, girl, don't break my neck. Save the pieces, will you? Come on, let's go."

She found a seat where she could watch Henry as they pulled away from the station. She was able to smile through her tears at the comical way in which he stood, impatient to leave, scratching crosses in the dust with his boot toe, yet looking up often to see if she were still there.

"He's going to be feeling much better when he gets us out of his way," said Byron.

"Byron! Look!" said Juliana, pointing beyond Henry to a black Essex that came to a jerking halt almost at the same instant a tall figure leapt from it. "Foster," she breathed. "Byron, let me by, I must go tell him good-by."

"You can't! The train's pulling out! There, don't you feel it? Just wave. It's all you can do."

Foster had started running, but stopped as he saw

the train moving. Now he stood beside Henry, his hat off, waving to the spot Henry said was Juliana's window—though all he could see was a blur of white.

CHAPTER 15

Pinedale
September 12, 1922

Dear Juliana,

I know I have been impatient with you, but it's only because you're the dearest one in the world to me. Now I'm hoping that you will forgive me for my harshness on my last visit, and let me begin again with a fresh slate. If I can't be everything to you right now, let me be what I can be. I once thought it was very unmanly to agree to be only friends with the one you loved, but that was before I knew what it was to love.

Your Mamma sends love to you, too, though by now you will have her own letter, for I mailed it myself. I went to your house to see if I could learn anything about you. She had not heard from you herself, so we comforted each other.

I had not realized how keenly lonesome it would make me to go to your house, and find no dear girl in blue tissue gingham smiling at me, teasing me into a laugh.

Your Mamma invited me into the front room, but seeing my downcast spirits, allowed me to talk with her in the dining room. It was just that I was going to miss you so much more in that room where we have spent so many hours listening to records and talking.

It is dawn now. Just light enough for me to see to write. It is the moment before even the pinkness shows through the screen of trees to the east, the moment when the birds go crazy with enthusiasm for whatever is to come (like another Little Bird I know), the moment when the light that is almost not light reflects off of night and brings form and color to what was only hunks and slabs of varying blackness.

Dear Girl, please write to me—write about anything you wish. And if you should at some time begin to have some deep feelings for me, let me know quickly. Now it is time for me to pull the weeds out of the myrtle bed before I start painting. Don't study too hard.

Always,
F.K.

"Juliana Hamilton!" The sharp voice jarred her from the peaceful world of Pinedale and the thought of Foster Kirk's dark head bent in concentration—jarred her suddenly back to the confines of the dormitory at Flora McDonald College. "Are you going to stand there all day mooning over that letter? I'm sure someone is paying dearly for you to come to school, and you shouldn't be dawdling your time away."

There were several things about the college that Juliana had disliked on sight. Heading the list was the woman with the strident voice who had met her upon her arrival. Lucretia Morgan had introduced herself as

177

the housemother in a way that seemed to indicate she had the authority of a judge and jury combined and would never be caught this side of death handing down mercy to anyone. Behind her back she was known as "The Morgue." She wore nothing but black, and found occasion to say something derogatory about the pretty dresses worn by the girls in her dormitory. Her heavy eyebrows appeared, whether they were or not, to be constantly drawn in condemnation. Her lips were thin and straight, and she smiled only when someone was in trouble.

Juliana soon found that, even if she rushed in from the library five minutes before the deadline, she would still be put on restriction. "The Morgue" always sat at her desk like a cat quietly waiting to pounce on its unsuspecting victim. Juliana was often that victim. As Miss Lucretia said, "Five more minutes, young lady, and you'd be put on restriction, so I'd better go ahead and give it to you so you won't forget."

Another bitter disappointment was the water. Not the drinking water, as bad as it tasted, but the streams, if you could call them streams. The water was so red it looked black from the iron content. There were no falls or rapids, no pleasant gurgles around stones. The water just sat there, and only if you studied it for minutes at a time could you see any flow, even if you threw in a leaf to measure it. This was most distressing to Juliana who loved the movement, the rushing, the forever seeking of the Clover Hill creeks and the Chattahoochee River.

But the main problem with the water was that it spoiled the girls' clothes in the laundry. Juliana's pretty white dress, trimmed with Mamma's finely made lace, was no longer really white. And her blue gingham, Foster's favorite, looked dingy in between the blue. It was no wonder, she told her roommate, that The Morgue wore only black. It was the only color that would come through the wash the same as it went in.

But some things more than compensated for the annoyances. One was her French teacher, who was very demanding but fair. Juliana found a challenge in the ''no English'' limitation, in writing original essays in French, in translating a French newspaper. Miss Gerard began calling her aside after class to have conversations in French, commenting that very few of her second-year students took such an interest.

''You have had very good language instructors,'' she said.

''Yes, my brother taught me Latin for one year,'' said Juliana proudly, ''and then my favorite teacher in Cornelia, Miss Shannon, taught Latin and French.''

''We will work hard,'' insisted Miss Gerard. ''You have much talent. It must not be wasted.''

Juliana said little about her French class in ner letters to Foster. She couldn't seem to write about it without sounding as though she were bragging, and, besides, she wasn't sure he would like it at all. He still didn't understand her burning desire to learn all she could, even though he himself was an avid learner.

Instead, she wrote to him about the silent movies, the lyceums, the art exhibits, the Highland fling, which was the one dance pronounced acceptable for students at this Scottish school. She wanted to be very honest with Foster, so every time Byron came over from Chapel Hill and brought a friend to escort her to the movie or concert, she told him about it. She didn't mention how boring the friends were.

Juliana was often the first to look for mail in the tiny room of pigeonholes behind The Morgue's desk. She realized one day that it wasn't a letter from Mamma she was most eager to find, but one bearing Foster Kirk's impossible scrawl. As she read, her cheeks would glow a soft pink. She hoped that only her roommate noticed, and not Lucretia Morgan!

She devoured Foster's description of Pinedale in autumn, and of Clover Hill where he visited often. Also, she enjoyed his character sketches of people whom he met while selling Essex cars in a new part-time business. Sometimes his letters bore a Florida postmark. He would tell about meeting a python at late dusk on his way through the scrub, or of killing a six-foot rattlesnake on the beach below his house.

"This is rough country," he wrote once. "Today we needed supplies, but it had rained so much it was necessary for me to walk into the village to get them. The Essex, as tough as it is, couldn't be expected to travel through that boggy sand. But I enjoyed the walk. The sunsets here make me ache to get them all on paper. Not one is the same as another. And, though I miss the hills of Habersham, there is a certain beauty in the swamp grass, the egrets, and the powerful, majestic, forever-rolling ocean."

"Please get your rest," he urged in another letter. "I love you so dearly that I simply cannot help worrying about you up there toiling over your books. I am living in the hope that you will decide one year of this is enough."

"What about *your* rest?" she responded. "You talk casually about getting up at 4:00 A.M. and working until dark, then reading and writing into the night. Since your last letter when you told me about the mushrooms you cooked up for breakfast, I've been wondering if I was going to hear of your having poisoned yourself."

Mamma enclosed a clipping from the *Constitution* of one of Foster's poems. "Far blue hills, apple hills, red clay hills of Georgia," she read and could see with a pang of homesickness not only the hills but the author, dark eyes intent, hands behind back, looking out from his hilltop to the twin slopes of Trey or the craggy-sided Yonah.

She had a cry in her tiny room when she learned that Henry and Martha had married and were living at Clover Hill with Mamma. How sad, she thought, that out of their big family only Richard and Mamma were there for Henry's wedding. She didn't like to think of how different Clover Hill must be now with a new mistress and no one going to school on cold mornings, or coming home to raid the warming closet of leftover baked potatoes and biscuits.

It was Mamma who told Juliana that Henry had sold John and that they were using either Black or Gray for the buggy now. The reason Henry gave was that John was too stubborn for the womenfolk to handle, but Juliana remembered how he'd said, "There's always a way to manage." She suspected he'd sold the horse and given up his own house plans so she could go to

181

school. Lucretia Morgan was right. Someone *was* paying dearly for her to come to school, and she vowed anew that it would not be in vain. She would make sure she made good use of this year and learned every bit that she could.

Juliana had the growing feeling that she was being watched closely at mail time. The Morgue's eyes seemed always to follow her every move, and once Juliana caught her holding a letter up to the window and peering at it intently, as if trying to read the signature through the thin envelope. Juliana impulsively snatched it from her, and was promptly put on a week's restriction. Not being allowed to go to the library meant she made a "D" on a research paper that was due.

She asked Foster never to send her any postcards, as she didn't want The Morgue to read them. She did not tell him about the time she was sitting in the parlor studying French when a young man kissed his girl, and The Morgue put every girl in the parlor on restriction. Even after the girl explained that her beau had just asked her to marry him and she had accepted, The Morgue smiled with her tight lips and pointed to the stairs.

One day she had a letter from Miss Delia Sweet. She thought it rather odd, but nice. She had wondered how she would ever live with Aunt De if she did marry Foster. It was encouraging to have a friendly letter from her, though she was disturbed to learn that Foster was doing very little painting now that his exhibit was over. He was working hard in the woods and selling only a few cars.

"Today," wrote Foster, "I am making pencil drawings of the English-style stone house I plan to build on Hilltop. I'm planning to use a lot of gables and arches. The structure will be of flint and granite hauled down from the mountains. Our Creator made flint stone in varying muted colors that change with the changing lights. Beautiful! I have my eye on a little used truck that will be just the thing for hauling. If only my lady love would say yes to me, and would help me plan this house. . ."

Why is it so frightening to think of planning a house? Juliana asked herself as she looked out at the flat, rain-bedraggled campus of Flora McDonald. *Or of planning a family? Having babies? I do want babies—just like Margo, and Baby Jack, and Peter. But—a dozen? I'm just not old enough. There are other things I must do first.*

Autumn seemed interminable, despite the variety of interesting activities. The day Juliana got the news that Foster was bringing Mamma to Brother's where she, Byron, and Sister would meet for Christmas, she could have turned cartwheels if there had been a place where she could be sure The Morgue wouldn't see her from behind some curtain. As the days drew near, her dreams were constantly filled with what she would say to Foster, how he would look, whether or not he might kiss her. She set to work embroidering a tiny picture of a bright red cardinal to give him, taking care that her stitches were even neater than usual.

Because of her schedule, Juliana was the last to arrive in Linden for the Christmas gathering. Brother and Byron met her at the station, full of descriptions of the wonderful dinner being prepared. "The people in my church heard my family was coming," said Brother, "and they must have felt quite sorry for me. They have been arriving by twos and threes with dishes of this and that—cakes, pies, a turkey, loaves of bread, even some butter. You'll feel as if you're back home at Clover Hill, Juliana."

She wondered why Foster had not ridden with them, but would not ask. She knew it must have been because Brother didn't want him to.

She had barely gotten out of the car at the house when a small figure flung itself into Juliana's arms, almost knocking her over.

"Margo! Don't be so rough!" commanded Brother.

"Oh, it's all right," said Juliana happily. "Margo, how I've missed you! And haven't you grown! Next thing we know, you'll be starting to school."

"And can I go to school with you, Judy? Wouldn't that be fun!"

"Yes, wouldn't it!" Juliana hugged the little girl while she looked over her shoulder, expecting any minute to see Foster striding toward her. Where had they hidden him?

Mamma, Sister, and Winnie holding Peter met her at the door. "Oh, you do look so like a college girl—I can tell by the way you walk!" exclaimed Sister.

"How do college girls walk?"

"Confidently, I guess. I don't know, but I am so

glad to see you. Come on, let's start catching up on everything.''

They were pulling her in, seating her in the living room, plying her with questions, and hardly waiting for answers. She kept looking toward the kitchen, then toward the outside door. He must be out walking.

"See our Christmas tree, Judy!" cried Margo.

"Tristmas chee!" echoed Peter, pulling at a colored paper chain.

"Juliana," said Mamma cautiously, "the boys did tell you, didn't they? About Foster not coming?"

"Not coming?" The announcement was too sudden for her to be able to cover her disappointment.

"He had to see about some urgent land business in Florida. He really was very sorry."

"This is for you," said Margo, running to her with a small package.

"Oh, Margo, you shouldn't!" said Winnie.

"It's all right," said Mamma. "I think Juliana needs it now. It's from Foster. He asked me to bring it to you. Go ahead. Open it."

For some reason her fingers shook as she undid the wrappings. She felt everyone's eyes on her, and she kept her own on what she was doing so they wouldn't see the mist of tears that had come. What was so urgent that he couldn't be here for Christmas? What was so terribly important?

When Juliana opened the box and saw the gold watch, her breathing stopped. Not quite believing, she touched it, then turned it over. It was engraved on the back with her name and the date. A small note, folded into a triangle, said, "To the one girl in all the world

185

for me, I give my love and this token of it. I am quite disappointed not to be with you to put it on you myself. But when you receive this, I'll be in hot Florida trying to iron out a land boundary problem. Please forgive me and know that I love you more than anything on earth.''

Brother didn't want her to keep the watch. He said it was the next thing to an engagement ring. and surely Mamma wasn't going to agree to that. Mamma said she had been with Foster when he picked it out, thought they had done a rather nice job of selecting it, and if she had not thought Juliana should have it, she certainly wouldn't have carried it all that way in her pocketbook.

"And, Juliana," she said, looking at her with a searching expression, "there is soon coming a time when you must make a decision about that young man. He cannot keep on waiting, though right now he may think he can. A man can only wait so long."

"Mamma! What are you saying? Juliana cannot marry Foster Kirk! Do you want her to be a widow half her life?''

"Brother," said Mamma, looking at him firmly, "it is Juliana's life, and we haven't the right to keep on making her decisions for her. If the two love each other, then they need to be together for as long as they do have.''

Brother walked out of the room, muttering something under his breath. Margo climbed into Juliana's lap so the two of them could admire together the beautiful gold watch. "Make the ticks start, Judy. Come on, make the ticks start beating."

CHAPTER 16

Dearest Juliana,

I'm back at Pinedale. The trees along the driveway seemed to reach down to welcome me.

What a precious little picture you made for me. I wish I could have had it to help me through the lonesome holidays, but then it is such a blessing to me now.

Darling, I am so glad you like the watch. If only you could realize that I would give you the world if I could. That is why I didn't come at Christmas—because I was securing an investment for our future. If I hadn't remained in Florida I would have lost half my acreage.

Your mamma and Henry are going to let me buy a little cow from them. She's a good one, Henry says, and I trust him. As you know, dealing with cows is not my strong point!

My Little Girl (thank you for letting me call you mine, even with reservations), let us be honest with each other. Our Lord has taught us to be trusting and trustworthy. Let us never break that bond between us. If another light comes into my life, I will certainly let you know (though I assure you it is highly unlikely). And you must do the same. I say that with a pain of fear in my chest, yet knowing that if you do not love me, I must accept that and go on living the kind of life that I will not be ashamed of when I meet you in heaven.

And now good night, my love. It is very late, but still a whippoorwill is singing, and I will not be alone as I lie awake dreaming of you.

Always,
Foster

Juliana wrote to him faithfully, sitting at her window, struggling to express her feelings. It seemed so easy for Foster to tell her he loved her. Yet, no matter how much she wanted to say it, too, her letters sounded either too bold or too stiff. So she would tear them up and write about The Morgue or the red water or the prospects of Scottish Day to be celebrated in the spring. "He will know when he sees me," she whispered to herself. "He will know that I love him when he sees me."

Clover Hill
January 25, 1923

Dear Juliana,

I hadn't planned to write tonight, but I do want you to know what has happened here, and to assure you that we're all quite safe.

As you know, we have continued to do what we could for the little German peddler. I had taken to giving him eggs and milk whenever he came, he looked so thin and white. Well, I'm very sorry to say that won't be happening any more, for he is dead, attacked on the road by a group of KKK's. It is so hard to believe that there are people right here around us who will do that. And as bad as that is, it isn't really the worst. There was one member of that group who hadn't enough sense to leave the scene and is now behind bars. ·Blake Davis. The wretched criminals pulled poor Blake into their evil work, and not a one is showing up to speak in his defense. Needless to say, Mrs. Davis is distraught.

Henry is doing what he can to help Blake, and also Foster Kirk is working in his defense.

I wanted you to hear this from us and know that we're safe, rather than to hear it from anywhere else.

Don't worry now. We'll be fine.

Love,
Mamma

Later Mamma sent clippings of the follow-up stories on Blake, who was pronounced not guilty by reason of insanity and sent to the state mental hospital at Milledgeville. To Juliana's relief, she read that the other KKK's were all brought to trial and found guilty. She noticed that the stories were handled well, with honesty and forthrightness, but without the use of scare tactics. It wasn't until she was sliding the clippings back into the envelope, however, that she saw the by-line—Foster Kirk.

Hurriedly she got out paper and pen to express her appreciation. Again she tried to write the all-important words he'd asked her to share whenever she could honestly say them: *I love you.* But the pen would not obey her heart, and the words did not come. She signed her name, then impulsively started a P.S. But

189

again she sat long in thought and finally wrote "Byron and a friend are coming this weekend. We're going to see 'When Knighthood Was In Flower'."

When Foster's letters stopped coming in March, she thought he must have had to make a sudden trip to Florida, or that he was extra busy with an art exhibit in Atlanta. But weeks passed and there was no word from him, though she kept writing him faithfully at Pinedale.

When she got a letter from Grange with a clipping of Foster at the exhibit enclosed, she had to fight the doubts and jealousies that rose inside her. In the picture of Foster and his paintings, Maureen was standing at his elbow. There was no mistaking her profile and the profusion of tight ringlets. He had said to trust, and she was trying. But why didn't he write? True, he wasn't smiling at Maureen in the picture; she could have just happened to be there. But she *was* there, and Juliana knew Maureen—her flirting eyes, her saucy mouth, her possessiveness of what she considered her own.

It became harder and harder for her to keep her mind on French or her other subjects, though she managed to keep her grades up. Miss Gerard was obviously aware that her interest had slipped, and kept giving her little lectures about reaching her full potential, not slacking when things got tough. But French class was right after the morning mail, and she was becoming more and more depressed at the absence of letters in her box. Mamma wrote and said Foster had been to see her and had asked about Juliana as if he hadn't heard from her in a long time. Her heart leapt with hope. Surely there had been a mix-up in the mail. She wrote him again, but still there was no answer.

Early one morning, when she got to the mail room, Juliana saw a letter addressed in a scrawly handwriting lying on The Morgue's desk. When she realized it wasn't to her, the disappointment cut like a knife. Inspecting the letter addressed to Mrs. Morgan, she realized that it wasn't Foster's hand at all, but more like his Aunt De's. Who could Mrs. Morgan know who wrote so nearly like the Kirks? She couldn't read the postmark, so she turned the envelope over to see the return address, but there was none. She was dropping it back on the desk when Mrs. Morgan's door opened, and she burst forth with a guttural, smothered cry. "How dare you molest my mail?"

"I—I thought for a minute it was mine," said Juliana, turning white, and backing away.

"Yours! There is no way you could think my name is yours. They are nothing alike. Young lady, I should report you to the authorities, but I won't—this time. Just take a week's restriction graciously, and get out of my sight this instant."

The week's restriction added to Juliana's misery. She could go nowhere except to the lunchroom and classes. Her friends were very attentive, but even that did not cheer her. Ever one to try to make those around her happy, she tried to play along for their sakes, but they saw right through her act. They had known the jubilant Juliana, and couldn't be fooled. Perhaps the streams, so sluggish all year, might be moving more briskly now that spring was here, but she couldn't go out to see. She missed, too, the fresh air and even the very tame flowers in their precise, unimaginative beds. She almost stopped eating, just nibbling enough so that The Morgue wouldn't take her lunchroom privilege away, too.

At the end of the week Juliana's spirit was so quenched that she could not bring herself to look for her mail. So her roommate offered to check it for her, assuring her again and again that Foster would write soon. In fact, said the roommate, Juliana might just get a whole bundle of letters one day that had been held up in the mail somewhere.

"Juliana Hamilton," spoke Miss Gerard at the end of French one day, "come to my room for a cup of tea."

Juliana was glad that she wasn't on restriction any more. Tea with Miss Gerard would be a bright spot in the midst of so many drab days.

"Juliana, my dear, whatever has happened to you?" asked Miss Gerard as she poured tea and then eased herself primly onto the edge of a delicate chair. "Your grades are not bad, but you have lost your spark. You are doing only what is required, not reaching hungrily for more. You always reminded me of a baby bird crying for more food as fast as the mother could shove it in. Now—now you are just like my other good but boring students. Juliana," she leaned forward and laid a blue-veined hand on her knee, "you have the ability to go far. After one more year of French, if you were back to normal, you would be good—so good that I could recommend you for foreign study. You could study in Paris. Ah! I see some of that old interest returning. I knew you would like that idea!"

192

"But, Miss Gerard . . ."

"Never before have I been able to recommend anyone for study abroad," said Miss Gerard, standing up and walking around her small finely decorated parlor with her hands clasped in excitement. "If it is money you are worrying about, I can do something about that. If we can't get you a scholarship, I will personally underwrite you. How would you like that?"

"But, Miss Gerard . . ."

"Oh, yes. I know it is a very great deal, but I have saved all my life and have never had anyone to spend it on. It will be as if—as if you are my very own daughter. Yes, that's it!" A spot of bright color in both cheeks betrayed her excitement. "Now, dear, what do you say?" She paused in front of Juliana.

"Miss Gerard, I cannot possibly accept."

"You *cannot?* But why?"

"I am going to be married this summer—I hope."

"Oh, no, no! Marriage! What a waste! No, no, love, think again. You must not throw away all that talent. You must not! Please don't do that to yourself! What about those brothers who have sacrificed for you to come to school? Think how proud they would be. And this young man, too—he would wait."

"Wait? No, I don't think so—not as long as he has waited already."

"But he does not know. You must tell him. Think about it, Juliana. This may be your chance to make your dreams come true."

Her dreams? What dreams? Was this what she'd waited for all these years—to study French in Paris? Her heart froze. Was she to become like Miss Gerard, living in a two-room apartment, teaching others and watching them go into the world, leaving her behind? Or maybe she would become a missionary in a French-speaking country, teaching many children who would never be hers. Her teacup rattled as she set it in the saucer.

"It's very kind of you, Miss Gerard, but I will have to let you know," she said softly.

"Good. You will think about it. The offer is open and will remain so. And in the meantime, do come out of the doldrums. If you are in love, let me tell you: no man is worth all that misery. I should know. I had a fiancé once who said he loved and adored me until, one day, 'The Right Person' walked into his life and snap! it was all over with him. I've learned, Juliana, that there are more important things."

"Thank you very much for the tea," said Juliana. "I must go now."

"But don't forget my offer. Think about it."

Scottish Day was only two weeks before school was out. Byron insisted on bringing a friend to escort Juliana to the various activities—the Maypole dance, Scottish bagpipes concert, and the singing of Scottish songs at midnight. She would have written Foster Kirk to tell him how much she wanted him to be there—not Byron's friend—but there seemed no use. She hadn't heard from Foster now in three months. Instead, she wrote to Grange, telling him all about the exciting day: how pretty the bagpipers' costumes were; what fun it was to dance with Byron's friend who somehow knew how to do the Highland fling, though he'd never done it before; and how cozy it was singing "Loch Lomond" by a bonfire with the stars overhead. She never once mentioned Foster Kirk.

As school drew to a close, Juliana was almost sick with excitement and anticipation. At last she would be returning to Clover Hill. There she could think with a clear mind about Miss Gerard's proposal, and maybe the ache inside of her would ease. Perhaps she would see Grange and he could tell her whether a "new light" had really walked into Foster's life.

CHAPTER 17

IT WAS A LONG, long train ride home from Red Springs. Byron would have come and traveled with Juliana if she could have waited one more day. But she could not possibly stay in that dormitory another day after all her friends left. Besides, maybe it was best to make the trip alone so she could think.

What had she done to make Foster stop writing? She carefully reviewed her letters to him as, almost unnoticed, the fields and foothills slipped past. She had been too careful not to tell him how much she cared. She knew that now. But she had been just as friendly as always, and he had always written back, even though he called her notes "cool and proper."

Maybe it had just finally been more than he could stand, as Mamma had warned. Maybe he had found someone nearer his age. Like Maureen. Henry, Brother, and Byron had worried so about her interest in Foster, because they said she would spend half her life as a widow. Now she knew that it just didn't matter. But Foster himself may have realized how awkward it would be introducing her to his friends in Atlanta and having them, one by one, comment about how she looked like his daughter instead of his wife. Juliana took a small mirror from her pocketbook and studied her reflection. She thought she looked pretty old now, and she could make herself look older if necessary. She could keep her hair up in a bun like Mamma.

It was dark as Henry drove her home from the train station, but he noticed at once the fatigue in her voice. "You sound like all the sparkle has gone out of you. Just wait till you see all the little new calves, and a mess of kittens in the barn, too. And Martha and I have a surprise for you."

"You're going to be—"

"You guessed it. A father! Come October."

"Oh, Henry, how very wonderful! I'm so glad for you both." Then recalling that he had sold his beloved horse, she added, "But I know you miss old John. I'm sorry about that."

"John? John who? Oh, the horse. Pshaw! The old scalawag had to go, that's all. He's on a good farm down toward Commerce. He's all right, and I'm happy. But I—I—won't be completely happy until my little sister is, too," he said gently.

"You mustn't worry about me, Henry. I'm going to be just fine—now I'm home."

But Juliana needed more than calves and kittens to cheer her up now, more than wild tiger lilies in the woods, or the chuckle of Jenkins Branch. The waters of Lorna Doone Falls simply made her cry. There was no joy anywhere.

One night after Henry and Martha were in bed, she poured her heart out to Mamma.

"I don't know what I did to ruin things between Foster and me," she said tearfully. "I wanted to tell him I'd like more than anything to be his wife, but it seemed too important to put on paper, so I decided to wait. Now I don't know what to do."

"It's strange you didn't hear from him," said Mamma with a puzzled frown. "Very strange. Because he came here several times and never once did he seem to have given up on you. Do you suppose . . ."

"Mamma," Juliana interrupted, anticipating the question, "that many letters could not be lost. You know they couldn't. Besides, this study that Miss Gerard wants me to go into . . . well, maybe that's what God wants me to do. Oh, I wish He would just talk out loud and tell me if it's what He wants."

Mamma tied off the threads on a piece of crocheting, smoothed the square in her lap, then looked at Juliana. "Juliana, God doesn't give us life tasks without giving us the desire to do them. He is no cruel taskmaster who holds out good things to us and then snatches them away. He wants you to have joy. How can you give joy to others if you don't have it within you? I don't mean that we can't expect to have hard times, big disappointments, changes in our lives that we can never understand. But the Lord gave you a good brain to learn with and make decisions with. You're just going to have to recognize what you truly want and go after it."

"Mamma, I have no doubt what I want. I want Foster Kirk."

"Anyone who accepts partnership with that man is accepting a calling," said Mamma quite definitely, laying her square on the table.

"But what can I do?" asked Juliana. "He won't answer my letters."

"Tomorrow you're going to Pinedale to see him."

"Mamma! After he hasn't written for weeks?"

"He says *you* didn't write. You go straighten it out. Take the buggy in the morning and go to town and take the train."

"By myself?"

"By yourself."

"You're sure?"

"Much more sure than I was the last time I let you go there alone."

As Juliana started out the next morning, she was tingling with the old feeling of anticipation—of expecting Something Big to happen. However, on the train ride to Clarkesville, she began to be apprehensive. As the train neared the Hill's Crossing stop, she almost decided to go on to Tallulah Falls, but pulled the bell at the last minute. The conductor was quite startled for some reason, and after helping her solicitously down the steps, he questioned her wisdom in coming by herself to such a lonely place.

"You haven't anyone to meet you?" he asked.

"No, it's a surprise," she explained, and waved him on.

It did seem very strange for there to be no Foster

and no Beppo at the stop—strange and very, very lonely. Juliana stood at the crossing as the train puffed away into the distance, and looked across at the big house where Maureen had stayed with her aunt. Wouldn't it be humiliatingly horrible if Foster had married Maureen—or someone—and now here she came barging in, uninvited. But then something Foster had said gave her courage to keep walking. He'd said, "I trust you, and I want you to trust me. No matter how things seem, we must be willing to trust each other."

Well, Mamma was right. She would never forgive herself if she didn't find out exactly how things were. So she walked on between waving Queen Anne's lace and then, in the cool woods, huckleberry bushes loaded with ripe blue berries. She came to a sudden halt at the sight of an old tin pot half full of huckleberries. Since it was at the edge of the path, it seemed that someone had just left it for a minute and would be back soon, might even at this moment be walking toward her. She stood listening, barely breathing, her lips parted slightly in anticipation. The woods seemed vast and filled with footsteps. But it was only the rustle of squirrels, a breeze through the leaves, or just inexplicable cracklings and whisperings of the woods. Finally she walked on—more slowly than before.

She had on the dress Foster had always liked the best, the blue gingham, though it was old and dingy now from Red Springs water. At least the hat was not spoiled. She loosened it now and fanned herself with it as she neared Hilltop. She would see the place he'd talked of building on, the place from which she could see Trey Mountain and Yonah—never-changing, never-moving sentinels.

The sound of a dog barking made her stop. Beppo? She tried to see ahead, but couldn't. The dog was barking quite wildly, she realized now, as she moved cautiously closer. When she saw Beppo, he was bouncing back and forth in a small semicircle, now and then jumping farther backward, scattering leaves as he did. Moving past an invervening tree into the hilltop opening, she gasped audibly at the sight of Foster Kirk, gun raised to shoulder, apparently aiming at Beppo.

"Stop there!" he commanded sharply, never moving the gun barrel an inch or taking his eye from his target.

"Don't shoot!" she cried, but at that very moment he did, and she closed her eyes, unwilling to believe what she'd seen. The explosion was followed by the insistent smell of gunpowder and an unearthly silence, uninterrupted even by the crackle of a leaf or a sigh of wind.

"You can look now, Juliana. I've killed it," said Foster heavily. "I was afraid he was going to get my dog."

She saw it then. A big brown moccasin with its head blown off. Beppo was standing over it, sniffing cautiously at the still-writhing, brown-patterned body.

"It was camouflaged so—I didn't see it," faltered Juliana, her hands shaking now that she knew everything was all right.

"You surely didn't think I was going to shoot my dog!" laughed Foster bitterly as he propped the gun against a tree beside an axe. "He's been my only joy for quite some time now. May I ask why you've come? To collect the picture, I suppose."

"Picture?" she asked stupidly. Then, with understanding, "Oh, no, not the picture! I came to see why you never wrote and answered my many letters."

"Why haven't I written, she says, Beppo boy. You must have a boxful of my letters, Juliana, or would have if you'd saved them."

"I haven't gotten any—since—since March. I wrote and wrote because I wanted you to know . . ." There was a tearful shake in her voice.

"Know what? That you've fallen in love with one of Byron's friends? That you've decided to be a career woman? That you want no more of an old man like me? Well, tell me now. Let me have it straight, and let's get it over and done."

She lifted her head and looked at him, towering above her, his cheeks thinner than usual, his eyes bright, his jaw set hard. "Foster Kirk," she said unsteadily, "I love you with all my heart."

"You—what?"

Encouraged by a leap of hope in his eyes, she put her hands up to his shoulders and said, "I love you with my whole heart." Only she had to finish it against the rough khaki of his shirt where he held her closely with strength and, at the same time, reverent tenderness.

"My little one, oh, my little one! I thought I might never see you again. My life has been so miserable these many months. Juliana, I love you. Nothing else on earth is more important to me."

The questions, all the questions, could wait. Right now, nothing mattered to Juliana except knowing that Foster loved her. Sometime later with Beppo beside them, they walked hand-in-hand down toward the cottage.

"Don't you want your axe—and your gun?"

"I'll get them later. I have more important occupations for my hands right now than killing snakes or trimming underbrush."

"Or picking huckleberries?"

"Yes, that, too," he said, looking down at her with a boyish grin. Then his face grew serious. "You say you haven't had any letters from me since March? And I've had none from you. I wonder who is holding them up."

"I'm afraid I know," she said sadly.

"Not Grange? He would if he could, the sorry rascal, but how could he? He's done his part, telling me every discouraging fact, such as the wonderful time you had on Scottish Day with some lucky guy."

"Oh, he didn't! And I wished so it were you, Foster! Truly I did, but . . ."

"Well, we mustn't worry now that it's over. Only . . . I wish I could get my hands on the person who held up our mail."

"I'm afraid—it must have been Brother and Mrs. Morgan. You have never met such a mean woman in your life, and I'm afraid Brother used her. I'm so ashamed."

He looked down at her, a warm light in his eyes. "I'm so very thankful that you've come to me, love, that I can forgive anyone. Maybe, after all, it helped you make up your mind."

"I knew for sure at Christmas," she said. "I was so horribly disappointed that you didn't come."

He stopped and took both her hands. "Are you really sure now, Juliana? Sure you won't be wondering later if there were some mission you should have gone into? I didn't think I could bear to lose you, but neither can I bear to have you commit your life to being my wife when you'd rather be something else."

Her smile came from the very depths of her eyes, as well as her lips, as she answered confidently, "I'm sure, very sure, Foster, that my mission is with you —to follow those bends in the road with you."

They were in another close embrace, Beppo patiently waiting nearby, when Aunt De's voice caused Juliana to jump back, blushing.

"So—" said Miss Delia Sweet, "my little scheme didn't work. Well, so be it. If I tried that hard to stop it and failed, it must surely be blessed of the Lord."

"Just what did you do?" asked Foster sternly.

"Just a little meddling. It wasn't at all hard to get that Mrs. Morgan to hold up the letters. The woman said you were quite a naughty child, Juliana, and she was very glad to help." Miss Sweet chuckled and reached down to pet Beppo. "Actually made me like you a bit to know you were naughty," she said, sheer mischief shining in her old eyes.

"Aunt De! How dare you!" said Foster, stepping forward.

But Juliana's small, firm hand on his arm stayed him. Looking up earnestly into his face, she said, "What did you say a moment ago? You'd forgive anyone? Did you really mean it?"

He looked down at her and his mustache twitched in a sudden grin. "You little witch!" he said, hugging her tenderly to him.

The Song of

the Nereids

Sandy Dengler

THE BEGINNING OF AN ADVENTURE . . . .

Singapore, Dusk, June 7, 1851

She despised rain. She despised warm rain even more, and no other kind of rain ever fell on Singapore. She despised Singapore, most of all, this waterfront. She ambled slowly along the pier. Rain rivulets ran down the planking to disappear in cracks between the boards. Boats flopped listlessly at their moorings. The wet air hung heavy with a hundred odors, every one of them foul. All the bustling city's waste flushed itself down here to the docks. A carabao swayed past her dragging a creaky wooden cart. Its half-sweet bovine smell added itself to all the other smells.

Two years ago in Chelsea, distant Chelsea, she had yearned to see exotic places and go adventuring. She had dreamt of warm tropical climes. The irony of it almost tickled her funny bone, though there was surely no real humor in the thought.

Above the constant rustle of rain a sailor shouted in English. Another answered. A bark of moderate size was just now tying up a few hundred feet ahead. Its flaccid sails drooped wet from their spars. Soaked and disspirited, the

5

Union Jack hung near the mizzen. *British ship. Home.*

Mooring hawsers thunked against the pier planks. She was constantly amazed by the sheer size of the ropes on ships. A section of the starboard railing opened; a gangplank was thrown out. It dropped—*kunnng*—against the pier. More shouting. Men docking a ship were much like hens laying eggs; neither could perform quietly.

She pulled her shawl closer around her head, but it offered scant protection against the rain. A lock of her hair plastered itself against her cheek—all sticky. It would soon be dark. She had best start back.

From the bark, a voice with a distinctive Scots brogue called, "God bless the lad, sir!"

A man wearing a black jacket and carrying a large bundle jogged down the plank. Two small, bare feet dangled from one end of the bundle and the man clutched the other end close to his shoulder. *A sick child?* It looked so. The man was walking rapidly, almost at a dog trot, directly toward her. She shrank back into the shadows too late. He obviously had seen her.

He paused right in front of her. "Can you tell me where I can find a doctor?"

His bundle was indeed a sick child. The little boy's face, normally weather-tanned, was flushed. Even in this half-light she could see ragged brown fever lines across his lips.

"A doctor? Yes. Go three—uh, leave the waterfront at that gray building and go north—" She shook her head. "Let me take you."

"I'm grateful. Thank-you." He fell in behind her as she turned on her heel and hurried off.

No matter how brisk her step, he kept up easily. Her back was to him, but his face haunted her nontheless. He was a rather handsome fellow. No doubt he had a girl in every port and only a few of them his wives. He was well built, but

6

then most seamen were well built. He had dark hair, but everyone in Singapore had dark hair except herself; her's was a warm brown. Tanned skin like his was common enough. It must be the eyes that moved her so. They were warm and dark, the largest eyes she had ever seen in a man—deep reservoirs of fear and worry. Was the boy his son? A cabin boy? A shaver? A total stranger?

She panted from the exertion. Barely twenty years old, she felt like sixty. Although he was only medium sized, as men go, she was petite enough that her head barely reached his shoulder. No wonder he so easily outpaced her. His long legs were taking two strides to her three. Salty sweat mixed with the rain on her face.

She felt confident, leading him to the British sector. Even if he were familiar with this part of Singapore he'd never find the right street and door.

Some of the more noxious odors had been left behind. They turned here at the chicken-seller's deserted stall. The fourth door on the left—here they were.

"This door right here. I assumed you'd want an English doctor rather than Chinese." She jogged up the wooden stoop and pounded the knocker up and down for him, since his arms were full.

He stared absently at the door knocker. The knocker, a brass lion with a ring in its mouth, stared absently back at him. Sun crinkles in the corners of his eyes etched deeply, as did the worry frown across his forehead. She wished she could watch his face when he was jovial. She could just imagine the sun crinkles bunching up as he laughed. How old was he? Thirty-five at the most, and probably not quite that.

The door swung open. A Chinese houseman stood in the gloom. "Yes?"

"Captain Travis Bricker. My cabin boy here requires a

doctor's attention immediately. He is very ill."

The man bowed elegantly. "Come in, Captain."

Captain Bricker stepped inside and followed the houseman down the long dark hall.

She had done her good deed. She should leave now. Instead she found herself following that jacket down the hall. She was sworn off men. She was through with the fickle animals. Why did this one fascinate her so? At the houseman's direction the captain laid his burden on a waist-high teak table and unwrapped the blanket.

Moments later the doctor appeared through a side door. A rotund man with muttonchop whiskers, he had to lean quite a bit to bend over his examination table. He slipped a stethoscope into his ears and studied the ceiling as he listened to this part and that of the lad. She hung back in the doorway watching.

The doctor grunted. "What medicines has he received today?"

"None. We tried to control his fever with quinine and the convulsions with laudanum, but we ran out of both two days ago."

"The proper medications. His fever waxes and wanes, so to speak?"

"Yes."

The doctor grunted and nodded again.

The captain stepped away from the table, stretched his back and rubbed his face with both hands. No doubt part of the sadness in his face was simply a lack of sleep.

"Your cabin boy, I presume. He receives good nourishment?"

"My cabin boy, yes. And he eats like any two seamen before the mast. His appetite matches Edward's, helping for helping." He sighed heavily. "Edward was cabin boy when this voyage began, but he's really too old for the work. He wanted to sail before the mast and I gladly signed him on as a seaman. I suppose if I can't find another cabin boy, I'll have to put Edward back in the stern again. I trust Gideon here won't be able to take up duties for a long time."

"Several months. In fact, he shouldn't be asea, assuming he lives."

"Leave him here?"

"I recommend it."

The captain paced about, rubbing the back of his neck. "We're due to meet a buyer; I diverted to bring Gideon here; can't lose much more time—" His voice trailed away.

She pondered the voice. He was not English, Aussie, or Canadian, yet there was somehow a touch of the Canadian accent.

"Very well. I have friends here where Gideon can stay awhile. And I'll just have to put Edward to serving again."

A brilliant idea dawned so suddenly it startled her. "Sir? Captain?"

He looked at her for the first time. "I'm so very sorry, Miss! Not only have I neglected to thank you, I've ignored you. Please accept my apology. I couldn't have found this place without you. How can I repay?" He was reaching into an inner jacket pocket.

She held up her hand. "Please, no. You're most freely welcome, sir. But I was just thinking: my brother is seeking work. He's younger than I, but too old to apprentice. And there are precious few jobs for a white boy in Singapore. He's never been to sea but he's accustomed to serving and he learns quickly. Might you consider him as cabin boy, please?"

"I'll be glad to talk to him. Send him around tomorrow morning. You know where we're berthed. The *Arachne.*"

"Thank-you. He'll be most pleased to hear about this." She hesitated. "You're an American?"

9

He smiled suddenly. Those sun crinkles did indeed bunch up, and in a most delightful way. "Yes. Millinocket, Maine. I may be doubly indebted to you if I can use him. What's his name?"

"Eric Rollin. Shall I tell him to bring anything?"

"References from other employers if he has them. And your name?"

"Margaret Rollin Rice. Good evening, Captain Bricker."

"Good evening. Thank-you again very much, Mrs. Rice."

The houseman bowed curtly and led her to the door. She walked the cool, dark hall, and paused as the houseman opened the outside door. She stepped into the warm and stinking night rain.

She despised Singapore.

CHAPTER 1

Singapore waterfront, Morning, June 8, 1851

The rain was ended, the early morning mist lifting. Travis Bricker appreciated the way this weather reflected his own good mood—improved, much improved, even say bright. Mist no longer muffled noise. His heels rapped hollowly on the boardwalk. The cacophony of a hundred native entrepreneurs hawking everything from chickens to finch cages was constant. Trapped between pier and lolling hulls, the murky water sloshed back and forth. He came abreast *Arachne* and strode up the gangway. It felt good to be home.

"Top o' the morning, sir!" lilted a familiar voice from the quarterdeck.

Bricker stopped by the mizzen to wait. Seamus Fisher tucked the sextant under his arm and came bounding down the starboard steps. *Should a more ebullent Irishman ever be born,* Bricker mused, *Bosun Fisher would still outbounce him!*

The cheery redhead brandished a slip of paper. "Ye'll be pleased to 'ear, sir, that Singapore sits precisely upon the coordinates touted for it. Not only is y'r chronometer in fine mettle, whatever ye did to the sextant corrected that problem as well.''

"Excellent. It'll be nice to know where we are again.''

Fisher followed him to the stern cabin door. "I can tell by y'r sprightly demeanor, sir, that the lad is faring well.''

"Doctor broke his fever last night. But he's too weak for sea duty. I'm going to ask Wang See if there's someone he can live with awhile. Given rest and good food he should be back to his usual high level of impishness in a few months. Is Mr. McGovern about?''

"Aye, and the candidate for y'r new cabin boy, sir.'' Fisher leaned forward and pushed the cabin door open.

"Already?'' Bricker stepped from muggy brightness to cool darkness and paused a moment until his eyes adjusted. He nodded toward his first mate. "Good morning, Mr. McGovern.''

"Morning, sir!'' The dour Scot never laughed uproariously, rarely laughed at all, and seldom smiled. He was smiling now. "Our lad's on the mend, aye?''

"Aye. And you must be Eric Rollin,'' he said as a mere wisp of a lad bolted to his feet.

"Yes, sir. I mean, aye, sir.'' He crunched his cap together in his hands and stood tensely, nervously, like a slave being inspected by a prospective buyer. Somehow Bricker had expected a larger boy than this, though size was surely no requirement for the position. And yet the boy seemed poised despite his nervousness, self-confident. His coppery brown hair, undisciplined, flew away all over his head; he needed a proper haircut. And his clothes fitted badly. But those blue eyes sparkled with the same mischievous twinkle that had rendered young Gideon so endearing. Bricker liked the boy instantly.

Bricker wandered over and flopped down in his favorite

12

chair. He was so tired he ached. "Tell me about yourself, lad."

The boy licked his lips. "Our parents were missionaries in the Far East here. Uh, God took them home untimely. You've met my sister; she married locally. But I wish to return to our native England to complete my schooling, though I'm in no hurry for that, I assure you, sir. I'll not jump ship the moment I see a white face and leave you in want. Nothing of that sort. I'll serve you well, sir. But England's my eventual goal."

"A worthy goal. Any prior experience?"

"None in this line, sir. I've no letters of reference. I serve my sister's and her husband's household. She taught me; they both did. For whatever it's worth, sir, my sister claims I'm quick to learn. She says it's never a waste to know a good line of work, whether I return to school or not."

"Divinity school? You mentioned your parents were missionaries."

"I've not decided, sir. Time enough for that, I'm told."

"True. You seem more mature than your size would suggest."

"Small for my age, sir. My brother-in-law assures me I'm just slow getting my growth. Hope he's right." The boy's big blue eyes met Bricker's squarely, hopefully, as if there were no doubt at all that he would make an absolutely splendid cabin boy.

Bricker glanced over at his first mate. McGovern gave the barest of affirmative nods. An accolade.

"Long months at sea, tedious work, scant pay, rough weather. Certain you want to do this?"

"Positive! Aye, sir!" He smiled warmly, broadly, expectantly.

"I certainly can't fault your enthusiasm, or your motives. The desire for an education is laudable." Bricker hauled to his feet and stretched. "Very well. Fetch your duffle aboard promptly. Yours is that closet there. I'll make arrangement for Gideon's keep this morning and return by noon, Lord willing. We sail right after the noontime meal.

The boy snapped a perky little bow. "I'll be back directly, sir. I thank-you very much for this opportunity. I promise I'll do my best to serve you well."

"I can't ask for more." Bricker started for the door. The boy darted ahead to hold it for him.

Bricker stepped into full-blown tropical sun. It burned his weary eyes but did not obliterate the approaching vision. The Scotsman grunted into Bricker's left ear in surprise, then whispered coarsely, "I smell money boarding, sir."

Bricker had never seen a waistline so slim, or a bustline so artfully sculptured. The woman's dress was the essence of European high fashion. Three or four acres of vivid blue silk swirled down over her crinolines. Draped silk, ruffles, and laces highlighted all the best parts of her form. Even the obligatory shawl was appropriate to this heat, a pale blue swath of some sort of see-through fabric. It draped her bare shoulders elegantly to blend with the silk of her sleeves. Her dainty bonnet and ringlets of dark hair completed the picture of perfection.

She did not walk. She glided, the silk rustling delicately with each dainty step. She paused and looked right at him with liquid brown eyes. "The captain, please." Her tone of voice intimated strongly that she owned this vessel, though Bricker distinctly remembered being responsible to two owners in London.

"I'm the captain, Travis Bricker. Your servant, madam. How can we help you?" He dipped his head.

Were a man to look him over as she looked him over now, he would have been angered by the air of cold disdain. Somehow in her he didn't mind it.

"Maude Harrington. Miss Harrington. I require passage to the East Coast of the United States, preferably the New York area. I understand you're going that way."

"Possibly, but not by a direct route. I have promise of cargo in New Zealand if I arrive there in time, but we'll be sailing contrary to the prevailing winds. We may call at Valparaiso before heading east around the Horn. The voyage will take the better part of a year."

"Very well. Then from New Zealand you'll sail north to Honolulu and San Francisco. The West Coast will do."

Bricker felt the hairs on his neck bristle a bit. "With all respect, madam, you'll not reach the West Coast aboard this vessel. Gold fever is hot in California. Were I to touch the coast there, half my seamen would change their occupation to gold miner and leave me with no crew. A hundred and fifty vessels lie rotting in San Francisco Bay right now for lack of a crew, and *Arachne* will not become one of them."

"You're overly cautious, Captain. Ships call at San Francisco constantly without being stuck there. Shall we say San Diego? Inconvenient, but I'll put up with the extra travel. Provided the Pacific passage is satisfactory. Book me to San Diego."

"No, madam." Bricker folded his arms. He tried to keep her obvious and lovely attributes from distracting him so. "I can put you ashore at Callao, in Peru. Or Panama. I understand gold seekers by the hundreds are pouring across the isthmus to avoid the Horn. There should be guides aplenty to lead you safely to the Atlantic side, and from there ships to take you anywhere you wish to go."

Her eyes snapped. "I can just see myself standing on some desolate Panamanian beach, where eager natives will crowd about simply overjoyed to help me," she said, with scathing sarcasm. "Surely you know Panama is in a state of rebellion. Between Panama's rebels and Colombia's regulars, I'd be in a pretty fix indeed. You will take me to America directly."

"I will not."

"Don't ever call yourself a gentleman where I can hear you, Captain. I shall book passage to New Zealand and make other arrangements from there. When do we sail?"

"Immediately. Will that be soon enough?"

How could such rich, dark eyes be so ice cold? "I've never really appreciated the Yankee sense of humor, such as it is. Your sardonic wit is wasted on me, Captain, and best not offered at all. A carriage will be by with my trunks." She adjusted her mouth into a cold and unfeeling smile. "Thank-you, Captain, and good day." All swishes and swirls, she flounced down the gangway. The dark pipe curls bobbed beneath the bonnet as the smooth, milk-white shoulders disappeared from view.

"Is a cabin boy permitted to voice an opinion, sir?"

"Only when asked to do so." Bricker glanced down at the lad, bemused. "And what is your opinion?"

"Charge her twice the fare, sir, for you'll earn every penny of it."

At Bricker's side, the Scot burst into a single raucous peal of laughter. His muttonchop whiskers molded themselves for a moment into interesting new curves. He clapped the boy's shoulder. "Ye've got 'er pegged, lad. Ye've got 'er pegged." He wandered off wagging his head.

"The voyage may prove interesting after all. Have you had breakfast, boy?"

"Not yet, sir."

"Nor I." Bricker led off toward the galley. "You'll bring your things aboard soon as you've eaten and I'll tend to my business ashore. Are those your best clothes?"

"Uh, my only clothes, sir. We're not wealthy."

"You know the Wang See chandlery near here?"

16

"I've passed it, sir."

"Stop by there and have Wang See outfit you properly, including oilskins. We'll be crossing the south forties in summer, but it'll be cold all the same. I'll leave word it's to be put on *Arachne's* tab."

"Thank-you, sir! Thank-you very much!"

"Don't thank me too profusely. It'll come out of your wages. Here we are." He ducked into the galley.

The Chinese cook peered into a big iron vat, frowning morosely. He shot the captain a perfunctory nod, all that was left of the elaborate bow with which he used to greet his employer. "Potatoes," he grumbled. "Cook, outside; inside, hard. Cook, inside; outside, apart pieces. Bah! Rice better." He looked at Eric and panic washed across his leathery face. "Gideon! Gone?"

"Very sick, but getting well. He'll stay here in Singapore until we can come back or send for him. Eric here is our cabin boy until Gideon returns. Eric, this is Wun Lin. Wun Lin, would you serve us both breakfast, please."

CHAPTER 2

Singapore, Midday, June 8, 1851

The morning flowed smoothly—delightfully smoothly, considering the way that Maude Harrington had started it off. Travis Bricker found the lady constantly on his mind as he wound through the stall-lined streets. Was she a supreme irritant or was she simply supremely lovely? There was a certain vulnerability, a desperation, behind the haughtiness. Bricker guessed she was a much nicer person than that first meeting would suggest. What grave concern did her pose as Queen of the Whole World conceal? What was the source of her conspicuous wealth? There was one sure way a white woman could come into a fortune quickly in Singapore, and Maude's superb face and figure would lend themselves to that means. Bricker realized belatedly where his thoughts were wandering. Mentally he apologized to the lady for thinking such evil thoughts about her, no doubt false besides.

He called upon the chandler, Wang See. The gentleman needed no clerks or warehouse boys, but the clerk of his friend Chow Chen had just married and moved to Kowloon.

Bricker called upon the chandler Chow Chen. Mr. Chow could indeed use a smart, quick boy. Could Gideon cipher? Affirmative. Could he read? Well, somewhat. The bargain was struck even before Bricker's tea had cooled enough to drink.

Gideon himself presented something of a different problem. Fever had left the boy less than alert. Bricker had a terrible time convincing him he was not being summarily abandoned. He explained to Gideon about the arrangement with Mr. Chow. He discussed the value to anyone planning to become a sea captain someday of a knowledge of chandlery. Once Gideon understood how ships' suppliers did business, he would know how to avoid being cheated or taken advantage of. That in itself would be worth the few months' separation.

Bricker promised to post a letter each time he called at a port. Several times over he solemnly pledged to return for Gideon—or send for him—as soon as health and trade permitted. Gideon would still have a berth aboard *Arachne* for as long as he chose. In saying goodby, Bricker held the boy close, firmly, for some minutes longer than really necessary.

He walked the long way around to the docks. Did that tiny streetside stall still operate on the Street of Bright Stars? It did. Did the wizened old lady there still sell those delectable bits of sweet curried duck? She did. The morning was absolutely faultless.

A block from Wang See's, the captain's brand-new cabin boy came popping out of nowhere, arms laden with parcels. Bricker was impressed all over again by the boy's quickness and charm.

The lad greeted him, jogged three paces ahead, and struck the exaggerated pose of a dandy gentleman. "Am I better attired now, sir?"

"Much better. Now don't outgrow everything before we raise England."

"I'll try not, sir." The boy marched along at his side a few moments. "Sir? You told Miss Harrington we'd be about a year getting to the North Atlantic."

"That's assuming no problems. I failed to mention to her that we were dismasted off the Society Islands not long ago, though we think we have the problem licked. But we haven't yet tried *Arachne* under a heavy press of sail. The Horn in December is usually as quiet as it ever gets, but it can always give you trouble, even on the west-east passage. We may call at Praia or Dakar, which would add a few weeks. London in June, Lord willing, as the roses begin to bloom."

"A long time, sir."

"A long way."

"Aye, a long way." The boy's voice faded, thoughtful. His eyes seemed misty. Was he saddened to leave the Far East or fearful of a new life alone in a different world? Bricker ought to get the lad talking.

"So you're going home to school. How much schooling have you had so far?"

"Not much, sir. A bit of Latin, but no Greek yet. And no geography. I could use some geography just now, to know where I am and where you're talking about."

"I'll try to remember that and be more informative."

The boy looked at him curiously. "Thank-you, sir. When you first said *'Arachne'* I thought you were saying *'Rackney'*. After all, ships have been given stranger names than that. But then I saw your quarterboards. Arachne was a Greek goddess, wasn't she?"

"No, a mortal. She considered herself the finest tapestry weaver in the world. This didn't sit well with Minerva, who was the goddess of such things. Arachne ended up challenging Minerva to a contest of tapestry-weaving skill. So Minerva stitched a big picture, telling how she gained control of Athens and had it named for her—her Greek name was Athena. And Arachne's tapestry pictured the gods' flaws and errors. Their shortcomings.''

"Wasn't very tactful, I daresay.''

"Wasn't tactful to challenge a goddess in the first place.''

"Who won?''

"Nobody. Minerva got fed up with her before they finished and turned her into a spider.''

"Why a—Oh! I see. That's why spiders are such incomparable weavers. So why did the owners name your boat *Arachne?*''

"Bark, not boat. Masts and tonnage of a ship but the mizzen fore-and-aft rigged.''

"I must learn all that?''

"It'll come. The owners had no prior contact with shipping. They came by her more or less by accident. Her rigging named her—that tangle of strange lines aloft. To them, her rigging was a web only Arachne could figure out.''

"Or Minerva.''

Bricker chuckled. "Or Minerva.'' He turned onto the street which led downhill to the wharfs. Food beckoned. The curried duck hadn't lasted long down there.

"I've so much to learn—ships and boats and barks, not to mention Minerva, who is Athens; no, Athena. And all that mythology. Sometimes I think—look! Isn't that Miss Harrington?'' The boy stretched out a burdened arm to point.

"It is!'' Bricker broke into a run without thinking.

Three-hundred yards ahead, Maude stood, flanked by two men. She shook her head violently. Her shrill protests were audible, even at this distance. Each man seized a blue-clad

21

elbow, and, as one, the three disappeared up a side street.

Bricker turned the corner so fast he nearly slipped in the mud. Billows of blue silk jounced along up ahead.

All three heard him coming. Miss Harrington twisted around. "Captain! Help me! Oh, help me!" She began struggling wildly, jerking, pulling, kicking. The elegant lady turned into quite a tornado.

Bricker didn't slow his pace. He aimed himself squarely at the taller of the two, then lunged aside suddenly to bowl the shorter over. He noted as an afterthought that the men were European, not Oriental.

Miss Harrington twisted free and, scooping up her skirts, ran down the street toward the docks. Bricker swung at Taller and missed completely. The man lunged at him, both fists flailing. Now Shorter was on his feet. With a soprano howl, Eric came flying through the air, parcels and all, and latched onto Shorter. The momentum carried the man down into the mud again.

Bricker slammed both fists into Taller's middle, struck again, and swung at the fellow's face. He connected this time, though not solidly enough. Taller tried to duck away, but was too slow. Bricker lined up a totally effective punch that slammed the man backwards into a jug-seller's stall.

Without pausing, Bricker wheeled to meet Shorter. Eric sat in the mud amongst his parcels, a splash of bright red on his mouth. Shorter was scrambling to his feet. A rolling water jug waddled into the edge of Bricker's vision. He snatched it up and flung it; he was quite as surprised as Shorter that his aim was true. The jug caught Shorter in the neck, giving Bricker time enough to reach the fellow with two good slugs. Shorter fell backward, his third roll in the mud.

Bricker grabbed two handfuls of shirt and hauled Eric to his feet. "Run, lad!"

Eric stared blankly at him, then snapped to life. He twisted around and scrambled in the mud, snatching up his parcels.

"I said run!"

"My things—"

In desperation Bricker grabbed the last bundle and shoved Eric in the right direction. The boy staggered before getting his feet moving. As soon as he was running strongly, Bricker gripped his arm and pulled him along. They were lucky for the moment; they must not push their luck or the Lord's good providence.

Bricker heard footsteps splacking in the mud behind them, but they were within sight of *Arachne* now. Bricker yelled. Up on the foredeck Halloran turned to look. They were safe now. Halloran came racing down the gangway as DuPres, aloft, jigged rapidly down the ratlines. The footbeats behind them ceased.

Bricker slowed to a walk. His lungs burned in the muggy air; sweat ran in rivers down his face. He let go of Eric's arm. The boy's knees buckled instantly. He sat in the mud a moment, swaying slightly, then stood. He slogged to the ship glassy-eyed, so winded he could not speak. The lad's face glowed alarmingly red. They both stumbled up the gangway with DuPres and Halloran right behind. Home.

"Halloran—Miss Harrington—Did she—?" Bricker sagged against the rail, unable to breathe either.

"Aye sir, She came running from upstreet there just a few minutes ago. Collapsed near the gangway into the loveliest pile of blue. Fisher's carried 'er aboard, but I've not been aft to know how she's doing."

"She didn't tell you to come help me?"

"Dead faint, sir. Never saw skin so white. A proper lady, I'd say, sir."

"Proper!" Bricker snorted. "Her trunks aboard yet?"

"Aye, all five of them. And the bags."

"Five?"

"Stowed 'em in the orlop, sir, except the two carpetbags. Opined she'd like them with her and stowed 'em in her quarters."

"Well done, Halloran. Tell McGovern and let's away. Send word when we're out in channel."

"Aye, sir!" Halloran jogged off foreward.

Bricker looked at his new cabin boy. The lad's face was still burning bright as a port light, but he could breathe somewhat. The blood on his lip and chin was turning black.

"You acquitted yourself well in that fight, lad. Waded right in. But when I give an order—any order—you're to obey instantly. Not when you get around to it, but instantly. Understand? As, for example, when I say, 'Run, lad!'"

"I'm sorry, sir." The lad gulped air. "Truly sorry." Those huge blue eyes drifted upward, totally repentant, to meet Bricker's. "I lost my head, sir." He took in another pound or two of air. "You said—all I could think of was—you said 'twas from my wages, sir."

CHAPTER 3

Entering Karimata Strait, Midday, June 10, 1851

The jib boom's tenor complaints betrayed its bobstays' need for retarring. The wind whistled under its soprano breath as it wove itself among the jib sails. The anchor bumped, baritone, against its billboard in rhythm with the rise and fall of *Arachne*'s prow. The cutwater's alto swish was soft and sibilant.

Bricker stood in his favorite place at the foredeck railing and braced one foot against the cathead, listening to this gentle symphony of hums and whispers. He knew every sound his ship was capable of making—any captain knew that—and these sounds pleased him most. They were the contented voices of a vessel doing what she did best, clipping along before a stiff breeze off her starboard quarter. *Arachne* was not often blessed with such a fair breeze, even less often on a day as sunny and clear as this. Bricker basked in the pure pleasure of the moment.

"Excuse me, sir. I completed all the tasks you mentioned. What shall I do next?"

Bricker turned to his cabin boy. "The serving closet is

cleared away? The cabin tidied? The lamp chimneys polished?"

"Aye, sir. I trimmed the wick in the lamp above the table. It was burning a bit smoky this morning."

"Mmm." Bricker settled back against the rail with both elbows. "Excellent, young Eric. Well, then, you're free to move about as you like till tea time."

" 'As I like'?" Eric cleared his throat. "Ah, sir? Would I be disturbing you if I stay right here?"

"Not at all. Welcome."

Eric flashed that quick and cheerful grin. "Thank-you, sir!" He leaned against the rail in partial imitation of his captain, though the position jacked his elbows up shoulder high. He presently stretched to tiptoe to peer over the side, watching their cutwater.

Such a simple thing, a boy watching a cutwater, but it instantly took Bricker back twenty-five years. He had been too short to reach the toprail then, and thus spent hours stretched out precariously across the jib. Most curious of all, that boyhood fondness persisted. He could still watch, fascinated, for hours on end.

Eric waved a finger toward the water. "I've heard it said, sir, that it glows at night." The eyes flicked up at him. "Is it true?"

"Yes. Sometimes in certain seasons and in certain waters. Phosphorescence. A gentle green or blue, very pale. Muted. But on a dark night it looks almost vivid. The color boils up and then fades as it moves out and away from the vessel."

"I'd love to see that sometime."

"I'll tell the watches to call you if they notice it."

"Would you really?" Eric stared at him a moment, apparently realized it was impolite, and turned his eyes back to the roiling water. "When will we lose sight of land?"

"Not for a while. These particular waters are riddled with little islands; almost always a few visible through the strait here."

"We're passing between Sumatra and Borneo, right?"

"Right. Sumatra lies west of the Java Sea, and Celebes lies east. We're paralleling the Indonesian Islands—Batavia's just about due south of us—but you won't see them. Too far away."

"I should think we'd see more ships, though, for all the tea and spices they send to the world."

Bricker smiled at the simplicity of his logic. "Just local traffic through here. Major trade routes follow the prevailing winds north from Singapore through the China Sea."

"China Sea. Pirates."

"Used to be. The pirates are pretty well suppressed. The Portuguese cleaned up the area around Macao, the British cleaned up around Sarawak and Borneo."

"So there aren't any anymore?"

"Oh, there are *some*. But it's not at all like it was."

"Then that's why you just stand here and look contented. I was afraid to ask, but now I know. You're relieved that there aren't any pirates to chase us."

Bricker laughed. "I've been chased by pirates, and recently. No, I'm just standing here feeling good because I gambled and won for once."

"You don't appear to be a gambling man."

"I mentioned the prevailing winds take ships north into the China Sea. I could have looped the long way around to my destination by following the normal wind patterns. I took a chance and headed straight east instead; much shorter, but that doesn't necessarily mean faster." He waved a hand. "The breeze is perfect; totally opposite to the way it usually blows at this time of year. Better than I could have hoped for.

27

"I see. Then you're standing here, gloating."

"And listening to the music."

The boy frowned, caught off guard. "Really! Music?"

"I attended a concert in London a few years ago. A Handel oratorio. The woman I escorted was enthralled by the way all the singers sang different things, essentially, yet it all fit together. One whole. I didn't say this to her, but I hear that every day. *Arachne* has her special set of voices. They change—for example, during heavy weather—but she always harmonizes with herself and with the Nereids' songs." Bricker glanced at his cabin boy. The frown had deepened. He smiled to himself. "Listen to the swish of water along the hull here. Hear the rhythm? And a melody of sorts. Nereids singing."

Eric strained at tiptoe. He dropped down on his heels and studied Bricker. "Little things singing down there? What are Nee-ree-ids?"

"More classical mythology. Learn the classics well. Much of literature refers to it; the planets and constellations all reflect it; even scientific names of many plants and animals come from it. Do you know what a nymph is?"

"A pretty maiden. A demigoddess."

"That's right. Nereids were sea nymphs, daughters of the gods Nereus and Doris."

"In the *Odyssey,* wasn't Calypso a sea nymph?"

"Very good. She was."

"I thought Neptune was god of the sea, not Nereus."

"Oceanus was, until the old Titans were overthrown and Neptune took the job. Nereus was Neptune's father-in-law. An aquatic elder statesman, you might say—a wise and well-spoken thinker. I'd like to think that at least some of his fifty daughters inherited that wisdom. That they know a sound vessel when she plies their waters and that they enjoy singing in concert with her."

28

Those splendid eyes were saucers. "You actually believe that?"

"No, I said I would like to think that. What I actually believe is that the one true God is Lord of the sea, as He is Lord of everything else in earth and heaven. In Jeremiah 31—somewhere around verse 30 or 35, I think—the prophet says the Lord stirs up the sea so the waves roar. And in Matthew 8, of course, Jesus stilled the storm at sea. And then there's Jonah."

A cool distance seemed to wash across Eric momentarily. Then he warmed again. "Nereids' singing. I wish you taught mythology in a school. Minerva, Arachne, Nereus—I'd study there. You make them seem alive."

"Why, thank-you." Bricker pondered what, exactly, the charm of this boy might be. He admired his captain quite obviously and that always endeared one. His intelligence and sense of wonder, his industry were all most appealing. Bricker admired those traits in any person, but that did not seem quite it. And the boy was physically attractive to the eye—slim, slight, pleasant features, even say pretty features. He'd never be a big man, but he'd be a lady-killer.

A dark cloud cooled Bricker's thoughts. He had never encountered the instance firsthand, but he had heard enough whispered stories—shipmasters who found a boy attractive and employed him for immoral purposes. Surely that wasn't possible here. Bricker would never even consider such a heinous sin. Yet the blackest of perversions must start somewhere, and perhaps, in just such innocent thought. No. No, the more he thought about it, the further Bricker put that sort of thing out of his mind. This boy, not nearly a man yet, was simply pleasant company.

His close attention bolstered Bricker's self-esteem; Eric listened. And his sensitivity made conversation a pleasure. Bricker did more than just put any impure thoughts out of his mind. He banished any further consideration of them. As time permitted he would enjoy the lad's innocent company. Then he would set the boy ashore in London and sign some other cabin boy for the voyage out, assuming Gideon was not with them.

Eric laid his chin on his arms. "When I complete my duties, as now, do I really have time all to my own, to do as I please?"

Bricker reminded himself that this boy, however delightful, was still a boy, and a clever one at that. "Within limits. So long as what you please isn't bound to get you into trouble if it's discovered. I know boys will be boys, but not aboard my vessel. I hope you've left any pranks ashore in Singapore."

Eric giggled. "I'd never pull pranks on you, sir. That Maude Harrington, perhaps—she deserves some trouble—but not you. Nor shall I bother her. I'll behave."

"You sound jealous, boy."

"Jealous! What have I in common with her?"

"Nothing, I would presume. That's why your general tone of voice puzzles me."

"I suppose it's her attitude, sir, as if we were all born to serve her highness. If I were a lady, sir, and not what I am—that is, if I were vying for your attention—I've heard that women may fight over a man that way—I'd say to her—" Eric drew himself up stiffly. "I'd say to her, 'Miss Harrington, you may have him!' Forgive my boldness, sir."

Bricker tried to hide his grin and almost succeeded. "And what fault do you find in me that I'm not worth fighting over?"

"None, sir. These crewmen all put out their very best for you and seem to enjoy doing it. That says what sort of master you are, though I've no experience as a seaman myself. I mean, I can't speak to that firsthand. There is, though—ah, I'm not certain I should say this—''

"I promise I won't remember it, let alone repeat it."

"Then, sir, my only objection is not a fault. It's, ah, that you tend to dwell on religious things. I've had religion pumped down me my whole life—my parents and my brother-in-law, all telling me God will punish me if I don't behave. They painted the picture of a huge ship with God as the Master, applying His cat-o'-nine-tails liberally to all His erring little crewmen. Frankly, sir, I've been rather confused about religion of late, and I'd like not to even think about it for a while. 'Twould be a pleasant change from what my life has been so far."

"I see. So you'd be happiest if I put God aside completely. Then you'd have no objections to me at all."

"I'm sorry, sir, but yes."

"Then I won't preach to you or require your attendance at the services we hold each Sunday. But I can't put my God aside any more than I can leave my left leg behind. He's part of me. However, I understand that you must work out—''

"Sail ho!" the lookout's voice interrupted from on high.

Bricker twisted around and called up into the straining canvas, "Where away?"

"Dead astern."

Bricker pushed away from the rail and walked briskly aft. Eric was running to keep up.

"Your duty, lad, is always to fetch my telescope when the lookout calls. I'll expect it without asking. It's on my desk."

"Aye, sir!" The boy ducked aside and in the cabin door as Bricker took the quarterdeck steps two at a time. He leaned on the taffrail to watch the white fleck on the horizon.

McGovern's square frame came to rest beside him. "In a

31

hurry, she is; evensay pursuing us. Pirates, mayhap."

"Or simply an English vessel wishing to send mail east."

Eric bounded to the rail and handed him his telescope. Bricker snapped it open and tried to pick out her colors, but she was still too distant. He heard the patter of light slippers behind him as he handed the glass off to McGovern.

Maude Harrington, her skirts flowing in the breeze, paused by his elbow. "You can outrun them, can't you, Captain?"

"Unless they be pirates, why should I?"

"You must!" Her eyes opened wide, fear-filled. The long lashes framed them in black, making their rich brown richer. "Please, Captain!"

"Miss Harrington, the men who accosted you just before we sailed were hardly waterfront ruffians out to earn a pound or two from a kidnapping. They were Europeans, fairly well dressed, and had seen a barber recently. I believe someone employed them, which means you're running away from someone or something."

"Captain, you'd best not be intimating that I'm a fugitive from the law or anything of that sort."

"I see her colors. British." McGovern squinted into the glass. "Arrgh! They just touched one off!"

Bricker saw the tiny puff of blue. The water splashed between his ship and theirs; belatedly, a muffled little boom floated in off their wake.

McGovern scowled. "Shall we come up?"

"No. Put on some canvas and let's see how we do. I don't trust her colors when she acts that uncivil."

"Aye!" The Scotsman almost smiled as he hurried off. Nearly as much as Bricker, the first mate loved a good run.

"I'm not familiar with the jargon." Miss Harrington watched the fleck, transfixed. "Does this mean we're running away?"

"For the time, at least. Pirates have been known to fly the Union Jack or some other friendly colors. Then, you see, they come roaring down unsuspected on their prey. But that vessel carries twice the sail area we do. I doubt we can outpace them for long."

Her soft lips trembled. "I see. Please do your best, Captain."

Bricker studied the lovely face, the milky skin. Those soft lips tightened into a thin, hard line. Her fingers diddled nervously. Sometime, under the right circumstance, Bricker would draw out of her the reason for this extreme agitation. For now he contented himself with feeling sorry for her. She was sorely perplexed. For all her aloofness, her coldness, she was so vulnerable. It touched him. He glanced at Eric. It wasn't touching his cabin boy at all. The lad watched her furtively, not the least bit sympathetic.

The royals snapped, luffed momentarily and spread to the breeze. McGovern was ordering Edward and one other to wing the spencer out wide. Never could Bricker ignore this lady—this vessel—when she was flying. When the breeze was right and *Arachne* was stretched out full like this she lost her status as an inanimate object. Some people claimed that the best captains always fell in love with their ships. In a peculiar sense it was quite true.

How long had he stood there absorbing the pleasure of her running? He snapped his attention back to the problem at hand—or was it a problem? He looked behind. Their pursuer was drawing closer by the minute.

CHAPTER 4

Off Cape Sambar, Teatime, June 10, 1851

Adrenalin flowing with the thrill of the chase, Bricker took the quarterdeck steps two at a time. Just as he reached the taffrail their pursuer fired another warning shot. Fisher came springing up the steps with his normal ebullience, and Eric bounded along right behind him.

Fisher greeted the helmsman in passing and draped himself across the rail. "Me insignificant opinion be that we'll not outrun 'er. And it's too early in the day to 'ope we can keep a'ead till dark and steal away."

"I agree. Miss Harrington is staying out of sight?"

"By 'er own request. She's absolutely certain that vessel's coming to lop off 'er dear sweet 'ead."

"The cabin is not sufficient. Hide her thoroughly and completely in whatever way your nimble mind contrives. Hide her well. If the vessel's legitimate and they've come seeking her, they won't get her unless they show good reason to have her. And if they're pirates, it's absolutely imperative she not be found."

Fisher glowed. "I consider it a privilege to render the lady temporarily invisible."

"And, Fisher. Tell Halloran to break out the guns and arm the crew—everyone save Eric here."

"On me way!" Fisher romped off across the quarterdeck and descended toward the cabin without touching the steps at all.

"Sir?" Eric's voice quavered a bit. "You really think they're pirates? That they might do something—ah—awful?"

"It's possible, but not probable. I told you piracy is dying out."

"On the main shipping lanes, you said. We failed to discuss the Java Sea."

Bricker smiled. "This is a major route west part of the year. Don't fret until fretting is necessary. Besides, they might kill the men and ravish the women, but they usually don't harm boys."

"Scant comfort that is."

Bricker raised his glass. "There's a crewman. Two. Both dressed like proper British seamen."

"But if they be pirates, do I fight, too?"

"No." He lowered his glass. "No, Eric. You did bravely with those two in Singapore, but compared to your average pirate they were inept. Sorry fighters. You'd be no match for a real cutthroat. So keep out of the way. Should shooting start, we don't want to worry about whether you might be in the line of fire. Understand?"

"Yes, sir," the boy barely whispered. Bricker looked at Eric's eyes. Intriguing. Brown is supposed to be warm and puppy-dog, yet Maude Harrington's eyes were cold. Blue is considered aloof and haughty, but young Eric's blue eyes were warm and soft. Obviously it was not color after all, so much as what lay behind the eyes.

"Sir?" Halloran came up behind and handed him his pistol. "And your two extra cylinders. Fisher put DuPres up in the rigging with the shotgun. And we have our instructions to forget there's a lady aboard.''

"Then spill our canvas and bring her about. Eric, make yourself scarce.'' Bricker slipped the ungainly pistol into his pocket. He let his hand linger a moment on the smooth, cool grip. "Death at y'r fingertips'' McGovern called it. McGovern detested guns of any kind, though this very pistol had once saved the first mate's life.

Their pursuer ranged alongside. No wonder she overhauled them so quickly. She had enough canvas aloft to shade a small city. Every man aboard her appeared to be a proper seaman and she was fitted as a proper merchantman. Her quarterboards said *Joseph Whidby*.

Fisher handed Bricker his bullhorn as he stepped up to the port railing, but he didn't need it. The merchantman wallowed less than fifty feet to port. At the rail beside her captain, a short, stocky Malay in some sort of paramilitary uniform called out, "Prepare to receive boarders!'' Already four seamen were lowering a jolly boat.

Fisher snorted derisively. "Friendly jack, aye? The sort of man whose wassail y'd love to sip on Christmas Eve.''

"He has six armed men coming over with him. Do you recognize the uniforms?''

"Nay, unless they be Singapore civilian militia. Constables. That'd be the governor's boys.''

"The guns look like muskets. Your guess sounds good.'' Bricker shouted, "What does Singapore's governor want with us?''

"We've come for Maude Harrington.''

"Begorra!'' Fisher mumbled under his breath. "Ye pegged that one right on the beacon!''

"She's well hidden?''

"Aye. And cleverly, if I do say so meself.''

Bricker watched the jolly boat bob toward them and recalled the desperation and fear in Maude Harrington's troubled eyes. Fisher and Halloran dropped a ladder over the side. In a rush the seven militiamen—or whatever they were—swarmed up onto the deck.

Their leader snapped a brusque salute. "Maude Harrington, Captain. A reliable informant assured us she's aboard."

"So Maude Harrington is a mortal woman. You must have a dandy reason to come storming after her like this commandeering a merchantman. Must be an intriguing story."

"We know she's here. Give her over to us now, or you can return to Singapore in irons and give her to us there."

Bricker felt his neck getting warm. "I doubt whatever authority you enjoyed in Singapore extends onto the high seas. You're proposing piracy, and we take a dim view of piracy. If you think you can pit six muskets against my armed crew, why, then I suppose you'll try to put me in irons. Bet you're smarter'n that."

"My authority is vested by the governor and, therefore, the crown." The Malay dropped his voice to a condescending purr. "I didn't commandeer the *Whidby* to pass the time of day with you. I do indeed have full authority to recover Miss Harrington by whatever means I must. You're not beyond jurisdiction of the Straits Settlements. You'll be wise to surrender her with no further fuss."

Bricker stepped back, in part to avoid the man's breath. "Mr. Fisher, Mr. McGovern; these gentlemen have permission to make a hasty search of our vessel. Follow them about, let them satisfy themselves as to the presence or absence of any Maude Harrington."

The commander eyed Bricker suspiciously. Suddenly he snapped something in Tamil. The six musketeers marched aft. Four of them disappeared into the stern cabin. The other two bounded up the quarterdeck steps. At a loss for anything impressive to do, the commander stationed himself halfway between Bricker and the aft companionway.

"Ohmigawsh!" Fisher snarled under his breath. "I forgot about 'er ditty! She must 'ave foofoo things scattered all over 'er quarters. They'll know for sure there's a lady aboard, and any moment now!"

Bricker seethed. He wanted dearly to explode on the outside, of course, but he dared not. He hissed, "I left that to you, Bosun, and hiding her possessions was surely a part of hiding *her.*"

The Malay was frowning toward them, trying to eavesdrop.

Bricker raised his voice a notch. "The next time we run out of my favorite coffee two days into a voyage, Bosun, you'll be deposited ashore at the nearest port of call. Is that understood?"

Fisher kowtowed so sincerely he actually tugged his forelock. "Ah, Cap'n, I cannae tell ye 'ow truly sorry I am! And I assure ye 'twill not 'appen again!"

The four came marching out the stern cabin with McGovern at their heels. They frowned at their commander with a negative little shake of the head and tromped down the aft companionway. McGovern and the other two followed. The commander snooped along the main deck, sticking his nose in here and lifting that.

Bricker studied Fisher and Fisher stared back. "Go tend your duties, Bosun. And our seven guests will not be staying for dinner. Let them eat aboard their commandeered vessel."

"I shall thus inform the chef, sir."

Chef. Wun lin a chef. Much as Bricker wanted to be enraged at his bosun he found himself smiling—almost. He casually wandered aft and pushed through the cabin door.

38

Eric was setting the table for tea. The guest cabin door stood open. The bed there was neatly made up and tucked in, the room devoid of any personal belongings whatever. Bricker yanked open a locker under the bed. Empty. The room had not been used for a long time. To the searching eye, Maude Harrington had never existed.

Presently Bricker wandered back out on deck. He ordered the main staysail set to keep *Arachne* a safer distance off *Whidby*'s beam. He delivered some course corrections to the helm and rapped his knuckles on the water butt. Full.

Finally, after half an eternity, the Malay gave up. In a very black mood indeed, he scowled up at Bricker as his jolly boat bobbed away, his six musketeers straining at the oars. They rowed like lubbers.

"Shall I wave bye-bye, Capt'n?" Fisher hauled the rope ladder in.

"I think not. You'd undoubtedly wave with your thumb to your nose, and that's not polite."

Fisher slammed the rail into place. "Ye've the general idea right enough. Cheeky fellow. Pity 'e'll never know 'e was right all along."

The jolly boat thunked against the flanks of *Joseph Whidby*. The oarsmen staved her off as the Malay hauled himself awkwardly up their ladder. The *Whidby*'s captain waved to Bricker, a hearty glad-it's-over saluting gesture.

Bricker waved back just as heartily. "Mr. McGovern, set our sails and get us underway again. Mr. Fisher, you may resurrect our passenger. Be prepared to tuck her away again, though, should they come about."

"Me pleasure, sir." Fisher cavorted off.

Bricker walked back to the stern cabin. It was well past teatime, but all their meals would be late tonight. Wun Lin had had to tear his galley apart for that constable—or whatever he was.

Eric set a steaming teapot on the table. "Your tea is ready, sir. Will the bosun and first mate be coming?"

"Mr. McGovern'll be late; save him some. Mr. Fisher will be here shortly with Miss Harrington. Eric, are you responsible for hiding her belongings?"

The boy smiled in guarded pride. "I wasn't sure I should, at first. But when no one else came to do it, I thought I'd better. Did I act out of line?"

"You did splendidly. Fisher thought of it too late. But where did you put all that stuff?"

Eric swung his closet door open. "The carpetbags are in my locker here. I jammed my oilskins into the tops of them to make them appear my own. Her soap and face paints are wrapped in her towels. I hid them among the other towels in the serving closet here. And her shoes are folded in amongst the shirts in your locker, sir, and her hair brushes are—" Eric's brow furrowed. "Now where did I put them? Ah, well, sir. They're about here somewhere."

Bricker laughed. He could see the *Whidby* departing, already far astern. The tension was gone, the situation relieved. They could enjoy the remainder of the voyage as it had gone thus far—pleasant and peaceful. There was no reason to suspect exceptionally foul weather this time of year. He would quiz Miss Harrington closely about this turn of events. Perhaps he would teach young Eric chess, or ask Wun Lin to teach him backgammon, or both.

Eric was glowing. "Rather exciting, wasn't it—I mean the suspense. Wondering if they might find her. Do you know where Fisher hid her, sir?"

Bricker heard muffled voices approaching. "No, but I'm sure we'll find out. Fisher's much too proud of his little *coup* to keep it to himself." He poured three cups of tea. Eric popped a tea cozy over the pot; his fingers were deft, quick, and very clean, unusual for a lad that age.

40

The cabin door burst open. Maude Harrington filled the cabin instantly with her strident shouting. "—so humiliated! Never! Nor shall I ever be again, you dimwitted Irishman!" She fixed her blazing eyes on Bricker. "And you—you ordered it! You condoned it! How could you?!"

Bricker stood, partly in politeness, mostly in surprise. "I don't understand your consternation, Miss Harrington." He glanced at Fisher but the answer wasn't there. Fisher shrugged in blank confusion.

"You don't understand?! *Look at me!* My dress is spoilt! Ruined! I'll never get this filth out of my hair! I reek! In a slop barrel, that's where he dumped me! A slop barrel! He poured slop on top of me and nailed the lid shut. I had to breathe through a knothole in the stave for two hours.

Fisher grimaced. "And lucky we are the barrel 'ad a knothole. We wouldn't 'ave been able to nail the lid down for fear of suffocating 'er. As it was, we—"

"*'Lucky'!*" She shrieked. She turned on Fisher. Her string of expletives included two Bricker had never heard in twenty-five years at sea. She stomped off to her quarters, shedding potato parings.

Bricker pointed to the floor. "Eric, clean up that garbage before someone slips or ma—"

"They're gone!" She came howling out of her cabin and stopped at the table, the picture of perfect rage. "Everything's gone!"

"Of course! I'd forgotten. Mr. Fisher, would you dig her shoes out of my shirt locker, please? Eric, fetch her carpetbags and towels from the closet. And try to remember what you did with her hairbrushes."

She pointed wildly at Eric. "You mean this hideous boy has been pawing through my private belongings? You permitted this half-sized waif to rummage through my personal things? How could—"

41

"You—you ingrate!" Eric exploded so violently that Bricker was momentarily dumbstruck. "The slop barrel's better by far than you deserve! If it weren't for the captain and Bosun Fisher you'd be on your way to Singapore in the clutches of a greasy little martinet, and good riddance! They risked much for you. They—"

"That's enough!" Bricker bellowed.

Even as he spoke, Maude had seized the teapot. She hurled it at Eric with perfect aim; it thunked against his chest, splashed steaming tea all down the front of him. He yelped soprano in pain and surprise.

Bricker waved toward the serving closet. "Go dash cold water on it, lad! Quickly!"

Eric wheeled and fled, slamming the closet door behind him.

Bricker did not bother to walk around the table. In one stride he was atop it; one more took him to stand on the floor in front of this deranged lady. "The boy spoke out of turn, but he's absolutely right. Your ingratitude is distressing and out of place. Not only could we have been saved considerable inconvenience by turning you over to them, we were no doubt outside the law in hiding you. And we did it knowing nothing about you. You probably deserve to be sent back. We could all be in irons right now, had they found you. And here you have the impertinence to scream at us for taking considerable risk on your behalf. For hiding you well enough that they scoured this vessel without finding you. You owe us a great deal more than the price of passage, madam, and if you can't repay with graciousness, you will at least repay with silence."

He clamped onto her arm and dragged her off to her cabin. He gave her a push through the door, not too gently, and slammed it after her. He called through the panel. "We'll put your belongings in as we come across them,

Miss Harrington. Consider yourself confined to quarters."

He took a deep breath, then another, for the first one failed utterly to control his ire. Fisher emerged from his quarters with an armload of shoes, chewing his lip.

"I compliment you, Mr. Fisher. You did well both in hiding her successfully and in keeping a civil tongue. You're an officer and a gentleman."

"Ah, well, thankee, sir. I knew I was an officer." Fisher raised a hand to rap on the lady's door, hesitated and turned. "I 'ope, sir, ye'll not consider y'r own reaction a breach of chivalry. 'Twas the perfect response for the occasion, sir. Couldn't 've said it better meself. And 'ere they claim we Irish 'as the gift of blarney!"

Bricker chuckled. "Thank-you, Bosun. Carry on." As he headed for the serving closet, he thought he heard Fisher mumble, "Wouldn't I love to" but he wasn't certain, nor was he about to ask. He stepped into the serving closet and closed the door behind him, lest the irate Miss Harrington storm back out and accidentally see young Eric in a state of undress.

Bricker froze . . . He stared . . . His mind went blank. Eric . . . was . . . Erica!

CHAPTER 5

Entering the Java Sea, Past teatime, June 10, 1851

Bricker knew some deepwater captains were famous for their flamboyance, their love of risk and high adventure. He was not one of them. He enjoyed routine, at least to a point. He approached life deliberately, evensay cautiously at times. And he vastly preferred the predictable. Surprises tended to incapacitate him, and he had just been struck by two surprises in a row.

The erstwhile cabin boy stood before him utterly naked. She flung one arm across her breasts and with the other hand covered her most private parts. The gesture was futile. Her breasts, the curve of her waistline and hips was enough to tell him her true sex.

After what seemed a century or two of being unable to think or move, Bricker wheeled and presented his back to her. All he could think to ask was, "Why?"

Apparently surprises paralyzed her also. "I had no other— I didn't— you don't understand. There was no other way— I—" Oilskins rustled; the stool creaked. Her voice had been reined in to some sort of control. "I am robed now, sir."

He turned cautiously. She sat perched on the high stool beside the counter. Her top was completely covered by her oilskin jacket, and her lower half was almost adequately swathed in towels. She stared at the floor. Tears streamed down her cheeks.

"You are the young woman who directed me to the doctor that night. The supposed sister."

She nodded and sniffled.

"I believe I deserve some explanation."

The huge blue eyes drifted up to meet his. "I'd rather not. Must I?"

"Yes, you must!" His voice exploded much too loudly. He cleared his throat and modulated his ranting. "At the very least you've betrayed my confidence. You've placed me in a difficult and compromising position. Should anyone else learn who you really are— I mean what you really are—"

"They won't." She was studying him almost in a calculating way, sizing him up. Did she realize to what a blithering idiot her little surprise had reduced him? It seemed she did. "I assure you, sir, they won't. I've been serving you well as a cabin boy, have I not?"

"Yes, you have. I can't fault you for that. But—"

"Then let it continue so." She raised a hand. "In the first place, I swear I'll throw myself overboard before I'll spend one minute with that witch in guest quarters. You've nowhere else to put me but here. So let me continue serving as I have been. You need a cabin boy and I do well to keep my identity a secret. What I'm trying to say, I suppose, is that you needn't make any hasty decisions right this moment. Nothing is lost by letting things go along as they have been."

"But you're not a— I mean you are a—" He stopped. She was right, for all her deceit. He could do nothing at this moment, but not because he wanted things to continue. He could think of nothing to do. His mind was blank. She sat, unmoving and quite composed, watching him, clutching that jacket around her.

"What's your true name?"

"Erica Rollin Rice. Margaret is my middle name."

"Where is your husband now?"

"Joshua Rice died about a year ago. I'm a widow."

"You're too young to be a widow."

"I'm twenty. I married at eighteen, which is not so very young."

Married at eighteen, nubile, still young and lovely, self-possessed—

Bricker turned away and studied the dishes on the shelf. The appearance and the thought of her were leading his mind astray. He'd best redirect his mind before his body got the notion to follow. "You haven't yet answered my first question. Why?"

"I saw in you my only chance to return home to England honorably."

"'Honorably.' A strange use of the word, Mrs. Rice. You lie and deceive in the basest way and call it honorable."

"I realize you think precious little of me just now."

"That is understatement."

"But you'd think even less of me if I poured out all the details of these last few years. Yes, Captain, I am honorable. Fortunately, my good honor springs not from what you think of me, but from what I am—and will be. Please don't press me further. Later perhaps. Sometime. But not now."

He was master of this vessel; his word was law. He could extract the truth from her by sheer dint of his authority. But would it be the truth? What, as Pilate asked Jesus, is truth?

He found himself saying more than he had intended, more than he ought. He turned to her. "I enjoyed talking to you very much. You make pleasant company. After dinner, as you readied the table and we were teasing each other, this morning on the foredeck—two days out and you were brightening the voyage already. I suppose that's why I feel so betrayed now. I'm sorry you are who you are. I liked Eric very much." He turned to leave but twisted around again. "I, uh, failed to notice. Your burns. Were you badly scalded?"

"No. No blisters. Just a bit of redness. I did as you said and splashed cold water on it. I suspect it will disappear in a day or so. Thank you for asking, sir."

He nodded. He had trouble saying that name now. "See to yourself, Eric. And check with Wun Lin about supper."

"Aye, sir." The voice whispered as if stricken. It sounded almost like the hushed swishing of the Neriveds.

Bricker closed the door behind him.

Fisher was down on his knees peering under Bricker's desk, his ear to the floor. He vaulted to his feet. "Sure'n I 'ope young Eric remembers the whereabouts of the lady's 'airbrushes, for meself cannae turn 'em up."

"She can live without them." Bricker was done with women of any stripe. *Bah.*

The volatile Irishman dissolved into instant worry. "The lad's badly burned, sir?"

"No. The burns are superficial. Be gone in a day or two."

The face rearranged itself to its customary grin. "Ah." He bounced across the cabin.

Bricker realized almost too late where his bosun was headed. He wheeled. "Mr. Fisher!"

Fisher paused with his hand on the serving closet door. "Aye, sir?"

47

"There's nothing you need in there."

Fisher frowned. "I thought ye mentioned the lady's bags are there."

"Eric can bring them out in good time."

The frown deepened. Fisher's shrug was a suspicious gesture rather than a resigned one.

Bricker groped for some reason, any reason— "The lad's undressed and he's still at that bashful age. Self-conscious. He'll be out when he's ready."

The face relaxed. "Of course, and well I remember. There was a while there, when meself was yet a shaver, I went through the same sort of thing." He strode toward the door. "Didn't want me own Mum to see me peeled. She put an end to that nonsense quick enough; claimed she changed me nappies long enough that me bottom 'eld no secrets for 'er." He disappeared outside.

The noise Fisher generated by his very presence left with him. The room was suddenly, instantly, dreadfully silent. Bricker took a quiet turn around the cabin. He heard dramatic sobbing from Maude Harrington's guest quarters and sniffling from the serving closet. He glanced out the casement window to the rear. *Whidby* had nearly disappeared. He flopped down in his chair. He tried to be God's man toward everyone in the whole world. Why was life so wickedly unfair in return? By slow degrees the silence cooled his jangled nerves and thoughts.

Fisher swooped back in the door with a new teapot from stores. The silence fled. Eric emerged, red-eyed, from the closet. He dropped a towel on the pool of tea and pushed it about with one foot.

Fisher handed him the pot. "Ask Wun Lin for a reload."

"Aye, sir." Eric left.

Fisher disappeared into the serving closet and returned moments later with the carpetbags.

48

"Eric says he put some of his own things in them to disguise them." Bricker reflected momentarily on the boy/girl's cleverness.

"Noticed, sir. Bright lad. I think I've removed everything not belonging to a lady."

That's what you think. Bricker watched him cross the room. Fisher knocked, announced his intentions and received some sort of muffled acknowledgment. He cracked the door open just far enough to scoot the bags inside and carefully, quietly closed it again.

Fisher turned. "Ye know, I'm sure, why every ship's a she. Moody. Unpredictable. Y'r source of pain and pleasure. Then about the time ye give y'r 'eart and soul over to 'er, she sinks right out from under ye and leaves ye to the bitter sharks of fate. Ah, but what would we ever do without 'em, eh?"

"You'll do without that one. She's very likely married, and I'll not countenance adultery aboard this vessel."

"O' course, sir. Furthest thing from me mind." He dropped to one knee and began mopping up tea. "Pitiful sight she is, too, all sprawled out upon 'er bunk so sad; one dainty ankle draped fetchingly over the end of it; the pale shoulders trembling as she sobs 'er little—"

"Belay that!"

"Aye, sir."

Eric returned with the tea and set it on the table. "Wun Lin promises dinner in two hours, sir."

"Thank-you."

A shaft of golden evening sun stabbed through the stern window and splashed across the floor.

Eric returned Maude's towel and toiletries to her. He/she seemed to share none of Fisher's awe and admiration for women. Now that Bricker reflected on it, Eric's attitude

49

toward Miss Harrington was nowhere near what one would expect from a boy. Boys fear strange women, hold them in abeyance. Eric despised her as an equal. Bricker should have seen that right away. What had blinded him?

The golden shaft widened out to a dazzling sheet of light. It reflected into Bricker's eyes.

Fisher glanced at his captain. "Shall I be mother of the pot today, sir?"

"Go ahead." Bricker hauled himself to his feet and shuffled to the table, feeling old before his time. He sat down as Fisher poured all around.

Fisher patted the chair to his left. "Eric, me lad, sit down 'ere. With all the 'uggermugger swirling about, ye deserve to be treated like a person this once. 'Ave some tea with us."

"It's all right, sir, really . . ."

"Sit."

Eric sat.

Fisher pushed Miss Harrington's cup in front of Eric. "Ye see, lad, it occurs to me belatedly that the chief reason y'r chest was scalded so is simply that ye were defending y'r ship's officers—a noble gesture. 'Ad ye let injustice reign and kept y'r mouth shut, ye would never 'ave come to grief. So therefore the captain and meself, we owe ye a considerable debt of gratitude. Aye, Cap'n?"

"Gratitude," Bricker muttered.

"Mmm. Well. Anyway. The captain at times fails to articulate 'is true feelings, but I take that as an opportunity to thank ye on behalf of us both. Y're a true and loyal mate and I for one am tickled pink y're aboard." He looked pointedly at Bricker. "Aye, sir?"

"Uh—of course. Tickled pink." Bricker glared at Eric. Eric stared at the table.

Fisher rolled on undaunted. "And from all this, lad, y've

learned two important lessons today. One is that ye never speak 'arshly to an irate female or call attention to y'rself, regardless 'ow lovely 'er form and figure. Sure 'n she'll nail ye one way or t'other. And the second: When something unexpected pops up, rest assured y'r captain 'ere is competent to 'andle it; but it does put 'im off. So when 'e's been dealt an unexpected card, just back off awhile. 'E'll sweeten up soon enough."

Fisher patted Eric's shoulder, his hand lingering a moment. *A man should never casually touch a woman, and even less so in such an intimate manner,* thought Bricker. Fisher wrapped his arm about Eric's shoulders and gave him a final avuncular hug. "Y're a member of the crew, lad, and welcome ye are."

"Thank-you, sir," Eric mumbled.

Bricker sipped his tea and burned his tongue. How long could this impossible charade go on before someone noticed that Eric was not what he pretended to be? The deception had been unmasked, at least to himself, in less than forty-eight hours. Would his crew believe he had signed Eric on unwittingly? Hardly. So far his best bet would be to protect Eric's secret as long as possible and listen for murmuring among his men. If the secret went undiscovered to that point he might deposit Eric at the nearest port of call without anyone being the wiser. Embarrassing, to have been taken in so easily by this deceit.

The cabin door banged open. McGovern crossed to the table and stopped. He looked from face to face, scowling. "What's wrong?"

Bricker sighed. "Nothing, Mr. McGovern. Have some tea."

CHAPTER 6

Java Sea, Morning, June 11, 1851

To Erica Rollin Rice her present position was a familiar one. She was sure she must have been born under an unlucky star. Or perhaps she was simply too immature and hasty in her decision making. Or then again, maybe she harbored an inaccurate perception of what adventuring ought to offer. Whatever the problem, she was doing something wrong. For every shining moment of these last few years she had suffered months of anguish.

She placed the napkins on the table and mentally counted items. What had she forgotten? *Butter*. From the little pantry locker she brought out the butter mold. Mold? The butter was formed into a simple hemisphere, the only shape it would hold in this tropical heat.

Captain Bricker came in the door, barely acknowledged her with a nod, and crossed to his desk to put his sextant away.

"Breakfast is ready, sir."

"Thank-you." His voice was cool, aloof. She wished she had the courage to throw something—preferably something very big and heavy.

Fisher breezed in with something heavy enough, but she couldn't throw the breakfast tray. Mr. McGovern trundled in behind him.

She smiled with what she thought to be a boyish grin. "Good morning, Mr. Fisher. You look cheerful enough today."

He handed her the tray of porridge and scones from the galley. "And why not? When I awoke this morning, I discovered meself is still alive. Reason enough to be 'appy, aye?"

"Aye, but if you ever wake up dead, you'll bound along for a fortnight before you realize the fact."

McGovern guffawed.

"Get on with ye, lad!" Fisher laughed. He gave Erica a friendly swat on the backside as she turned away, a jovial and innocent gesture.

She glanced at the captain as she entered the serving closet. He was standing there, livid at the intimacy, but unable to say a word.

Maude Harrington's door creaked open as the captain was about to sit down. She wore a clean dress and had pulled her hair back into a quiet, austere bun. Her eyes were puffy and red. "May I come out, please, Captain?"

"Yes. Good morning, Miss Harrington."

"Good morning." She stood there hesitant, as if such a brazen hussy would ever be uncertain of anything. She crossed to the captain and paused before saying, "I ask your forgiveness for my scene yesterday. I'm very, very sorry."

The captain held out his hand to her. "It was a trying situation. We were all upset. You're not only forgiven, the scene is forgotten. Will you join us for breakfast?"

She accepted his hand and turned to Fisher. "And you, Bosun. I wronged you so. Please accept my deepest apologies."

"Y'r lovely face makes apology unnecessary, milady, but I accept it all the same. And a gracious good mornin' to ye." He seated her beside him, across from the captain. Grudgingly, Erica put a place setting before her.

She looked up at Erica with wonderfully repentant eyes. "Eric, I apologize to you also. I hope I didn't hurt you."

"No, ma'am, you didn't." *Bite your tongue, Erica! This floozy certainly did hurt you. If it weren't for her, things would still be as they once were. And the pain is far from over.* Erica served Wun Lin's scones as soon as the captain had completed his morning prayer at table. Pointedly she placed the teapot on the captain's side of the table.

Miss Harrington patted her hair with both hands. "I had difficulty arranging my hair this morning—no hairbrushes. I trust I look presentable enough."

Fisher cooed something almost worshipful. Erica served the porridge, and it was all she could do to keep from dumping the boiling gruel in the Irishman's lap. *Disgusting it is, the way some men fawn all over women.*

"I owe you an explanation, Captain." Miss Harrington dug into her porridge hungrily.

"If explanations were money, I'd be a wealthy man when all that was owed was paid me." He was looking right at Erica. "Eric, is there any marmalade?"

"I think so, sir." Erica slunk off. So she could expect little potshots, eh? Very well—she could shoot, too.

Miss Harrington cleared her throat. "I wish I had some excuse for the fit I threw. I can't believe I did that. And after all you risked for me. You see, I find myself very anxious—more than nervous—terrified—when I'm confined in a small space. I can't ride in a closed carriage for more than a few blocks. I have trouble sleeping with bedcurtains drawn. When Mr. Fisher nailed that lid down—I can't tell you how terrified I felt. Panicked. I was

54

trapped. I was reduced to such a wretched state I would gladly have given myself up just to get free of that barrel. But every time I took a deep breath to cry out, I gagged. When he finally let me out, I— I just— I'm so deeply ashamed.''

Fisher waggled his porridge spoon in the air. ''DuPres's like that exactly, Cap'n. 'E's the best man aloft I've ever seen. Makes monkeys look like donkeys up there. But never send 'm below into a crowded lower 'old. 'E'll come popping out abovedecks like a champagne cork in two minutes flat, and shaking like a slack jibstay. Wild-eyed.''

The captain smiled at Miss Harrington. ''If you're discussing some experience I should be familiar with, I must have forgotten it. I'm sorry. Old age, I guess; things of no consequence slip my mind.''

Erica clunked the marmalade on the table.

Maude smiled more than a smile. She radiated. She glowed. ''You gentlemen are magnificent, all of you!'' She reached for a hot scone. ''For some reason that escapes me, there's a dress in my quarters all soiled. How does one go about handling laundry aboard ship?''

''Give it to Eric here. He's had some experience laundering dresses.''

Erica recognized the meaning. Potshot number two.

Fisher swallowed. ''Aye, of course. 'Is sister's.''

Maude sipped her tea and laid her spoon down. ''Are you familiar with the name Franz Bilderdijk?''

The captain nodded. ''Wang See has mentioned him. Calls him 'that Dutchman.' I assume he's a Singapore businessman who drives a hard bargain.''

She made a derisive noise. ''His public monopoly is shantung and brocade. No such fabrics leave the island until he's had his cut of their profits. And his private monopoly is, ah—'' She glanced at Eric. ''Ladies. He controls all the gaming parlors and hotels frequented by Europeans. His influence extends throughout the Straits Settlements nearly to Australia. Perhaps farther."

"Sounds like a charming gentleman."

"I realize you're being sarcastic, but, yes, he is charming. He's handsome, suave, wealthy, and knows exactly how to impress a lady. He's also abusive, given to strong drink, sadistic, possessive. I could think of adjectives all morning if I cared to. I don't."

"And you're running away from him."

"Yes. Until I declared my freedom by boarding your ship, I belonged to him. Don't you see?" Her eyes locked onto the captain's. "By leaving his house, I openly defied him. He is not a man to let defiance go unpunished—not among his associates, his hired help or his women. There will be no mercy for me if I fall back into his clutches, and as I said, his clutches extend very far." She straightened. "But they don't extend to the New World."

"You're an American."

"Born in Chicago, yes. I have no idea what my status as a citizen is any more, but that's the least of my concerns."

Fisher wagged his head. "And that explains why the governor's militia could commandeer a merchantman just to search for a woman. Big money. Evensay a reward?"

The captain shot him a dirty look. "Mr. Fisher tends to relate much of life to pound notes, or whatever the local currency might be. Why didn't you tell me this before?"

"I was afraid you wouldn't risk it—meddling with the Dutchman. Besides, I've learned to trust no one—not his henchmen, not his associates, not even my so-called friends. I couldn't trust you, Captain, until you proved yourself yesterday."

"You took a big risk, not giving me better reason for hiding you."

The lovely shoulders heaved. "I knew what I wanted—what had to be—but not how to go about it exactly. Where was the line between saying too much and not saying enough? But I had to do something. Run. I couldn't take his infidelities and denigrations and—and he was so certain, so confident that I was trapped. His forever."

"You're still his by law regardless where you run. You referred to yourself as his woman. Are you legally married?"

Her voice was low and husky. "I've never married."

Fisher brightened perceptibly. The captain looked disappointed. Erica could have told him so. She had known from the beginning this woman was immoral. But on the other hand, if the bare facts of her own story were laid out, she would appear every bit as fallen as Maude.

Erica was not by choice immoral. She had been trapped, just like Maude claimed to be. She studied the woman's face in a new light. Was Maude as much a victim of circumstance—of men—as she herself? Apparently. She was a changed woman today. Either Maude Harrington was a consummate actress or finding someone to trust had shattered her façade of haughtiness.

Maude was continuing in a soft, feline voice. "I believed, too, that I was trapped. And I despised myself more every day. Then I learned you were about to sail. The Dutchman was outside town on the west end. It seemed the perfect opportunity. In fact, you were my only chance."

Her only chance. The captain had been Erica's only chance as well. Poor Captain Bricker—did he realize how many fallen women were clinging to him to escape their fates?

Captain Bricker buttered another scone. "How did you hear about us? We were in port less than a day altogether."

"Doctor Bigelow. He was treating me for a— ah— a

57

plantar wart. Not a very romantic malady. He mentioned in passing that a sea captain required a cabin boy; did I know of anyone appropriate? I didn't know any boys who might be interested, but when I heard you were sailing east— immediately I got the idea that—" She frowned. "What's wrong?"

Fisher and the Captain were staring at each other grimly.

"Would ye say," Fisher asked, "that this Dutchman's the vindictive sort?"

"To say the least. And petty. Extremely petty. What are you two scowling about?"

The captain answered, "Gideon."

"Who is Gideon? Your sick cabin boy?" She shook her head. "Surely there's no way the Dutchman would connect me with him."

"There are half a dozen ways. His man didn't find you, but the Dutchman suspects you're aboard this vessel. He knows *Arachne* and he knows my name. All he need learn is that *Arachne*'s cabin boy is in Singapore, and he could get that from Chow Chen, Wang See, the good doctor or anyone who saw me come ashore that night—and puts two and two together. Your Dutchman must have a thousand ears on the waterfront."

McGovern grimaced. "Wang See'd never sell the lad out."

"Not intentionally. But perhaps inadvertently. Especially if he didn't know in time that the Dutchman is hoping for revenge against us. And I don't know a thing about Chow Chen. Gideon could go to the highest bidder."

Erica refilled the teapot. "Will that be all for now, sir?"

"I think so. You're excused."

She tiptoed out the door and into bright morning air. The cabin air was so dark and heavy. No, the morning was not bright when she looked twice. The sky was overcast but not thickly enough to bring rain. The cloud cover made the water a bleak sort of gray, matching the gray sky. She looked aloft. In this light the sails appeared dirty; in sunlight they gleamed white as snow.

She wandered foreward to the foredeck railing. She stood with both feet on the cathead, the better to watch the whitewater boil up along the prow. Nereids. Only now did she fully realize how much had slipped through her fingers. Her eyes burned hot and wet.

She thought of the captain's eyes that first night ever she saw him, anguished for the boy Gideon. And now Gideon might well lie in grave danger, and all because of that Maude. Erica's sympathy for Maude chilled again. And yet Maude couldn't help it. She had acted quickly and without thinking, exactly the way Erica had acted. If there were a victim here, it was not Maude or Erica or even that fevered little boy. It was Captain Bricker, who wanted only to do right before men and his God and to lean here on the rail, listening to His music.

Erica had lost interest in Nereids. She came down off the foredeck and ambled aft. As she passed near the mainmast she met the larboard watch; Edward the towhead, fifteen and lanky, draped casually over the port rail.

He grinned at Erica. "Hi, Eric."

"Hi, Edward."

"Hey, I'm off at sundown. Wanna play a couple hands? Cribbage maybe, or euchre?"

"Maybe." Erica shrugged and kept going.

Fisher and McGovern came out the stern cabin door, heads together in earnest conversation. She must go clear breakfast dishes away now. The captain emerged, but he didn't come forward. He jogged up the steps to the far side of the quarterdeck and stood at the taffrail. He was watching the horizon behind them. He was looking toward Gideon.

She walked quickly, not to the cabin but up onto the quarterdeck. Quietly—but not too quietly—she leaned beside her captain at the taffrail. He made it plain he was ignoring her.

"You're still angry with me, aren't you?"

He shifted a little. "No. *Angry* isn't the word. I was never actually angry with you, as such."

"Then why so cold? Yesterday you were warm. Open. And now—what can I do to restore your good humor toward me?"

"Nothing. You are what you are and you can't change that." He looked at her for the first time that day. "A man earns respect by his conversation—that is, his walk through life. A woman deserves respect simply because she's a woman. Regardless this sham of yours, I do hold you in a certain degree of respect."

"And you didn't respect the person Eric?"

"Of course, but that was different. He was male, not much more than a child, really, just barely beginning his walk. Different."

"I'm not *that* old!"

"Neither are you Eric."

She was going to speak but she chewed her lip instead. She dwelt upon the marvelous camaraderie of yesterday. Without in any way compromising his authority as this ship's master, he had accepted her freely, held her in a kind of nonsexual affection. It was an uncle-nephew thing, a father-son thing. She relished those moments and savored them. She yearned for them and they were gone. He was now a gentleman, addressing a lady in the only way he knew.

Mentally she tried to restore that open feeling as she stood beside him. But camaraderie requires two participants and he was no longer participating. By "respect" the captain meant "cool reserve," the proper distance at which any proper gentleman held a lady—proper or not.

The full picture was unveiled, a picture spoiled past mending by Maude. She saw in the picture that what she yearned for and what she could achieve were two completely different things. Ah, well, she could cry over spilt milk (or beans, as the case may be), or she could continue her adventuring. Her impetuous nature had gotten her into this. It could get her out. Perhaps she could even make some amends for her contribution to this man's burdens.

"Uh—sir? It's true you can't take *Arachne* back to Singapore?"

"True. Not with Miss Harrington aboard. We're committed, now, to taking her on to safety. And there's still the goal of reaching New Zealand in time. Cargo is scarce and hard to find. If we don't take the load, it will go to some other vessel."

"But you can send me back. Call at the nearest port where I can find passage to Singapore, or flag some passing ship."

"I thought you wanted to continue serving here as you have been."

"I do! Even under the present conditions I'd much rather be here. But I can help you in Singapore. Consider: I know the city fairly well. I wouldn't be suspect, so to speak, to that Dutchman. I can spirit your little Gideon away and book passage to New Zealand or wherever. If he's too ill to travel, we can spend a few weeks in that little room I was renting. Don't you see? I'm the perfect person to go rescue your lad out from under that Dutchman's nose—before something terrible happens."

"And this is all your own idea."

"I think it's a magnificent idea. My dream back in Chelsea was to go adventuring. I see now that adventure

61

doesn't come to one. It must be sought out—pursued. And the very best adventuring is one with high and noble purpose. Like rescuing a child." She expected him to brighten at least a little at the idea. Perhaps he would even see her sincerity and concern.

Instead, he both looked and sounded disgusted. "I realize it's the common province of women to be devious. But when you listen at the door, why not just come out and say you did? Why this blatant little fiction that you have a bold new idea? If you think you can handle the job better than Fisher, come right on out and say so."

"Fisher! What has he to do with this?"

He glared at her. "As if you didn't know. He's the one who came up with that idea. And I'll send him back to Singapore, not you. He's quick and clever—not that you aren't—but in a dangerous situation he can fight if running is impossible. He's a first-class barroom brawler. I used to count that against him, but it could work in our favor if he gets into a sticky situation. I'll give him all my contacts and he has quite a few of his own in the seamier establishments. Do you?"

"No, I'm sorry. I do not frequent seamy establishments. There is a line to be drawn when adventuring." She felt her anger bubbling to the surface. She should not talk back to the captain, but here it came pouring out. "I don't care if you are my captain; you shall hear this. I was being completely honest with you, sir. I did not listen at any door. I was up on the foredeck listening to your silly Nereids. And since you need proof now for whatever I say, ask Edward; he's larboard watch. The idea was wholly mine because I like you and I wanted to help you. I cared about you, but I see now that was foolishness. In return, the only thing you care about is looking and acting stuffy and proper. And I feel sorry for you, but not too sorry. After all, much of your anguish is of your own manufacture. Respect indeed!'' She turned on her heel and flounced off to the steps.

Difficult as it was to flounce when not wearing skirts, the whole scene gave her a perversely satisfying feeling. Maude was to blame in a way, but Captain Bricker was to blame in another way. *Men! Bah!*

CHAPTER 7

Java Sea, Mid-morning, June 11, 1851

The biggest problem in Erica's ill-starred marriage to Joshua Rice had been her temper. When she lost patience with a person (and especially a person she cared about), she became angry almost instantly. Obviously she hadn't changed a bit in that respect.

She roared into the stern cabin, fresh from her tangle with the starchy captain, and started scooping up porringers. She burned.

Maude Harrington still sat at the table. She folded her napkin. "Ah, there you are, Eric. My dress is in the corner of my room. See to it promptly."

"My pleasure. How many pieces would you like it returned in?"

"What!"

"And what color? The color of the slop spots or the color of the vomit spots? They won't wash out of that silk, you know, so we'll simply change the color of the rest of the dress to match. No matter, of course. Blue is blue. Let me know when you've decided." She carried her armload of dirty dishes to the closet.

"You just watch your impudence, young man!"

Erica returned to the table. "A word to the wise, madam: Haughtiness does not become you. Your mask of contrition looked much better." She snatched up the marmalade jar so carelessly she nearly spilled it.

Maude was glaring at her. The glare softened. "I apologized to you, you know. But I did treat you badly, so I apologize again. I think I may have somehow damaged your position with your captain."

"More than you'll ever know." Erica shook out the captain's napkins with a snap and tucked it in its ring. She looked at Maude. With puffy eyes and scant make-up, Maude looked almost human. "How did the Dutchman keep you, exactly?"

"That's none of your business, boy."

"I know it's not. But it's important to me for reasons you aren't aware of. You're a strong woman. You know how to get what you want and make demands. Why couldn't you just—well, assert yourself? Simply say to the Dutchman, 'That's enough of this nonsense. I'm leaving.'?"

Her laugh was abrasive. "You'll learn that life is never that simple."

"Oh, I've learned that much already." Erica sat down across from her, perched earnestly on the edge of the chair. "How could he coerce you so fearfully if you weren't tied by the marriage bond?"

"So you can trap some innocent little girl yourself when you grow up?" She studied Erica. "No, probably not. You just don't seem the type . . . Do you know if the captain keeps any whiskey around handy?"

"He doesn't approve of spirits. Fisher said so. But the crew gets their daily ration of rum—those who want it."

"Rum. Ugh!" She laughed, mirthless. "Why am I laughing? I might be reduced to that before this trip's over.

65

So you want to know how the Dutchman hangs onto his women. Pass the sugar.'' She poured another cup of tea.

"When you said 'trapped' it meant something to me,'' Erica said. "My sister was trapped against her will. But the man literally kept her in chains. She could say 'I'm leaving' all she wanted, but she couldn't go anywhere.''

Maude snorted. "The Dutchman's a little more subtle than that. You old enough to know what a paramour is?''

Erica considered a moment. "I trust you understand that when I say 'yes' it doesn't mean I consort with them.''

Maude guffawed. "You're gonna outtalk that glib-tongued Irishman if you don't watch it. Well, I was one for a while. How I got to the South Pacific is a long story. When I met the Dutchman I was doing all right in Macao, in the Portuguese quarter. But I wasn't happy; didn't like myself.'' Her face sobered. "Know what really trapped me? My own dreams.''

"I don't follow.''

"Don't blame you. When I met the Dutchman at a New Year's Eve party, we liked each other and, lo and behold, he started courting me. I dreamed of being able to leave the past behind and begin life all over. Have genuine respect as the wife of a respected businessman. I think that's what got me in the end more than anything else.''

"You mean you let him court you and stayed with him, hoping that you'd have a respectable life eventually?''

"Something like that. And he's charming—a real heart-stealer. He seemed like he'd be the perfect husband—wealthy, well-thought-of, courteous.''

"Like Captain Bricker.''

"Your captain isn't wealthy.'' She smiled sadly. "But then, wealth is the least of it, though it took me a long time to realize *that*. When the Dutchman invited me to Singapore, I couldn't say yes fast enough.''

66

"Did he forgive your past or did he ever learn of it?"

"I'm sure he must have known, but I never told him. I was afraid he'd drop me. Shoulda told him and I'd have been lucky if he did. How did he trap me?" She took a heavy draught of tea and stared glumly at the cup. "Just isn't the same without a shot of whiskey," she mumbled. "He trapped me by promising wonderful things. I sat around a long time waiting for them; hoping for them. He trapped me with pretty words. He said things I wanted to hear and I was afraid I'd never hear them if I weren't with him. He trapped me by being the most powerful man in Singapore, and that includes the governor. I couldn't say anything, do anything, go anywhere but that he heard about it. Every soul in Singapore's afraid of him."

"I see. Even if the Dutchman let you go, everyone in Singapore would be afraid to associate with you."

"Afraid the Dutchman might change his mind and want me back. Afraid I might be his spy. Your sister was lucky. Only *one* chain. I had hundreds."

"Didn't you ever love him?"

Maude drained her cup and stared morosely at the dregs. "Funny, isn't it? In a way I still do." She looked up at Erica. "And now you're going to go running straight to the captain with everything you just heard. Buy yourself back into his good graces with dirt about dear old Maude."

Erica shook her head and sat back. "No. No, you guessed right about the captain's opinion of me. Damaged past mending. Not just because of you. There's much more to it than that." She shrugged. "I'm very good at keeping secrets—mine and other people's."

"You? Secrets? You're not old enough to have secrets. Not big ones." She leaned forward toward Erica. "But you're still respectable. Hang onto that. I'd give anything—my life itself—to be considered respectable by polite society. And I shall, too." She sat back. "Tell me something. Yesterday when I lost my head the captain got howling angry, but he didn't hit me; didn't even try. And for some reason I never had the fear that he might, even though he was mad enough to breathe fire. Is he always that gentle?"

"I don't know; I guess so. I only just signed on this ship in Singapore."

"Really?" Maude frowned, perplexed. "You two seemed so close—so comfortable with each other, like you'd known each other a long time. You fit together so well I assumed either you were related to him or had worked here for years."

"Yes. We fit well together." Erica's loss welled up inside her anew.

"Your captain got a wife or girl friend or something?"

"He never mentioned any, but that doesn't mean much."

"No, he seems to play everything pretty close."

"I don't understand—"

"When he kisses, he doesn't tell."

"If you knew that, why'd you ask me?"

"Just checking. I like to know what I'm up against." She stood up and glared at Eric, instantly contemptuous. "When a lady stands up to leave, the gentleman stands up also, boy."

Erica shrugged. "You're no lady and I'm no gentleman." Little could Maude guess how true that was!

She smirked. "Brassy brat. See to my dress." She minced out the door, apparently dismissing the fact that she had just confided her most intimate secrets to a virtual stranger—and a young boy at that—for all she knew.

Erica could sense the woman's intentions and it enraged her. The position of captain's wife is a highly respectable one. Maude's claws were out; Erica just knew it.

She stood up and finished readying the table. *Men! Bah! And women! Double bah!* Erica wished she were quit of them both. She stopped suddenly in the midst of her busyness. Or did she wish that? Once she had sworn off men. But the captain haunted her. She was afraid he would succumb to the wiles of the likes of Maude Harrington. She was afraid he would find an attractive lady, perhaps someone who appreciated Handel oratorios, and—those eyes.

She marched on to the serving closet and stacked the dishes. No, she would forego men forever. They took so much pleasure and offered none in return. She had been badly used by them—well, by a few of them, and they were all alike.

Captain Bricker strode in the door and crossed to his desk. He pulled a chart and spread it out on the table. He stared at it a few seconds. "Eric, I need the chart that's in the pigeonhole immediately to the left of this one."

"The left. Aye, sir." Erica trotted over to the chart rack, the dozens of cells filled with dozens of protruding ends of rolled paper. How did he always know just which roll to choose? They looked exactly alike. A faint and distant bell was tinkling in her memory. What was it?

She pulled the chart from the cell to the left of the empty cell. Two heavy blue weights came, leaping and sliding, out of the roll of paper. One of them fell on her foot; the other clunked on the floor. Aha! Now she remembered.

The captain turned and frowned at her, irritated by the noise.

She picked up the two blue objects and waved them shoulder-high for him to see. "Maude Harrington's hairbrushes, sir."

CHAPTER 8

Java Sea, Evening, June 11, 1851

Erica hung up the dishtowel. She wiped the counter off and positioned the tall stool just so. Now what? She could look up Edward and play some cribbage. She could choose a book from the captain's shelf to read. She could wash Maude's dress again and hope more of the stains would come out—what a mess. Or she could just mope around on deck feeling sorry for herself.

Moping seemed by far the most attractive of her options. She left the serving closet, crossed through the dark, deserted stern cabin, and stepped out on deck.

The wind had shifted. Until now it had blown from behind, scooting them along. Now it came almost exactly out of the east, the direction in which they were headed. She could tell because the setting sun dipped low behind them, gilding the sails.

Crewmen were just finishing the onerous task of rearranging the sails. There was no doubt a word sailors used for the extreme angle at which these spars had been set, but Erica knew none of the terminology. But the sails were turned so far aside they nearly paralleled the sides of the ship. *Arachne* canted slightly aport.

Erica looked up behind her. At the quarterdeck rail the captain was watching his crew work. Beside him, Maude snuggled in close. Now and then he would point to something aloft. Obviously Maude was receiving detailed instruction about tacking against the wind. Occasionally she would also point or wave a hand. Erica simply couldn't believe her interest was genuine. At intervals she would look up at the captain with bovine eyes. Couldn't he see through her artifices? The whole sight made Erica angry and frustrated. No, it made her jealous. That was it and nothing less. The captain deserved far better than that harridan.

Erica turned her back on the lovely twosome and wended her way foreward. She stepped cautiously across a coil of rope too big to step around and continued on. Even ropes considered small on these ships were huge!

There stood Fisher and Mr. McGovern by the foremast. They were peering aloft, discussing some rope or sail. Mr. McGovern pointed and Fisher nodded earnestly. Erica paused beside a pile of rope and looked up, also. What did they see that absorbed them so? To her it all looked alike up there.

The second sail up on the foremast made a funny growling noise and began to flutter.

"Arrgh! There she goes, I bet!" McGovern wagged his head, grimly. "If she fouls the forecourse it's all gang topsail teery. Kelso! Grab the haly—"

With a mighty shuddering moan, the sail tore slowly and majestically from top to bottom. The ragged edges whipped backward; the ropes tied to them writhed, serpentine. Erica gazed fascinated. Everything aboard a ship operated on a grand scale, bigger than life, including the things that went wrong.

71

Mr. McGovern ran over next to Erica and began hauling vigorously on a line. The coil at her feet shrank as the line snaked up into the rigging. She watched entranced, as the torn topsail twitched downward inch by inch. Other seamen ran over to haul on selected lines, all a mystery to her.

Fisher shouted a warning. Something hard and scratchy seized her ankle. It couldn't be Fisher; he was over there and running this way. Her ankle was yanked up off the deck. She flailed her arms for balance. Her left leg jerked upward by degrees and flipped her toes-over-ears. Her head clunked against the hard teak decking. A careless shoe trod on her fingers. Two or three men yelled at each other.

Here was Fisher grabbing her around her body and lofting her high. She could neither see nor think. Fisher's arm wrapped tightly around her breast; did he notice that her body was softer than a boy's chest ought to be? He shifted her and jacked her higher. Rough hands tugged at the rope around her leg; her leg was free.

"I got 'm! All's well." Fisher toted her away bodily. He flipped her and clunked her bottomside-down on the forecastle steps. Surely he was angry with her, and Mr. McGovern must be enraged. Erica had disrupted their work at a moment when speed was essential. And soon her captain would come roaring over, angrier still.

But Mr. McGovern was shouting orders from behind the foremast as if nothing were wrong beyond the problem at hand. And Fisher's face was creased with genuine care and concern. He seemed not the least bit angry with her.

"'Ere, lad. Ye settling down some inside?"

She nodded. "I bumped my head."

"Aye, ye did. I 'eard the clunk so loud, meself thought we'd run aground a reef."

"What did I do?"

"Naething. Ye 'appened to be standing on the wrong coil

72

is all. A loop tightened around y'r leg. As the foretopsail came down, yerself went up. Why, 'ad we not decided to turn ye free, ye'd be 'anging like a 'aunch of beef from the topmast cap there."

"Then I'm glad you decided to free me. But you shouldn't have. I messed things up royally with my carelessness."

"Fret not, lad. Things were messed up sufficient all by themselves. Topsail parted at exactly the wrong time. Let's see y'r leg there. Drop y'r drawers."

"I'd rather not really." Instinctively Erica grabbed her pantwaist.

"Ah, that's right; captain mentioned it." He flicked his pocket knife open. "I'm gonna open y'r pants leg up along the seam there. Ye'll 'ave to sew it back together then, or else go through life with y'r pants flapping tag-end to the breeze."

He slit the inseam up past her knee. She cringed; men simply do not do such things to women, and the fact that he was completely innocent of her gender did nothing for her discomfort.

He pressed his fingertips to her knee. "Bend. It 'urt?"

"No, not my knee." She flexed it up and down.

"Good. No need to work y'r ankle for me. 'Tis swelling up already. Begorra, what a beauty!"

He was right. The side of her left ankle was turning a greenish-blue color and rope burns drew sticky red lines around the bottom of her shin.

She licked her lips nervously. "You said the captain mentioned something about me. Mentioned what?"

"Naething much. He allows as 'ow ye feel a wee bit self-conscious about flaunting bare skin before the world. 'Tis natural; don't think a thing of it. When y'r old and 'ard calloused like meself, ye'll not think twice about letting the breeze kiss it all."

"You're not old. You can't be thirty yet."

"Older'n y'rself, lad, and in more'n one way." He commenced twisting his kerchief into an elaborate wrap around her ankle. "Why, I bet y've not yet taken up with the ladies, aye?"

"Not yet." Erica felt her neck and cheeks turn red. She reminded herself that for all Fisher knew, he was engaging in sly conversation with a boy and would never speak so to a lady.

"Now there's something to do when we raise New Zealand. I know a charming little place a few blocks up from the waterfront. Not y'r usual den of thieves as caters to the seafaring class. Officers more'n common seamen gather there, quaff a cup 'r two, and there's some lovely ladies 'anging about. Ye'll be me guest."

"The captain go there, too?"

"Eh, nae. Lots of masters but not our captain. 'E goes with local businessmen to their clubs and such, but it's all very proper and hoity-toity. Fact is, 'e don't much associate with the ladies atall." Fisher frowned. "Doubt there's anything wrong with 'im, if ye catch me drift. Hit's just that 'is scruples keeps getting in the way of 'is pleasures."

Erica smiled. "And you never let scruples get in the way of your pleasures?"

Fisher chuckled. "Meself takes great pains to keep each in its proper place. Now stand on that. 'Ow's it feel?"

Erica came down off the steps, one-shoe-off-and-one-shoe-on. She walked, *click-bip, click-bip,* a few paces across the deck. "I'm sure it'll be fine, Mr. Fisher. Thank you very much."

"Eh, y're welcome, lad. It'll do till the captain sees it and wraps it up proper. Ye'd best support it for a few days till it mends."

"The captain has to see it?"

"Aye, 'e checks out all injuries and logs only the serious ones. Not this'n, likely. We'll not disturb 'im now, though. Saw 'im disappear into the stern cabin with the lady just before ye were wafted into the sky there."

"Oh. I don't think they are, uh—you know, uh—do you?"

"Likely not. But I'll not be taking any chance of popping in on 'em unannounced."

Here was one isolated instance where it was to Erica's advantage to appear the boy. Talking about man-things to a man, she could say things which under any other circumstance she could not—not politely.

"Does the captain have the first choice in such matters, so to speak?" she asked. "I mean—do you know what I mean?"

"Aye, I know, and the answer is aye. Y're speaking generally, I trust, of just any ship afloat and not just *Arachne*. Captain takes 'is choice of anything from victuals to company. Privilege of rank." Fisher studied the rigging aloft. The wayward sail had been gathered up against its spar but for one stubborn end. Of the four men standing in the footropes handling it, Erica recognized only DuPres.

Fisher looked down at her. "'Ere now, lad. Y're still shaking. Let's stop off at the galley for a spot of Wun Lin's toe-curling tea. 'Twon't cure what ails ye, but ye get so muckle worried that it might pickle y'r taste buds. Y'll forget all y'r other ills." He wrapped his arm around her shoulder and drew her against himself. Erica hobbled at his side, leaning into him, and his warm presence against her made her feel much better.

"Tell me something, Mr. Fisher."

"Fish. Friends call me Fish. Not in the captain's presence, understand, when we're being all formal and polite. But times like these, I'm plain old Fish."

"Very well. Tell me something, Fish. Are you considering courting Miss Harrington? I mean if the captain should decide he doesn't want her?"

His pleasant little chuckle rumbled. "Courtin' be not the exact word, since it suggests the 'ope of marriage at its end. Old Fish is not about to be bound down permanently to one lass. But if the lady mourns and languishes for a gentleman's company—and ye know me meaning—sure'n I'll consider it me duty to ease 'er pain, captain or no. 'Tis the least I can do for a lady of questionable associations. And a gorgeous one at that."

"What do you see in her exactly that appeals so?" Erica had often wondered that of men.

"Why the 'ole cut of 'er jib, lad. Fair skin, ample bosom, high-tone air, well-turned ankle—" He laughed. "I could do without 'er general temperament, which tends to being testy and short, but nobody's perfect, meself foremost. And in a lady that lovely 'tis an easy flaw to dismiss." His voice dropped a notch. "I'll wager from the words she knows that the Dutchman's not the only man what's 'eld 'er close. An encouraging observation, I daresay."

Erica almost revealed part of Maude's conversation and bit her lip just in time. That was privileged information, shared with her alone, though Fisher guessed it well enough.

They stepped into the smoky gloom of the galley. A single lantern swayed from the ceiling; the shadows on the walls pulsed and undulated. Wun Lin was hanging up the last of his copper pots.

"Tea, Wun lin?" Fisher grabbed Erica around the waist and perched her on the counter. He backed up to its edge and hopped up, sitting beside her.

"Tea. Yes. Rum?" asked Wun Lin.

"Why not, aye, lad?"

"No, thank-you," Erica put in hastily.

Wun Lin snickered pleasantly at some secret joke. He poured from a pot already prepared. Erica noticed his own half-empty cup on the other counter. He reached for the rum, but Fisher raised a hand with a "Don't bother."

From aloft, the lookout announced a ship in the distance. Mr. McGovern responded faintly and barked something about signaling.

"Ah!" Fisher tasted his unspiked tea. "May'ap that's me ride back to Singapore."

"How do you know it's not a ship headed in the same direction we are?"

"We're not about to go over'auling anyone with our fore topsail down. Nor would the mate 'ail a vessel going the wrong way."

Erica nodded. "I have a lot to learn. Including how to keep out of the way." She extended her hand. It held steady. "At least I've stopped shaking. I'm sorry. I wouldn't have thought being dumped upside down would put one off so."

"No need to apologize, lad. 'Ow were ye to know that coil was unwinding? Ye be a lubber yet, though I allow ye catch on remarkably fast. Won't be a lubber long." He gave her a brotherly hug.

At that very moment a shadow blanked out the open doorway. Captain Bricker stepped into the galley lamplight. "Wun Lin, would you—" He stopped cold and stared. Erica squirmed.

Fisher, of course, had no reason to squirm. His voice lilted cheerfully. "Join the party, Cap'n! We're celebrating the parting of the fore topsail. Young Eric must've appreciated 'ow we were bringing it down in a 'urry; 'e really got caught up in it." He laughed enthusiastically at his own wit. The captain was staring. Fisher's laugh died aborning.

"They're bending a new sail to it now, sir. Be in shape in no time. The lad 'ere tangled in a line and was swept off 'is feet. All's well now, as ye see."

The captain must have stood there for a count of twenty. He looked at Fisher, at Erica, at the kerchief around her sorry foot. Thrice he opened his mouth to speak and all three times shut it again.

His eyes finally met Erica's and stayed there. "Can you walk comfortably?"

"Aye, sir. No problem."

"Then bring a pot of tea back to the stern for Miss Harrington and myself. Fisher, we may have found your way west. Come with me." He wheeled and left.

Fisher stared after him. "Now what's all that, I wonder?"

"I don't know what it is." Erica hopped down off the counter. "But I know what I *wish* it were." She watched Wun Lin clap the lid on another steaming teapot. She remembered how it had bothered her when the captain and Maude stood so close together, arm pressed to arm. Wouldn't it be grand if he felt just as jealous when she and Fisher were pressed arm to arm?

But it would never be. She picked up the pot and limped out the door toward the stern cabin.

CHAPTER 9

Singapore, Evening, June 14, 1851

Seamus Fisher prided himself on many things and rightly so. Most of all he prided himself upon his superlative skill at creating opportunities where otherwise none existed. It was a gift, this ability to find just the right happenstance at the consummate moment. Unfortunately that moment was eluding him; or perhaps the happenstance was out of joint. He stood on the Singapore dock as life bustled about him, stymied. He must find a vessel, any vessel, about to sail east. Wind and currents favored passage north this time of year. No one—not a solitary one—was considering an eastward route.

Fisher's captain claimed the old Roman gods were mere magnifications of human beings replete with the flaws, whims, and foibles so common to humankind. Well, count Lady Luck a member of that crew. She had bent over backward being kind to humble Bosun Fisher. Not twelve hours after *Arachne*'s officers had discussed sending Fisher back here, the wind had changed to speed passage west and the captain had flagged down a willing vessel. Luck! Lady Luck had wafted him here to Singapore about as swiftly as anyone could go that distance. And now apparently the Lady had traipsed off to parts unknown and left him standing here all alone, bereft of fortune. Or perhaps she was simply averting her petulant face, or turning her lovely back, showing her sloping alabaster shoulders. Lady Luck and Maude Harrington had much in common.

It would be dark in an hour or two and he'd been prowling these wharves for hours to no avail. Mayhap he should seek out young Gideon first. No, that would not do; some vessel going east, a vessel which up to now he had missed, might get underway in that brief hour when he was uptown. And once he had the sick lad, he wanted to be able to tuck him immediately into a comfortable berth.

Most of the square-riggers were now at his back. This end of the waterfront was where the junks tied up. He was not keen on booking passage in a vessel so ponderously slow. Aunt Fanny in her rowboat could overhaul a well-laden junk. Still, with Lady Luck in such a snit, he ought to wander through this end of the docks for lack of any better plan.

Within minutes he was awash in a sea of Oriental faces, all a handspan closer to the ground than his own. Here his captain had one on him. Bricker did not seem to note the color of a man, and he could count fast friends among three foreign races Fisher knew of. Fisher felt uncomfortable when his was the only European face in sight. He paused with unpainted warehouses to his left and slopping, fetid water to his right. He could smell both. He perched like a pelican upon a mooring post and pulled out his pipe and makings.

Here was another point of difference between himself and his captain. Bricker did not approve of alcohol and tobacco. A dull man in many ways was Captain Bricker, but an able man, and fair. Fisher would cheerfully limit his use of tobacco to shore for the privilege of serving under him. Able men and fair were hard to find among deepwater captains.

Fisher packed his pipe but he never got around to lighting it. Ahead there, moored between two Foochow pole junks, lolled a trim little red vessel with yellow poop and forecastle. He grinned to himself. A *lorcha*. The germ of an idea planted itself in his mind. Even as he watched, three Chinese seamen of disreputable appearance came off her. Fisher pocketed his makings and followed them upstreet.

Lady Luck, who till this time had turned her darling countenance away from him, gave him a broad smile, for the three were entering a tavern known to him. The Palace of Delight of Mai Foo See was known amongst Anglo seamen. He watched from the doorway until the three had chosen their table, then walked to the bar.

Every female who worked in this tavern called herself Mai Foo. Probably one of them was the Mai Foo of ownership, but just which was as closely-guarded a secret as the whereabouts of the Ming treasure trove. Mai Foo the bartender looked up and smiled with teeth stained yellow by betel nuts. "Ah! Feesher. You back so soon."

"Top of the evening, Celestial Lady. Might Mai Foo be about? I'd be pleased to treat 'er to the beverage of 'er choice."

Mai Foo studied him blankly.

Fisher held up a one-pound note. "Buy 'er a drink?"

"Ahhh!" The jaundiced smile returned. She grunted in baritone like an overworked water buffalo.

From some dark corner the desired Mai Foo appeared. She bowed respectfully. "Toppee dee evening, Meester Feesher."

Fisher returned the bow and escorted her to the table next to the three seamen. He hoped he could complete this ploy

81

before they decided to puff a little opium in the back room. Once they stood up, the game was lost. He seated his escort with her back to that table, enabling them to eavesdrop more successfully.

"May Foo, ye look exquisite this evening."

"Is that good?"

"As near perfect as mortals attain. Aye, very good."

She giggled.

"Meself was feeling low and I'd like to sit and talk a bit. Got the time?"

"Always time for Feesher."

"Bless ye." He sighed heavily. "Ever 'ave one of those—"

Mai Foo the bartender brought two glasses of something rather noxious-looking and took the pound note with her.

"—those days when what ye desire most just slips right through y'r fingers?"

She frowned a little. "Aye."

"That's me problem, right there. As ye well know, Delight of the Eye, the thing closest to me 'eart is money—save for y'rself, o' course. The king's coinage. The more, the merrier. And me captain, 'e just turned down the most splendid opportunity for making a very pretty penny, and all because 'e fears it might be just a wee bit illegal. Were it only 'is own pocket, I could see it. But it's all ours—the 'ole crew's. Sometimes meself feels like shipping out aboard some other tub, but I never seem to put me thoughts into action."

One of the three with his back to Fisher had been hunched over on his elbows. He was sitting up straight now. Lady Luck was smiling sweetly again.

"Awwww," Mai Foo purred. "Poor Feesher."

Fisher plunked both elbows on the table and cradled his chin in one hand. "And that's not the worst of it. Ye 'eard 'ow the Dutchman's looking for 'is lady, that—oh, what's 'er name—the one 'e commandeered the *Joseph Whidby* to go fetch.''

"Aye. I hear bout that. Many boats, all sorts boats go look for her.''

Fisher smiled inwardly. He had suspected half the smugglers and brigands in Singapore would have gone off treasure hunting, and Mai Foo just confirmed it. "Aye. And the reward for 'er—''

"Beeg reward.''

"Aye. The captain would 'ave no part of that, either. Claimed 'e didn't want to get involved. Why, we 'ad as much chance of finding 'er as anyone. Though I admit this last is a richer prize by far than the Dutchman's lady.''

Mai Foo wagged her head. "Sad thing. You wanna come to back room, forget troubles, aye?''

"I'd love to, Lotus Flower on a Crystal Pool, but I've scant funds at the moment, being impecunious.'' He paused. Her face was blank. "No money.''

"Ah. So sad. Maybe you get pay soon.''

"Aye. Arrgh! 'Ow I'd love to be chasing after that prize!'' He sighed heavily again.

Behind Mai Foo the three men stood up. Were they leaving, or were they rising to the bait? If Lady Luck were grinning before, she was absolutely jubilant now. The tallest of the three, a tough-looking scoundrel with a red silk pillbox hat, mumbled two nasal syllables to Mai Foo.

She hopped to her feet and bowed deeply. These Orientals did know how to train up obediant women. "I must greet new customers now. Very good talk to you, Feesher. Come back, aye?''

"Aye, Mai Foo, and I appreciate y'r letting me unload.'' He paused. "Thanks for listening.''

"Ah.'' She bowed again. "Good day.''

"Good day, Jasmine Petal." Instantly he was surrounded by potentially lethal sailors of piratical persuasion. He nodded to the gentleman in the red hat. "Seamus Fisher at y'r service. Do sit down."

Stool legs grated and rattled as they sat. Fisher felt a bit more comfortable; at least they were eye-level now.

The red cap nodded. "Hwang Ahn. My compatriots." He waved a hand. "We did not intend to overhear. But we are at the next table, and to overhear was inevitable. We are distressed. A fellow man of the sea is distressed, and that distresses us. We would like perhaps to be of service. Is such possible?"

Fisher brightened a bit, then frowned, disconsolate. "Ah, thankee, no. Y'see—well—a junk just isn't fast enough. And we'd be quartering against the prevailing winds, which'd slow y'r junk even more. This project calls for a fast vessel. Fast and maneuverable."

"Faster than British frigate."

"Ye got the picture clearly, mate."

"Macao lorcha is fast enough?"

Fisher grinned brightly. "Now y'r talking! Ah, but what I 'ear, they were built for smoking out river pirates. Coastal trade at best. 'Ow does she do in deep water with that flat little bottom of 'ers? 'Ow does she wear in 'eavy seas?"

The man tipped his head. "We get there. You wish to sail east. She does well."

For the briefest moment Fisher feared this man knew too much. Then he realized that in mentioning quartering against prevailing winds, he had revealed his intended direction. He rubbed his chin. "And y're sure y're game for sticky business if need be?"

"Perhaps. We are, of course, law-abiding citizens."

"Of course, as is meself as well. 'Ere's the story in part. Understand I cannae give ye the 'ole of it. Briefly, a very wealthy businessman, a trader, from San Francisco was over on this side on business when 'e met a charming Portuguese lady. As it turns out, there was a boy child born of the, ah, friendship. Now the trader 'as died in Frisco and left no issue, save this one lad. If ye think the reward for the Dutchman's lady be 'andsome, ye should see what they're offering for the lad. Ye see, there's an un'oly fight over the estate. Some wants the boy found and others wants 'im destroyed. There be a big race on to locate 'im.'' Fisher leaned in closer. "And I know where 'e is. But can I convince me captain to enter the race? 'Ardly.''

"Where would the lad be delivered?''

"Depends. The businessman's solicitor is sailing west from Frisco. With luck we might encounter 'im 'twixt 'ere and there; get a jump on the competition to boot. At the farthest, 'Onolulu. Possibly New Zealand. Most likely not that far.''

"To whom specifically?''

"Ah. That's me own bit of information. Sure'n ye understand.''

"And our portion?''

"''Alf and 'alf across the board.''

"We are nine and you are but one. One-tenth, each man.''

"But I know the lad's whereabouts and the contact to deliver 'im to. Tell ye what. One part for meself and three for the lot of ye. That's still five years' wages for meself and only a few months' work.''

They exchanged glances. The inscrutable faces were impossible to read.

"When do you wish to depart?''

"Sooner the better. I'd pick up the lad and we'd be on our way.''

"You would say, perhaps, that time is of the essence.''

"Took the words right out of me mouth."

The man stood up. "Join us. See where our vessel lies. Then bring your lad. We shall discuss specific amounts at our leisure as we sail east."

Fisher stood also. He extended his hand, a distinctly western gesture but one the man would understand. Hwang Ahn accepted it. Fisher bowed slightly just to top off the performance and followed the red cap out the door. Lady Luck was jumping up and down for joy.

CHAPTER 10

Singapore, Dusk, June 14, 1851

Dealing with the more polite and cultured European elements of Singapore was not one of Fisher's strengths. He vastly preferred the simpler life of a seaman along the waterfront. True, there were tricks to avoid being robbed or taken advantage of, but such were true in any area of living. Fisher knew most of the tricks for survival on the waterfront. He knew very little about the machinations of uptown business tycoons.

He stood now, scanning a row of British houses and feeling surprisingly ill at ease. In the half-light of dusk they all looked pretty much alike along here. There was the one he wanted—little brass name plate and a lion's head door knocker. He jogged up the stoop and slammed the knocker up and down.

A houseman answered the door. "Yes?"

"Seamus Fisher to see Dr. Bigelow, please. Important business."

"Very sorry. The doctor is not available at this time. You make an appointment, please."

Fisher heard Anglo voices in a distant room. "I'm just as sorry as y'rself, but me business cannae wait."

The door started to swing shut but Fisher countered it with his shoulder. It thumped to a standstill, and with his full weight behind it, opened. The housekeeper said something insistent, evensay impolite, but Fisher was past him and charging down the long dark hall toward the voices. This was it—this door here. He rapped once and entered.

Of the three men in the room, Fisher recognized the doctor from his captain's description. The second man was small and dark and square-built, probably half Malay. And the third stood nearly a head taller than Fisher and was twice as wide. He was a handsome cuss, nattily attired in the whitest of ruffled shirts, the trimmest of European-cut trousers complete with the stirrup to keep them taut, the latest cut of waistcoats and ties. His fair face was clean-shaven and framed by a mane of sandy hair. Even being found in a doctor's office, the fellow was the picture of robust health.

It dawned on Fisher just who this might be. He'd best confirm his guess anyway. He nodded toward the doctor. "Dr. Bigelow, good evening. And you, sir." He turned to the rosy-cheeked giant. "Might ye not be the gentleman they call the Dutchman, Franz Bilderdijk?"

The half-Malay stepped forward as the Dutchman looked at the doctor. "Do you wish him removed?"

Fisher talked fast. "Y're a legend in y'r own time and the talk of the wharves, sir, posting such an agreeable sum for the return of y'r mistress. She must be one magnificent woman."

The man's eyes burned into him. "She is my wife, not my mistress, and the mother of my three children."

"Oh? Well, ye know 'ow waterfront gossip distorts such things. Mr. Bilderdijk, sir, this is extremely important, though I cannae divulge why this moment. But be ye truly married? Church wedding and all the legal trimmings?''

"Of course, truly married. Would I sire children by a harlot? What information do you haf about her? Why did you ask that?''

"I 'ave none, save what I've 'eard on the docks, and none of that concerning 'er whereabouts. Me captain's got 'igh scruples. 'E'd not bother seeking a mistress, but a mother with responsibilities—ah, that's another thing, regardless 'ow poorly she's been treated.''

"You may tell your scrupulous captain she's been treated fairly and kindly. She is wearied of marriage; no excuse.''

"I'll tell 'im that at me first opportunity, sir. And now, Doctor, I'd like to pay a brief visit to a lad in y'r care named Gideon. I sail shortly, so I've not much time, or I wouldn't bust in thusly. Just a minute with 'im, by y'r leave.''

The doctor snorted. "You want to abduct him also, no doubt.''

Fisher barely stopped himself from gaping. Abduct? How could this man have guessed? "Eh? Nae, not lest ye wish to be rid of the shaver.''

The Dutchman planted himself directly in front of Fisher, towered over him, cast him in a broad and menacing shadow. "What's your business with the lad?''

Fisher kept his voice light and friendly. "A year ago I was in Praia—that'd be y'r Cape Verde Islands off Africa near—''

"I am familiar with Praia.''

"Course ye are, sir. I met a lady there, a very proper lady, 'oo's little son ran off to sea. She described 'er boy in detail. The lad fits the description of a young tad shipped aboard a bark, *Arachne,* in Praia about that time. Now I 'ear that very lad's 'ere in Singapore, but I learned it almost too late. If indeed this be that widow's son, I can tell shortly by quizzing 'im. Does 'e by chance, Doctor, speak Portuguese?''

The doctor frowned at the Dutchman. "I used the boy three days ago to translate for me when a Portuguese sailor from Macao was brought in. He's fluent."

"Where is *Arachne* now? What is her destination?" The Dutchman could thunder like Vulcan when he wanted to intimidate a person. It worked, too.

Fisher shrugged amiably. "Gone, save for the lad, I 'ear. Me business is less with *Arachne* and more with the lad, so I asked not where she be bound."

The Dutchman's leonine head loomed above him. "Is there a reward for the boy, and who's offering it?"

"No reward I know about, sir. The lady's not wealthy. Me only return is in seeing the lad 'ome safe with 'is loving mother. Or at least telling 'er 'e's alive and well. Or recovering."

The Dutchman traded gazes with the doctor. He turned back to Fisher. "The lad is gone. Begone yourself, back to your ship before it sails. Go." Beyond him the half-Malay moved closer. If the Dutchman hired as a bodyguard a man half his own size, that man must be tougher than any three pirates plus a Sumo wrestler.

Fisher backed off. "Gone? On 'is own two feet?"

"Taken. So leave. I'm sorry, you've nothing here."

"Then I takes me leave. Y'r houseman'll see me to the door, I trust. No need to bother y'rself. Good evening, gentlemen, and me best wishes to you, Mr. Bilderdijk, in finding y'r lady safe."

The houseman held the door open. Fisher backed through it, nodded again and turned to step into the dark hallway. He did not look back, but he knew the half-Malay would be watching, for the door behind him didn't close until he had walked the length of the corridor.

The moment he heard the latch click, he flattened the houseman against the wall and grabbed an ear in each hand.

"Where's the lad? Speak quickly!"

"Taken. We don't know. Taken."

"By whom?" Fisher gave the ears the slightest twist.

"The Dutchman seeks him but a Chinese gentleman got him first. He came to visit the lad and, before we could stop him, he carried the lad away."

"The Chinaman's name, if ye wish any 'earing left."

The man's eyes bulged. "We don't know. We don't know."

He was telling the truth; Fisher could see that plainly enough. So a Chinaman had beaten the Dutchman to Gideon. In a false rage, well acted, Fisher stomped out the door.

Chinese, eh? Wang See or Chow Chen. Wang See was Captain Bricker's close friend and a wise and clever gentleman in the bargain. If he heard the Dutchman was seeking *Arachne,* and the reason, he might well have reasoned as Bricker had—that the Dutchman would use Gideon to reach Bricker, at the very least to work revenge. Fisher would call first upon Wang See. He took a few extra loops around the streets to make certain no one was following. Then he slipped around to the rear of Wang See's chandlery.

The store itself would be closed now, but lamplight drew feeble yellow lines down the wooden shutters in the back. Wang See was in his residence. Fisher knocked at the back door. A stifled cry from inside made the nape of Fisher's neck prickle. Politeness be hanged—he would barge in now and apologize later. For the second time that hour, he slammed his shoulder into a door. Fortunately, for his shoulder was getting a bit tender, this one opened easily.

Fisher knew this room. He had dined here before with his captain. Like any truly elegant Chinese home, this one was austere but for the gold leaf on the upright chests, plain but for the ornate wall hangings, and scrupulously clean. Mrs.

Wang, terrified, crouched in a corner. See, on his knees in the center of the room, looked composed and dignified despite his bloody nose. One of the biggest Orientals Fisher had ever seen brandished a cap-and-ball pistol; another toted Gideon like some sack of potatoes.

Gideon glanced over his shoulder and squealed, "Fisher!" He commenced squirming and flailing. He was a handful, even for so huge and brutish a thug.

Without thinking Fisher yanked his sheath knife. He held it wide, balanced lightly in his hand. "Gentlemen, and good evening to ye. I wager we're all after the same end: to return little Gideon 'ere to 'is rightful place, aye?"

Gideon's abductor took a step toward the door behind him. Fisher knew that door opened out into the store.

"No! Pray bide a moment, gents, and think: Ye got one shot in y'r pistol there and I got but one knife. Ye can drop me if ye 'it me just so, but I guarantee I'll take one of ye with me. I further guarantee I can pick off either one of ye without any chance of 'arm to the lad. Anyone care to challenge me assumption?" He looked from face to face. "'Ow much is the Dutchman paying for the tad? I'll double it."

Wang See climbed to his feet, a bit rocky. "I did not give the doctor my name. How did they find us?"

"Y're good friends with the captain. A thousand people 'ere on the wharves know that. They'd guess without thinking that y'r friendship with the captain might lead ye to protect 'is cabin boy. And we're mightily pleased ye did, See. But a few questions, a few loose tongues, and these rascals knew the very place to come, aye, lads? Now I've asked ye to be naming y'r price."

See wagged his head. "They are not for the reward itself, which is but twenty pounds sterling. They plan to hold the child for ransom, assuming he is worth more to the Dutchman than the reward would indicate."

"Ah. So the price is up. Well, then, gents, 'tis beyond me 'umble reach. Y'd best just take the lad and fly. 'Ere. Let me 'old the door for ye." He opened the door behind him and stepped aside.

The two started not for this back door but for the front door into the store, as Fisher had known they would. What he wanted was to be near enough the little charcoal brazier to grab a pot of hot whatever-it-was, and, stepping aside, did that. Taking his chances that his hand would be burned, he snatched the pot and flung it at the gun-wielder. The pistol blammed but the huge Chinaman's aim was spoiled. Mrs. Wang's shrieks broke the silence following the gunshot, as Fisher lunged after the two.

Gideon's abductor made it out the door. Fisher snatched up an ornately carved teak armchair and heaved it. It caught the pistol-wielder behind the ear and helped him out the door considerably faster than he would otherwise have gone. Fisher jumped the falling miscreant and kept running.

The store was almost totally dark. Fisher knew his way around in here to some degree. Did the kidnapper? Apparently not—the fellow splacked into a stack of something. Oaken sponge pails went crashing. Fisher saw the abductor's silhouette in the gray-black of the doorway.

Gideon, bless the clever lad, was making life difficult for the man lugging him. He flexed his body violently back and forth. Suddenly he changed directions and threw his torso from side to side. His weight shifted his captor off balance, slowing the burly Oriental enough that Fisher could reach him.

Knowing his captain frowned upon antisocial acts such as murder, Fisher resisted the temptation to drive his knife between the villain's ribs. His free hand brushed a coil of rope in passing. He latched onto it. His grip almost failed; his hand pained him viciously because of the burns from that pot, but it held long enough to allow him to swing the coil. It caught Goliath in the side. Fisher punched wildly at the darkness, only half-aiming. Three or four half-effective blows are worth more in the long run than is one good swing that misses.

Gideon fell away and tumbled into the doorway. Fisher snatched the boy up and started running. He must stay on the main streets and resist the temptation to cut through alleys; he'd trip for certain over some fool thing left lying about.

Gideon clamped to him like an octopus. "I knew you'd find me, Fish. You 'n the captain."

Fisher gulped air. "Listen. No English. 'ere me? Ye—don't—don't speak English."

He was so winded when he reached the wharf he could not speak any language at all. By the time he stumbled drunkenly aboard the lorcha, his legs were rubber. A pirate rescued Gideon out of his arms lest he drop the boy after bringing him safe thus far. Gasping like a hounded fox, Fisher sprawled on his back on the deck and let himself pant and sweat and drift.

There was that old bromide about the frying pan and fire, and idle talk about rocks and hard places. This was it. If Lady Luck could keep her smile pasted on her lovely kisser a few days more, they would sail relatively clear of this dragnet of bandits seeking Maude and the lad. But now Fisher had willingly placed the boy and himself in the hands of pirates who would as soon feed them to the sharks as take a breath. He must thread his way carefully from this point on—very carefully indeed.

CHAPTER 11

Approaching Celebes, Afternoon, June 15, 1851

Erica gathered the last of the dishes from the noonday meal by stacking them up her arm. The fewer trips between table and serving closet, the better she liked it. She wasn't being overworked, nor was she genuinely weary. Far from it. The captain assigned her no job that might entail lifting or struggling. Her weariness was a sort of weariness with life in general, and she could not explain it.

She backed through the closet door and sloshed her dishes in the waiting dishwater. She wedged the door open with a spoon to better watch her captain. He was alone in the cabin, seated at his desk with his back to her. He had finished writing in the ship's log and now he was writing vigorously in his personal journal.

She would let the dishes soak a few minutes. She brought the steamy dishrag and a towel out to the table. She wiped it off and toweled it dry.

The captain must have eyes in the back of his head. Without glancing her way, he said, "Thank-you, Eric," and abandoned his journal. He pulled a chart and brought it to the table.

Until that moment Erica had planned to go back to her dishes. Now she lingered beside the table. And when he rolled out his chart, she quickly and voluntarily held down one curling end.

"I bemoaned a general lack of knowledge about geography, do you remember?" she asked. "And you promised to show me where we were going—to tell me about the places we went."

He frowned. "I said that?"

She smiled and shrugged. "Something close to that."

He looked askance at her. "Well, this isn't the chart to show you on. We're still off it—somewhere out west of its left edge." He thumped the tabletop, then pointed to the map. "We'll enter the chart about here. This big round island is Borneo; and this spidery one, Celebes. Celebes is mountains and volcanoes and jungles, for the most part. Nearly the whole population lives along the coast. We're headed east, this direction."

"Why then we've very nearly crossed the Java Sea. Celebes is at its far eastern end, right?"

"Right; not so wonderful an accomplishment. The Java Sea isn't all that big, and we have had favorable winds much of the way."

"You said we're going to New Zealand. So we'll just sail right on between these islands here. Oh. That's Australia. North of Australia, then."

"Yes. Pretty much so." He measured with his two-pointed instrument (a caliper), not across the open sea space but to a dot on the long spider leg of the island he called Celebes.

She frowned suspiciously. "What's that dot?"

"The port of Macassar."

"What's there?"

"Oil. Know how all the young men in England slick their

hair back? They glue it down with Macassar oil."

"And we're stopping there."

"Just briefly."

"To bring all the young men in England more hair dressing?"

He kept his attentions pasted to the chart. "To put you ashore."

"To run an errand for you?"

"To find yourself another ship—another gullible dupe. It won't be easy; apparently I'm about as gullible a dupe as you'll find."

She sputtered, flabbergasted. "You can't do that to me! You said I could go all the way to England with you."

He snapped his caliper shut. "And you obtained that contract under false pretenses." He walked back to his desk to jot down meaningless numbers on a scrap of paper.

She urged her stunned feet into motion and parked herself as close as practical to him. "Please. I beg you to let me stay."

"The decision is made. I believe duties are waiting for you. You're dismissed."

You're dismissed. He said it so easily. He brushed past her and walked outside. Alone, Erica scuffed disconsolately back to the closet. *You're dismissed.* Wasn't that the truth! She grabbed the door and yanked it shut viciously. *Pung!* That spoon went flying against her ankle. She had forgotten the spoon. She picked it up. It was bent in half and twisted, a deformed, useless little Quasimodo of a spoon. Is this what Erica was, a useless parody of neither boy nor girl?

Tears were coming again. She wiped them away impatiently and plunged both hands in the hot, soapy water. If anyone besides Captain Bricker had dismissed her she wouldn't feel so bad. She could just picture the bouncing bosun letting her go—all apologetic. And the dour Mr.

McGovern would simply sound and act a little more solemn than usual. But the captain—she didn't want to leave this ship. No, being honest, she didn't want to leave the captain. She wished she could have admired Joshua Rice this much. She wished she could have enjoyed simply watching him do whatever he was doing, the way she enjoyed watching the captain.

The twisted spoon lay there forlornly. She wedged the handle into a drawer and tried to bend the bowl back up. Her fingers weren't strong enough. The spoon was ruined.

She was just as ruined. Her career as a boy was nearing its end and with this short hair she could hardly go back to being a girl.

She *could* explain short hair to the world by saying doctors had cut it during a severe illness. That sort of thing happened frequently and mysterious maladies abounded in this tropic corner of the earth. Perhaps if she looked more like the young lady she was, the captain would see her with new eyes. She had one skirt and blouse with her, jammed in the bottom of her duffle. She could—

Forget it! Erica told herself. *Both garments are shabby. They will never pass muster next to Maude Harrington's elegant silks.* In fact, the captain would never notice her at all so long as Maude hovered at his elbow. Maude was beautiful, well endowed, and totally feminine. Even in a skirt, Erica would still carry the vague odor of "cabin boy." Her slight build was neither well-endowed nor elegant, though people used to say she was pretty. No, so long as Maude provided a comparison, Erica could not hope to attract the captain.

Erica finished the last of the dishes and leaned on the countertop to think. Dare she "borrow" a dress from Maude? There were those five trunks, all unlocked, in the orlop. She ought to know. Yesterday, driven by curiosity, she had devised a story that Maude sent her there to fetch something (should anyone question her). That was just a story; in reality, she had wondered what could require five trunks.

One thing that Maude did *not* possess, she learned, was a gift for packing. She had thrown things in willy-nilly. Had she packed with care and planning, she could have come aboard with two trunks. And what she did possess was unexciting—clothes, some empty japanned boxes—not worth the effort or the risk of getting caught. And as Erica thought about it, none of the dresses was plain or simple enough to be altered to fit her. There were none she would want to borrow. Just as well. Even if Maude didn't realize whose dress it was, Erica's conscience would pain her. Pangs of conscience had made her stop snooping, halfway through the first trunk. *Bothersome things, consciences,* she thought, smiling ruefully.

Her duties were about done here. Should she wander about on deck awhile, perhaps to listen to the captain's Nereids? Neither the overcast sky nor the blustery wind would help her gray mood. Besides, the captain was out there. She felt uncomfortable being near him even as she longed to. *You're dismissed,* he had said.

Well, she was not about to spend the afternoon cowering in this stuffy little pantry. She had her hand on the door handle when she heard the stern cabin door open. The captain was coming in. He was laughing, a warm lilting chuckle as if he hadn't dismissed anyone for twenty years. Maude Harrington's giggle sounded, too. Erica waited, listening.

Maude cooed, "Well, I didn't know what to do. Fortunately some little old lady came waddling by. She bought the chicken from me on the spot and saved me no end of embarrassment. I'll never go near a market again, let alone nod my head." There was what sounded to Erica like a calculated silence. Maude spoke again. "Captain, I should think you'd get so lonely out here. I mean—you know—*lonely*. Were you ever married?"

Erica listened intently.

"Yes, some years ago in Maine. I was working coasting schooners between Vinalhaven and Philadelphia."

"Is she—did she—?"

"She died in childbirth."

"That's very sad. You know what's even sadder? That you never tried again; instead, you married yourself to this ship."

"It's a very pleasant ship. And as ships go, *Arachne*'s a charmer. Great character."

"You're playing at words with me, Captain. You know exactly what I mean and you're avoiding my whole intent."

He replied, but Erica was too angry to listen carefully. He was using that teasing tone of voice on Maude, the same he used with Erica when talking about Nereids and Neptune and all that. Maude didn't deserve his cleverness and attention—not in the slightest.

Both voices had dropped now to an intimate murmur and Erica could catch only occasional words. The foolish captain must have indeed spent his whole life at sea. A man who had any contact at all with women would see immediately what this siren was doing. She was blatantly, disgustingly obvious with her cooing and purring and soft velvet giggles.

But then perhaps he wasn't falling for her charms, after all. *Perhaps he was inviting them.* The thought shocked Erica at first, then angered her. Who was the seductress and who the seducer? If the captain were the moral paragon he thought himself to be, surely he would not condone this woman's wiles, let alone encourage them. But then,

100

perhaps, he was blinded by having known love and then living years without it. Yet he mentioned escorting a lady to a concert in London. So he must have some experience resisting women's machinations—or inviting them.

Erica's thoughts turned ajumble, but they certainly were not favorably inclined toward this two-faced man, this animal typical of the species. She realized suddenly that complete silence reigned beyond the door. Had they left? No, for she had heard no door close. Then—

Whether the captain recognized a scheming woman when confronted by one or not, surely he must recognize when the situation had proceeded from words into action. By letting himself be allured by this floozy, he was as guilty of seduction as was that clever Maude. He was as guilty as every other man under God's blue sky. *Bah! Men! Triple bah!*

Erica opened the closet door carefully, ever so quietly, and peeked out to confirm her suspicions. The two were wrapped in a firm embrace, kissing, it seemed, with abject enthusiasm. It was a modest kiss as private kisses go, with no hands where they ought not be. Of course, all such kisses were surely precursors to less modest things to come in the immediate future. The fingertips of his left hand lightly massaged the bare nape of her neck. The neckline of this maroon brocade dress was exceptionally wide, and her milk-white shoulders curved toward him, around him.

Erica slammed the door as she came marching out. They both jumped a foot and disconnected instantly. It was comical, in a perverse way, but Erica was in no mood to laugh. She was so irate, so put out, her tongue stumbled.

"You—you two—you— Miss Harrington, you may have him!" She stormed out the cabin door.

CHAPTER 12

Entering Karimata Strait, After dark, June 16, 1851

Fisher had never before appreciated his captain's insistence against the use of tobacco in the stern cabin. Heaven forbid *Arachne*'s cabin should smell as foul as this lorcha's! Surrounded by Oriental seamen of half a dozen minor subraces, Fisher sat cross-legged on the floor. Hot, stagnant air hung heavy with acrid tobacco smoke and opium haze. Despite their sorry state, they were listening raptly to Fisher's performance.

He rapped on the deck with his left hand, then held it up as if it were speaking. "Innis! Be ye 'ome, lad?"

He held up his right hand and made his voice fainter. "Maybe. What ye want?"

After each exchange, Hwang Ahn interpreted.

Left hand: "We found a dory afloat with a dead body in it, about y'r size. Afraid it might be y'rself."

Right hand: "Oh? And what was it wearing?"

Left hand: "Checkered shirt and dungarees, high-top shoes, as me memory serves."

Fisher put an edge of worry to his voice. Right hand: "Checkered shirt, ye say. Be it a bright red check, or a bright blue check?"

Left hand: "Lest me memory fails, a bright blue check."

Now the voice was really worried. Right hand: "Blue. Be ye certain?"

Left hand: "Eh, nae. Wait. 'Twas a green check with little blue lines."

Fisher's voice crowed, awash with relief. Right hand: "Ah, saints be praised. 'Tweren't me."

Titters preceded uproarious laughter as the crew, one by one, caught the punch line. It was one of Fisher's favorite stories and he felt gratified that he'd gotten it across to these fellows of foreign mentality. But he was fast running out of jokes, stories, and anecdotes. Even his supply of war stories from far-flung ports and ocean storms was nearly dry.

He rubbed his hands together. "Gentlemen, entertaining as this little soiree may be, I'm about ready to call it a day." He translated for the translator: "Gonna go to bed."

A few sailors stood up and walked off or simply sagged forward, their thoughts turning inward.

Hwang nodded. "Very late. One thing before you go, Fisher."

"Aye?" Already halfway to his feet, he sat back down.

"We left Singapore in haste, without provisioning. Food is low. We must call at Batavia or Badjarmasin or Macassar."

"Make it Macassar; I've a friend or two there, can get a good deal on victuals."

Hwang nodded. "Satisfactory. Concerning the cost of provisions: We lacked time to trade, to sell, to otherwise earn the wherewithal to purchase supplies."

"I 'ear ye. I've got a wee bit with me, enough to stock up on rice and beans and a pig or two."

Hwang smiled. "You are a most pleasant man to deal with. I appreciate this opportunity to know you and to be of service."

"No more than do I. Well, if that's all, a good night to ye."

He nodded. "Good night, Fisher."

Fisher stood and stretched. He'd best look in on young Gideon. He wandered to the far end of the deck cabin and pushed the light cotton curtain aside. Separated from the bustle of the main poop cabin by draperies, Gideon's bed seemed too small to hold a real person. Yet the boy was shorter than the pallet. Fisher could not imagine being this little, though of course at some time in his life he must have been. Somehow, as he charged through life, he always felt ten feet tall.

Gideon stirred in his sleep. Fisher sat on the edge of the pallet to listen to the boy's breathing for a few minutes. The movement awakened Gideon. The big eyes stared a few moments, blank, before the lad's brain made the connection.

"Fisher?" he whispered.

"Aye. Just checking." Fisher laid a hand across the lad's head—warm but not hot. He spoke louder. *"To eres awake'o. Como estas esta noche, Chiquito?"*

"Mejor, gracias." Gideon replied. He dropped his voice to a faint whisper. "Fisher, tha's not Portuguese. Tha's not even good Spanish."

Fisher grinned and whispered, "Good enough for the occasion. I'm 'oping our captain 'ere doesn't know Portuguese from Spanish anyway. Just ye remember, no English. Aye?"

Gideon nodded. "You know one of the sailors came by this afternoon. He speaks Portuguese real good. Guess he was checking to see if I really know the language."

"Mm. Guessed as much; shoulda warned ye."

Gideon grinned. "I played dumb and used my Cape Verde accent. He seemed happy."

"Ye're a clever lad. Keep it up." Fisher patted the boy's arm and stood up.

Gideon smiled. *"Bones noches."*

"Boneez nocheez," Fisher pushed back the curtain. He patted his pockets, located and dug out his makings, and headed for the forecastle, or what passed for a foredeck aboard a lorcha.

He greeted the larboard watch and climbed to where he could sit with his back against the foremast. Just above his head, the battened sail whispered. The moon was entering its third quarter; it hovered at water line and made sky and sea glow together, so that the line between air and water merged into a continuum reaching from here to heaven. Fisher rather enjoyed these moon-misted tropical nights.

Several thorny problems could stand the light of contemplation. Through no small fault of Fisher's, these cutthroats were now under the distinct impression that Gideon was worth five hundred pounds to someone. There was no way on this earth that Fisher or Bricker or any of Fisher's other friends could come up with five hundred pounds. But one could safely bet that these particular pipers would be paid.

Apparently these brigands had not heard that the Dutchman was offering a reward for the cabin boy from the *Arachne*. But they, along with the rest of the world no doubt, knew that the Dutchman was posting a reward for Maude Harrington. Wharf scuttlebutt tied Maude to the name *Arachne* and Fisher must assume these men were aware of that. Indeed, the Dutchman's interest in *Arachne* was such that a price might also rest upon the handsome and august head of the good Captain Bricker as well.

Now should Fisher by some miracle raise *Arachne* out here on these wet salt wastes, what convincing story could he possibly feed these lascars to convince them they should let him board her with Gideon? Any other ship would pose no problem; it would simply be the very one carrying that trader's solicitor from San Francisco. But the name *Arachne* was tied to the name Maude Harrington, a most suspicious circumstance.

And there was the matter of Mistress Harrington herself, not a problem so far as Fisher was concerned, but something to mull, nonetheless. The tone of the Dutchman's voice, and his indignation—his whole demeanor convinced Fisher that Maude was indeed his through legal matrimony. The captain was innocently abetting a runaway wife, albeit a woman of supremely appealing endowments who might conceivably feel burdened to be tied to the service of a single man for a whole lifetime. Fisher's memory lingered on her smooth white skin, the saucy curls (attractive even when laced with potato parings), the pouty mouth—he realized his thoughts were skating close to adultery and reluctantly shifted them onto other things.

On the northern horizon a red light gleamed faintly. *Arachne* was bound east, so that couldn't be her. In fact, Fisher held scant hope of catching them short of New Zealand and perhaps not even then. How he wished, though, that he could hail each passing vessel and confirm, for his own peace of mind, that he was not passing his own ship and master in the night.

This Java Sea was vast, but vaster still lay the South Pacific. And somewhere on that endless expanse, itself only partially charted, floated one tiny dot. *Arachne.* An infinitesimal speck bobbed on the biggest ocean in the world, and Fisher must somehow find it.

And that was the thorniest problem of all.

CHAPTER 13

Macassar, Late morning, June 18, 1851

Erica folded her oilskin jacket one more time. She shoved with all her might, hunching the jacket down into her duffle bag far enough that she could draw the string tight. She shouldered the bag and walked out on deck. The sky was still overcast, still sulking. She appreciated the mood.

Captain Bricker was coming down off the foredeck. She paused by the gangway to wait for him, and glanced back and up to the quarterdeck. Maude Harrington stood there. And her catty, smug look—the knowing, victorious look—made Erica wish dearly for a dagger or a sword or a gun or a cannon or perhaps a rocket sling of moderate size.

"Ready?" The captain started down the gangway without waiting for her reply. Disconsolate, she fell in beside him. They walked up a crowded little street. Were all South Seas ports like Macassar here—bustling, alien, huddled? He was walking briskly again, as he did when he was worried or upset. She was nearly jogging to keep up.

"Slow up, please, sir. Your legs are too long. Or perhaps mine are not quite long enough. Are you absolutely certain this is what must be?"

He slowed his pace to half. "I'm certain. I've studied this a great deal. I appreciate that you don't have to take my advice, but I'll give it to you, anyway. Address the world in your proper gender. If you're a woman, be a woman. Abandon this sinful theatric."

"'Sinful theatric,' you call it. You're being just a bit judgmental for one unfamiliar with the facts of the matter."

"It took me awhile to find the passage. It's buried in Deuteronomy. Verse 22:5. A woman who wears men's clothes, or a man who wears women's clothes—both are an abomination before God. If I'm being judgmental, I'm voicing God's opinion, not mine."

Here he was off on religion again. She had best change the subject. "I know I should have begged harder. When you hailed that ship and sent Fisher back to Singapore? It really should have been me. You need a bosun more than you need a cabin boy. Now you have no bosun and no cabin boy, either."

"I have Edward and Mr. McGovern, and I'll get by just fine." His voice was curt and cool.

She cast him a sidewise glance. "I know why you're doing this. You'll feel more comfortable about making time with that hussy if I'm out of the way. After all, who fancies chaperones popping out of closets! That's why you're dumping me. Oh, I admit she presents a perfect opportunity for a casual dalliance, and such things don't happen all that frequently. Why, I'd venture to say—"

"Belay that."

"No." She stopped suddenly in the middle of the street. "No, I think not. Since I am no longer in your employ you are no longer my captain, and I *shall* speak my mind. You are a worthy man in spite of your glaring shortcomings and you deserve better than that strumpet. She's as transparent as a crystal goblet and I don't understand why you can't see

108

what she's doing. Notice I did not say 'trying to do.' *Doing.* And now you—''

"*Miss* Rollin. *Mrs.* Rice. Erica. Whatever you think your name is at the moment. Let me—'' He paused and looked about. "We're in the wrong place. Come with me. And belay that constant blather.'' He took her arm, not as he would a woman's, but in the grip reserved for an errant schoolboy. He piloted her two blocks up a side street.

Erica would not have thought the exotic trade city of Macassar would boast a city park, but this seemed to be one. Rimmed all about with clustered shacks, a vast greensward stretched nearly a quarter mile. She realized from the variety and number of dungpiles that were she a farmer bringing her goat or carabao to town, she could graze it here. No matter, it was a pleasant place all the same. A clump of trees on a little copse studded its middle. The captain led her directly toward the copse. There the dense trees coupled with the overcast to make the shaded little hill a dark place indeed.

He released her arm and turned her to face him squarely. "I determined to dismiss you here in Macassar long before that, er, that incident. That had nothing to do with it.''

"Miss Harrington thinks it does. You should have seen her face as I was leaving.''

"I don't care what Miss Harrington thinks. Am I correct in this? That you picture me as some innocent babe being manipulated by a gold digger far more sophisticated than I?''

·"Well, ah, I certainly wouldn't phrase it quite that way.''

"Who is more acutely aware of unchaste women than a sailor? And I have been twenty-five years asea. Please give me credit for at least a modicum of discernment in such matters. But I'm not certain ab—''

"How old are you exactly?'' she interrupted, frowning.

"Just short of thirty-four. I shipped aboard a packet as a cabin boy at age eight. But I'm not certain about you. Maude's kind I've seen before, but not yours. If you're spotless, why are you so reluctant to explain this strange impersonation?"

"For one thing, I didn't think you'd take me aboard if you knew all in advance. And in the past—" She bit her lip. She could not do it. "The past is dead."

"Your state now will be no worse than when you latched onto me in Singapore. And if you're escaping from someone, it may even be better."

"Escaping from whom?"

"I don't know. Maybe you're running away from this Mr. Rice just as Maude's trying to get away from the Dutchman."

"Joshua Rice died of malaria fourteen months ago."

"Then maybe you're looking for a husband of means. Rather than take Maude's route to that end, ship aboard as a boy. Look the officers over and make your choice. Then when you've sufficiently ingratiated yourself, unmask your little deception."

"How dare you think such a thing!"

"You see my three options? You're either soiled or running or headhunting. Any way it goes, you're trouble. I face enough troubles in the course of a voyage. I don't feel like volunteering for more by deliberately shipping trouble aboard. Rest assured, therefore, that Maude Harrington had nothing to do with this. I'm dismissing you strictly on your own merits—or lack of them."

"Merits! You speak of merits! I don't see you dismissing that harridan. If you're so resolute about avoiding trouble, she should be the first to go."

"She's a paying passenger."

"And I can just imagine her mode of payment." Erica

110

stopped. She may already have said too much. He looked enraged enough, insulted enough, to strike her.

But he did not. He did take several deep breaths, composing himself. She could watch the subtle changes in his face, the minuscule shifts in those fascinating sun-crinkles at the corners of his eyes. He did have a magnificently expressive and attractive face.

"I admit, I let her get a little ahead of me there, that one occasion. I wasn't thinking. I have no intention of taking immoral advantage of Miss Harrington."

Of course not, not at the moment. He keeps forgetting Maude Harrington can shape and change intentions. What about tomorrow and the next day and a week from now when her white shoulders and cheap perfume beckon to him in the lamplight? But Erica said none of that. To what use? Particularly, why should she care if he made a fool of himself before his God?

Perhaps that was it. Why did she so want him to look good in the eyes of his God? She did not care beans about gods, either his or Joshua's or, supposedly, hers. When she ought by all rights be very angry, she felt only confusion.

He spoke again, but his voice was softer. "I have to buy cargo, and I won't be selling anything in significant quantity until we enter the North Atlantic. So I don't have an excess of money. But I do have your wages here, fairly earned—" He pulled a fat envelope from his jacket pocket. "And a bonus. Your fine service earned that, also." He thrust the envelope into her hand.

She felt her eyes brimming. "I suppose it's only fair to remind you: You were to take my bill at Wang See's out of my wages. It doesn't look here that you did."

"I didn't forget. Consider it part of the bonus."

She was nearly whispering. "I'm pleased my service was satisfactory."

111

"I put a letter of recommendation in the envelope there. It may help you get a position if you decide to continue your charade."

"That's very good of you. Thank-you." She looked up into those wonderful warm deep eyes. "I hope Fisher is successful and they both rejoin you safely."

"If prayer carries any weight at all, they'll fly out on eagles' wings. I'll keep *you* in my prayers, too."

She could make no reply. She studied the front of the crackly yellow envelope.

"Well—" Did he seem reluctant to leave? It almost sounded so. "Uh, goodby Eric." He extended his hand in a gentleman's handshake.

She accepted it. She even found herself saying, "God be with you." She took a breath. "Now that was redundant. Of course He is. You're His person. Goodby, then."

"I hope sometime you become His person, also." He nodded, uncertain. "Godspeed." Suddenly he turned and walked out into the lighter gray beyond the shade. He hesitated halfway across the green. At its edge he stopped and turned to look at her another moment. Then he walked quickly off, swallowed by the crush of crowded, steep-roofed buildings.

Her brimming eyes overflowed; hot salt tears cascaded down her cheeks. Almost instantly her nose was running. That was what she hated most about crying, the runny nose. She fumbled for her handkerchief. She leaned against a tree a few minutes until the first rush of tears had abated. She blew and wiped her eyes. The crying was done. She must get on with life.

But why was she crying? Her mind buzzed in disarray. She must first get her thoughts in order. Clear thinking would follow from there. She remembered several signs in English and Dutch along a major street. She would find an

112

accommodation, deposit her duffle, and take a long, brisk walk. Nothing clears mental cobwebs like a brisk walk.

Several hotels, some of them permanent-looking buildings, lined the main street. She chose one at random, took the smallest room available, and jammed her duffle bag beneath the tiny bed. She divided her money into four portions that she might seem only one-fourth as rich at any one time. Within half an hour she was on her way out of town along a narrow, rutted little dirt road.

See? She had walked less than three miles and she felt better already. The road, more a trail, wound along the flanks of a rather steep slope. But she could see nothing of the terrain. Dense forests and a thousand sorts of fronds hid the nature of the land. She heard the ocean off to her right from time to time, and gulls mewed everywhere. The trail apparently followed the coastline. She left the road along a faint path and walked down to the edge of the sea.

She found herself out on a point, a small headland that poked itself almost apologetically out of the forest wall. Working her way out onto the nethermost rocks, she sat down.

She could not see Macassar to her left, for the coast curved back. But a variety of ships, moored out from the city, lolled at anchor within view. There were several European square-riggers of one kind or another. A few small sampans bobbed about on the light swell, pretending they were not nearly as seaworthy as she knew them to be. The one really large native ship looked like a vessel built of odd parts from other boats. Its low deck houses were roofed with bamboo mats like the houses ashore. Its prow of unpainted shakes was narrow and pointy. Its stern, though, a hulking square box painted in bright red, green, and yellow, perched rather haphazardly up on the back.

Out on the open sea directly before her was a native boat,

coming in. Of plain wood, it was long and pointed at both ends, with none of this bright-stern nonsense. Its squarish sail looked ridiculously wide for the size of the vessel. And its deck house, too, was roofed with those reed mats. Gull-like, it soared gracefully shoreward. The sail spilled and it drifted the last few feet to a bobbing halt.

Only now did she notice its destination at her extreme left, a small village crouched on the thin line between green jungle and gray sea. All its houses perched on stilts at the water's edge, a full story above the restless surface. People in canoes commenced to go meet the huge gull.

These people were all happy. They had very little in a material way, and none of European comforts. But they were happy and Erica was not. She thought of the Malay and Chinese faces she had seen in Macassar, in Manila, in Singapore. They were open and cheerful and free of dark concerns. She was laden with dark concerns. The gull wallowed. Its two long spars swung slowly around until they nearly paralleled her keel line. They dropped lower by jerks. Nearly a dozen outriggers gathered around her now. Erica was too far away from them to hear voices or laughter, but she knew it was there. It was always there with these people.

But surely the same basic things happened to these people as to anyone else—births, deaths, illness. No doubt they fell in love just as intensely as any European and no doubt occasionally with the wrong person. Still they smiled.

Erica remembered smiling. Those first few months as Joshua's bride were all smiles. So was the first part of the voyage out of Chelsea and the last part of it as they neared Mindanao. And there was one other recent occasion when her heart smiled and sang—with Captain Bricker at the foredeck railing. Those moments, so few and so intense, were augmented by other moments here and there those first days of her service. Put plainly, Captain Bricker made her feel good inside—very good.

Fine. That was established. Now why did he make her feel so good? True, he was attractive, as men go. But she liked to think she was not so shallow as to make appearances a decisive factor. He was strong—not just physically strong but morally strong, Maude Harrington notwithstanding. His strength lay with his God. He apparently subscribed to the same deity Joshua did, but the Captain's God was more a partner than a disciplinarian and taskmaster. He feared his God, but it was a wholesome, friendly fear. *Is there such a thing?* Perhaps she was thinking nonsense.

Erica went through the Bible verses she had grown up with, and the definitions she had memorized all those years, looking for a cogent description of Captain Bricker's God. *"Casting all your care upon Him for He careth for you. Be sober, be vigilant . . ." Peter something.* The captain was sober and vigilant, as was Joshua—well, most of the time. *"Ours is a God of mercy." "By the grace of God ye are saved." "For our God is a consuming fire." "Vengeance is mine, saith the Lord."* The more she tried to piece together the nature of God, the more any sensible description evaded her. She managed to confuse herself completely. She must get her mind off pigeon-holing God and tend to more mundane things, more fruitful endeavors—for instance, the reason she had broken down crying on that copse.

It could be that she had just lost, and she hated to lose at anything. She had lost to Maude in a big way. In a bigger way she had lost her fine plan for traveling to England, and it had been such a clever plan, too. Yet she was unmasked in half a week, thanks to that Maude. *Maude, Maude, Maude!* Why did that woman always insert herself in

Erica's life and thoughts? The upshot of it was that her act of whim—and that is what it was—had gone sour, and now she was pouting about it.

She might have been crying simply because she had enjoyed life aboard *Arachne*. It was a pleasant time she would never have again. That was worth shedding a tear right there.

She should start back soon. The sun would be down, quenched in the sea for another day, and darkness comes quickly in the tropics. She stood up, stretched, and worked her way back across the rocks. With difficulty she found the path to the main trail. It was almost dark already in these gloomy forests. She must hurry.

The road was heavily traveled now and she found herself moving against traffic. Constantly she had to pause and stand aside or else be trod upon. Guiding oxcarts, pushing handcarts, with bundles balanced on their heads, Malays of all sizes were returning home from a day at the market. They eyed her curiously, the young girls in particular. She realized belatedly that they were seeing her in her male *persona*. She was still not accustomed to being a young man.

She took in the sights and sounds and the feel of the warm, muggy air. She let her mind wander. And her mind, thus turned loose to follow its own paths, sorted out deep inside the facts she could not sort out on the surface of her thoughts. Her mind put two and two together, as it were, and summed them up:

Captain Bricker.

Love.

She stopped dead in the road as that summation struck her in all its enormity. She and her girlhood friends in the parish had discussed love a million times, though none of them knew the least thing about it. In the Bible and also in the

116

streets of England, men murdered for love. The love of Helen and Paris had started a whole war. Always she had looked at love as happening to others, never what it might feel like in the first person. *Well, Erica, this is it.*

She began walking again, rapidly. Of course he made her feel good every time he spoke to her. Of course his face and eyes—everything about him—fascinated her so that she never wanted to turn her eyes away from him. Of course she was concerned about his relationship with his God; that was of prime importance to him and, therefore, to her as well. Of course she detested Maude. Maude was not simply an unsavory person; she was a rival—a full-blown, uncompromising rival. Of course Erica cried when he walked away. The only man in her whole life who had never tried to exploit her in any way, the only man she had ever felt— well, this way—about, was dismissing himself from her.

She arrived back in town well after dark, outrageously hungry. The little stalls were all closed, as was the hotel's sleazy little dining room. She finally found an old lady down the street who was trying to sell the last of her *trepang*. Erica was so starved she easily forgot what live sea cucumbers look like. She found her hotel again with some difficulty.

It was too late to seek out *Arachne* tonight. She would return first thing tomorrow morning. She would lay out her past, her whole past—in as much detail as he cared to hear—before the captain. Then she would beg him, implore him, plead with him to take her back. Would he condemn her or forgive her? His was a God of mercy; she would point that out to him if need be. Perhaps he would forgive her. He seemed wise and fair enough. She did not care any more whether she would be Eric the cabin boy or Erica the cabin girl or simply another passenger.

She felt as happy as a Malay as she drifted off to sleep.

117

CHAPTER 14

Macassar, Morning, June 19, 1851

Erica stepped from musty gloom into cheerful morning sun and let the louvered hotel door swing shut behind her. Yesterday's clouds had dispersed, but for a pallid haze. She shouldered her ditty and marched with springing steps toward the waterfront.

She liked Macassar, at least more so than she had the preceding day. The sunshine showed it to be a rather bright little city—not nearly as dirty as some she'd been in, Singapore included. The houses with their steeply pitched thatched roofs were crowded shoulder-to-shoulder along the street. Almost every house boasted a little shop on its ground floor. The keepers, mostly Chinese, were rolling up the storefront shutters, preparing for this new business day.

The closer she got to the wharves, the more she worried. She had doubted a little, when she first awoke, that the captain would accept her story, her presence, and her apologies. She deliberately forced herself to dispel such doubts. He had forgiven Maude's outburst, had he not? But now that doubt and others were returning.

Most pressing of her worries was: *Have they left already?* The captain called this a brief stop and he had wasted no time leaving Singapore. Yet Mr. McGovern's first excursion ashore when they docked yesterday told the captain there was oil to lade, though not a lot. Surely the canny captain wouldn't turn down certain cargo, would he?

Also worrisome: *Can I find them again?* The waterfront was easy enough to reach. She simply walked downhill. But now she must sort through a forest of masts, a press of hulls. Tiny crafts of myriad sorts crouched among huge, stately junks and a few European vessels. She walked quickly along a dressed-stone pier, looking for anything familiar among the mélange of vessels beside her.

"Madam, please! The captain told ye to stay aboard!" That was Mr. McGovern's voice not far ahead, and he sounded exasperated. "Madam!"

Erica broke into a jog.

Here she came, down a familiar gangway. With her head high and her reticule on her arm, Maude flounced out across the pier in a swishy sky-blue dress—not the soiled one. How many did she own?

Selfishly Erica was glad the woman had gone. Now she could speak to the captain without fear of interruption or distraction. *Wait!* Erica paused to think. *Mr. McGovern could not come ashore to stop Maude. That means he is officer in charge aboard* Arachne *and* that *meant the captain himself was not on board.* Were the captain anywhere around, surely Mr. McGovern would have come blazing down the gangway to retrieve the errant Miss Harrington.

Erica couldn't talk to the captain now, anyway. On the other hand Mr. McGovern needed help. Already Maude had disappeared upstreet. By the time the first mate found someone below decks to follow her, she might be tucked away in some little shop, virtually unfindable. Erica would follow her, and when she saw an *Arachne* crewman coming, she would tell him where Maude was.

She broke into a run. Skirts were feminine and lovely and elegant, but when it came to running, boys' trousers were much easier to race in and didn't have to be hitched up. Already Mr. McGovern had left the railing in search of a crewman. Erica dropped her duffle on the wharf at the foot of the gangway and sprinted away upstreet.

She stopped in the middle of the narrow street. Maude was gone. No! There she was, just popping out of that little shop. The billowing blue skirt swayed as she turned and walked to another door close by. Erica moved closer. She looked all up and down the street and saw no familiar faces from *Arachne*.

Almost as quickly as she entered, Maude came out. She continued around the corner. She was certainly a hard shopper to please. Erica rounded the corner as Maude flounced into still another little shop. She moved in close to the door, curious as to what was so difficult to buy in Macassar. She could hear Maude's voice clearly.

"Cosmetics. You can't be entirely stupid. *Cos-met-ics!*"

A cheery little Chinese voice replied. "Aaah, yes, yes. Now I understand. No, no."

"What do you mean, no, no?"

"In all Macassar, no lady paint. No cosmetic."

"This whole sty of a town is nothing but shops. Surely some little hole-in-the-wall carries European goods of that sort."

The Chinese voice chose words carefully. "Seek. Go; seek. When you no find, come. I sell you this. Here. And this; see? Lady paint, no. These, yes. Many European lady come in, buy these. Make lady paint."

"You mean I must make my own?" Maude's voice was getting just a bit strident.

Erica grinned openly. So Maude had run out of cosmetics, and was desperate to buy more. Did that mean she was getting nowhere with the good captain? Erica most fervently hoped so. And now this little shopkeeper wanted to sell her, apparently, ingredients. Erica could just envision Miss Do-It-For-Me compounding her own powders and rouges. That would slow down her beauty campaign considerably. Erica almost giggled aloud.

"I can't believe this!" Maude fretted. "Oh, very well. I'm in a rush. I haven't time to go wandering all over, and the shops I stopped at thus far seem to agree with you. That and that and that; wrap them up."

"Very good, Miss. At once. Thank-you, Miss."

Erica could picture the gentleman's whole upper body, bobbing up and down in the unique Oriental half-bow, half-nod. Was that a secret to constant happiness—this exquisite politeness? She looked up and down the street and jogged to the corner to check the other street. Still she saw no sign of anyone she knew.

Should she reveal herself to Maude and cling closely, or simply follow from a distance? She saw no real advantage either way. What she wanted most was to be done with her completely, and here she was nursemaiding the woman. When her greatest desire was to explain her past and her actions to the captain, she was tagging along behind a spoiled, willful Jezebel. Ah, the ironies of life. Erica pressed back flat into a doorway.

In a complete grump, Maude appeared in the street. She glanced up and down, frowning. She started one way, paused, turned, and went the other way. Surely she couldn't be lost. Erica followed.

It occurred to Erica within a few minutes that she was not the only one following. Three men, who had simply been standing about idle on a street corner, were now walking along in Maude's wake on the other side of the street, moving at Maude's speed. They were mumbling together, nodding and smiling. Erica feared the look of them. All three were hideously unkempt—ragged, unwashed clothes on ragged, unwashed bodies. A white scar angled down the face of one of them; his sunken eyelid was sewed shut where the scar crossed his left eye. Another had no toes on his right foot. Erica noticed right away because, despite his mutilation, he was barefoot. Their bandannas probably had been brightly colored once, long ago.

Why would they want Maude? *That's silly, Erica. Of course you know why they want Maude. Yes, but could they possibly know she is Maude Harrington, and the Dutchman will pay well to get her back? Would the Dutchman pay to get her? Certainly, that's the way things get done in Southeast Asia.* Erica calculated briefly. *Arachne* had come directly from Singapore except for that half day while the Malay searched the ship and another three hours when Fisher transferred to the westbound vessel. But for those eight hours, *Arachne* was moving, and usually before a fair breeze. But then, any other vessel would be enjoying the same fair breeze. And the commandeered *Joseph Whidby* had overtaken *Arachne* in less than two days by crowding sail.

Were the Dutchman to spread the word on his waterfront that he wanted his lady, at least a few bored ship's masters would hear the huntsman's bugle and go off sniffing after the fox. And if such a vessel were to sail east to Macassar, it might easily have arrived within the last few days. Erica imagined idle ships and cutthroats swarming out from Singapore, if not east to Macassar, then surely north to Manila and Macao, to Brunei and Kuching, perhaps out to Vlaardingen and New Guinea. *Who knows how far the tentacles might extend?* A sudden jolt of fear pulsed through her. If the Dutchman were that powerful, not only Maude but the captain himself was in real danger.

No doubt she was overreacting. These three wretched thugs simply saw an unescorted white woman whose appearance suggested a dubious reputation. After all, a woman of unassailably spotless reputation would certainly be escorted. Erica moved in closer, and kept a close eye all about for any seaman from *Arachne*.

Totally unaware of the parade behind her, Maude paused, studied a little shop and disappeared inside. The three gathered at its door. They were certainly more than a little interested in her, all right. Erica walked on to the next corner and looked up and down. The cross street curved around the hill and she could see very little. She started back toward the shop.

Here came Maude, more put out than ever. The three surrounded her instantly. Erica was close enough now to see and hear well.

A burly churl with yellowed teeth smiled. "By some far stretch of the imagination, y'r name wouldn't be Maude 'Arrington, would it?"

She stared at him for only the slightest moment. "Not by any stretch of the imagination. Stand aside, sir." She started to move but they blocked her way.

"Then what might y'r name be, I be so bold t' ask?"

She did not hesitate. "Adrienne Bricker. I said stand aside." Again she tried to pass.

The scoundrel absolutely gloated. "Y' 'ear that, mates? Bricker is the very name we got an ear for."

"Ah, missy," purred the lout with the scar, "the Dutchman's not in the least gonna like the idea that y'r foolish captain's taken ye to wife."

"I have no concept what you're talking about, and you'll cease harrassing me or I shall call for the constabulary."

123

"Ah, the fine words ye know. Keen music to the ears of any edoocated man, I aver. Now open y'r sweet mouth with the least bit of noise and we deliver ye dead. The reward is very nearly as high and not worth the difference, I assure ye. Come along now, there's a good girl." The three bunched in close around her and began moving her by sheer force of bodies down the street toward Erica.

The horror—the abject terror—on Maude Harrington's face erased any hostile thoughts Erica had ever held against her. Panic-stricken herself, Erica looked wildly about.

There! Up the street two blocks behind them, a familiar dark jacket stepped into view from a cross street.

Erica began shrieking. "Captain! Here! Help! Here!"

The three blackguards stared at Erica confounded, then looked behind them. He heard! He was running this way! Maude twisted around to see and began screeching, also.

Maude should not have started shrieking. Erica saw the man with no toes pulling a dirk from a sheath on his belt. Whether they managed to keep her or not, they would not leave Maude behind alive. She ought to know that.

"No!" Erica must not stop to think or she would run away. Mindlessly she plunged forward and grabbed No Toes's arm. She twisted around, her back against him, and gripped that arm in both hands. Calloused fingers clamped across her face and gouged at her eyes. Erica was beginning to fathom the captain's understatement that she was no match for real pirates.

She stamped as hard as she could about where his left foot ought to be. She felt a crunchy pop beneath her heel. He howled; the fingers loosened. Prim and ladylike persons would never dream of hitting below the belt—of hitting at all, for that matter. This was no time to be prim and ladylike. Erica let go the knife-wielding arm, whirled, and swung her knee up. Her aim was satisfactory, but her legs were too short; she did not even half the damage she had hoped. It slowed No Toes to a temporary standstill, however. Erica grabbed his hand and tried to wrest the dirk away.

The group beyond No Toes exploded; the captain must have arrived. The dirk dropped. Erica scrambled for it but someone else's foot struck it, kicked it away. She could not see where it went amongst the tangle of struggling legs. Someone, purposely or not, whacked the side of her head. She felt herself rolling, falling. She tried to stand. The toeless foot lashed at her, caught her in the side and lifted her waist-high. She fell away, paralyzed.

The skirmish seemed remote, abstract. Erica wanted desperately to dive back into the fray, but her body refused to obey what her head instructed. She dragged herself to her knees; the dirt street wavered beneath her. She saw No Toes hobbling off down the hill, both arms wrapped around a wadded billow of blue. She must make sure the captain knew they were absconding with Maude!

She heard a hoarse cockney voice: "He's worth more alive!" The captain came hurtling backwards straight at her. She lost her balance ducking aside. Yellow Teeth, who moments ago grinned so gratuitously, was now snarling. He came roaring down upon the prostrate captain, swinging something, striking again and again. Erica stared, stunned. Her captain wasn't moving.

He had lost.

The third lubber grabbed handfuls of arm and coat and yanked. As if Captain Bricker were no more than a sack of rice, the huge man hoisted him to his shoulder and lumbered away. Erica saw now that Yellow Teeth had used an ungainly dueling pistol of some sort to strike the captain. He was pointing it now—not at Erica but upstreet. She lurched to her knees and twisted around to look. Two small Malays

125

in European-style uniforms were speaking rapidly. They stopped simultaneously, frightened.

" 'Tis just a friendly little fight amongst fellow shipmates. Interfere and y'll regret it. Y' understand the queen's English?'' Without taking his eyes off the two, Yellow Teeth scooped up the dirk and tucked it into his own belt. He grabbed Erica's wrist. "Ye'll do for an 'ostage, should I need one. Come along, lad,'' he yanked.

On her way to her feet, Erica bumped into Maude's parcel. It had burst open, no doubt trod upon. A pile of brilliant vermilion powder fairly glowed in the morning sun. Without realizing why, Erica snatched up a handful of the red dust.

With occasional glances over his shoulder, Yellow Teeth dragged her along. He did not really seem very interested in her, but seemed to be bringing her along more to tidy up the fight scene. His grip was so lax that if she twisted just now she could no doubt wrench free and duck away. And his dueling pistol, she knew, contained only one shot. He would surely not waste a bullet on a fleeing cabin boy when he might need it shortly in his own defense. But she did not struggle, and she could not imagine why she did not struggle. This was most unlike her—by nature she was a fighter.

She looked behind them. Not only were there no familiar faces in sight, the two constables had decided not to interfere. They stood in the distance watching, the cowardly clods. Only when she noticed splotches of red on the ground did she realize the vermilion powder was leaking from her clenched fist. From that point on she trickled vermilion through her fingers in niggardly amounts. She ran out of powder at the gangway of the cutthroats' ship.

CHAPTER 15

Noon, June 19, 1851

There is darkness and there is blackness, Erica mused. This was blackness wherein no light gleamed, no star twinkled, no gray smudge promised more light to come. "Black as a ship's hold" was more than just an adage. She abhorred sitting in this ship's hold now in such utter, abject blackness.

The weight in her lap moved slightly. Her captain was waking up again. She took the opportunity to raise herself from the floor and flex her sore backside muscles. She felt numb from sitting motionless on the deck planking so long. She settled down again and leaned back against the rough boards.

She groped for his collarbone, and from there, ran her fingers up the side of his face to his temple. Still sticky, but not wet—the bleeding had stopped.

He took a deep breath and muttered something she could not quite catch.

She followed his shoulder and arm down to his hand, checking. The fingers were still clammy cold, as they had been. But they turned now and wrapped around hers. He held on for several minutes.

The hold here was so silent that her whispers sounded like shouts. She kept her voice very low, though there was no one else to hear. "I'm not going to ask you how you feel. I think I have a general notion."

"Eric?"

"Very good, sir."

"Did they catch Miss Harrington? Could she get away?"

"They did and she couldn't. I suspect at least one of them kept a good tight grip on her the whole fight, though I couldn't see. She certainly tried to free herself—struggling, squirming, shrieking like a banshee."

"Where is she? I don't hear her."

"Nor will you. I would imagine she's up in the stern cabin with the other elite of this scow. Her proper place. They didn't throw her in this hold at any rate."

"How long have we been down here?"

"I've been wondering about that. No more than two hours, I suppose. But it seems much longer. You started to wake up once but it didn't last. They brought us aboard immediately after that little brouhaha. And you can't believe how terribly delighted they all were to see the two of you. I gather they hope to turn a handsome profit by dragging you two back to Singapore. They emptied your pockets—had to make sure you were the captain in question. Took your matches, I gather so you can't burn up their ship. And they took that pretty little pocket knife.

"And they made all these, well, ugly comments. Incidentally Maude tried to talk her way out by claiming to be Mrs. Bricker. I don't think that will help your cause much. I was snuffling a little. I felt very low, as you may well imagine. Some smelly person with a tooth missing in front jabbed my arm like this—" she demonstrated gently

"—and said 'Stop y'r sniveling. Be a man!' Fat lot he knows. They were getting underway even while all this was going on. In a muckle rush they were."

"Mmmm." Another deep sigh. Was he drifting off again or struggling to return to something of his usual alertness? Perhaps she'd better keep him talking.

"You were going to look for oil to round out your cargo. Did you find any?"

"No." He paused, then amended his answer. "No, I didn't look for oil, and, no, I didn't find any."

"What did you do all the rest of yesterday, then? And this morning. You weren't aboard this morning, were you?"

"I was looking for you."

"Really! Should I be flattered?"

"I hope so. I worked for days to convince myself that dismissing you was the best thing to do. But when I got back to *Arachne*—sat down in my chair—you weren't in the pantry, you weren't bouncing around anywhere; I knew then it was a terrible mistake. But you left the green before I got back there. I looked everywhere in the city for you. It was as though you'd evaporated."

"I went for a walk. So sorry I missed you. I had a great deal of thinking to do, as you can understand, and I needed some solitude. What is a rather long ship that's thin and barren-looking in front and square and brightly painted in back?"

"A prau. I've heard them called flying praus, too. Usually pirate vessels, usually well armed. Where'd you see it?"

"Tied out from the city a ways. And what is a ship, long and thin at both ends with an absolutely enormous sail? Local design, I should guess."

"One mast with a very wide spar? Caracor. Has an outrigger."

"That's it. It put in at a little village as I watched. Have you ever noted how happy these Malays are? The villagers and all?"

"Uh-huh." He sounded more as though he were talking to Eric than to Erica. Despite their position, she felt elated. On the other hand, he didn't sound interested in the fine points of local shipping or the joys of being a Malay.

To use a nautical phrase, she took a different tack. "Do you remember when you first discovered my, ah, secret and you said you felt betrayed because I had brightened your voyage? Is that accurate?"

"That's pretty accurate."

"And then you said 'I'm sorry you are what you are. I liked Eric very much.'"

"I don't remember my exact words. That was my feeling at the time, though."

"Eric isn't gone, you know. He never left. I didn't change. Do you realize that, in fact, you called me Eric a few minutes ago when you weren't really all that awake yet? The person you explained the Nereids to is the selfsame person you confronted in the serving closet. I am me. And once upon a time you seemed to like me very much. Do you understand what I'm trying to say?"

"Yes. I do." He heaved another of those heavy sighs. His head must be throbbing terribly. Suddenly he turned to face her, though of course no one could see anything in this blackness. "How thoughtless can I be? You were in the thick of the fight. Are you hurt?"

"No. Not really. A couple of bumps, a thump in the side. No blood spilt, which is more than you can say. He beat on your poor head with a dueling pistol. Did you know that?"

"He was going to fire the ball into my belly and not a thing I could do to stop him. But his chum yelled something."

130

"I believe he said something to the effect that you're worth more alive than dead."

"Wonderful." His voice dripped bitterness. It softened. "You're sure you're not hurt at all?"

"Quite certain. Thank-you. Of course, that is in reference to the immediate effects of the skirmish. Excuse my saying so, but my posterior aspect is in disastrous straits at the moment. I'm afraid I really must move, at least for a minute or two. Here." She pulled off her cutaway jacket and waistcoat. She rolled them into a loose wad to pillow his head. She wiggled out from under him and tucked the roll where her lap had been. "Is that all right for you?"

"Fine. It's—what is it, your jacket?"

She might as well have a bit of fun with this. "Jacket and shirt and all. We must keep you comfortable, musn't we?"

"Your shirt and—now, look! Just because it's dark—"

"It's absolutely pure, pitch, Stygian black and who's to know?" She giggled. "However, I overstated slightly. It's the jacket and waistcoat only. Your propriety is preserved."

Was he angry? She couldn't tell. When he spoke she knew he wasn't. His voice had regained something of that lilt she had liked so much that day on the foredeck. He was feeling better. "You obviously weren't spanked enough when you were young. You don't have an ounce of respect for man or beast or moral law."

"Respect? I certainly have. But I remember more than once you took devilish delight in teasing. Sauce for the goose and all that." She mused a few moments. "On second thought, perhaps you're absolutely right. I at least lack the respect to hold my peace just now, but I'm too anxious to know: After you dismissed me, did Maude, ah, approach you, and did you rebuff her advances? Not just yesterday, but before that, too."

"Why do you ask?"

"She came ashore to buy cosmetics, which led me to deduce that (a) her supply was becoming exhausted and (b) she felt the need of additional ammunition in her fight to win you. I suppose *seduce* is a closer term than *win*."

He chuckled, that loose and rippling laugh. She could just imagine his sun-crinkles bunching up. "Very shrewd of you. That painful incident, when you came clanging out of the serving closet like a blamed jack-in-the-box, served one good purpose. It reminded me, speaking frankly, of my fleshly responsibility toward my Lord. It reminded me to put my guard back up. She tried half a dozen times to pick up again where we left off. She's a most enticing woman."

"I think I can understand at least a little the temptation. Not only beautiful but willing and, ah, shall we say knowledgeable in the ways of pleasing a man?"

"I think we could say that. Yes, a temptation. And you were right about her thinking that incident was the reason you were fired. Then after I put you ashore and returned, she said something to the effect that now our blankety-blank chaperone is gone, let's get to know one another better. Those weren't her exact words; I'm very poor at repeating exact quotes, and that includes Scripture verses. But you get the idea."

"Clearly. Funny. I would never have guessed anything good at all could come of that—what you called a painful incident."

"I suppose the standard cliché applies here: The Lord works in mysterious ways."

He was silent a few minutes.

She walked in tight little circles, stretching her stiff limbs and rubbing her aching backside.

His voice came so suddenly in the silence it startled her. "You said, as I recall, that perhaps you might explain yourself sometime. Is this the time?"

132

"It's half a day past time. When I saw Maude coming down your gangway, I was on my way to you to tell you everything, beg your forgiveness, and entreat you to take me back. Had you been available, and had Maude not gone cavorting off, you would have heard the whole story hours ago."

"Start by sorting the fact from the fiction. Were your parents actually missionaries?"

"Yes. But they were not serving here in the Orient when I was born. They had returned to their parish in Chelsea. I was born in England. The part that they died untimely is true also. Smallpox. I was thirteen. The vicar made me a ward of the parish. I worked as a sort of charwoman in return for keep and some education. It was a rather nice arrangement, now I look back, but at the time I loathed it."

"Cleaning? That kind of thing?"

"Helping the regular charwoman. Cleaning the brass and silver in the sanctuary, washing the vicar's vestments, pulling weeds in the garden out back, rubbing out the initials small boys carved in the choir loft. Such chores as that."

"Joshua Rice came to the vicar when I was seventeen—just barely seventeen—and wanted to train for the mission field. He was intensely dedicated and eager to go. He was pleasant, polite, well-behaved; the vicar liked him. So did I. When someone suggested a married man would be more appropriate in the field, so to speak, the idea just sort of fell together that I would marry him and we'd both go."

"That was all there was to it? I mean—no love?"

"What did I know about love? He was scrawny but rather attractive, and I liked him. I was looking for no more than that. I suspect now I was in love most of all with the chance to get out of the vicarage. No more dull, dreary toil in a dull, dreary place. Chelsea is what you'd call drab under the best of circumstances. I wanted to see exotic places like my parents had. Go adventuring. You know—*do* things. I mean, things besides polishing four-hundred-year-old candlesticks."

"At eighteen."

"Yes. The voyage to Manila was our honeymoon cruise."

"Very romantic."

She licked her lips. "Since you were speaking frankly in reference to Miss Harrington, I shall also. Neither Joshua nor I had the least notion of what married couples, uh, do. We weren't even certain whether anything is permissible or if sin began where good behavior left off. And besides, there are many other difficult aspects to marriage—molding your life to that of another when you're both of independent spirit. Oh, we would have succeeded in marriage. We were both determined enough."

He rustled in the blackness.

"Are you getting up? You shouldn't, you know."

"Just sitting. I'm all right. Keep going."

"Well, the end of it is, I have a much healthier respect for how much marriage requires of one. I've lost my casual attitude toward it."

"And you say he died of malaria?"

"A fortnight before our boat was to sail from Manila to China. We spent some months in Manila learning Chinese. Well, he learned Chinese. I never did get the hang of it; the words all sounded alike to me. Anyway, suddenly he was gone. I had a little money but not enough to get back to England. I didn't know what to do. The local church was very poor. They couldn't really help. And with my background I was dreadfully afraid to ask them; to even speak to them. Anglicans and Romans—Henry the Eighth and the

134

Pope—you know. So foolish of me. I see that now.

"Obviously the thing to do was earn enough money to get back to England—or perhaps America or Canada. A man offered to hire me as a maid and nanny. He was Spanish, smaller than you, and very dark-complexioned. He gave me his address so I could come be interviewed by his wife. Well, when I got there, I found there was no wife and he, ah—" Here it came. Here it all came and Erica just knew it would shatter the fragile rapport they had established in this black hold. "He, ah, intended to violate me. Keep me. He said so in so many words, and he threatened me great harm if I should tell a soul. I couldn't fight him, so I pretended to be amenable to the idea. I suggested that I would step in the next room and disrobe. Oh, he liked the idea! So I stepped into the other room and out the second-story window, worked my way down the tile roof to some gnarled sort of tree, climbed to the ground, and ran home. I abandoned the apartment quickly lest he come find me."

He was chuckling. "I can just picture that, knowing you."

Erica frowned. He could afford to chuckle. The worst was yet to come. "Then I met this nice man, an older man, a man of means. He was a trader and ship's master, just like you. He offered to take me back to England. By now, you see, I was all for going home to England. I'd pick up again at the vicarage, find some nice young man with a farm, get married, and forget this ridiculous urge for adventure. The shipmaster would give me cabin space, he said. He rather intimated it would be a service to the church."

"What's his name?"

"Abram Sykes, *Cartagena*. Do you know him?"

"I met him once." His voice sounded subdued. "Let me second-guess your story. His free offer had strings attached."

"That's putting it nicely, to say the least. He had no intention of sailing anywhere near England. Almost a year later, we were still in the South Seas. He chained me to his bunk whenever we were in port and only let me out of the cabin if he was with me. That's slavery, you know."

"Given to drink? Captain Sykes, I mean."

"Only one of many vices." She sat down carefully nearby, she hoped. "How close am I to you?"

"Oh, about this close."

"Very funny." But his voice had given her a more precise fix. She wriggled in a bit closer. Her foot bumped against her discarded jacket and vest, and since he wasn't using them, she put them back on. "There was one young man, his seaman. I found him alone on one occasion and begged him to help me. He seemed such a decent sort and sympathetic to my plight. But he wouldn't help. He said the captain's business was the captain's business and he wouldn't interfere. The captain was master."

"That's right. Not a man among them would have lifted a finger for you, no matter how much they'd like to. Calling the captain on a moral issue is as much mutiny as calling him on a point of authority."

She buttoned her waistcoat. "Then Miss Harrington posed a far greater temptation than I suspected. You mean you could have done anything you wished? And the crew would simply turn their faces away?"

"Anything I wanted. Nobody's business but my own. And God's, of course, but that too is my own affair, not the crew's."

"Of course." There he was again, on religion. Yet the tone of his voice was not one of fearing God's wrath but rather one of fearing disappointing Him. It was a fine line, but clear. Curious. She must ask him about it. "We were coming into Singapore a few weeks before I met you,"

136

Erica continued. "There are those outer islands, you know, off to the left of the ship as you're coming around from Malacca. Anyway, I saw we'd pass rather close and he hadn't chained me up yet. So I gathered a change of clothes into a bundle, and stripped to my unmentionables. I broke up a locker door and squeezed both it and me out the porthole. I don't know what I would've done had I got stuck halfway—or what he would've done, for that. It was late evening, nearly dark. If the watch saw me they didn't say anything. I kicked and floated ashore on the broken-up wood."

"God was good to you. Those offshore waters are thick with sharks. The villages are constantly losing trepang divers."

"Well, I made it. But do you know, within a week I very nearly made the dastardly mistake of trusting another such fellow? I just barely escaped having the same horrible thing happen all over again. So do you see, Captain, why I could not bring myself to trust you?" She wanted to be able to see his face just now and she could not. "Now that I know you, I realize I could have come to you with my story and you would have given me passage to England freely and clearly. But I didn't know you then. And those other experiences—I was trapped, I was half a world away from home, I was sick to death of tropics and exotic places. And you needed a cabin boy." The telling wearied her. She drew her knees up and rested her arms and chin on them.

"As you said, an honorable way home to England. And I refused to believe you." A hand bumped against her arm. The fingertips ran down it to find her hand. He took it in his. His own hands were warm again. "I apologize for not accepting you. I had no evidence to distrust you and you claimed your honor. I should have respected that."

"Why? As you so rightly pointed out on that greensward,

my refusal to explain anything to you made me suspect, and quite reasonably so. I see that now. But then, I just couldn't bring myself to tell you all this. I mean, intimacy with Joshua—well, it was natural and proper. But Abram Sykes soiled me. He defiled me. I was afraid—''

"But if he victimized you, it certainly wasn't your fault."

"Regardless of the blame, I am defiled all the same, don't you see? And I was afraid of what you would think of me. It matters to me just as much now—maybe even more—but somehow now I can talk about it, and then I couldn't. Do you suppose it's because of this darkness and we can't see each other, or because the danger above is so imminent?"

"I have no idea." His hand released hers and traveled back up her arm. It cupped around her head just behind her ear. The fingers pushed up into her short hair. "I immensely admire your gift for plunging ahead and burning your bridges behind you. You got this idea to pose as a cabin boy and less than twelve hours later, you're sitting in my cabin with your story and your plan all worked out. And you couldn't very well go back to being Erica once you whacked your hair off like this, could you?"

"It wasn't all courage, believe me. I cried for two solid hours after cutting off my hair. You're right, though; I'm impetuous. Always have been. Marrying Joshua like that—impulse. Decide this, decide that. So it breeds trouble? Well, charge on forward and find some more trouble. I suppose if you want to spend a life out adventuring, it's a handy character trait to have. But it does cause wear and tear and pain."

"All the same I should have more of that impulsiveness. I'm too cautious, too slow at times."

"And I must learn to take better heed; you're really a

very good model for me. I must think things through more carefully."

"Are you familiar with the difference between the Gospels of Luke and John?"

"I, well, I presume they were written by two different men."

"True." He chuckled again. "They complement each other, dovetail their information. Except for a few passages, they talk about different things altogether. We complement each other that same way."

She leaned her head into his hand. "I never thought of that. It's quite true. You're steady; I bob about like your Mr. Fisher—"

"Not as bad as Fisher."

"No one bounds through life like Fisher. You know what I mean. You're very proper and careful, and it is glaringly obvious that I am not. And as you say, there's that matter of impulsiveness."

"Impulsiveness. Yes." He was drawing her head over toward his voice. It took her a moment to realize what was coming. Somehow she could easily picture Maude kissing just any old pair of lips that wandered into range, but this was different, very different. This was the straight captain and the cabin boy/girl who perplexed him so, his partner in a quite probably lethal dilemma. Surely—

Their lips met softly; his aim in this pitch dark was extraordinary. He wrapped around her, encased her in the strength of his arms. She melted against him and let him pull her in close and tight. Her body, her spirit, all her senses hung suspended in the blackness. How long did she float in this happy oblivion, and did he float as happily? In due time his lips left hers, brushed along her cheek and kissed her neck. His hand pressed her head against his shoulder.

She murmured, "Excellent impulse. You learn quickly."

"Not impulse. That was very carefully considered." Those gentle fingertips massaged her neck behind her ear. She would have liked to rest her hand on the nape of his neck, but she feared she might accidentally bump a sore spot.

She snuggled deeper in against him. "How long considered?"

"I told you. When I came back aboard after leaving you yesterday, I sat down in my chair, remember? And the cabin felt empty. It wasn't the lack of, ah—" Ever gentlemanly, the voice stumbled, groped for words. "The lack of a man-woman relationship. Maude Harrington was available up on the quarterdeck if I were so inclined. It wasn't the absence of someone to set the table. Any man aboard could be pressed to that service. And the emptiness was complete. Hollow. Almost frightening. It took me a while to realize just why the emptiness was there, and that you hadn't really left my mind since the voyage began. As Eric—or as Erica—you were all I thought about."

"Puppy love," she lied. "You'll get over it."

"At my age?" He paused. "Why did you come back? The truth, please. The real reason."

"Because I had determined on my long walk out to some rocky little point southeast of town that I, too, am a victim of whatever this may be."

"Why did you stay and fight? They didn't want you."

"I don't know."

"You could have run, found help—"

"Help came—a couple of gendarmes—but they decided not to get involved. Besides, I couldn't just watch them drag you off not knowing—I mean—oh, I don't know what I mean. I suppose it would have simplified matters considerably had I broken away. Impulse again."

140

"You should have saved yourself."

"Well, I didn't. But I have a better suggestion. Let's both save ourselves now. Any ideas?"

He took a breath. A little chuckle rumbled down inside. It exploded as a cheery, lilting laugh. The fingertips moved up to her ear and both his hands cupped around her head. He held her face as if he were looking at her eye-to-eye. Incredibly, they locked eyes in spite of the blackness; her imagination filled the dearth.

His voice was warm and happy with the pleasure of her. He had forgiven her past—he didn't have to say so—and her heart sang. "Do I have ideas! However dark it may be, my Lord is watching over my shoulder all the same, and I know He wouldn't approve of the idea I favor most. Besides, the faster we look for a way out, the better our chances are."

"A way out? Two hatches and the companionway, and I'm positive someone unsavory and ominous will be waiting on the other side of any of those exits."

"Possibly. We'll go exploring." He hauled himself by degrees to his feet. He rocked a bit, unsteady, so she pressed close—to keep him upright, of course.

"Exploring, eh? More adventuring. Very well, you take the lead. It all looks alike here to me." He was leaning on her, however slightly, and it gave her great pleasure to be of help. "The fruit of all this: I'm learning quite a bit about adventuring. Do you know, for example, that its charm is almost all in whom you do the adventuring with?"

"I concur. Absolutely."

She wanted him to kiss her one more time before they went plunging off through the blackness, but she was too short to initiate it. If they were to kiss, he would have to bend down to her.

And he did.

CHAPTER 16

Java Sea, Afternoon, June 19, 1851

Most of the Anglo seamen Fisher knew looked askance at native vessels—considered them crude and haphazard arrangements of ill-fitting boards. The appearance of these weathered craft would tend to foster that impression; Fisher could see that. And at one time he, too, had looked down his nose at Oriental watercraft. But now that he was serving aboard one, he was altogether impressed. Efficiency, maneuverability, comfort—this lorcha had all the best qualities of any seaworthy vessel. And now that he knew, he could see those qualities in the ponderous junks and feathery outriggers as well.

Perhaps, should this Maude Harrington/Gideon/*Arachne* business fall apart completely, he might simply stay on with Hwang Ahn here. There were far worse things in life than plying the South Seas in a worthy vessel. Moreover, now that he was surrounded with no one else, all these Orientals didn't bother him at all. Professionally speaking, these seamen were as skilled as any Fisher had ever known, and that included DuPres. He even enjoyed his turn at the tiller.

Why, he hadn't handled a tiller since he sailed dories off Knockadoon Head when he was just a wee shaver.

Thoughts of his own pleasant childhood reminded him of Gideon. In a way Fisher was glad he had never married. This one lad was a heavy responsibility. Imagine the onus of a whole houseful of tads, not to mention the little wife to keep happy.

And what if he accidentally yoked himself to someone like Maude Harrington? Ah, a splendid body had Maude Harrington, and without doubt she knew how to use it for purposes of pleasure. But if the Dutchman were only half speaking the truth (and the Dutchman's whole mien suggested truth spoken in anguish), Maude was cutting out simply because she had tired of responsibility. If Fisher ever married he would marry the responsibility along with the woman, and Maude apparently didn't feel that way. How could he know for certain that the girl he wed was ready to stick it out? Marriage was an incredibly complex contract, to be undertaken only by a wise man capable of seeing into the future.

Yet even without marriage, Fisher found himself responsible for the lad Gideon. The responsibility had been thrust upon him, but he would discharge it cheerfully. He would protect the child and succor him, and if need be, see him safely into his teens when he would go off on his own. All in all, it was a rather pleasant prospect, this matter of having someone so bright and precocious and affectionate utterly dependent upon you. Unlike marriage, this responsibility was limited and its end visible.

The glaring sunlight must have washed some sky color into the water; it rendered the sky pallid and the water a deep, rich blue.

Hwang wandered foreward and a few minutes later came wandering aft again. He stopped by Fisher's side at the larboard rail. He smiled and pointed off abeam. A large bird, from this distance no more than a thick white streak, soared a few feet above the swells. As they watched, it dipped in closer, swooped gracefully, heeled starboard, coasted in so close on the lorcha's wake that Fisher could see the color of its eye. The wings must span three yards at least.

Hwang leaned out to watch it better. "Remind me, please, its name in English."

"Albatross. 'All wings and appetite,' me mate McGovern calls it."

"Al, yes. Albatross. Good fortune, they say."

"Aye, so I 'ear."

"And like good fortune, very rare. I have only seen one or two my whole life at sea."

"Rare in these seas, aye. If ye sail much down in the roaring forties ye'll see 'em aplenty. They seem to like blustery weather and choppy seas. In fact, meself cannae recall ever seeing one this deep up into the tropics before."

"Indeed. An omen of luck, then, perhaps, to come this far north."

Fisher grinned. "Wouldn't it be grand."

Albatross. Lady Luck. No—divine providence, Captain Bricker would insist. Fisher was not about to argue the fine points of difference, if any. Right now he could use the ministrations of albatross, Lady Luck and God—all three.

Total darkness renders everything exactly alike—no beauty or ugliness, no shades of gray. Erica pondered the equalizing effect of pitch black as she gripped the tail of the captain's jacket. He was groping his way along the belly of this ship. Apparently he had some notion where they were; at least, so far they hadn't bumped into anything insurmountable.

"Now where are we?" she asked.

144

"Still moving aft. I can't say exactly because I don't know how long she is or where we were to start with."

"How do you know we're moving aft?"

The jacket went slack. He had stopped. "Let's sit a minute." He plopped down rather hard.

She settled close beside him. "Are you certain you're all right?"

"I'm fine. Remember when we were standing on the foredeck that morning and I was weaving the yarn about Nereids?"

"The highlights of my life. And since it's totally dark you can't tell from my face that I'm telling you the absolute truth."

"I believe you. From now on I'll believe you when you say something—within reason, of course."

"Until that moment I was convinced that all the men in the whole world—except the vicar, maybe—were exactly alike. Vermin. You changed my life with those Nereids of yours."

He was quiet a moment. Apparently he had decided not to comment on that. "The wind then was to our backs—actually more off to one side. That was unusual. The prevailing winds quarter from the other direction this time of year. We were enjoying a rare occurrence when the wind was right for a change."

"Very well. So?"

"Assuming that fair breeze wouldn't last, and the wind is, therefore, pretty much what it usually is; and assuming this vessel is bound for Singapore—"

"A likely assumption with Maude up there in the stern cabin."

"Precisely. Then feel the ship's cant, how she's tilting."

Erica scooted her legs around to her right a bit. "I think now I'm facing downhill, so to speak."

An arm reached out and bumped her legs. "That's right. So from the tilt of the ship and knowing the way the wind usually blows, I'm assuming that aft is to my present left, your right."

She sighed. "It must take a lifetime to learn all these things."

"Now here's why we're moving aft. Feel the litter on the deck?"

"Litter?" She patted the floor beside her. She felt occasional bits and chips, something soft like bark.

"And the last clue, smell the air."

"Smells like wet wood. This entire hold smells like it. I assumed that's normal since it's built of wet wood."

"This vessel has been hauling teak logs lately—the bark chips, the distinctive teak smell. If so, it may be fitted with sternports for lading the long lengths of lumber."

"What are sternports?"

"Little doors at the very back under the transom."

"Doors!" Erica beamed so happily she half expected the hold to light up. "A way out! Open the doors to admit some light, fashion a raft and launch it well after dark. Excuse my lack of chivalry, but we leave the fair Maude to whatever fate awaits her."

"Maude. I don't see how we can possibly rescue Maude unless they decide to toss her down here with us. You didn't happen to see the name of this vessel as you were brought on."

"No. I'm not even sure it has a name. Oh, surely it must."

"Well, let's find the sternports first." He moved, rustling in the darkness.

She stood up and bumped into him. "Sternports do stay in one place, don't they? Don't sneak about?"

"Of c—now what are you getting at?"

"Well, if we needn't rush right over and leap on them, perhaps there's time for one short kiss."

He laughed. The artificial wall he had constructed between proper ladies and proper gentlemen was gone, gone to the last brick. Was it the darkness, or the point she made that she and Eric were the same, or simply their present danger? Would the wall reerect itself once they were safe somewhere, should that happen at all? She didn't want to lose this oneness again. She pressed against him as his lips brushed her cheek, their aim slightly off, but quickly found together.

She must shore up this fragile unity now, the more so, if by chance, Maude would indeed be sent down here. Maude was much less resistible than Erica; in a contest of physical attractiveness, Erica would lose. From what she knew of men, there was one certain means of buying a man's temporary allegiance. The captain's God would just have to turn His back a few minutes, that's all. Erica was not voluptuous like Maude, in fact hardly endowed at all, but she pressed her small body hard against Bricker's.

He gripped her shoulders and broke the kiss off instantly. "Don't." He whispered hoarsely. "Please don't. I'm closer to the brink than you know."

She let a sob slip out. *I'm so unattractive I can't even seduce a man who claims to like me!* She sniffled. Maude could have done it. She would have purchased or bribed his devotion somehow. She had both the gift and the equipment to take what she wanted from men. The tears edged up and over and out.

"I'm afraid."

"I don't blame you." He wrapped his powerful arms around her. "Try not to be. We'll get out of this."

"It's not this I'm afraid of."

His hands moved up to cup around her head again. His

147

thumbs stretched out forward and wiped the tears from the corners of her eyes. He was looking into her face again, through the blackness. "What are you afraid of—that I'll forget about you?"

She nodded in his hands.

"Don't ever be afraid of that, Erica. Don't ever be afraid of that."

"Even if Maude steps back in—or someone like her? There are inordinate numbers of Maudes, you know—multitudes and multitudes of them."

"And there is only one Erica. Which is more desirable, one unique diamond or many common pebbles?"

There was silence in the blackness, long moments of it. Then he was kissing her, at once firm and pliant, soft and fierce. The tears dispersed. No, she would not have to offend his God by pulling any of the little tricks in a Maude-like repertoire. She felt suddenly light-headed—from the kiss? Or from the giddy revelation that Erica was being loved for what she was—herself—and not because she happened to be a convenient female?

He relaxed his ardent bearhug eventually, topped off with a final little peck, and found her hand in the blackness. There was no more hanging onto coattails. He led her by the hand as they worked their way aft in silence.

They bumped into a stack of crates and struggled together, moving them aside; Erica was sweating profusely by the time they worked through the pile. She heard the gentle thunk of his hands against—against what sounded like thick wood. He grunted with exertion. Metal creaked on metal and set her teeth on edge. A white vertical line streaked the darkness. Hinges groaned and brilliant searing white sunlight blasted in. It overwhelmed her eyes. She clapped her hands to her face and peeked by degrees through her fingers.

She knew she must not speak loudly, for human ears were

just a few yards overhead. Yet she wanted to scream joyously and jump up and down. He pushed the door open a little further and hung onto the frame as he leaned out. After studying the situation overhead, he pulled himself back in.

He kept his voice low. "The counter's deep enough that they can't see us, even if the door here swings out wide."

Raucous voices drifted down from above. Someone laughed.

Erica's eyes were adjusting now. She pointed out to sea. Far astern a blob of white canvas and a dark cutwater followed them. "Look at that."

He studied. He squinted. He grinned broadly. "Guess who!"

"*Arachne?* But how—? That means we're saved!"

"Not yet. See our shadow on the water? The mizzen? This ship is larger than she and full-rigged. They don't have to work hard at all to outdistance her. She's not catching up; I'll wager she's falling behind."

He sat on the frame leaning out, staring at the side. She stuck her head out, too. He seemed to be studying the rudder. He looked up. She looked up. The shadowy hull of a little boat swayed back and forth above their heads. Nothing suggested itself to her, but obviously he was scheming.

He sat back and leaned his head against the frame. She had forgotten he must still have a dreadful headache. She sat down on the frame across from him, half in the hold and half in the open air of freedom. Their wake gurgled and boiled beside her.

He was studying her thoughtfully. "You're not strong enough to muscle a jolly boat around by yourself. But you are impetuous and clever—"

"I believe we established at least half of that."

"Can you dream up some story to get above decks, back here to the quarterdeck? There's a light dinghy above our heads, the captain's boat. It hands by light line from davits, out over the water. Can you cut it free?"

"It drops in the water, we both hop in and we sail away." Her face was alight with the dawning of his plan.

"That's half of it. While you're up there I'll be down here finding something to jam their rudder with. If I can skew the rudder, *Arachne* will walk right up to us." He sat up straight. "The Lord has been with us this far. Let's do our best and pray the continuation of His favor."

Religion again. She raised a finger. "Listen."

He frowned, expecting trouble.

She pointed to the wake. "Nereids. Would they be singing this cheerfully if we were doomed to fail?"

He was going to say one thing, apparently, and decided upon another. "Sure they would. They're just happy to see sunshine on your face again. Bunch of aquatic romantics down there."

She leaned over suddenly and gave him a quick kiss, the sort of fast peck married folks give each other as one is going out the door. She hopped down off the frame, started away, stopped, and turned to him. "I love you." It was whispered, it was sung. She ran because she could not simply walk. She grinned irrepressibly because she could not feel serious.

She remembered in one of the vicar's homilies that he read from the Bible about charity. He claimed charity was a translation for the Greek (or was it Latin?) word for *total love.* He said it was ever patient, kind, forgiving, and giving; he said love was never rude, irritable, or selfish. *What a terrible burden love places upon one,* she had thought at the time. That showed how little she had known about it. Right now she wanted to be all those things to Travis Bricker and more.

The last shaft of light disappeared. Again she was moving

150

through complete blackness. But all the blackness was on the outside. Inside, her heart glowed bright as midday.

How long could she remain in this state of euphoria before the pirates above their heads killed one or both of them? She would leave that problem to Captain Bricker's God and bask in this heady new delight as long as possible.

She pressed on through the darkness, groping—

CHAPTER 17

Java Sea, Late afternoon, June 19, 1851

It occurred to Erica as she stumbled through the blackness that she had not the least idea what she was doing. She had never actually been in the hold of a ship before. Was she on the deck just below the surface deck? Was she deeper still? How was she to tell when she passed a hatch? With the covers on the hatches they were all just as black as the rest of the hold. She stopped and peered all about. It was as if she were under a thick blanket. She continued on.

Her searching hands rapped into something immovable. She patted it. It seemed to be a wall. No, on ships they were bulwarks, not walls. Or was it bulkheads? She was no sailor. She groped along toward her left, a random direction. Something whacked her on the ear. She reached for it and felt—a ladder. She scrambled up.

The hatch at the top was covered but she removed the lid easily enough. The hatch opened onto another deck, equally black. She remembered to put the hatch cover back on. She didn't want to fall into it during her gropings and wanderings.

She explored what seemed a long time before she found another ladder. She climbed it and tried to push the cover aside. It wouldn't budge. She felt around the inside edges. Whatever latched it held it from the outside. She knocked on it. She thumped on it. She pulled off her shoe and pounded its heel upon it.

Long moments dragged by. She had started to pound again when she heard strange scratching noises. The cover lifted. Blaring sunlight dumped into her eyes.

"Ho. It's the lad." One of the three ugliest men Erica had ever looked upon peered down at her. The other two stood near him.

"Might I come up, sir? Please? He's dead. My captain's died and its frightening down there." She sniffled and ran her sleeve across her nose.

The blackguard stared at her a moment, reached down, and yanked her up by one arm. She stood by obediently as he fastened the cover down again.

His breath was foul. "So 'e's dead, eh? 'E was nae good color when we put 'im down there. Suspected as much. Be ye sure?"

"Wouldn't be standing here if he weren't. I can't abide touching dead people, and he's cooling off already." She shuddered.

The three traded glances.

Erica took a deep breath and straightened. "Might I sign on as cabin boy? I'm very good at serving, sir."

All three laughed.

"Don't 'ave much trouble switchin' loyalties, 'ave ye."

"Ships is all about alike, sir."

"Come along. Got a thing to show ye. 'Sides, the old man's got questions ye may 'ave answers for." He gave her a shove in the right direction.

She stumbled and jogged ahead, her shoe still in her

hand. She would put it back on when she found the time. *So far, so good.* Captain Bricker's God was holding them in continual favor. She almost smiled at herself. Just listen to her! She was talking about his God much the same way he did, as if his God were a very real presence. She almost slowed down, thinking about it: *What if Captain Bricker's God were really a living entity right here on the Java Sea with us? We've gotten this far safely, haven't we?* That was some evidence of His helping hand, at least.

She had no time to think further. She got an additional prod up the quarterdeck steps. Three or four scruffy sorts were lolling against the taffrail, passing a jug amongst them. *Arachne* seemed smaller now in the distance. The captain was right; she was losing ground.

The ugly seaman dragged her up before a man with a blue rose tattooed on his cheek.

"'E says Bricker's dead."

"'E did, now. And 'ow does 'e know that?"
girl. She glanced past the dinghy's davits, not permitting sexton back in Shropshire. He plants 'em all the time."

Ugly chortled. "'E wants a sign on with us."

The tattooed one grunted and grabbed Erica's chin. He twisted her face aside, looking at the dried tear-streaks. "Who wants a crybaby? Not me."

"'M' father might plant 'em, but I don't like 'em all the same, sir. Not sittin' next to 'em as they gets cold, and no daylight." She tried to sulk as a boy would sulk, not as a girl. She glanced past the dinghy's davits, not permitting her eyes to rest long on any one spot. She scanned the array of sabers and belt knives and dirks which ringed her. She certainly had her choice of cutting tools, if only she could grab one.

Tattoo-cheek raised his telescope to his eye. "Reckernize that vessel out there, lad?"

"No, sir. They all look alike. Specially at that distance."

"Hit's y'r own *Arachne* out to rescue the captain. Losin' way. I don' mind sayin', though, that she's a few knots faster'n a bark-rigged vessel like 'er ought be." He turned to Erica. "The lady in my cabin back there claimed to be Mrs. Bricker. That'd be the captain's wife. Be they married all legal-like? The Dutchman'll wanna know."

Erica shrugged. "Don' know, sir. I wasn't ring-bearer at no wedding, is all I know."

There was a general display of merriment, no doubt encouraged by that jug. Erica seemed to be playing it right so far.

"Well, lad, was they bunkin' in the same cabin?"

Now how should she answer that one? She was trying to think of something innocuous and noncommittal that would protect the captain's good name, should it be spread abroad. As it turned out, she didn't need an answer.

Behind them the helmsman yelped. "M' hand's broke!" The great wheel moved all by itself as the fellow exploded with a string of oaths.

The deck tipped starboard high and port low—slowly, gracefully, inexorably. A couple of the seamen, their equilibrium already altered by inebriation, tumbled downhill to the far port railing. The jug shattered against a rail post and two men moaned simultaneously.

Tattoo-cheek was sliding away from her. Erica reached out and snatched the closest hilt at hand, a small saber at his side. She jumped up on the taffrail, surprised that no one thus far had noticed her. She glanced over her shoulder. Those sailors still on their feet had dived for the great wheel. Three or four of them were tugging at it, trying to swing it back aright.

Down at the port railing, at least four men were tumbled together into a tangle of churning arms and legs, all

155

generating an overbearing quantity of foul words.

Erica swung out, hacking at the davit line in front of her. Two swipes parted it. The dinghy's stern dropped from sight. She side-stepped, crablike, downhill along the taffrail. The dinghy hung forlornly by its pointy nose. She slashed out at the remaining line.

The line parted and the dinghy disappeared just as Ugly realized what she was doing. He charged at her with a snarling oath, and Yellow Teeth came boiling up the quarterdeck steps. She swung the saber at Ugly, not really wishing to do him harm. He howled and fell back, but she didn't pause to see what she had done or not done. She took one big step to the top of the taffrail and leapt out into empty air.

She hung suspended in space for an inordinately long time—seconds and seconds, it seemed—before the sea slammed into her. Instantly frigid salty water engulfed her, pierced her clothes and drenched her nose and ears. She remembered now that she had forgotten to take a deep breath. Her nose and eyes burned. She began to kick wildly, furiously, blindly. It occurred to her also that she had never learned how to swim. Her only real experience in water (save for that horrifying night when she escaped the clutches of Abram Sykes) was paddling about in the culvert near the parish. This was not the same thing at all; there was no mucky, gooey, safe bottom to touch.

Erica's view of life from water level was frighteningly different from that just a few inches above waterline. Even when she surfaced she felt submerged. She couldn't get her head far enough out of the water to see properly. She was choking and coughing too hard to kick.

From nowhere—from behind—an iron-hard arm clamped around her neck. Her head was locked back and she was being dragged through the water by forces far stronger than she. She gripped the sleeve for dear life. A gray something loomed just inside her peripheral vision. She reached out, flailing, and grasped a protruding ring. The gray something bobbed on the swell, but seemed otherwise solid. The arm released her and disappeared, so she clung to the ring. A strong hand gripped her back; she could not fall away.

Another spate of coughing partially cleared her lungs.

He was beside her, right beside her. "All right?"

She nodded vigorously and coughed again. "Oh, no! Our boat! It landed butter-side-down! I did it wrong!" She stared at the captain, panic-stricken.

He was grinning. He looked immensely, totally happy with her. "You did it right. In fact, you just achieved the impossible. What did you ever say to those . . ."

Someone from the ship was firing a gun at them. The little boat jerked as slugs struck its other side. Well beyond them, the ship was still arching in a smooth curve to port. Even as she watched, the sails spilled and the ship skidded to a casual halt. Its canvas flapped uselessly as it wallowed.

"Better right this thing before they put a longboat down and come after us. Hold on right there." He slapped the wood.

She gripped the rough wooden gunwale and asked no questions. He worked his way around to somewhere else. Suddenly the wood ripped out of her hands. She grabbed it again, panicky. The boat was bobbing low in the water and right side up.

His voice called, "Climb in over the transom there."

She had no idea whether this was the transom, but this was where he had left her. She hauled herself up, squirmed and wiggled, kicked and tumbled into the boat. It was nearly as full of water as was the ocean. She struggled to sitting on the forward seat.

157

An oar came flying up over the side, then another. She looked toward the pirates' ship. It wallowed, its masts marking huge, lazy arcs. The brigands were indeed lowering a longboat just as the captain feared, but they seemed to be having considerable difficulty. The launch project was not coming along well at all; the longboat jerked about, remaining virtually in place.

The captain's head appeared above the transom; disappeared momentarily; came shooting straight up. He tucked and landed in the bilge. The little boat tipped side to side perilously, its gunwales nearly awash. He came up grinning and plopped onto the center seat. "Frankly, I never dreamt we'd get this far this smoothly."

"Smoothly? Our little boat is nearly at shark level and I almost drowned."

"Minor problems."

"And wasn't this supposed to be the plan?"

"Cooking up an idea as wild as this and actually accomplishing it are two different things. Here. Bail some of this." He pulled his jacket off and folded it roughly. He scooped bilge once in demonstration, and tossed her the coat. He clunked the oars into their locks in one swift motion, dipped one oar deep and pulled with the other. The little boat pivoted in place. He leaned on the oars and started them moving sluggishly away from the pirate ship, toward *Arachne*. He grunted. "A boat full of water hates to move."

Erica scooped madly. She seemed to be making some progress. They had a good three inches of freeboard out there now. They bobbed toward *Arachne,* up swells and down. More gunshots cracked from the ship.

"You asked her name. Did you see a name?"

He shook his head. He was sweating. "No. Apparently they aren't telling."

She paused from bailing, winded, to look back at their kidnappers. The pirates must have abandoned their idea of putting down that longboat, possibly because it now dangled from one davit, useless.

"Stand up and wave my coat. Be careful; don't tip us."

She looked toward *Arachne*. She stood up, teetery, and flung his jacket back and forth joyously. *Arachne* was coming straight toward them under a heavy press of sail. The gleaming canvas billowed bright, drum-taut. Oh my, she was a lovely ship. Erica looked back again. The pirate vessel didn't even have the same colors of canvas in its sails. They were patchworks of white and yellow.

The captain glanced over his shoulder. "They see us. Sit before we capsize."

Erica clung to the rough wooden gunwales, too relieved and happy to do much bailing. *Arachne* was close enough now that she could see the frothy cutwater. Nereids must be scattering in all directions!

Nereids. They were silent out here among the smooth swells. Or were they? As the water drained from her brimming ears, she could hear more than just the loudest noises. The Nereids were here, accompanying this tiny craft as it undulated across their world. She could hear them now as she listened carefully, soft and tender, whispering.

CHAPTER 18

Java Sea, Late afternoon, June 19, 1851

Fisher took in a deep breath of clear and sparkling sea air. *"Una boneeta día, verdad?"*

"Sí. Muy bone-eeta." Gideon seemed to have resigned himself to Fisher's tortured Portuguese-*cum*-Spanish. He only snickered a little at it now and then. In fact the clever lad, almost equally fluent in Spanish, tempered his own good Portuguese to make it sound more like Fisher's fumbling polyglot. This brilliant lad was indeed a pleasure to be responsible for.

Fisher and Gideon walked the length of the lorcha's deck from stern to stem. Fisher scooped the lad up and perched him on the forecastle roof. They were now far enough removed from Oriental ears that they could murmur *sotto voce* in English awhile and actually communicate.

Fisher cuffed the boy affectionately. "Y're doing splendidly, lad. Now listen quick 'ere. We may call at Macassar in the next few days to pick up supplies. Soon as we get anywhere near a dock, y'r to jump ship and disappear."

"What about you?"

"Ye needn't worry about old Fisher. Meself can talk me way clear of any foul weather. Ye just make sure ye escape clean."

"Whatever you say." Gideon sprawled on his stomach to look over the side as the water boiled up around their hull. "The Old Man ever tell you 'bout Nereids, Fisher?"

"I've 'eard of Calypso and 'er lot. 'E's got a book about mythology in 'is quarters, ye know. Ye should read it sometime. Exciting stuff."

"Yeah. Soon's we find him."

"Aye, lad. Soon as we find 'im." Fisher grimaced.

Gideon knew how big the Pacific Ocean was. There was no fooling the lad, no lulling him into thinking everything was hunky-dory. Chances varied from slim to impossible that they could successfully reach New Zealand and the *Arachne*. Gideon knew pirates when he saw them, too, and sensed at least to some extent their present predicament.

Fisher realized that sooner or later he would talk himself into some pickle he could not talk himself back out of. But Gideon's safety and well-being were quite another matter. If Fisher lived or died by virtue of his wits, it was Fisher alone. This innocent child must not die for Fisher's flaws. Responsibility has its limits. Perhaps Fisher ought to bare all to some trusted seaman here and extract from him a promise that Gideon would be spared and given haven. Hwang, the crook, was not the person to approach thus. In fact, in this boatload of crooks there was not one Fisher could begin to trust. He could only hope they would raise Macassar before Hwang became suspicious. Gideon was quick enough to do well if only he could escape.

The afternoon was starting to wane. Fisher noticed that this was the first day that the boy was not excessively tired by this hour. He was waxing stronger. What would he say when he encountered the usurper Eric? No matter just

161

yet—he was nowhere near strong enough to take up his duties. There would be plenty of time for them to work some arrangement. Difficult choice, though—as much as Fisher liked Gideon, he really liked young Eric immensely, also. Eric was bigger than Gideon. Perhaps they could shunt him into some more responsible position.

Fisher smiled at himself. Talk about your optimistic outlook! Here he was making long-range plans concerning Gideon and *Arachne* and Bricker and Eric and—*that's the spirit, Fish, old top! Keep a bright eye to the future!*

One of the lookouts shouted something only the heathen Chinese could understand. Fisher peered at the horizon and saw nothing.

"Alla." Gideon pointed almost dead ahead. Sure enough, a white speck floated on the line twixt sea and sky. They glanced at each other. Both knew the other's thoughts even without words, for they shared the same wish. Might it by some impossible chance be *Arachne?* Fisher knew it couldn't be; *Arachne* was headed east beyond Australia.

Fisher patted Gideon's knee. *"El sitt-o 'ere-o, Chico."* He wandered aft. Here came Hwang with a big brass-bound telescope. "Might I take a peek through that when y're through?"

"With my pleasure." Hwang walked over to the rail, studied the approaching ship briefly, and handed the glass to Fisher.

"Lovely piece. European, eh? German?" Fisher wondered what poor packet the blackguards lifted it from, but would not be tactful to mention such thoughts aloud. Fisher spoke loudly enough for Gideon to hear easily. "I see—ah. Aye, there's a cro'jack. Full rigged. And no colors. Know 'er, Hwang?" Full rigged. It was not a bark—not *Arachne*.

Hwang retrieved his glass and studied the ship further. The question was no longer of interest to Fisher. He had identified who she was not, and that was identification enough. Hwang purred, "Ahhh." Apparently he enjoyed the challenge of identifying random vessels of no consequence. His first mate came wandering up and they exchanged a few words concerning the approaching ship. Hwang handed his glass back to Fisher. "Do you see anything unusual about her?"

"Unusual?" Fisher peered through the glass. " 'Er canvas is brought 'ome fair; mainsail's goose-winged; seems to be making the most of the breeze. I see naething remarkable about 'er. What does y'rself see?"

"Examine her canvas."

"Looks good. Spencer and flying jib look to be sewn up of two different lots of canvas—top's yellowish, bottom's whitish." He lowered the glass, frowning. "Many's the time a sailmaker 'as to stitch together two unlike bolts. That be not so unusual."

"If you inspect that gentleman's sail lockers, you will find his spencers and flying jibs to be of like manufacture."

"That be 'is mark, y'r saying. Ah, then ye do know the vessel."

"The record shows the Norwegian ship *Stavanger* ran aground near Port Moresby, and two weeks afterward the derelict was broken up during a typhoon. That is the record. In truth, she ran aground but her captain and all but two of the crew foolishly abandoned her, thinking her beyond salvage. Her present master used the high storm tides to help lift her free and made her his own. To speak with strictness it was an act of piracy; he dispatched the two crewmen in order to claim her."

"I see. But the captain feared to make an issue of it, lest 'is own poor judgment come to light. So 'e wrote 'er off as lost aground."

"Exactly."

"Then I venture she's seaworthy and then some."

"Her reputation is for speed." Did Hwang's even voice carry a slight tinge of irony, perhaps of bitterness?

"May'ap y've locked 'orns with 'er master."

Hwang frowned, puzzled.

Fisher translated. "Ye've 'ad a fight or two with 'im. Or per'aps a race ye lost."

Hwang chuckled. "Astute, Fisher, and better spoken than you realize. We are rivals, not enemies. But races? Many. He takes great pride in the speed of his ship, and in the fierceness of his crew. He and I are engaged in the same occupation. We pursue the same trade. He considers anyone of Oriental race, ah—" Hwang waved a hand, "beneath his level of excellence; beneath any European's. He feels this particularly so in our mutual field of endeavor, or pursuit of trade." Hwang glanced at Fisher. "On rare occasion, this pursuit transgresses the boundaries of law. I look at it as a necessary risk when reaching for high profits. He considers himself above the law. You see the difference.

"I follow ye. Met a few of them sorts meself, 'oo views the Irish in a similar dim light. And y're itching to do 'im one better, but so far 'is own ship 'as outpaced y'r lorcha. Of which, as ye say, the bloke be insufferably proud."

"Insufferably. One day, rest assured, I shall surpass him. I shall obtain a prize that he might consider his. Perhaps I shall even bring him to his haughty knees, and with no small degree of glee. My men are able, my vessel strong."

The erstwhile *Stavanger* was swift indeed. Already it had approached closely enough that Fisher needed no glass to see details. But he raised the telescope to his eye anyway, just to be certain of what he saw.

"Ah, Hwang. That albatross wasn't just luck for meself. 'Ere may be y'r chance to sail circles around 'er. Looky there, will ye." He pointed.

The distant ship had altered course. She was turning slowly, majestically, to port, veering away from the lorcha. Should she veer just a few degrees more without resetting her sails she'd lose way completely. Aye, and there she went. The canvas luffed and spilled; she wallowed helpless in the swells.

Hwang very nearly smiled. "An unusual maneuver in open sea. You are knowledgeable about such craft. A problem, perhaps?"

"I'd say something in 'er rudder. A steering chain parted, or some pintles sheared. Something of that sort's crippled 'er rudder, prevents 'er from 'olding 'er rudder true."

Hwang nodded. A little half-lift raised the corners of his mouth. He spoke in Chinese and the mate at Fisher's left laughed out loud. Hwang purred, "I believe we shall approach her closely enough to express our condolences. How unfortunate we are in too much the hurry to actually remain at her side and render aid in this time of, of—crisis." He shouted nasal orders to his crew and to the man at the tiller. With hearty good cheer, sailors scurried all over. Apparently the rivalry was not only between captains. The lorcha leaned slightly astarboard.

Gideon came flying down off the forecastle. "Fisher! Look! There's a ship a-chasing, her, Fisher, coming on hard! It's her, too! I just know it's her!" He ran up to Fisher and snatched the glass from his hand. He dashed to the rail and peered through the telescope, his arms nearly too short to manage it. "It's her, Fisher! *Arachne!* I'd know her anywhere!"

Hwang's slanted eyes narrowed to a dangerous squint. "Portuguese?"

"I'm, ah, teaching the lad a bit of English. Right smart little shaver, ain't 'e? Catches on so fast."

Gideon had forgotten everything in the world save the joy

165

of seeing home. "It's her all right. There's the black splash down her foreroyal, where Halloran dropped that bucket of tar!"

A sharp point pricked Fisher's back just above the kidney area. He jumped, startled, then steeled himself. It was the mate's dagger. Instantly another pirate materialized behind him.

Hwang stood just behind his elbow now. "You have not been completely honest with us, Fisher, though we have long suspected as much. Perhaps it is best we discuss right now the true connections between you, this humble lad with the gift for foreign tongues, and the bark *Arachne*."

CHAPTER 19

Early evening, June 19, 1851

The scaling apparatus, a rope ladder, came snaking down the vast, flat black impenetrable, unscalable fortress wall of the ship's flank. Erica stood up and snatched at it. She caught it on the backswing. "Straight up. There you go." The captain was hanging onto a light line as their little dinghy sloshed beside the slippery, towering hull of *Arachne*.

She clambered up the ladder. Half a dozen strong hands grabbed her arms and the seat of her pants and hauled her over the rail. Men were grinning and laughing all around her.

"Here he comes. Easy, lads!"

The captain's head appeared above the rail. He almost fell back, but the gaggle of willing hands dragged him inboard. His feet hit the deck, his knees buckled. For some reason Erica glanced at McGovern, the stoic. The dour Scot's face was twisted in pain concern, as if this were a favorite son rather than a master. The captain straightened and leaned back against the rail. He glanced around. His eyes rested on Erica.

She smiled and waved, an "I'm-fine" sort of gesture.

The captain rubbed his face wearily. "Break out the guns. Maude's still aboard there."

McGovern patted the pistol in his belt. "We're ahead of ye."

"You? With a gun?"

McGovern shrugged. "We were fixing to bring ye off by force of arms if need be. Don't know how ye did it, but we're mightily pleased."

Yes. Erica looked around. They were indeed mightily pleased, every jack here. Travis Bricker was more to them than a mere sailing master.

"It's the Lord's providence and none of our own doing." He inhaled deeply. Even from her distance, Erica could see he was looking better. "Range in closer. It won't take them long to figure how their rudder fouled, but it should take them awhile to right it. We have a few minutes left to work."

"Aye." Mr. McGovern started to turn but Halloran was already off shouting orders and calling to the helm. The first mate peered closely at the side of his captain's head. "Mmph. Found blood at the site, but we were hoping it weren't yours. See we were wrong."

"How did you know to pursue us?"

"Fifteen minutes after ye left, the lady insisted on going ashore to buy cosmetics. By the time I sent DuPres and Lampeter after 'er, she was gone. They found a parcel lying in the street—talcum and foofoo things. And, lo, here's a string of vermilion blotches here and there down the street. Led DuPres straight to the wharf and the very berth. He saw y'r vessel moving out into channel and we were underway and giving chase in no time atall. From the tracks around the fight we knew ye were with 'em, but we didn't realize about young Eric."

"You kept up with her well."

"She's fast, but we've the breeze to our quarter, the lady's best side. Lucky we kept as close as we did."

"Luck, Mr. McGovern?"

The Scot forgot himself and smiled. "Providence. My mistake. But having this particular old girl beneath our feet didn't hurt, ye know. Ah, she loves t' fly! Here's Edward! Splendid. Soon as we saw ye commandeer the dinghy, I sent him to brew coffee." McGovern relieved the towheaded young man of two steaming coffee mugs. He handed one to the captain. "Here ye go. This'll put ye to rights quick enough." He looked all around. "Ah, Eric. There ye be. This one's for y'rself, lad."

Erica crossed and took it, gratefully. "Thank-you, sir!" Though the tropical heat was drying her soaked clothes, it cooled her so quickly she was almost shivering.

"And how did yerself fare in that fight? Did ye get any good licks atall or did ye stand by and watch?"

"Got kicked in the side. I'm fine, sir."

"Strip y'r shirt off there. Let's have a look."

Erica clamped her elbows against her sides so tightly she almost spilled her coffee. "Oh, I'm sure it's fine, sir. Ask the captain. He already—ah—he, uh—questioned me closely about it. I'm fine. Really."

McGovern nodded. "Let one of us know if ye've trouble breathing or if the pain hangs on for days."

The captain's jacket was bobbing about in that dinghy yet, somewhere in the Pacific. His light sweater must have been cooling him off also as it dried. He wrapped both hands around the hot coffee mug. "We heard shooting from both sides. Anyone hurt?"

"Nay, they were loading that deck gun on their forecastle. DuPres managed to squeeze off a couple good ones with your Sharps rifle. Discouraged 'em from hanging around their cannon."

From aloft a lookout called, "That batten-sail craft, sir. She's ranging close in; might be trouble."

The captain frowned, puzzled.

"One of those trim little flat-bottoms the Portuguese built for snuffing pirates."

"A lorcha?"

"Aye, that's it. We spotted 'er some time ago but thought nothing of it." McGovern was peering off beyond the tangle of shrouds beside him. "Arrgh. It's right here among us. Don't smugglers own most of 'em now?"

"Never heard of one in the hands of an honest seaman." The captain leaned out a little, watching it.

Erica strained on tiptoe at the rail beside him. It was a rather pretty little boat if you didn't mind that business about dishonest seamen. Its hull was earthy red; its cabins fore and aft, a cheerful yellow. The little deck house in the middle, somewhat discolored, probably had started out white. She could distinguish faces there. It seemed to be an exclusively Oriental crew.

The captain sipped at his coffee. "Mr. McGovern, we know she's not with us. And if they left Macassar in a hurry, it's doubtful she would be with them. But if she did mean to join them we can't fight two crews to a standstill. Maude may need help, but I won't risk the lives of my own crew to get her out of there."

"We're willing to go after her. Our own decision. In fact we all agreed on it before ever ye came off their vessel. Unanimous."

"I know you're willing, and I appreciate it, but—"

"Your bullhorn, sir?" Edward wedged between Erica and the captain.

Arachne had swung about. They were now broadside the nameless ship and not a hundred yards away. Erica could make out some facial features. Ugly was among them, so she must not have hurt him too badly.

"Very good, Edward. Mr. McGovern, try to keep their vessel between us and the lorcha until we know more about her."

"Aye, sir." McGovern trotted off.

"Edward, I want every free hand aboard to line up along our rail with a gun easily visible. You might mock rifle barrels up with some mop handles, too. We want an impressive show of force."

"Got it, sir!" The towhead grinned and ran off.

Halloran filled the spot Edward vacated before Erica could move back in. "Don't suppose ye'd find this 'andy, sir." He extended the big ungainly Paterson.

"Thank-you, Mr. Halloran." The captain lifted his bullhorn to his mouth. "Ahoy the ship." He separated each word carefully. "Surrender Maude Harrington unharmed and we'll let you go your way. No complaint, no retaliation."

A laugh and some sort of expletive floated across from the crippled ship.

Halloran rubbed his hands together gleefully. "A demonstration, aye, sir?" He turned grinning to Erica. "DuPres's a good sharpshooter, but the Old Man here's better. A joy to watch."

The captain had wedged his coffee mug between two deadeye lanyards by his shoulder. He raised his pistol with both hands. "The swells aren't making this any easier."

His gun blammed and spit smoke. Erica flinched. The ship's port running light exploded in a little burst of red glass. The crew crouched lower behind their gunwale.

Captain Bricker brought his bullhorn up. "Maude Harrington, gentlemen, or I pot-shoot skulls instead of lanterns."

Erica whispered, "Would you really?"

171

"No, but they don't know that. As Paul wrote to Titus, to the pure everything is pure, but the defiled think in defiled ways. They assume I'm cut of the same bolt they are, and they wouldn't hesitate to blow us all out of the water if DuPres would let them get at their cannon."

There he was, quoting Scripture again.

Halloran grinned even wider. "I do believe they're considering it. And that lorcha's hove to. Just sitting there. Wonder what she wants."

"All we can do is wait and watch."

Up and down the rail, half of *Arachne's* crew stood sober and ready, brandishing guns and mop handles of all descriptions.

Erica had some time to think, it would seem. She folded her arms on the rail and rested her chin on them. Item: *The captain's relationship with his crew was most revealing.* He held them in great esteem and they, him. Moreover the captain not only cared about them but trusted them utterly. He trusted his God even more. The men beneath him were trustworthy; it was logical his God was also. Esteem probably followed the same lines.

Item: *I may not know this God personally but the captain very obviously does.* And because he did, it followed that his God was knowable on a personal basis. It further followed—if he could, she could.

Item: *The captain resisted my clumsy advances not because he did not like me—his kiss proved otherwise—but because he did not want to offend his God.* Not once did he mention fear of punishment by some harsh Jehovah. Erica did not doubt that an all-powerful God could wreak whatever havoc He wished on those who displeased Him, but the captain placed fear secondary. Most of all he wanted to please his Lord. This idea was new to her.

Item: *The captain is firmly convinced his God provided*

our way out of the pirates' clutches. He certainly was a better judge of such matters than she. And now that she thought about it, they had indeed achieved the impossible. He had single-handedly crippled their ship. She had successfully fooled a crew of wily connivers long enough to steal a boat out from under their noses. Ridiculous. Impossible. It couldn't happen. Yet here they both stood safe.

She mused awhile over all the little odds and ends of evidence she had picked up since meeting this man, evidences of his relationship with the Almighty. Her mind seemed almost as muddled as the time she had tried to work out the nature of God. But something within her had changed. She was now less concerned with knowing about God and more concerned with knowing God. She knew Joshua, like the captain, had known God. But he had never really asked her about her own convictions and she had never volunteered, lest she spoil her chance to go adventuring.

The man farthest aft called, "They've righted their rudder, sir. It's swinging free to both sides."

The captain raised his gun again and steadied it two-handed against the deadeye by his ear. Hunched low and skulking, the crewmen across the way were moving to their stations.

"She's gonna run for it, sir!"

The captain's gun blammed blue smoke again. Erica knew it was coming, but flinched anyway. Aboard the other ship a voice yelped and a belaying pin shattered at the main fiferail. The line it held swung free.

The captain raised his sights somewhat and squeezed off another one. A heavy block dropped to deck, bringing several lines with it. From somewhere around the forecastle, DuPres's rifle cracked. More fiferail lines fell loose.

"Mr. McGovern! Bring us athwart hawse of her; give her

173

the choice of veering off or ramming us. We'll engage her rigging if we must.''

"What about the lorcha, sir?"

"She hasn't raised a finger to help them so far. Let's take the chance she's neutral and waiting to prey on the victor. They may not—"

A minor cannon blasted. A blue-gray cloud of gunsmoke lifted off the lorcha's deck. From aloft the ship with no name, the far upper fourth of the middle mast creaked. It tipped slowly, with excruciating grace. Casually, languidly, it creaked more and began its topple. Upside down it came, still with that easy grace. It plunged like a sword through the orderly web of lines, parting a few of them, fouling others. It stopped, hopelessly tangled, ten feet above the deck. It bobbed up and down.

A faint voice, barely audible and clearly Irish, came over from beyond the stricken vessel. "Put Maude over the side, laddies, or we bring y'r mizzen down next."

Erica frowned. "That sounds like Fisher."

Mr. McGovern pressed in close beside her. "What's an Irishman doing aboard a batten-sail? They ship with their own, the Chinese."

A flurry of blue appeared near the ship's stern. They were bringing Maude Harrington to the rail.

"Would ye look at that! Shall I block 'em off or give 'em a moment?"

"Give them the moment. But let's make sure that's really Maude and not a Trojan Horse."

A whitish sort of doughnut ring was jammed down over the blue. Suddenly the whole blue billow came flying over the rail. Maude wore lace pantaloons under her crinolines. She hit the water shrieking in strident soprano. Erica recognized a couple of the words as being part of her basic repertoire.

174

The two men spoke simultaneously. "It's Maude."

The captain nodded. "Order arms, gentlemen. We said we'd let them go. Lower a boat and bring her aboard."

Arachne's crewmen made their guns a little less visible—reluctantly, it seemed to Erica. One by one the sails on the other ship—those few with rigging intact—spread and filled. Like an aged old crone, the ship dragged herself forward.

Her master leaned against his taffrail. Erica could make out the blue tattoo only because she knew it was there. His voice was easily audible without a bullhorn. "I'll not forget this, Bricker!" He turned toward the lorcha. "Nor you, Hwang!"

Erica could see a Chinaman aboard the lorcha bow in perfect courtesy. She could also see now why the vessel with no name might consider itself outgunned. Not only were the *Arachne* crewmen well-armed and irate (and demonstrably good shots), the Chinese boat sported two menacing deck guns, both level point-blank on the ship. The struggling vessel was making a little better way now.

Arachne's longboat splacked into the water. Erica peered over the side to watch it. Halloran and another seaman took to the oars. It pulled away toward Maude.

Mr. McGovern gasped, totally startled, totally incredulous. "Captain, do ye ken any Chinese sailors with red hair?"

"Red ha—you don't suppose he managed to—praise the Lord!"

Fisher moved to stand at the lorcha's rail beside her master. A dark head appeared beside him, barely rail high.

"And the bairn," breathed McGovern. "He's got the lad with him. Providence, captain? Nay, a miracle. Nothing short of a miracle. If I was an infidel a minute ago, I'd be a believer now."

Erica stared wide-eyed at Mr. McGovern, and at her captain. It was not just what these two had just said, it was the intensity with which they believed every word. McGovern did indeed acknowledge a miracle. And her captain was indeed praising his God for an abundant providence. Erica remembered vaguely the vicar saying that one must approach God in prayer by first making confession. *General confession: Almighty God, Father of our Lord Jesus Christ, Maker of all things, Judge of all men; We acknowledge and bewail our manifold sins and wickedness, Which we, from time to time most grievously have committed, By thought, word and deed, Against thy Divine Majesty, Provoking most justly thy wrath and indignation against us.* . . . No. This would not do. She could recite the *Book of Common Prayer* end to end, and she had never once thought what she was saying. She must pray sincerely now, not deliver a recitation. Later she would study what she had been saying all these years.

She had all manner of things to confess, but what weighed heaviest was that sinful attempt to seduce the captain, God's faithful servant. What hurt most was that she had so lightly and glibly set out to offend God. She must put that first in her confession; already she vowed to do her best to avoid future offense.

The oarsmen hauled Maude indelicately up over the transom. She sat on the floor of the longboat, a sorry, sagging, soggy blue pile.

The lorcha bobbed in closer. Its two deck guns were now trained upon *Arachne*.

The captain's voice rumbled beside her, strong and steady, reassuring. "If it comes to a firefight, lads, shoot for the gunners on their cannon and stay clear of Fisher and Gideon amidships."

Erica would confess later. Pressed by a vague but insist-

176

ent urgency she simply asked whoever was listening that the God of Abraham, Isaac, Jacob, Joshua Rice and Travis Bricker be her God as well. She would do as His Son Jesus commanded because He wanted her to. And she certainly remembered well enough Jesus's own words, "I am the Way and the Truth and the Life. No one comes to the Father except by Me." Or however that line went. She would try from here on to please God, not in fear of punishment (though knowing full well it lurked as a possibility) but because she wanted to please Him. She would follow her captain's example in that regard. And in her confession, when she got it worked out, she would mention her hard-heartedness. She was sorry about that, too. If it took a miracle to bring her to God, well, that's what it took. Still she should not have been so recalcitrant.

What was involved in this commitment? She did not know yet. But once she set her mind to something, she followed through. She always followed through. The captain would help her. Scripture would help most. She had determined her course now, and she would stay upon it. For some reason she could not fathom, this latest decision pleased her immensely.

The longboat clunked against *Arachne's* flank.

From the lorcha, Fisher called, "Captain! Before ye ship 'er aboard—"

Captain Bricker leaned over the side. "Hold a moment, lads. Aye, Fisher?"

"Captain, Hwang 'ere is considering ye might wish to swap Gideon and me for the fair lass in y'r longboat there."

Maude tilted her head up. The curls, once saucy, were now bedraggled ropes. "You surely wouldn't consider it!"

Fisher called, "She's married, captain. Mrs. Franz Bil-derdijk."

"He's lying!" she snapped. "Can't you see he's lying to

177

save his skin? He has to say that to convince you to trade.''

"No, Miss Harrington," said the captain quietly. "Fisher can prevaricate instantly. He can lie like a barge at anchor. But in this situation he does not—he would not—lie to me.''

Fisher's voice floated in. "She's the mother of three little ones. Got it straight from the Dutchman's mouth.''

"That's not true!" Her voice was rising. "You mustn't believe that lying knave. He'll say anything—anything at all—to get off that stinking boat. You know that. Don't you dare listen to him!''

The captain was looking at her. That was all, just looking. She averted her eyes suddenly and turned on Halloran. "You don't believe him, do you? Please! Don't let them do it!''

The captain's voice was so gentle and sad Erica had to fight the impulse to hold his hand in sympathy. "I'm very sorry, lady. Your marriage is a commitment in which I cannot interfere. Mr. Halloran, make the trade.''

Grimly, sadly, Halloran nodded. The longboat pulled away.

Maude shrieked a string of invectives that turned the air as blue as her soppy dress.

Aboard the lorcha Fisher and Hwang were bowing politely to each other. Fisher appeared to be paying him some money. They bowed again, then shook hands. Fisher laid his arm across the little boy's shoulder. Then they climbed out over the side and hand-over-handed down a light line into Halloran's boat. Fisher tied the rope around the violently resistant Miss Harrington and called "'Aul away, lads.'' By the time Maude's feet touched deck, Halloran was halfway home.

The lorcha's main sail tilted suddenly and caught the breeze just right. Like a dipping petrel she heeled, showed a bit of her flat bottom, and turned on the wind, bound for Singapore.

Erica pitied Maude in a way. *Was she truly married?* If the captain believed Fisher, so would Erica. Still, if Maude felt so very trapped that she would go to these lengths to escape her marriage—whether right or wrong—well, Erica did feel sorry for her. Maude had lost either way.

Halloran's longboat shouldered affectionately against the bulging wall of *Arachne*. Fisher set Gideon on his shoulders and climbed the rope ladder. Eager hands scooped the little boy over the rail; he was smothered instantly in hugs. Grinning and laughing, he greeted each man by name. A precocious lad, this—he seemed not at all intimidated by the noise and attention. Here came even the Chinese cook to greet the prodigals.

She stood back away from the cluster of exuberant well-wishers. She was not a part of this. She was not one of them. Oddly enough, she did not really want to be a part of it. Jealousy? The captain's arms were wrapped around the lad now and the boy was inquiring anxiously about the spectacular marks on the captain's head. Erica, as Eric, had enjoyed exactly that sort of wholesome intimacy. Was she jealous of a scrawny stripling? *Yes.*

McGovern dispatched sailors hither and yon. *Arachne* ceased wallowing as her sails filled one by one. She lurched and pressed forward, under way again.

Fisher overflowed with words. "I thought we were zonkered for sure. But then ye pealed out on y'r bull'orn there, telling the blackguards to 'and over Miss 'Arrington. 'Aha!' cries I to Hwang. 'She's aboard there. 'Elp convince 'em to give 'er up and ye can 'ave the pleasure of turning 'er in for the reward. All yours. What ye say?' And Hwang bought it. So if ye 'adn't used y'r bull'orn, we'd not known Maude was available for the plucking. That Hwang, Captain—'e 'as 'is own set of ethics, but 'e takes great care to follow 'em. A gentleman 'e is—a proper gentleman.''

The captain scooped Gideon into his arms and he and Fisher walked to the stern cabin. Erica fell in behind them.

The verbal torrent flowed relentlessly on. "Soon's we figured Maude was obtainable we worked the swap. The reward for 'er is considerable, ye know. Considerable. Hwang was dee-lighted, I aver. Sez 'e always wanted to pull one out from under that particular rascal. I suspect *Arachne's* guns 'elped considerably in changing the blackguard's mind for 'im. Ye looked formidable there with y'r lineup on the rail. Where did ye get all the extra rifles?''

Erica hopped ahead and held the door for them.

"The mop locker. What's the vessel's name? We should keep an eye out for her.''

"*Stavanger* before she wrecked. She's a salvage; don't know 'er name under 'er present larcenous ownership.''

The captain set Gideon on his feet. "You look like you were pulled through the hawse-pipes feet first. You're overdue for a nap, scamp. You'll have the guest quarters until you're strong enough to take over your duties. Off you go.''

The boy's feet dragged he was so tired. He paused in the doorway to what was once Maude's bailiwick. "Sure good to be home. Thank-you, sir.'' He disappeared inside. The door closed. The bunk ropes creaked.

"Mr. Fisher, give Mr. McGovern a hand, please. We may not raise New Zealand in time to earn that cargo, but we can make a first-class attempt at it.''

"A little extra canvas maybe, sir? Short watches and long rations?''

"See to it, Mr. Fisher.'' The captain smiled. "Glad you're back.''

Fisher left, words still tumbling out of him.

The cabin was stuffy. Erica pulled open the transom windows. The one to port stuck halfway. She wanted the soft air, the cooling breeze. But mostly she wanted to listen. So the cabin boy was back. The ship was functioning fully. They didn't need Erica now. The captain's world was righted; the people he held dear surrounded him again. Did he still need Erica at all? Or was what happened in that oppressive hold merely a product of the moment, of the temptation, of the disorienting effects of his injury? She sat down with her ear by the opened window. Did that bunch of aquatic romantics down there sing any hope for her at all?

. . . AND THE ADVENTURE'S END

A bit later, June 19, 1851

Arachne was stretching out to her full speed now, drawing the most from her canvas. She heeled only slightly aport, charged ahead with power and purpose. Her wake, rather skimpy before, was now a firm, smooth vee. Erica's side ached where she had been kicked. Her backside was still stiff when she flexed the muscles there. And she felt incredibly weary. Her eyelids drooped. She laid her head against the window sash and let the breeze stroke her face. The Nereids were putting her to sleep.

She raised her head. She could feel him standing near her. She could actually feel his presence, a curious sensation. He was simply looking at her, thinking apparently, with his thumbs hooked into the corners of his pockets.

What should she say? She didn't know. Her head grew too heavy. She leaned back against the sash again and watched the rippling wales of their wake. "I'm glad your friends are back safe. The people on this ship fit together and there seems to be something out of joint when you're not all together." She tilted her head around to look at him squarely. "I'm sure I'll be looking for excitement eventually. But I've had quite enough of adventuring for a while. Peace and quiet has an inviting ring to it now."

"Yes, it certainly does." Was the captain at loose ends? He shifted his weight from one foot to the other and folded his arms, a sophisticated adult version of a shy schoolboy called upon to recite. "Maude doesn't have the presence of mind to lay a trail of vermilion powder. Was it you?"

"Yes. But you can see that I wasn't going to pipe up and say so. It would sound as if—I mean—you know."

"I know." Silence. Then: "Uh, how long was your hair before you cut it?"

She twisted a little and held her hand flat near her tailbone. She smiled and shrugged. "It'll grow fast."

"I hope so. The Scripture says a woman's long hair is her glory. If all of it was the color of what you have left, glorious is an understatement."

"Thank-you." She felt her cheeks get warm. Had she thought of him as a schoolboy? Anyone would swear by her behavior that she was still in the little parish grammar school. She came around with her back to the water in order to sit and look up at him comfortably. "Do you know? I didn't find that irritating at all."

"Find what irritating?"

"Your reference to Scripture. It used to annoy me. Religion, religion, religion. I, ah, apparently have had quite a profound change of heart, more so than I had suspected. I hope that doesn't sound maudlin, but—"

"Maudlin! It sounds wonderful!"

"I'm glad you think so. I haven't had time to really sit down and work it out inside my head. I'd like to do that first. Organize a little."

"In other words, you'd rather not talk religion now."

She smiled. "Every time I try to convince myself you're

183

nothing but another of those callous, uncaring men, you surprise me with your sensitivity.''

"I have to sit down." He walked across the room and picked up his favorite chair. He half dragged it over and plunked it down three feet from her. He melted into it. His legs and arms drooped, flaccid, in all directions. His day had been rougher by far than hers. Wouldn't he rather shut himself in his quarters and sleep the next eighteen hours away? She was not about to suggest it. Selfishly, she did not want him to go. She said nothing.

He shifted in his chair and leaned on one elbow. "Forgive my staring. It's not polite, I know. Now that I look at you—I mean, really look at you—I don't understand how I could possibly have mistaken you for a boy. Your face, your form—there's nothing masculine anywhere. Not even a hint.''

She chewed her lip a moment. A small light dawned. "Perhaps it's because you wanted to. A lady you must hold in abeyance. But as a boy I was, ah, more immediate. Talk, joke, act normal, one might say. I mean—there are, you know, things your head thinks about down so deep you don't realize it. Like that vermilion powder business. My head thought it out, but it was two blocks before I realized what I was doing. Do you understand what I mean? Here was a person whose company you enjoyed; and you could enjoy it much more comfortably if that person was a boy. You needn't be so infernally and constantly polite, you see. So guarded.'' She frowned. "Does any of this make sense at all? I'm so tired I can't think clearly.''

"It makes very good sense.''

She was staring past him now, looking at a rain-wet wharf in Singapore at dusk. "That first night, when you brought little Gideon ashore—it was the eyes. I'm certain it was the eyes. They were so large and they said so much.

Not to say the rest of you is not attractive, understand. You see, I had promised myself no more men—to forget men. Enter a convent or something—preferably not a cloistered order, should I wish to take up adventuring again. Men were scum. And then—" She tried to snap her fingers. They wouldn't snap. "There you were. Am I speaking out of turn?"

"What's your feeling about men now?"

"They're still scum, all but one. Only one. With him I could be happy. All the rest can stand by and watch me walk in through the convent gate." She sat up straighter. "Why speak in veiled terms? I refer to you. That first day, when I was still Eric to you—it was so very pleasant, for both of us. Loose and free and open. I beg you, please let us go back to that. If you really try, I'm sure you can treat Eric like—like Eric. I so want to stay on here, to recover that—that—that feeling. It's the thing I want most."

He shook his head. "It would never work. You can't roll time back like that. You might call it a time of innocence. I was ignorant of who you were and you were still innocent of any deep feelings about me. But now I know, and you know, and we can't erase what we know. It's changed, Erica. Permanently."

She sagged back and let her eyes fall shut. They felt hot. She certainly hoped she would not make a fool of herself by weeping or by any other such schoolgirlish behavior. "You're right, I suppose. Still, it destroys the only thing I want."

"Is it the only thing you want?"

She opened her eyes. "I don't know what I want, except to regain that special relationship and hold onto it. You know, where there was no wall of propriety. I don't mean something improper. Not something your God would frown upon." She paused. "Actually, it's our God now, to be

185

more accurate. Anyway, I mean when we—''

''I understand.'' He cut her off. The sun crinkles were starting to crowd together a little. It was not quite a smile, not yet, but his face had a sly twinkle about it. ''When a ship loses way she loses helm. That is, to steer a ship and go where you want to go, you must keep her moving forward. It's an excellent rule of life as well. We can't go back, but we can move forward.''

The door opened at the other end. Mr. McGovern stepped out of sunlight into gloom and crossed to the captain's chair. ''Arrgh. Y're just sitting here. Ye ought to be closeted in y'r quarters, getting some rest. Ye look like death in a thundermug.''

The sun crinkles bunched a little tighter. The expression on his face suggested that he knew something Erica didn't. Erica knew he knew something Mr. McGovern didn't. ''Mr. McGovern, I think I shall make you captain for a day. Two days. No, a week. Captain for a week.''

''I accept the temporary promotion with pleasure, sir. Ye can do nicely with a week's rest. Ye deserve it. Indeed, 'twill take the better part of a fortnight just to rid y'rself completely of that headache, I'll wager.''

The captain was smiling at Erica. Would she ever be able to bring herself to call him Travis? She could not imagine it. He was her captain. He was speaking not to his first mate but to her. ''I believe you know, Eric, that while on the high seas, captains are empowered to perform marriages. But I suggest it would be distasteful, if not illegal, for a captain to officiate his own nuptials. Does that answer your question?''

''Aye, sir. It surely does.''

''Mr. McGovern, pull up a chair and sit down here, please. I have a story for you that will jar your teeth loose and curl your toes.''

Erica found herself grinning so widely her cheeks were getting tired. His proposal was, to say the least, unusual. But then, even that was fitting; this whole relationship was unusual beginning to end. End? Not yet. Beginning. Just beginning. She drew a foot up onto the sill (the one still without a shoe; she could not for the life of her remember when she parted company with her shoe), crossed her arms across her knee, and buried her mouth in the crook of an elbow, lest she accidentally give something away. What she wanted most was to leap up and kiss her captain roundly and extensively, but that, of course, would spoil his grand revelation. And the laughter in his eyes told her he was preparing an absolutely lovely surprise for the dour Scotsman.

Were her eyes laughing, also? He had locked onto them with his own and through them was bespeaking love across the silence. And he was grinning now, irrepressibly. They both reveled in their secret these last few moments before it became common knowledge.

Suspiciously the good Scotsman clunked his chair down nearly between them. "And now what's going on here, ye two magpies? Y're acting like knaves of hearts, the both of ye."

"Mr. McGovern, you'll remember I told you how Eric's sister asked me to consider him—"

She sat back and watched out the open window. The sun perched at such an angle now that their wake danced with white and yellow flecks of brilliant light. Did Nereids wear jewels in their hair? Of course the captain was relinquishing his position for a week. Who wants the burden of command on what is essentially a honeymoon cruise?

His voice was rolling on, nearing the dramatic moment. She listened with one ear. At just the right time she would turn, smile sweetly, and wink at the astonished Mr.

McGovern. You see? They fit together so well they could pull a splendid little prank with no rehearsal. And yes, she could listen to that voice for a lifetime. She waited for the perfect moment, and with her other ear listened to the bubbling wake, the breaking whitecaps, the Nereids' song.

Ransomed Bride

Jane Peart

CHAPTER 1

"PLEASE, CAPTAIN, COULD YOU TELL me where I might get the next stage to Williamsburg?"

Amos Dagliesh, Master of the sailing vessel, the "Galatea" turned his sea-weathered face to his questioner, one of the passengers on the ship whom he had just brought safely across the Atlantic from England to the Virginia colony.

A frown deepened the line between his bristling, brick-red brows as he reluctantly took his attention from overseeing the unloading of cargo to the slender, young woman looking at him with dark, anxious eyes.

He regarded her intently for a moment before answering.

The rose-lined bonnet she was wearing framed a rounded oval face with a porcelain pink complexion. She had a small arched nose with tiny flared nostrils and her parted mouth, rosy and sweet, revealed pearly teeth.

7

He had been curious about her the whole trip. She had been a late arrival, boarding the ship with only an hour to spare before they had sailed. During the long journey she had kept to herself, never mingling with the handful of other passengers. Her ticket identifying her as Miss Dora Carrington, had entitled her to one of the few single cabins and there she had remained, emerging only for meals and a twice-daily walk around the deck.

Their crossing had been fairly smooth, except for a few stormy days midocean. Although several of the passengers had been seasick, the young woman had proved to be a good sailor.

In one rare instance when he had engaged her in conversation, she had told him she was going to relatives in America. Yet there had been no one to meet her when they docked in Yorktown harbor.

Strange! for such an obviously well-born young lady to be traveling such a great distance alone. His frown increased almost to a scowl as he replied.

"You'll have to ask at the Inn, miss," he replied. "You'll find it easy enough—just up the hill from the dock. There's a sign. I'd have one of my men escort you but, as you can see, I cannot spare one just now."

The girl straightened her shoulders and looked in the direction he pointed.

"Oh, I didn't expect assistance, Captain," she said quickly. "Thank you just the same. I'm sure I will find it with no trouble."

A practical Scotsman, Captain Dagliesh was

not a man much given to idle curiosity and yet he found himself following the slim figure of his departing passenger with narrowed, speculative eyes. Though simply dressed, she held herself like a princess, he mused, confident, composed for all her youth. This thought quelled the small prick of conscience he felt in not sending one of his officers to accompany her through the crowded seaport town.

Then some clamor below decks caught his straying attention and he shrugged and resumed his command.

The object of the captain's speculation felt none of the confidence he had attributed to her. As she descended the gangplank, her heart was thudding within her, her pulses racing. Everything about her was new and frightening. She had never seen black people before, and the sight of the dock hands shouting to each other in an unintelligible lingo as they unloaded cargo was terrifying.

The heat of the Virginia sun this spring morning beat down upon her mercilessly as she picked her way carefully through the cluttered dock, holding her wide skirts with one hand while balancing a small wicker reticule with the other.

At the edge of the dock, she paused uncertainly. Accustomed to the cooler English climate, she dabbed daintily at the moisture on her upper lip with a lace-trimmed handkerchief. Then tucking one straying damp curl back under her bonnet, she squinted in the glaring sunlight toward the long hill she must yet climb.

Behind her loomed the tall ship from which she

had just disembarked that for the last six weeks had provided her some small measure of familiarity, security. Ahead lay only an unknown future.

Fighting the tears that threatened, a spontaneous prayer welled up fervently: "O Lord, protect me, lead me, guide me in the way I should go." Her own words—but drawn from her will-learned Scripture. The Psalms had been her sustaining comfort and strength all through this perilous journey.

She bit her lip to keep it from trembling, then shifted her reticule to her other hand and started up the cobblestone street. As she neared the top she saw a rambling, slope-roofed building where a wooden sign swung on a post in front. That must be the Inn where she could obtain the information she needed.

Warm and breathless from the climb, she paused at the top and shielded her eyes against the dazzling sunlight. Looking forward she saw the figure of a stocky man, leaning against the doorframe of the entrance. He glanced up, regarding her curiously as she approached. But his countenance was cheerful, she noted with some relief, and his ruddy-complexioned face seemed kind. Sandy-gray hair was queued carelessly and he was dressed in a homespun shirt, a worn leather vest, stained breeches.

At her question about the stagecoach, he replied jovially. "You're in luck, miss. The stage for Williamsburg will be leaving within the hour. They're hitchin' up the team in my stables just now."

"Could I send someone to fetch my trunk off

the 'Galatea' just docked?'' she asked getting out her little drawstring purse and noting with alarm how light the contents were becoming.

"Shure! I'll send my boy fer it.'' The man extended his hand slyly.

Quickly she handed him a coin, which he took, fingering it and turning it over with narrowed eyes. "And in what name should the boy be askin' for the trunk, miss?''

Thus preoccupied, the innkeeper failed to notice her moment's hesitation.

"The Captain will know. My belongings are in the name of Passenger Dora Carrington,'' she answered quickly. Then to avoid further questions, she asked, "Is there some place I may wait?''

The man nodded toward the door that stood ajar. "Inside, miss. There's the tap room and the keepin' room.''

As she ventured a few steps into the Inn, the sounds of voices raised in raucous laughter assailed her ears. Then the smell of pipe smoke mingled with airless heat, and she instinctively recoiled. The innkeeper looked sheepish for a moment, then giving her shrewd look he pointed to a rough-hewn table and bench to the side of the building under a shady tree. "You could sit over there out of the sun, miss, if you'd like.''

"Oh, yes, thank you,'' she sighed gratefully.

"And might you be likin' something to drink whilst you wait?''

"Some tea, perhaps, thank you.''

He shook his shaggy head, "No, tea, miss. Sorry. Just ale.''

She looked surprised. *Of course! How stupid of me!* she thought. *This is America, not England!* A new country, new customs, a strangely unfamiliar dialect, a different climate! She was terribly thirsty after the long walk in the searing heat. She must have something to cool her parched throat. *If ale it must be*—she mentally shrugged.

But when the tankard of foamy, dark brew was placed on the rustic table and she raised it to her lips, the warm, malty smell almost turned her stomach. Gamely she took a sip, but the bitter taste revolted her. She wrinkled her nose in protest. Setting down the mug, she reached instead into her skirt pocket for one of the last of her lemon drops and popped it into her mouth.

At least it was more comfortable out of the scorching sun; good to sit in the leafy shade of the huge tree, to set down her wicker basket that had become heavier with each step she had taken.

Loosening the satin bow under her chin, she let her bonnet fall back, then raised her head so that the breeze rustling the leaves overhead could blow on her face. With one hand she lifted the bunched ringlets from the nape of her neck, feeling a delightful coolness.

Soon the bustling activity and astonishing sights around the Inn claimed her full attention. On the busy thoroughfare in front, wagons trundled by—some filled with hay, others piled high with produce, still others loaded with braying sheep or squawking chickens. Roughly dressed people milled about, greeting each other or calling to their animals in voices accented with a peculiar soft sibilance quite different from the crisp tones of English country folk. And yet, she had to admit, the entire scene was not unlike that of Market Day in any village at home.

She became as interested in all the proceedings as if she were watching a play, and it was not until she saw the stagecoach rattling around the corner that once more she felt the uneasiness that had become her constant companion since she had ventured out upon this journey.

Unconsciously she murmured her sustaining prayer for protection from the Psalms: "I will trust and not be afraid," and from Isaiah, the comforting reassurance: "I am the Lord thy God, who leadeth thee by the way thou shouldst go."

The coach had now drawn to a stop in front of the Inn, the horses, stamping and snorting and rattling their harnesses while the driver barked orders.

Shortly the innkeeper appeared, followed by a group of prospective passengers. At first glance it seemed that all her fellow-travelers were to be men. But eventually a lone woman, or portly proportions and moving more slowly than the rest, emerged from the Inn, with a younger man in attendance.

From the look of it, most of the male passengers had been refreshing themselves generously while awaiting the arrival of the coach, and there was much jovial bantering among them as the baggage was loaded. The driver, his helper and the innkeeper hefted the pieces onto the top of the coach where they were strapped in an ill-assorted heap.

Disturbed when she did not see her small trunk among them, she left the bench and walked over to join the ragged line forming to board the stage. Anxiously she peered down the steep hill toward the harbor. She could see the mast of the "Galatea," but no sign of the servant the inn-keeper had sent to fetch her trunk.

"Ho there, driver!" called a voice from behind her and, momentarily distracted, she turned to see a tall young man elbowing his way through the crowd. "Say, have you room for one more passenger?"

His voice was deep and pleasant, with the same soft slur in his speech that she had already begun to notice in other conversations.

"If you don't mind riding with me on the box, sir!" the driver shouted back.

"That's the choice seat, I'd say! I'll take it!" came the laughing response. The young fellow looked around, saw that he had an audience and broke into a grin, showing square, white teeth in a tanned face. As his glance swept the circle, it rested on her for a long moment.

As their eyes met she drew in her breath involuntarily. A rushing warmth tingled through her to the tips of her toes, and she hastily lowered her eyes. But not before she had seen the frank admiration in his look and had observed how extraordinarily handsome he was with the sunlight glinting on his bare head.

In that brief glance not a detail had escaped her eye. She had noted russet-brown hair drawn back from a broad forehead and tied in back with a swallow-tailed black ribbon. Obviously feeling the heat, the young man had removed his jacket and slung it over one broad shoulder. The sleeves of a white linen shirt were rolled up from his wrists, exposed bronzed forearms. His legs in buff-colored breeches were long and muscular, and he wore good if well-worn black leather boots.

How big and strong and healthy looking he was! He was a man who obviously spent much time in the saddle and out of doors, she speculated. A farmer's son with the manners and dress of a gentleman? An uncommon combination in England, to be sure, where most gentleman were pale as women and much given to concern for dress and fopperies.

As their eyes had met for that single second, unknown to her, he had experienced a puzzling sensation. It came and went so rapidly he thought he might have imagined it, for it was indefinable—a certain quickening of his senses, as though something quite wonderful was about to happen.

But there was no time for contemplation, for in the next moment the coachman's helper was bellowing to the driver below, "Is that all the baggage, then?"

"'Pears so!" the driver shouted back. "We'd best be on our way."

"No, not quite," the innkeeper retorted, with a jerk of his thumb in her direction. "This young lady's luggage hasn't got up from the ship yet."

At once she was the target of several pairs of

eyes—some impatient, some curious. She twisted her handkerchief in anxiety and stood on tiptoe to peer down the hill. There at last she saw the young boy from the Inn trudging toward them, her small trunk hoisted over his shoulder.

"Miss Carrington's box, sir!" he panted as he heaved it into the innkeeper's arms.

But the handsome latecomer, who was standing nearby, picked it up easily. Turning to her he gave her a rakish smile and arched an eyebrow. "Is this all, *Miss Carrington?*"

Her face flamed. Perhaps he thought himself clever in initiating an introduction, she fumed silently. Yet she was only too aware that his gaze had fallen on the clearly marked brass initials *LEW* atop the hump-backed leather trunk.

She nodded with as much dignity as she could manage, and replied coolly, "Yes, that is all."

Even as she did so, the familiar stirring of panic rose within her. It must indeed seem peculiar for a young woman to have come so far with so few belongings. If he only knew the full truth of the haste with which she had packed, to say nothing of the circumstances under which she had left. . . .

She returned his direct gaze with a tilt of her chin. She had learned in a very short time neither to explain nor to excuse herself. It was by far the safest way. To answer no more than necessary, to give no more information than required, to be reserved without seeming mysterious and thus arousing suspicion. These were the rules of the dangerous game she was playing.

The moment of tension ended abruptly as the

driver climbed up on his box. The horses moved restlessly and the coachman's helper opened the carriage doors.

"All right, folks, let's be on our way!"

"May I assist you?" The young man gave her a little bow and extended his hand with a courtly gesture.

Other passengers waiting to board pressed forward impatiently, so there was nothing to do but to place her small, gloved hand in his large one as she lifted her skirt to take the high step into the coach.

The other woman, already seated by a window had spread her voluminous skirts and was busily arranging them, chattering to her companion.

The window seat on the opposite side was vacant so the girl sat there, gathering her own skirts close as the other passengers pushed in. The interior was unbelievably cramped and stuffy. She put her head out the open window to catch whatever breeze was possible on this early spring, yet summerlike, afternoon.

From the window she saw the intriguing young man swing himself gracefully up to the seat by the driver.

"Better close that, miss," came a sharp, querulous voice from the other female passenger. "Once we get started, the dust will be dreadful!"

Glancing about, she saw that the speaker had pulled a heavy veil over her bonnet, thus protecting her face. Probably an experienced traveler. Since her own knowledge was limited, the girl began trying to pull the window shut. But it stuck stubbornly.

As she struggled an oily, masculine voice beside her suggested, "Allow me." And a hand reached past her to yank it closed.

She drew away instantly, recoiling from the aroma of cheap cologne combined with strong drink. Allowing herself a sidelong glance at her fellow passenger, she saw that the man was dressed in the flashy, shoddy style of a commercial traveler. His face was barely inches from her own when a sly smile parted his lips, revealing two rows of badly discolored teeth. She prayed the trip to Williamsburg would be a short one!

After accomplishing his task the fellow must have felt he had earned the right to initiate conversation, for he inquired, "Will you be visiting in Williamsburg long?"

In a low tone she answered in well-rehearsed words, "I am recently bereaved, sir. If you will pardon me, I am not inclined to converse." Delivered in a firm voice, this reply usually discouraged further attempts at discourse, she had learned.

It had the very same effect now, she noted with relief. In the enforced intimacy of the crowded carriage, all the other passengers could not fail to hear both question and answer, and an immediate silence descended.

Of course, in a way it was true, she rationalized. Even though her father had been dead these three years, she still keenly felt his loss. She felt a twinge of sadness now, remembering how close they had been. Much closer than she had ever felt to her mother, she recalled with a certain wistfulness.

If her father had not died, everything would have been quite different. Certainly she would not be making this terrifying journey, not be alone in this foreign land, thrust among strangers! She closed her eyes momentarily, fortifying herself with the promise of the Psalmist: "The Lord watches over strangers; He keeps the fatherless. . . ." *I must believe that,* she reminded herself. *It is all I have.*

Shortly afterward, they heard the shouts of the driver, urging his team forward. There was a sudden lurch, which sent all the passengers lunging against one another. Then, with a few more jolts, the heavily laden coach began moving and pulled away from the curved apron in front of the Inn. Within a few minutes more, they were clopping through the Yorktown streets, toward the outskirts of town.

Thus spared any more questions from the curious, she settled back against the ill-padded seat and looked out the window, absorbing the scenery.

Only a few miles out of Yorktown the vista changed abruptly. Every vestige of civilization seemed to have been left behind. The countryside, while spectacularly beautiful, was almost frightening in its wildness. The forest appeared to have swallowed all but the narrow strip of road upon which they were traveling, and there was not a sign of a house anywhere. She felt a momentary shudder ripple down her spine.

Well, at least she was on the last lap of her long journey, she sighed, with an inner release of tension. To this point everything had gone well, with no mishaps. There were still hurdles ahead, of course—perhaps the most important ones. But the imminent danger of being apprehended had passed.

The crucial test was awaiting her in Williamsburg, she knew, but she had had time to prepare. On board ship, through the long days and nights at sea, she had done little else but practice. Now her role was letter-perfect, her lines memorized, her performance polished.

Still she knew she must be cautious, take no small detail for granted. It would be so very easy to make the fatal slip that would betray her daring charade. For a moment her pulses pounded erratically. Gradually, however, her weary body, deprived of rest by sleepless nights and hours of anxious anticipation, was lulled by the swaying motion of the carriage, and she slept.

Later—how much later she could not be sure—she was awakened by a restless stirring within the coach and a sense of rising excitement on the part of her fellow passengers.

"We're coming into Williamsburg!"

Already the coach had slowed and the horses' hooves beat out a measured cadence as they made their way through the heart of town. She sat up, blinking, a curious mix of emotions churning within. Pressing her face against the window, she looked out.

Williamsburg! What a busy, active place, pulsating with commerce and with its medley of wagons, carriages, and pedestrians. The town appeared to be as thriving as any market town in Britain, with well-kept shops bearing brightly painted signs declaring their owners to be apothecaries, barbers, wigmakers, milliners. There were bakeries, too, and chandleries, liveries, and leather goods stores.

The coach finally came to a jarring stop in front of a handsome building, The Raleigh Tavern. Some of the carriages were as elegant an any she had seen on the streets of London, and the people as stylishly dressed. She had heard the Colonies spoken of disparagingly by some people she knew, like the Fairchilds, and the Headmistress at school, and some of her mother's friends. But, surely, they had never visited this splendid town, or they would have known otherwise.

"Duke of Gloucester Street!" someone called, and she saw they were entering a tree-lined street of fine brick houses surrounded by trimly clipped hedges and flowering gardens.

Suddenly her throat went dry. She was here at last! The end of her long journey, undertaken in reckless haste. The next few hours would decide her fate.

CHAPTER 2

HEART HAMMERING WILDLY within her breast, she alighted from the coach and looked about as if in a daze.

"Will it be possible to obtain lodgings here?" she overheard one of the passengers inquire of a servant who was helping unload luggage.

"Can't be sure, sir. Some of the Burgesses are coming into town early for the opening of the Assembly. You'll have to ask inside."

Indeed, the Tavern seemed to be a hub of activity. She watched a constant flow of prosperous-looking gentlemen arrive, descend from fine carriages, then, deep in animated conversations, enter the doorway over which was mounted a lead bust of the illustrious Sir Walter for whom the establishment was named.

Most of her fellow passengers had already joined the throng mounting the steps into the Raleigh and were off in search of refreshment or

23

a night's lodging. Waiting for her trunk to be brought down, she stood uncertainly, wondering what she should do next.

The young man who had assisted her earlier swung down from his place beside the driver and gave her an appraising glance. He paused for a moment as if debating whether or not to speak. Then, as if thinking better of it, gave her a sweeping bow, put his tricorne on his head and went whistling down the street. She had heard him tell the coachman he was going to get his own horse, stabled at the livery while he had been in Yorktown.

"This yours, miss?"

She turned to see the driver holding her small trunk.

"Yes."

"Should I carry it in yonder?"

"Might I leave it with you until I can send someone for it later?" she asked hesitantly.

"Yes, miss," he nodded and thrust forward an outstretched palm. "There's a keepin' fee, o' course."

"Of course," she murmured and opened her purse, hoping the fellow was honest and would not pocket it for himself. There was no way but to give him a coin, further diminishing her meager nest egg. She certainly could not lug the trunk with her on her mission.

"It will be safe 'til you call for it, miss," he assured her with a beaming smile, and she wondered if she'd overpaid him. Ah, well, it couldn't be helped. In the whole scheme of things, it made little difference. What mattered was what kind of reception would be hers when she made her contact.

The afternoon shadows were lengthening as she started down the shady street toward the neighborhood to which she had been directed. The pleasant, tidy look of it seemed oddly familiar—perhaps because it had been described to her so often. She walked slowly, glancing from one side of the road to the other. The houses, were painted white or yellow or blue, with slanting roofs and dormer windows, shuttered in contrasting colors. Brightly blooming gardens flourished behind neat picket fences or boxwood hedges.

Then, quite suddenly, she saw it. She would have known it anywhere, she thought with a little catch of breath. Would have recognized it from a hundred dreams. She moved closer, read the little lettered sign on the gate, THE BARN-WELLS, and a rush of tears stung her eyes.

With her hand on the gate latch, the panic she had known in small, frantic moments all day clutched her now. This was the time of decision—to turn back or to take her chances.

She took time to still her quavering heart, to breathe a silent prayer, "Be with me now, Lord. I need Thee more than ever!"

Remembering what awaited her in England if she faltered now, she lifted the latch resolutely, pushed open the gate, and walked up the flagstone path to the house. At the fan-lighted front door she paused once again. Then with a trembling hand, she raised the polished brass knocker and let it fall twice.

Behind it she heard the sound of footsteps, the rustle of skirts on a polished floor. Then the door opened and a handsome, rosy-cheeked lady with silver curls escaping a ruffled cap, stood before her. She was plump and dressed in lavender silk with a frothy lace fichu and ruffled sleeves. Snapping blue eyes sharply regarded the pretty young woman on her doorstep, taking in every detail of the stranger's gray, pink-lined bonnet, the plain, but stylish merino traveling dress and pelisse. A puzzled frown puckered her smooth forehead, for she knew almost everyone in Williamsburg and she had never seen this girl before.

"Yes?" she asked briskly.

Overcome with nervousness the girl's mouth went dry.

"Yes, my dear?" the woman repeated more gently, seeing the visitor's evident distress. "May I help you in some way?"

With great effort the girl, swallowing hard, cleared her throat, "A–are you the lady of the house?"

"I'm Elizabeth Barnwell," she nodded.

"I–I am Lorabeth. Lorabeth Whitaker. Winnie's daughter. *Your* granddaughter."

There was a moment of stunned silence. Then a startled intake of breath, followed by a cry of "Oh, my word! It can't be! And yes! Yes, I do believe—oh, my dear! However did you get here?" Betsy Barnwell took a step backward, "Laura!" she called "Laura, come here at once!" Then she held out her arms to the girl still standing at the door. "My very dear child! Come in, come in!"

26

With that she was caught to Betsy's soft bosom, enveloped in the delightfully intriguing fragrance of rose sachet, starch and fresh linen. She was hugged hard. Then Betsy gently held her at arm's length and cocked her head.

"Let me look at you! My, how pretty you are! But you don't look a bit like Winnie! Oh, dear me, what a shock—but what a lovely surprise. I must hear everything—how you came, when, and all about it. How is your dear mother? We hardly ever hear from her!" Her arm about Lorabeth's waist, Betsy led her farther into the wide, center hall. As she did, she called, "Laura! Come at once! You'll never guess!" She shook her head, her curls bobbing. "But Winnie was never much for letter writing. Oh, my dear girl, I cannot tell you how I've longed to see my granddaughter all these years. We kept hoping Winnie would come home for a visit and bring you but—Laura! See here! Winnie's own child, all the way from England!"

A rustle of taffeta along the hallway and the slim figure of another woman came hurrying forward toward them.

"It's Lorabeth, Winnie's little daughter!" Betsy exclaimed.

The lovely woman, her blond hair silvered at the temples held out both hands and smilingly greeted Lorabeth. In the flurry of excitement, of explanations and delighted laughter, the three of them interrupted each other with fragments of sentences and startled gasps.

"We're just about to have tea, my dear. And you must be exhausted after such a journey.

Let's go in and you'll tell us all about it," Laura said, still holding one of Lorabeth's hands as she drew her into the parlor.

The room into which Betsy Barnwell led Lorabeth was bright with late afternoon sunshine. She had the impression of quiet elegance—pale blue walls, masses of fresh flowers, graceful polished furniture. Over the white-panneled fireplace hung a portrait of a bewigged, portly, rosy-cheeked gentleman.

Betsy took a seat on a small, high-backed sofa covered in floral needlepoint and patted the cushion beside her as she beckoned Lorabeth to sit beside her.

"While your Aunt Laura goes to fetch another cup and tell Essie to brew more tea, we'll have a nice catching-up chat. Mercy! I can still scarcely believe you're really here. You don't know how we've conjectured about you, my dear, wondering what you looked like and—Winnie never so much as sent a miniature!" Betsy sighed. She shook her head in exasperation. "But, that's Winnie. . . ." Her voice trailed away significantly. Then she placed her hand over Lorabeth's. "But enough of that. Let's talk about *you*, my dear!"

Betsy paused to take a breath while regarding Lorabeth with rather puzzled scrutiny.

"There's not a bit of family resemblance that I can see! Winnie was fair, of course, but the features—take off your bonnet, dear," Betsy directed.

Obediently Lorabeth untied the ribbons under her chin, let her shovel bonnet fall back and put up one fragile hand to smooth her pale blond hair.

"Now, I want to know how it is you came to travel all this way alone? The last we heard from your mother, you were off at boarding school and she had taken a position as housekeeper to some fine family in the country after your father died— the Fairchilds of Kent, wasn't it?"

Just then Aunt Laura came back into the room, followed by a black woman wearing a blue, stiffly starched apron, bright calico dress, and white turban. The woman was carrying a tray, which she set on the round table behind which Laura had seated herself. Then she turned a frankly curious gaze on Lorabeth.

"Essie," Betsy addressed her, "can you believe this pretty child is Miss Winnie's daughter, all the way from England?"

Essie grinned at Lorabeth and bobbed a curtsy. "Pleased to meet ya, Missy. No'm," she shook her head. "She sure doan 'semble her mama, do she? But she maghty pretty jes' the same.''

Lorabeth smiled and murmured a polite "Thank you." But she was greatly surprised by the display of familiarity between mistress and servant. Certainly this friendly interchange would not have been countenanced in the Fairchild household where even the housekeeper was treated with haughty condescension. And in their own small cottage, Mama ordered about their little maid of all work, Lilly, without a thought for her opinions. How different it was here in the Colonies, Lorabeth mused.

"Here, dear." Aunt Laura handed Lorabeth

29

one of the eggshell thin cups into which she had poured the fragrant, steaming tea, then said to her mother. "Now, Mama, let us allow Lorabeth to have her tea in peace, not ply her with questions. She must be tired from her trip—and hungry, too."

"Quite right, my dear," Betsy agreed, and after urging Lorabeth to help herself to the plentiful delicacies, she turned her attention to her own tea and well-filled plate.

As Lorabeth sipped the deliciously hot, aromatic tea, she felt its gentle stimulation gradually penetrate her lightheadedness and the feeling of dread that had oppressed her since entering the Barnwell house. The fear of being rejected had been quickly dispelled by the warmth of her welcome and the cordial atmosphere.

When she tasted the spicy nutbread and freshly churned sweet butter, she realized how hungry she was. She had had nothing since the ship's breakfast of hardtack and watery tea. During the last two weeks aboard the "Galatea," the meals had become monotonous repetitions. Slowly Lorabeth's healthy appetite and good spirits revived.

Soon the irrepressible Betsy's curiosity reasserted itself and she resumed her questioning.

"It is still hard for me to believe you are really here, Lorabeth. It has long been my desire to have you for an extended visit. In fact, I wrote your mother several times to allow you to come to us—after your father's death, for instance." She paused for a moment to replenish Lorabeth's plate with strawberries the size of small plums, then hurried on, "I'm sure things weren't easy for Winnie or for you, either, after your father's untimely death. The house the school provided for the headmaster had to be given up for his replacement, your mother said in one of her infrequent letters. So, at that time, I strongly urged her to come back to Virginia—make her home here with us! But . . ." Again Betsy shook her head sorrowfully.

"Mother!" Aunt Laura admonished gently, as if to warn her to abandon this line of conversation.

But Betsy ignored her. "Why didn't your mother come with you?" she persisted.

"She has a very responsible position with the Fairchilds, Grandmother. They depend on her. Especially since old Mr. Fairchild's stroke—"

"But why ever did she allow you to come so far alone?"

This was the moment, above all others, that Lorabeth had most dreaded—to be confronted with the reason she had undertaken this journey alone. In the class of society to which the Barnwells belonged, such a thing was rarely done and then only under the most severe of circumstances.

Even though Lorabeth had rehearsed her reply dozens of times, as she looked into those blue eyes gazing at her with such affectionate concern, her throat constricted painfully. Her face felt hot, her hands grew clammy, and she was suddenly tongue-tied.

It was Aunt Laura who rescued her—at least temporarily—for she rose and chided her mother

31

laughingly. "Mother, dear, isn't it enough that Lorabeth is here! No matter how or why! Let us give her a reprieve from all these questions.

"I'm sure Lorabeth would like to go up to her room, Mama, and freshen up, perhaps even lie down for a rest before dinner." Turning to Lorabeth, she said, "We'll send our boy, Thaddeus, to the Raleigh for your trunk right away."

"That's very kind. If you're certain I'll be no trouble—"

"Trouble!" exclaimed Betsy, thoroughly shocked. "*Trouble? my own granddaughter*, my own flesh and blood, under my roof for the first time, *trouble!* I should say not! A *pleasure*, my dear child! An undreamed of pleasure! Now you go along. Laura will take you upstairs to the room your own dear mama had when she was a girl. We'll have plenty of opportunity to visit, for I intend to keep you for a long time!"

Lorabeth followed Aunt Laura out to the hallway and up the curved stairs to the second floor. At the end of the upstairs hall Laura opened the door to an airy, spacious room.

"Here you are, dear. Essie will bring up hot water and clean towels later. Why don't you lie down and try to get a little nap. We don't dine until eight. And I'm afraid Mama has quite worn you out with all her questions. Don't let it bother you. She is so delighted you're here, as am I. We'll probably both spoil you!" she said with a light laugh. Then kissing Lorabeth on both cheeks she went out, closing the door quietly behind her.

Lorabeth let out the breath that she had been

holding unconsciously in a long sigh of relief. She had managed to evade her Grandmother's direct question for now, but she knew there would be a time when she could no longer avoid giving the answer she had prepared so carefully. Her reprieve was only temporary. Inevitably would come the day of reckoning.

Lorabeth moved like one in a trance to the middle of the room and looked around. Everything was so bright, so fresh and delightful. Crisp, flowered chintz flounces on the tester of the four-poster bed matched the deep dust-ruffle along the bottom; a white crocheted coverlet and white muslin curtains at the windows accentuated the airiness. A high armoire and kidney-shaped dressing table were of mellow golden maple. There was a wing-chair and stool opposite a little writing desk on either side of the fireplace; on the washstand, a bowl and pitcher of rose-painted China.

It was all very different from the surroundings in which she usually found herself. She had grown up in an underpaid Headmaster's house, furnished with cast-offs and without color or taste. At boarding school the rooms for "scholarship girls" were as bare as monk's cells, with a narrow single bed, washstand, study desk and chair.

Suddenly Lorabeth began to tremble. Her knees felt wobbly and she sat down shakily on the small fiddle-back chair next to the door. She clasped her arms around her slight frame, shivering as if from cold. She had not realized how tightly wound every nerve had been until now, when she could not seem to stop their quivering.

She glanced around her almost warily. It was true. She was here. She had got this far without a slip. No one had seemed suspicious, manifesting only a natural curiosity occasioned by the strange circumstances of her unexpected arrival. These lovely people—her very own kin—had accepted her easily and simply, with a warmth she had never before experienced.

Wearily Lorabeth closed her eyes.

In spite of all she had endured, she told herself, the long journey to Virginia had been worth the risk. And, whatever the cost, she meant to stay.

CHAPTER 3

UPON COMING DOWN TO DINNER that evening, Lorabeth was surprised to see that both Betsy and Laura were elegantly gowned. Virginians, it appeared, enjoyed a more gracious way of life than did the same social class in England, for both ladies had changed from their daytime frocks into more formal attire. In comparison to Betsy's mauve taffeta and Laura's lilac silk, her own simple blue merino, though trimmed with fluted linen and edged with cotton lace, seemed almost Quaker-plain.

Caught up in the charming customs of her relatives and the comparative grandeur of her surroundings, Lorabeth did not fret long.

At first she wondered if the ladies might have been expecting company, but when they entered the dining room, softly aglow with candlelight, she saw that the table was set for only three. Lorabeth glanced around with pleasure. The sheen of silver, the gleaming china, the center-piece of fresh yellow daffodils all satisfied her inner yearning and appreciation of beauty.

Everything was new and interesting. Even the dishes served were an intriguing experience— especially the assortment of vegetables that Betsy told her were grown in their own garden and the fluffy mounds of rice that she had never tasted before. The succulent chicken and hot breads, too, were expertly prepared and Lorabeth ate heartily.

Thankfully she was not plied with too many questions during dinner; certainly, none requiring careful answers. There seemed to be an unspoken agreement that she should not be taxed on this, her first night in Williamsburg.

Lorabeth found herself relaxing in the gentle atmosphere. This house, like all others, reflected the people who lived there, she decided. She had felt the coldness in the Fairchilds' huge mansion, the bitter melancholy that haunted the little house she shared with her mother after her father's death. Even when they had lived at the Headmaster's house while he was still alive, there had been an indefinable air of tension. Perhaps it had been her mother's constant complaints and dissatisfaction that was the cause or, to be charitable, the reverse.

But here the environment was one of serenity and cheerful order. Undoubtedly Betsy's benevolent personality and Laura's sweet spirit were responsible for the aura.

Studying Laura with her lovely cameolike features, the masses of silvery blond hair, Lorabeth wondered why she still lived at home, why she had never married. Was there some secret sorrow in her past?

As she listened to the two older women softly conversing about friends and local happenings, Lorabeth recalled once again that, back home in England, she had often heard Virginia referred to as an "untamed wilderness of rogues and ruffians." Certainly this description did not take into account the culture and refinement she had found, carved out of that wilderness. Strangely even her mother, although born and reared here, had never spoken in defense of her homeland.

Just as dessert, a cool lemon sorbet, was being served, there was a loud rap at the front door. Before anyone could answer its summons, the door swung open, admitting someone with a brisk stride and a hearty greeting.

"Anyone home?"

At the sound of that resonant male voice, Betsy and Laura exchanged a smile and a knowing look.

"Cameron!" exclaimed Betsy. Winking at Lorabeth, she put a finger to her lips. "Come in, dear. We're just finishing dinner."

Lorabeth's back was to the entrance of the dining room so she could not see who now stood in the doorway. But for some reason she felt a pang of alarm.

"Sorry if I startled you, Auntie B. And my apologies for barging in like this without an invitation—especially now I see you have company. But I've come to beg pity! I find myself stranded in Williamsburg too late to start back for Montclair. May I stay the night?"

37

"Too long lingering at Raleigh Tavern, I've no doubt!" Betsy retorted with mock severity. "And of course you never need an invitation here, dear boy. Come—do sit down. I'll have Essie bring another plate. And I want you to see *our* surprise!"

To Lorabeth she said, "My dear, this young rascal is Cameron Montrose." Lorabeth inclined her head slightly as a tall figure strode to the opposite side of the table and made a gallant bow.

When she saw him, she very nearly fainted! It was the same young man who had made the trip on the coach from Yorktown that morning—the one who had boarded late and had ridden beside the driver all the way to Williamsburg.

Her heart leapt into her throat and remained there, pounding violently, preventing her from swallowing or speaking. Her fingertips gripped the edge of the table.

"Cameron, meet your cousin, Lorabeth Whitaker," Betsy said triumphantly.

The young man's eyes widened, one eyebrow lifted.

With a sinking heart, her stomach knotted tightly, Lorabeth remembered he had heard her addressed as "Miss Carrington" when her trunk was brought up from the ship.

Would he expose her? Demand to know why she had traveled under an assumed name? To know what she was doing here under his relatives' roof?

"This is your Aunt Winnifred's daughter," Betsy continued.

Cameron bowed, a smile tugging at the corners of his mouth.

"My pleasure, *Cousin* Lorabeth," he said. Then, turning to Betsy, he remarked archly, "This must have come as a great surprise, Auntie B."

"Indeed it was!" Betsy chuckled. "A far pleasanter surprise than the one her mother gave us twenty years ago!"

Cameron pulled out a chair and sat down, not taking his eyes from Lorabeth's pale face.

"Ah, yes! Runaway Winnie!" He looked directly across at Lorabeth. "Of course, you probably know that if things had been different, she might have been my mother. Or at least my father's bride. What strange turns life takes, wouldn't you agree—*cousin?*"

Were his eyes twinkling mischievously or was there a hidden threat in their depths? Lorabeth wondered frantically.

"Ring for Essie, Laura, dear. Cameron needs to be fed," Betsy suggested, looking at her great-nephew solicitously.

Laura lifted the silver bell by her glass and gave it a jangle. Essie appeared as if by magic, bearing a plate heaped with chicken, rice, and vegetables, and placed it with a smile before Cameron.

It was clear he was a favorite with both servants and mistresses of the house.

"So, now, Cameron, Betsy beamed at him fondly, tell us what brings you to Williamsburg and all the events of your day. Knowing *you,* I've no doubt it has been filled with adventure and interesting encounters."

"Intriguing adventure, unexpected encounters! Ah, yes, Auntie B., my day was certainly filled with those. And surprises as well. None nicer, I might add, than finding I've a cousin I've never met!"

He gave Lorabeth a knowing glance that sent a stiletto of fear into her heart. She twisted her napkin nervously. What if he should recount having seen her in Yorktown, the initials on her trunk conflicting with the name to which she had replied?

But her worst fears were not realized. Cameron led the conversation to those of people she did not know and of a place called "Montclair." It soon became clear he had no intention of bringing up the fact of their earlier meeting or its puzzling circumstances.

She was aware, however, that his eyes rested often upon her, although with a studied casualness. Whenever his gaze met her own, her breathing became shallow and her pulses throbbed. It would be disastrous if she should be found out now—after all she had been through.

In spite of the sustained tension of the long day, when the conversation turned to topics that did not concern Lorabeth, she felt herself growing drowsy, and her eyelids began to droop. It was Aunt Laura who noticed her weariness and immediately suggested she be excused.

"It's been a very exhausting day for Lorabeth," she said in explanation to Cameron as she rose and went to Lorabeth's side, placing her hand gently on her shoulder.

Cameron also got to his feet. Bowing slightly

from the waist, he said, "Welcome to Williamsburg and to Virginia, cousin. I hope soon we can also welcome you at Montclair. I'm sure my mother will send a message to that effect as soon as she knows of your presence here."

"Yes, indeed. We must have a real reunion!" declared Betsy, bobbing her head in agreement. "Now, run along with Laura, child, and get a good night's sleep. There will be plenty of time later for visiting and getting to know one another."

Laura lighted her candle and accompanied her to the foot of the stairway. Then, leaning her soft cheek against Lorabeth's, bid her "sweet dreams."

Lorabeth accepted the candle in its brass holder and slowly mounted the steps. At the bend of the staircase, she looked back. Through the dining room door, she could see the three still seated at the table, and the low murmur of their voices and the muted sound of laughter floated up to her. A feeling of melancholy touched her. To belong to such a family would be a very special thing, she thought.

Once in her room she took the candle to the bedside table and began to undress. Her movements were slow and stiff; her limbs, weighted by fatigue. She was much too tired to think through the events of the day. For now they remained a muddle, fraught with anxiety and excitement and, yes, with fear.

She could still scarcely believe she was actually in Virginia, in the Barnwell house—welcome, accepted, safe! She looked now at the bed, draped with mosquito netting. Someone had turned down the coverlet, and it beckoned invitingly.

Lorabeth had never been pampered in her life, and now the tenderness with which she was being received brought tears to her eyes. Suddenly she was overwhelmed at the thought of providential protection through all the events of her life that had brought her to this moment, and she sank to her knees beside the high tester bed.

She had already taken her worn little Bible from her trunk. Now she opened it to the Psalms and, by the light of the flickering candle, she read from the 138th: "In the day when I cried thou answeredst me, and strengthenedst me with strength in my soul. . . . Though I walk in the midst of trouble, thou wilt protect me. . . . The Lord will perfect that which concerneth me."

Yes, in the time of her need, He had cared for her, had made the rough way smooth, had opened doors and lighted her path. Surely His goodness and mercy had followed her here to Virginia.

"And the Lord shall fulfill his purpose for thee."

Lorabeth believed that with all her heart, and clung to that truth. He would not have let her come so far only to have to return to the horror she had left behind.

It would be all right. Things had a way of working out. In a few days she would talk to Betsy, tell her the whole story, seek her advice, her help. . . .

Lorabeth lay long awake that night in the room

that had belonged to her mother. The worst was over, she told herself. The panicky trip from school, boarding the big ship, the long and frightening ocean voyage, the journey from Yorktown to Williamsburg, her meeting with Betsy and Laura—all had gone remarkably well. All except the unexpected appearance of Cameron Montrose and the information that the handsome stranger was her *cousin!*

Ever since she had first set eyes upon him, everything about him had fascinated her—his long-legged height, his Virginia drawl, his slow, enigmatic smile, easy-going manner and his laugh, so spontaneous, so joyful. There was a reckless vigor about him. She had never known anyone who radiated such a love of life, such energy and enthusiasm.

But she was afraid. What was Cameron really thinking? What did he intend to do?

Perhaps he had already told Betsy and Laura about their meeting earlier in Yorktown when she had been called *"Miss Carrington!"* No, somehow, Lorabeth did not think he had. He could easily have betrayed her when Betsy had introduced her as "Lorabeth Whitaker." There was no reason for him to keep silent. Yet he had. Maybe for reasons of his *own,* he had remained silent.

Whatever those reasons Lorabeth recalled with a sudden breathlessness that, in that very first glance that had passed between them in Yorktown that morning, there had been an instant of something akin to *recognition!* A shock had passed like lightning through her very being

43

when those deep-set blue eyes caught and held hers. She had seen a glimmer of that same look again this evening as those eyes had sought hers again and again during dinner.

Was she mistaken? Could it be only her imagination? Or was there something real, if inscrutable, in those glances? More than curiosity? More than a natural interest of a young man for a pretty girl? It seemed to her, even in that first moment, there had been either a challenge— or a promise.

Had he felt it, too? Was Cameron Montrose as inexplicably drawn to her as she was to him?

CHAPTER 4

ON HER FIRST MORNING IN WILLIAMSBURG Lorabeth was awakened by Essie, bringing her a tray of tea and biscuits and reminding her that it was Sunday and that her Grandmother expected her to accompany them to church.

It was tempting to linger a little longer in the lavender-scented sheets among the soft, smooth linen pillows, but Lorabeth did not give in to the inclination. She washed and dressed quickly, and hurried downstairs.

Her grandmother and Aunt Laura were having second cups of tea when Lorabeth made her entrance into the sunny dining room. Cameron was just helping himself to a generous portion of ham slices and eggs at the massive mahogany buffet, where there were covered dishes of hot breads as well as a crystal bowl of fresh fruit.

They all turned smiling faces in her direction, asked her how she had slept, and urged her to eat a hearty breakfast.

"Church services are at eleven, Lorabeth, so there's no need to rush," Betsy said, jerking her head toward Cameron's tall figure, she scolded the feigned disapproval, "Cameron, naughty boy, is not attending with us. Says he has to get started back to Montclair right away."

"It's true, Aunt B. You know it's a hard day's ride to Montclair, and if I don't leave soon, it will be nightfall before I reach home. And with the news I have to tell once I get there! Lorabeth, have you any idea what an object of curiosity and speculation you have been all these years?" He threw her a teasing glance. As she blushed, he laughed and asked in mock astonishment, "Or didn't you know your mother's running off with her French tutor was the 'scandal of the century'?"

"Now, that's quite enough, Cameron!" reprimanded Betsy. "You're embarrassing Lorabeth. Don't pay him any attention, my dear. He's a frightful tease."

With that remark of dismissal, she turned her attention to Lorabeth's blue woolen gown. "Didn't you bring anything lighter to wear child? It's almost summerlike today—and I'm afraid you'll be much too warm in that frock."

"I'm afraid not, Grandmother. England is so much cooler this time of year. . . . I never thought . . ." Her voice trailed off anxiously. "Won't this do?" She was only to aware of her meager wardrobe. There was little choice.

"Oh, it's charming, my dear. I'm just thinking of later on as the weather gets even warmer."

"Well, if you ladies are going to start talking

clothes and fashion, that is my cue," said Cameron, getting to his feet. "I really must be off now, Aunt Betsy. Thank you for your wonderful hospitality, as usual. Goodbye, Aunt Laura. And, Lorabeth, I know my mother will want to have you out to Montclair for a good, long visit very soon."

Cameron kissed his two aunts, made a little bow to Lorabeth and strode from the room. Aunt Laura went to the window and stood watching his tall figure swing into the saddle of the horse the stable boy had just brought round.

"What a dear boy Cameron is," she said, sighing. "Such a charmer, so gentle and yet so strong and manly. Such a pity, though, about Malinda. She certainly doesn't deserve such a prize!"

"Who is Malinda?" Lorabeth asked innocently.

"The little minx he's engaged to!" Betsy snapped.

"Malinda Draper. I still don't know quite how it came about. I doubt if Noramary and Duncan do either," Laura said, shaking her head.

"Her mama, of course!" supplied Betsy. "Felicia Draper knows a good catch when she sees one. She had Malinda paired with Cameron while they were still in their cradles. Remember last year at the Christmas Ball? Malinda had just returned from England with all her airs and the newest fashions. Cameron was quite dazzled and from then on, she held all the cards. But Mama is the one who played them so cleverly."

Lorabeth felt a strange, sinking sensation at

this exchange of comments between her grandmother and aunt—a feeling of dismay that was totally irrational given her short acquaintance with Cameron. So what if this utterly charming young man was engaged, spoken for, all but married! Why should she suddenly feel so devastated? After all, wasn't he her first cousin? They could never have been anything more than friends, at best.

Lorabeth rode with her grandmother and Aunt Laura to church in an open carriage. Surprised by the warmth of the early morning, she gazed with delight at the beauty of Williamsburg in April. Flowering trees and bushes gave the aura of a pastel painting. The air was perfumed with the scent of many flowers; the day, tinted with pale yellow from row upon row of primroses bordering gardens and hundreds of daffodils peeking from behind the picket fences of houses that lined the road to church. Even the salmon-colored brick of the steepled church itself seemed to glow with mellow light in the glorious sunshine.

Just as they pulled into the churchyard, the bell was tolling. Grandmother's coachman sprang down lightly and assisted the three ladies from the carriage. Other churchgoers, also on their way into the service, greeted them, including Lorabeth in their friendly smiles and nods, although there was no time for introductions.

Lorabeth had barely settled herself between her grandmother and aunt in the Barnwell family pew when the rector emerged from the vestry to begin the service.

Lorabeth noted with some surprise and not a little delight the cheerful atmosphere in the church. There were smiles and nods among members of the congregation as they got out their hymnals. The first was joyful in melody and lyric and was sung loud and enthusiastically—a far cry from the solemn Sundays at Briarwood School chapel, where the hymns were funereal dirges and the sermons long and full of admonitions on wickedness and repentance.

With a great rustling of skirts and adjusting of plumed bonnets, the congregation settled down for the sermon. Lorabeth was curious to hear what kind of message would be given to this pleasant and apparently godly group. To her astonished heart, it spoke directly to her! Or at least that was the way she felt when she heard the cherubic-faced minister's words.

"We are taking our text from Matthew 25 this morning," he said, and proceeded to read from the Gospel of St. Matthew. When he came to the part—"Come, ye blessed of my Father, inherit the Kingdom . . . for I was hungry and ye gave me to eat, I was thirsty and ye gave me drink, I was a stranger and ye took me in"—Lorabeth sent a grateful glance in Betsy's direction and felt unexpected tears.

The service over, Lorabeth followed her grandmother and aunt into the churchyard, and was amazed by the holiday air of the after-church crowd. Why, it was like Fair Day in an English village, she thought in surprise, with a great deal of laughter, warm greetings, kisses among the ladies and hand-pumping among the gentlemen.

The whole congregation seemed to linger, unmindful of time, mingling, visiting, gossiping, exchanging news, extending and accepting invitations.

While her grandmother and aunt were busily chatting, Lorabeth noticed the approach of a tall, elegantly dressed lady accompanied by two strikingly handsome young men. The trio was headed right in their direction.

Instinctively Lorabeth stepped back, shielded by her grandmother's bulk, as she heard Betsy exclaim, "Why, it's Jacqueline Cameron and her son, Bracken, but who is the other young man?"

"I believe it's their houseguest, a fellow student of Bracken's," whispered Aunt Laura.

"Good day, Mistress Cameron," Betsy greeted the dark-eyed beauty.

Jacqueline Cameron was one of those fortunate women whose age would forever remain a mystery, mused Lorabeth. Although she was the mother of a grown son, the lady's face was remarkably smooth, her brown eyes sparkled with youthful gaiety, and her smile was as animated as her conversation. Her slender figure and graceful movements were those of a young girl.

"Ah, Mistress Barnwell and Miss Laura! How good to see you." Mrs. Cameron spoke with a slight accent that Lorabeth recognized as French. She embraced the two Barnwell ladies, then turned her lovely smile on Lorabeth.

"My granddaughter has just arrived from England," Betsy proudly made the introduction. "Winnie's daughter, Lorabeth Whitaker."

50

Mrs. Cameron's eyes widened but she politely suppressed her surprised gasp. "Ah, yes—Winnie! And this is her child! But she doesn't resemble the Barnwell family at all, does she?" Then she smiled reassuringly at Lorabeth, who was beginning to feel uncomfortable under the scrutiny of both Jacqueline and the two young men at her side. "But is it not better to be oneself, *n'est ce pas?* To be one of a kind. Not to be compared to anyone else. *Voilá!*"

Jacqueline then lowered one eyelid in a sly wink. With one graceful hand she made a sweeping gesture. "And now may I present these two rascals, who were so restless all during the service, craning their necks, peering over their hymnals, paying no attention at all to the oh-so-profound sermon—for a glimpse of the *très jolie jeune mademoiselle* in the Barnwell pew this morning."

Lorabeth felt her cheeks grow warm under the steady appraisal of the eager young men waiting to be introduced.

"My son Bracken and his friend, Blakely Ashford." Bracken had inherited his mother's brunette good looks and was no doubt the handsomer of the two. But to Lorabeth, Blakely had an endearingly boyish charm that was most appealing.

He was tall, almost awkward as he bowed over her hand, holding it longer than etiquette required. His clear blue eyes were as guileless as a child's and in them Lorabeth saw an immediate worshipful gaze that startled her.

She felt herself flushing under it and turned away to hear Mrs. Cameron speaking to Betsy.

"Does Noramary know of the little English cousin's arrival?" she asked. "If not, since we are returning to the plantation tomorrow, perhaps I can carry the so good news?"

"She knows now. Cameron was here only yesterday and left this morning. I'm sure he has lost no time in telling her," Betsy smiled.

"I hope you will allow me the pleasure of entertaining for this enchanting child at Cameron Hall. I would so much love to give her a party—a ball perhaps? And a Midnight Supper on the night of the first full moon—*très romantique, n'est ce pas?*" Jacqueline shrugged her elegant shoulders.

"I am sure we shall see a great deal of each other while Lorabeth is with us," Betsy nodded, smiling complacently. She had not failed to notice the effect Lorabeth had had on the two young gentlemen. That rogue, Bracken, about whom there had been many romantic rumors, was not suitable for Lorabeth, she decided. But young Blakely—now there was a real possibility. The Ashfords were a prominent family, with fine heritage and great wealth on both sides. Neither had Betsy missed the flush that had suffused Blakely's countenance as he bent over Lorabeth's hand. The girl's unique beauty had struck a ready target, if she were not mistaken.

And, of course, in matters of the heart Betsy Barnwell was rarely mistaken.

The next day there could be no doubt of it. A bouquet of lovely spring flowers in a starched lace ruffle was delivered to Lorabeth with a note from Blakely asking for permission to call.

The promised invitation from Montclair was prompt in arriving, also. And as soon as the acceptance was written and dispatched to Montclair, by way of the Montrose servant, Lorabeth witnessed with amazement the unexpected flurry that followed.

Immediately she was summoned to Aunt Laura's sitting room, where her grandmother and aunt began to discuss plans for the visit to Aunt Noramary's plantation home—"Montclair."

"Lorabeth, my dear, we must see to replenishing your wardrobe at once! Noramary has many plans. She is giving a gala party to introduce you to society, and of course you will be needing a lovely gown. But that will be just a prelude to a round of parties and other invitations you will receive. The summer season will be starting soon, and you will be attending ever so many festivities for young people. So, come along, we'll take a look through what you have and then decide"—Betsy got up, motioning Lorabeth to follow—"what we must do."

She marched straight over to the armoire and began taking out Lorabeth's dresses one at a time with a great deal of clucking of her tongue and shaking of her head.

"Oh, this will never do," Betsy declared. "All your things are much too heavy for Virginia summers, my dear. We must do something about it at once. Light muslins, dimities, and voile are all one can be expected to endure in this weather . . . and only two petticoats . . . cotton stockings. . . . We'll pick out some materials this very afternoon and have Mme. Luisa make you some dresses right away."

What was Winnie thinking of, Betsy wondered, to send her daughter off with such a meager supply of suitable clothes? How did she expect her to put her best foot forward in Virginia society without a proper wardrobe? She did not want to hurt the precious child by displaying her indignation and shock. So tactfully she used the excuse of the climate.

Meanwhile Betsy's matchmaking mind was spinning with plans. Had she not arranged prestigious marriages for two of her daughters, to say nothing of Noramary? With the exception, of course, of Laura and Winnie—but no matter. Lorabeth had all the qualities of beauty, grace and charm to launch her into society and Betsy was determined this time not to fail.

Lorabeth, who had never owned more than three dresses at one time, except for the drab gray school uniform with white linen collars and cuffs cut down from her mother's old ones, was speechless. She listened in silent wonder as her grandmother and aunt made lists, alternately adding other necessities. Never in her short life had Lorabeth been the subject of so much attention.

From that day until their departure two weeks later for Montclair, her days were crowded with a myriad of appointments, fittings, and shopping tours, shepherded by Aunt Laura. Grandmother had engaged the services of *Mme.* Luisa, a fine seamstress in town, to make Lorabeth's new wardrobe. To the impoverished girl, it was a dizzying whirl of activity.

But if her days were filled, her evenings were less so.

Blakely Ashford, who had been so flatteringly attentive after meeting her, had left with the Camerons for their plantation home, Cameron Hall, and his frequent calls were temporarily suspended. Her grandmother always retired early and Aunt Laura kept busy with the management of the household, often into the evenings. In the long twilight of the Virginia summer, Lorabeth spent time in the lovely garden, and she found her thoughts often dwelling on Cameron Montrose.

For the time being, she pushed aside the necessity of telling her grandmother and Aunt Laura the real reason she had come to Virginia.

For now she allowed herself the luxury of living in the present. It would take several weeks yet for any word from England to spoil this idyllic interlude. After all she had been through, Lorabeth justified the postponement and was determined to enjoy this most pleasant phase of her life.

She was looking forward to the visit to Montclair, the Montroses' plantation mansion on the James River. She was curious to meet Noramary, who had taken her own mother's place as the bride of Duncan Montrose.

But in her secret heart she had to admit that, most of all, she wanted to see her charming cousin Cameron again.

CHAPTER 5

LORABETH'S FIRST VIEW OF MONTCLAIR was
through a veil of white dogwood blossoms as the
Barnwell carriage made its way up the winding
road leading to the Montrose estate. Just as they
rounded the bend and entered the gates, the rays
of the late afternoon sun touched the treetops
surrounding the house, enveloping it in a shining
radiance.

The large U-shaped structure of native stone
and white clapboard was of simple, even austere
architecture. But it evoked a serenity, a dignity,
a tranquility that touched the young girl deeply.

Nearing the house Lorabeth's heartbeat quick-
ened. She leaned forward eagerly, suddenly
aware of a peculiar sensation, a definite feeling of
"homecoming."

That first evening brought a mélange of impres-
sions for Lorabeth. Aunt Noramary was warm
and welcoming in her greeting; Uncle Duncan,

quietly dignified but cordial. They were a handsome couple and more than that, Lorabeth had noticed the obvious bond of deep affection between them—a glance exchanged, a smile across the parlor, the touch of Noramary's small hand on his arm, Duncan's eyes following her adoringly when she had acquiesced to the request to play the harpsichord after dinner. If the match had been arranged due to the default of Lorabeth's mother on her betrothal promise, the marriage had worked out very well.

Immediately a Scripture verse leapt into Lorabeth's mind: "And we know that all things work together for good to them that love God, to them who are the called according to His purpose."

Guests had been invited from neighboring plantations to meet "the little English cousin," and Lorabeth was almost overwhelmed by this manifestation of "Virginia hospitality." As Grandmother Barnwell had predicted, invitations of all sorts were proffered, with promises of follow-up reminders as to date and time and type of event.

Dinner was a sumptuous affair. The long table, set with gleaming goldrimmed china and shining silver, seated more than twenty and the conversation was as sparkling as the crystal.

Cameron, the one whom Lorabeth had been waiting to see, arrived only a few minutes before dinner was announced, making the excuse to his mildly disapproving mother that he had ridden to the far end of the plantation that afternoon and had only now returned.

"I abused my horse, I'm afraid, racing to get

back by sundown, but I wouldn't have missed Lorabeth's first evening at Montclair on any account," he had declared with a mischievous grin. "Welcome to Montclair, cousin!"

He bowed gallantly to Lorabeth and raised her fingertips to his lips.

She was struck anew with his splendid looks. His vitality and masculinity, combined with an easy charm must have quite a devastating effect on women. His eyes, so alive, sparkled with good humor and interest in whomever he was talking with at the moment. The fact that it was now she on whom attention was riveted quite took her breath away, to say nothing of anything witty or amusing she might have thought to say.

It was Cameron who escorted her into the dining room and leaned down to whisper, "My mother has designated me your official escort while you're at Montclair. So shall I have the pleasure of your company on a grand tour of the place tomorrow?"

"I should like that," Lorabeth managed to sound casually interested, more in the promised view than in her escort, she hoped.

"Tomorrow morning, then. The earlier the better. Or are you a 'slugabed'?"

"I'm used to getting up quite early," Lorabeth relied truthfully. She could not explain that it was the charity students' job to trot down to the school kitchens in the morning in order to fill the water pitchers for the sculleries to carry up to the paying students' rooms.

"Fine—right after breakfast."

Lorabeth could scarcely sleep that night, despite the soft embrace of the feather bed. The evening breeze was scented with the perfume of a hundred varieties of flowers, and it drifted, like a caress, through her bedroom window from the gardens below. When at last she slept, her dreams were of Cameron.

She was awake before dawn, made her toilette, and dressed hurriedly. Taking up her little Bible as was her custom each morning, she sought its familiar pages for some answer to the tumult within her at the thought of the tall cousin to whom she had been inexplicably drawn since first setting eyes on him. She was comforted somewhat by the frequent references to "waiting on the Lord." He had carried her through many a crisis. Surely He would not fail her now.

Nevertheless, she was trembling with anticipation as, dressed in the riding habit borrowed from Aunt Noramary who was very nearly her same size, Lorabeth sat at the window watching for Cameron.

Then she saw him! He was riding a chestnut horse whose flowing mane was almost the shade of its rider's rich brown hair. A lovely dapple-gray mare, on a lead, trotted alongside.

Lorabeth put both hands on the sill, then leaned out to call a greeting. Smiling, she turned, ran across the room into the hall and flew down the winding staircase, her boot-shod feet barely touching the steps.

Cameron proved a knowledgeable guide. His pride in the land was evident as they rode over the surrounding fields, along woodland paths that bordered the river at the edge of the property.

"Well, what do you think of Montclair?"
Cameron asked at length, breaking a long silence
between them.

"It's so—huge! All these acres and acres!"
Lorabeth searched for a way to explain why she
had made virtually no comment throughout the
long ride. "England is such a small country.
Even the manor houses are not so impressive.
It's a bit overwhelming, I must say."

"The original King's Grant to my great-grandfather and his brother was two thousand acres.
Each of them planned to build a house on his
portion; raise tobacco, corn, money crops, as
well as food—each plantation to be self-
sufficient. But when his brother died suddenly
without marrying nor developing his land, my
great-grandfather sold parcels. The Cameron
family bought some adjoining acreage, and now
the Montrose property is only about fifteen
hundred acres."

"*Only* fifteen hundred acres!" echoed Lorabeth. "My ·goodness!"

Cameron laughed at her amazement. "Virginians think big."

They halted in front of a pasture. Dismounting,
the two young people leaned on the top rail of a
white board fence. Mares grazed contentedly in
the sweet grass, their frisky colts gamboling
nearby. After a few minutes, Lorabeth and
Cameron walked their horses back to the stables
and turned them over to the grooms, then started
back toward the house.

"There's so much more to see," Cameron
said. "Much more I'd like to show you." He

opened the gate that led to the garden Lorabeth had admired from her bedroom window.

She looked about with delight. It was a perfect replica of many of the old-fashioned gardens in England—fragrant with roses, miniature apple trees, borders of iris, daffodils, and grape hyacinths.

"This spot is Mother's pride and joy." Cameron cupped Lorabeth's elbow in his hand, guiding her through the winding flagstone paths.

"It's very like a formal English garden."

"She meant it to be. My mother loves all things English." Cameron paused and regarded Lorabeth curiously. "That still seems strange to me, you know. You, growing up on the other side of the ocean; I, never knowing you—"

Just then Noramary, carrying a reed basket overflowing with fresh-cut roses, came round the hedge.

"We're just admiring your garden, Aunt Noramary," Lorabeth said.

"It is lovely just now, isn't it? Everything is at its peak—the roses especially." She picked one, still sparkling with dew, and handed it to Lorabeth.

Noramary smiled. "But you look like a rose yourself, Lorabeth, straight out of an English garden."

With a wave of her hand, Noramary turned down one of the paths and disappeared from view.

Cameron and Lorabeth strolled on, stepping onto the lawn, green and smooth as velvet and shaded by poplars, maples and tulip trees. The area, bordered by flowering bushes, and extended on through a meadow as far as the eye could see. On the horizon there was a sparkling ribbon of light, where the sun kissed the river. With unspoken but mutual assent, they walked along some distance from the house until the river was in full view.

Cameron took off his jacket and placed it on the grass for Lorabeth. Lifting her modified riding skirt, she sank down gracefully, sighing as she removed the tricorne hat and loosening the ribbon that bound her thick curls.

Observing the gentle bends and curves of the river, its sunlit surface shimmering, Lorabeth murmured, "What a lovely view."

"*Mine* certainly is!" Cameron said, frankly admiring her delicate profile.

She turned to look at him with an expression of sweet surprise. Amazed that he would speak so openly, she thought to herself, *And so is mine,* taking in his chiseled features, the thick, wavy hair, the generous mouth, his skin, tanned and glowing.

Then Cameron rushed on impulsively. "You know, I wish I'd thought to say what my mother said . . . about your looking so . . . like an English rose. I'm afraid she bested me that time, but then you've probably been told hundreds of times that you are"—his voice dropped—"quite beautiful."

As he continued to regard her, Lorabeth felt a tingling breathlessness. She was stunned by the impact of Cameron's words, yet she could not turn away from his steady, intense gaze.

Then, almost in spite of herself, Lorabeth asked softly, "What are you thinking?"

"I was thinking that if you'd never come to Virginia, I might never have met you."

There seemed to be no answer for that and again silence descended for long moments before Cameron spoke again.

"I never imagined there was someone like you."

"But—we hardly know each other, . . ." she protested.

"That's true, and yet in another way I feel we've known each other from the beginning of time. Don't you? As if we'd met somewhere, sometime before?"

A warm responsive tide of emotion washed over Lorabeth at the implication of his words. So he had felt it, too, she thought with wonder— that melting, sweet sensation, that tender yearning, the longing to hold and be held. She had never before felt like this and yet she recognized that it was as old as humankind and as eternal.

Lorabeth stared at him, transfixed. Something was spinning so fast within her that she could neither name nor understand what was happening. To both of them, for she saw something of what she was experiencing reflected in Cameron's eyes.

"Why didn't you come to Virginia before I— before this?" he asked. "After all, your mother was a widow. There was no real reason for her to stay in England, was there, with all her family here in Virginia?" He frowned. Scowled would be more like it, Lorabeth thought. Then, pulling viciously at the blades of grass, he muttered something under his breath. "Even so, I guess it wouldn't have made any difference...."

Whatever more might have been said was abruptly terminated by a shout from across the meadow. Cameron got to his feet and turned to receive a little black boy running toward them. "Marse Cam'run!" he was calling as he ran. By the time the boy had reached them, he was panting breathlessly. "Mistress done sent me to fetch you. Axes that you come back to de house right now. Company here. Mistress Draper and Miss Malinda. They all waitin' fo' you, suh."

"Blast!" Cameron muttered under his breath. "All right, Matt, I'll be up presently."

Turning to Lorabeth, he said, "I guess we'd best go." He held out his hands to her, she placed hers in them, and he helped her to her feet.

"Is there some way I can get into the house and slip upstairs to make myself presentable before meeting your guests?" Lorabeth asked, brushing off her skirt.

Cameron glanced at her, started to say something, then pressed his lips together firmly.

"Yes, we'll go in around the kitchen garden. Then you can go up the back staircase to the second floor and to your room."

They walked the rest of the way in silence. Both felt there was so much to say, so much left unspoken, and yet, perhaps, better not said at all.

CHAPTER 6

LORABETH REACHED THE GUEST BEDROOM unde-
tected. Breathless from running, she leaned
against the door for a few minutes, until she
could breathe easily again.

Feeling flushed, she poured some water from
the pitcher into the bowl and splashed her face
several times. Still she felt the rosy heat rise into
her cheeks, remembering some of the unsettling
things Cameron had said to her. And her own
response—so immediate, so spontaneous, so
unexpected! And yet—almost from the first—
she had sensed something between them. . . .

Cameron's words came back to her as she
stood patting her face with a linen towel. Had he
meant them? And if he had, to what purpose?
They were cousins. He was engaged—engaged
to the very girl who was downstairs waiting for
him at this moment and whom Lorabeth herself
was about to meet. Would she share Aunt

Laura's opinion of Malinda Draper? A minx who did not deserve Cameron?

Both dreading the encounter and anticipating it with perverse curiosity, Lorabeth proceeded to get dressed. For the first time in her life she was faced with the decision of which of several pretty dresses to wear. One by one she removed them from the armoire and, standing in front of the full-length mirror, held each of them against herself, eyeing the effect critically.

At length she chose a muslin sprigged with blue cornflowers, threaded with eyelet lace, and frilled with ruffles at the square neck and elbows. She brushed back her hair and tied it with a blue ribbon at the nape of her neck, letting the curls bunch in ringlets. Then she surveyed her reflection.

Against the backdrop of the luxurious bedroom, beautifully appointed in rosewood furnishings and damask bed hangings, and with a soft flowered rug beneath her feet, the girl in the mirror seemed almost a stranger to Lorabeth. It was as if she now moved in a dream world that had no substance. Cameron, she reminded herself, was part of that world.

No matter what undercurrent of feeling had passed between them, nor what had been said this afternoon, the entire episode must be put away from her waking thoughts as one puts away a dream upon awakening.

With a sigh that was almost a shudder, Lorabeth turned from the glass and opened the bedroom door to the hall. She paused at the curve of the balcony. From there, she could see through the half-opened louvered doors into the drawing room beyond.

Cameron was standing, hands clasped behind him, in front of the sofa. His lean, broad-shouldered figure blocked the view of the woman to whom he was speaking, but Lorabeth glimpsed the ruffle of a hoop skirt. She heard the murmur of conversation, the tinkle of soft laughter. Placing one hand on the bannister and drawing in her breath, she slowly descended.

The minute she crossed the hall and stood on the threshold of the drawing room, Aunt Noramary, beautiful in a French muslin dress embroidered with tiny red rosebuds, rose and came over to her immediately. Lorabeth noticed at once the intricately set ruby brooch she wore at her breast and matching earrings that sent out fiery sparks as she moved her head. These must be the same ones she was wearing in the portrait that hung on the stair landing. It was the portrait that had been painted of Noramary as a bride during the first year she lived at Montclair. Lorabeth marveled at how little her aunt had changed in appearance in the twenty-five years since.

"How sweet you look, my dear," Noramary said, squeezing her arm. "Come, I want to introduce you to our guests."

Lorabeth's eyes moved past her aunt to the sofa beside which Cameron stood. Their glances touched briefly before she saw the dainty, doll-like creature with whom he had been talking, and a plump, petulantly pretty woman seated beside her. *Malinda Draper*, Lorabeth thought, and her "formidable mama."

As Noramary made the introductions, Lorabeth noticed that Malinda's china-blue eyes narrowed slightly.

"So! You're Cam's English cousin! How very odd that you should suddenly appear when nobody knew you were coming!" she said, artlessly slipping her hand through Cam's arm.

Malinda carefully measured Lorabeth, taking in the slender, graceful carriage, the rose and cream damask complexion—God's gift to English girls—the sweet curve of the mouth. Nor did she miss the charming dimple nor the dark eyes with sweeping lashes, shadowing gently curved cheeks.

After this unnerving scrutiny, Malinda turned away and began chatting animatedly to the group at large, but kept her hand firmly locked on Cameron's arm.

Lorabeth had learned that it was not at all unusual for the mistress of Montclair to entertain on an impromptu basis. And that evening sixteen extra guests, in a festive mood, gathered around the dining table. As the guest of honor Lorabeth was seated to the right of Duncan Montrose. Far down the table, at his mother's left hand sat Cameron, across from Malinda.

It was not until after dinner when the gentlemen had joined the ladies in the drawing room that Noramary suggested perhaps the younger members of the company might like to go into the parlor while some of the others settled for an evening of cards.

Servants were lighting candles at the small game tables and the group of young folk, which included Bracken Cameron and Blakely Ashford who had come from Cameron Hall earlier, drifted together across the hall.

"Cards bore me! I can never seem to remember what had been played!" said Malinda, as if it were a virtue.

"Someone as pretty as you needn't bother about such weighty problems," Bracken Cameron said flatteringly but with a mischievous sparkle in his dark eyes.

"Let us play charades," she suggested, making a little pirouette in the middle of the room that sent her wide skirts spinning, her curls dancing, and her unfurled fan fluttering. Every young man in sight—was charmed by the effect—and Lorabeth suspected that was just the intent.

"I'm far too gastronomically overindulged for that," said Bracken languidly, sitting down on one of the wing chairs and stretching his long legs out in front of him.

"The exercise will do you good!" she retorted flippantly, affecting a pout.

Bracken groaned and, speaking in a dramatic tone, demanded sternly, "*Et tu, Brute?*"

"That's an idea—how about a game of 'Quotes'?" Cameron suggested. "That doesn't take much energy."

Malinda seated herself with a little flounce, patting the pillow beside her on the smaller of two sofas for Cameron to join her.

"I'll begin," said Cameron, accepting the seat beside her. Then, turning to Lorabeth, he explained. "Someone recites a familiar quotation,

71

and the next person must name it, supply an ending, or top it with another—"

"Oh, that's much too hard!" Malinda pouted.

"Of course it isn't! You've played it before...." He seemed a bit annoyed with her. But there was no edge in his voice as he asked Lorabeth, "Is this a game that is known in England?"

"No, but it sounds like fun. . . . I should like to try."

Taking Bracken's off-hand comment as his cue, Cameron pointed at the young man lounging in the chair and scoffingly quoted, "Even such a man, so faint, so spiritless, so dull, so dead in look, so woebegone—"

Bracken rose immediately to his own defense. "Shakespeare, Henry IV, Part II," he shouted, then laughingly countered. "Try this one—

In all thy humors, whether grave or mellow,
Thou'rt such a testy, touchy, pleasant fellow,
Hast so much wit and mirth and spleen about thee
There is no living with thee nor without thee."

Cameron frowned, and Lorabeth offered tentatively, "Addison?"

Bracken leapt to his feet, gave her a sweeping bow. "Right, dear lady. Now, your turn."

Lorabeth pondered a minute, then quoted, "If I had been present at the creation, I would have given some useful hints for the better arrangement of the Universe. . . ."

"Come now, Lorabeth. That's too obtuse," scowled Cameron.

"And even heretical, wouldn't you say?" teased Bracken.

General laughter. "Give us something simpler," begged Blakely.

She put her chin upon her hand as if in deep thought. Then: "I must be cruel only to be kind."

"Aha, Shakespeare, Hamlet," crowed Bracken triumphantly.

The game got off to a slow start, then grew more lively as both Blakely and Bracken, so recently back from their year at the university, began vying with each other. Quote followed quote in rapid succession. The rules included not only identifying the author of the quotation or play from which it was taken, but also contributing a line or rhyme or stanza or proverb contradicting the one just given. There was much merriment contradicting the one just given. There was much merriment as the young people rose to the challenge.

"Wine maketh merry, but money answereth all things," quoted Bracken at his turn.

"Shakespeare, Falstaff?" Blakely suggested.

"Wrong!"

"Proverbs?" suggested Lorabeth.

"Right. Your turn again, m'lady," conceded Bracken with a little salute.

Dimpling and with a mischievous look in her eyes, Lorabeth tried, "*Il n'y a pas de heros pour son valet de chambre.*"

"No fair!" Cameron said indignantly. "Only English spoken here."

"*If* the lady can speak French—" Blakely came to Lorabeth's defense. "Did anyone declare a ban on another language?"

73

"Oh, please!" Lorabeth held up her hands in mock horror. "Please, no fighting. I'll take it back"—she made an insinuating pause—"since you are all so ignorant. . . ."

Hoots of protest and laughter followed this remark, and Cameron said haughtily, "I know what it is: No man is a hero to his valet—of course."

"*Of course!*" the other two men chimed.

"Well, is it my turn again?"

"Cameron's."

With a dramatic flourish, he quoted, "As the great scholar and poet has said: *One* tongue is sufficient for a *woman!*"

Lorabeth put her hands on her hips as if dreadfully offended and said, "I resent that, indeed, *and,* sir, the quote is from John Milton."

"Ah, Lorabeth, you are too clever." Cameron shook his head sadly, but his eyes shone with admiration.

"Go ahead, Lorabeth," Blakely said respectfully, obviously impressed by her skill.

She thought a minute. "When in Rome, do as the Romans do, when elsewhere, live as they live elsewhere."

The tempo of the game picked up, with quotes and their sources flying back and forth like shuttlecocks, each person eager to guess the right author or to baffle the others.

Lorabeth, whose father had delighted in teaching his quick-minded daughter from his own love of the classics, was in her element. As the evening progressed, no one seemed to notice that Malinda, with her small store of knowledge of such things, had dropped out of the game.

Once, at Blakely's turn, looking directly at Lorabeth, he recited:

"There is a lady, sweet and kind
Was never face so pleased my mind
I did but see her passing by
And yet I love her till I die. . . ."

"Thomas Ford, 16th century poet," Cameron responded curtly. Then he, also looking at Lorabeth, quoted:

"Twice or thrice I love thee,
Before I knew thy face or name."

At this, Malinda darted a quick look at Lorabeth then at Cameron and with a little flounce she got to her feet, and gave an exaggerated yawn, half concealed behind her fan.

"Oh, for pity's sake, that's enough, Cam. Such a silly game, so childish! Come along, let's see if your mother will play for us a bit so we can dance."

"I am sure the grapes are sour," said Bracken, sotto voice.

To which Lorabeth spontaneously replied, "Aesop's Fables, 'The Fox and the Grapes,'" then quickly colored, aware that Bracken was criticizing Malinda for breaking up a game in which she could not keep up with the others. She was stricken, for even though she did not care for Malinda, she would never have deliberately hurt nor embarrassed anyone.

With unconcealed reluctance, because he had been thoroughly enjoying the contest, Cameron got to his feet. Malinda slipped her hand possessively through his arm.

The girl was pulling Cameron away when he shrugged and said over his shoulder, "When fate summons, even monarchs must obey!"

"Dryden," retorted Bracken. "But that's no excuse, my lad: Each man is the architect of his own fate," he called after the departing couple.

They could not hear Cameron's reply, if any, and the game ended abruptly, leaving Lorabeth with the two young men.

"I suppose we should join the others in the drawing room, too," she quickly suggested, rising.

"Where did you become so learned, madam, if I may ask?" Bracken stood also and offered her his arm.

"My father was a schoolmaster, and a teacher teaches!" she said lightly.

"And what a bright pupil you must have been."

"And lovely as well." That was Blakely at her other side, extending his arm.

With a smile, Lorabeth accepted their escort into the drawing room. But beneath her smile lurked the nagging feeling that she had somehow, by her skill at the unimportant game, earned Malinda's enmity.

For the rest of the evening Malinda very deliberately monopolized Cam, making it impossible for him to rejoin the group. Blakely, who was totally taken with Lorabeth, seemed happy to be without competition for her attention and spent the remainder of the night at her side.

It was not until after midnight, when everyone

76

had left and Lorabeth was in her room alone, that she found the note Cam had managed to slip into her fan case.

She held the piece of paper in shaking hands.

Meet me at the stables early in the morning. Montclair is lovely at dawn. I want to show it to you.

A quicksilver tremor slithered down her spine—a premonition of danger. Lorabeth felt caught between caution and longing.

She blew out her candle and crossed to the window, where the moon was shining in onto the bare floor in dappled patterns of light. She thrust it open and leaned on the sill, savoring the sweet-scented air of the garden below.

She recalled the evening—the repartee, the sharp meeting of her mind with Cam's as they played at "Quotes," the unspoken communication that each had conveyed to the other. Could all that have been happenstance only? Or were they, in some mystical way, meant for each other?

She put cold hands to her flaming cheeks, shaken by the dawning recognition. Yet could the emotions she and Cameron had stirred in each other be any kind of meaningful love? They barely knew each other. Such things occurred only in storybooks, fantasy romances, she reminded herself. And . . . romantic love for a *cousin?* That was a forbidden kind of love—as star-crossed as Romeo and Juliet, Lorabeth thought ruefully.

As Juliet had cautioned Romeo about their

sudden awakening: "It is too rash, too unadvised, too sudden. Too like the lightning, which doth cease to be, 'Ere one can say it lightens."

On the other hand, Lorabeth countered, what harm would it do to go riding together? Perhaps she was presuming something on Cameron's part that did not even exist. Why should she deprive herself of her cousin's delightful company? It was all probably her own imagination, she decided, yawning.

CHAPTER 7

BUT THE NEXT NIGHT AS LORABETH dressed to go to the Camerons' ball, she knew meeting Cam at dawn had been a mistake. She was in a state of exaggerated excitement, her head whirling with the enormity of her dilemma. Over and over every detail of what had happened between her and Cameron that morning came back to her vividly.

"I must be calm! I must" she told herself nervously as a tap on the bedroom door and Aunt Laura's soft voice reminded her that the carriage was waiting to take them to Cameron Hall and that Grandmother Barnwell was already inside.

Picking up her lace mitts, her fan and shawl, Lorabeth glided across the room and, with her hooped skirt sliding on the polished stairway, hurried downstairs and out into the soft spring evening.

Betsy Barnwell looked at her granddaughter

with approval, allowing as how her flushed cheeks and unusually bright eyes were from happy anticipation of the evening ahead.

Betsy, of course, had no idea that instead of looking forward to the gala party, Lorabeth was dreading it. She did not know how she could bear seeing Cameron again after what had passed between them this morning.

Was it too late to remedy anything? Her heart clutched as if being wrung with cold hands. Oh, how hopeless it all was!

Oblivious to the chaos in Lorabeth's heart, Betsy regarded her admiringly, thinking, *How pretty Lorabeth is. Far prettier than Winnie ever was,* she conceded rather guiltily, observing Lorabeth's exquisite profile, the rounded perfection of her small bosom, the sheen of her pale blond hair. Yes, she would be quite a sensation at the ball this evening, Betsy was sure. The blue gown, beautifully fitted through the bodice that emphasized her slender waist, the silk forget-me-nots sewn about the décolletage, the ruffles of starched lace and the loops of lace banding the skirt was a perfect complement to Lorabeth's delicate beauty Betsy observed with satisfaction.

How badly the poor dear had needed a new wardrobe, she thought. How could Winnie have sent her off on her journey so poorly clad? Betsy frowned. *There is more to this than meets the eye,* she mused. Perhaps Winnie would explain more about Lorabeth's unexpected arrival when next she wrote—*if* she wrote. In the twenty-odd years since Winnie had eloped with that dastardly Jouquet, she had heard infrequently from her daughter. Betsy sighed. *What's done is done,* she reminded herself philosophically. *What is past repair is past tears.*

A long line of carriages had already pulled up in the drive as the Barnwell party approached Cameron Hall. Elegantly gowned ladies and well-dressed gentlemen were alighting and moving up the broad stone steps of the house. The Montrose carriage took its turn in the parade.

Cameron Hall was larger and far more splendid than Montclair, Lorabeth thought, entering the many-arched front hall. A myriad of candles in crystal chandeliers glittered like hundreds of diamonds, and standing to receive their guests were Judge and Mrs. Cameron, resplendent in a wide-skirted yellow satin gown. Beside her stood Bracken.

He smiled as he greeted Lorabeth. "Welcome to Cameron Hall." His dark eyes swept over her. "I know *someone* whose happiness will be complete now that you have finally arrived. Someone who has been watching the doorway all evening."

Lorabeth blushed, knowing he meant Blakely Ashford. But Blakely was far from her thoughts. It was Cameron she both longed, yet dreaded, to see.

In the downstairs parlor in which the ladies were to leave their wraps, Lorabeth delayed as long as possible, reluctantly entering the center hall where she knew Blakely would be waiting her appearance. She stood at one of the mirrors, not seeing herself at all, but Cameron's face as he had looked that morning. Immediately the whole scene was vividly alive.

That morning, while the household still slept, Lorabeth slipped quietly downstairs and out to the stables. There she found Cam, who had the same saddled gentle mare for Lorabeth to ride.

For a while they trotted companionably down the road that led from the stables. At the edge of the woods, however, Cameron took the lead, pursuing a carpeted path of pine needles through the woods where the sun was just beginning to burnish the tops of the tall trees.

The sound of horses' hooves as they crossed a tiny arched bridge was all that disturbed the peace of early morning.

When they reached a clearing just beyond, Cameron reined in his horse and turned in the saddle, pointing to a small house nestled deep in a circle of cedars.

"That's 'Eden Cottage'," he told her. "It's the model for the big house. Mother named it." He smiled and shrugged. "No one knows exactly why she chose that name, except that she and Father spent the first night of their marriage there. Actually they were on their way to Montclair but were caught in a storm. A flash flood washed out the bridge . . ." He paused. "But then you should get *her* to tell you their love story."

They rode on a little farther before Cam suggested stopping beside the stream to let the horses drink. In one fluid motion he was on the ground, then hurried to Lorabeth's side and extended his hand to help her dismount.

Still holding her hand in his, he led her to a fallen log where they sat down. The woodland solitude wrapped them in a gentle mantle, with only the ripple of water over rocks and an occasional birdsong to break the stillness.

It was Cameron who spoke at last. "I love you, Lorabeth," he said slowly, lifting her small hand to his lips and kissing each fingertip. "I'm not sure when or how it happened—only that it did. Maybe the first time I laid eyes on you."

Shocked by the sensation of his touch, Lorabeth withdrew her hand as if his kiss had singed it. Quickly she rose and took a few steps, putting distance between them. Her breath was quick and shallow.

He followed instantly—his arms going around her waist, his head bending against her cheek. "I know. I know all the reasons this shouldn't have happened," he whispered. "But I don't know what to do about it, because it *has* happened."

Lorabeth's heart was pounding now. Every nerve was tingling, responding to his nearness. Yet every instinct told her she should resist him. His arms tightened, and she closed her eyes, biting back the impulsive words that sprang to her own lips.

Gently he turned her so she was facing him. They looked into each other's eyes as if for the first, or perhaps the last, time. Some bond was forged in that look that neither had felt before.

She tried to break away. Her heart fluttered in frantic warning. But before she could protest, he had clasped her firmly to him. His mouth was warm on hers in a kiss that was at once tender and demanding. In spite of herself, her longing overtook her caution, and she responded, winding her arms about his neck, her whole body trembling as she returned his kiss.

A lifetime of longing for love was fulfilled in the passing of a moment! Then, her lips still feeling the warmth of his, Lorabeth drew back, staring at Cameron in disbelief. Slowly she shook her head, reached up and touched his cheek with her hand.

"This—shouldn't have happened—it cannot be. Don't you know that?"

Cameron frowned fiercely. His arms loosened about her. "You mean because of Malinda?" he said.

"And also . . . even more impossible. Because we are, after all, cousins."

"Cousins do marry," he blurted out stubbornly.

"*First* cousins?" she reproached him gently. They both knew the tragic results that had sometimes come of reckless intermarrying.

"I don't want to think about that," Cameron said, crushing her to him. She could feel every muscle in his body stiffening.

"I only know what I feel and I know I love you!" his words sounded as if they came through clenched teeth.

Then, still holding her with one arm, he tilted her chin with his other hand and searched her face with an almost desperate yearning. An endless moment followed as they looked into each other's eyes, asking the same question, receiving the same answer. The next thing Lorabeth felt was Cam's kiss, infinitely sweet and tender. She did not resist.

Finally, with great effort, she pulled out of his arms.

"We'd better be getting back now," she said shakily.

"I know," Cameron sighed. "Lorabeth, maybe I shouldn't have said anything. But . . . I knew . . . I thought you felt the same and . . ."

He held her horse's bridle while she mounted, then stood looking up at her.

"No matter what, I can't take back the words. I *do* love you, Lorabeth, cousin or not."

She looked away from those searching eyes, because she could not bear to see the ardor he could not conceal. She felt the sting of quick tears, turned her horse and, with a light flick of her small crop, started her cantering along the path back to Montclair.

Cameron caught up with her. She was trying to control the trembling that had beset her at the hopelessness of their situation. He reached over and took her reins, bringing both horses to a halt.

Then he jumped down from his horse, came over to her, put his hands around her waist and lifted her out of her side-saddle and into his arms. There was no defense. Lorabeth clung to him helplessly, her emotions in turmoil.

He stood there, holding her for a long moment before she eased herself from his embrace and slipped to the ground, as loath to leave him as he was to let her go.

He helped her mount and climbed on his own horse. They walked the horses for a distance, as if to prolong their time together. When Montclair came into view, Lorabeth urged her mare into a canter, and they rode into the stable yard.

As the stable boys led the horses away, Lorabeth and Cameron took the path through the kitchen garden to the house. As they moved along the flagstone walkways, he bent down, snapped something from his mother's herb garden, and handed it to Lorabeth.

"There's rosemary, that's for remembrance, pray love, remember—" he whispered.

And Lorabeth whispered back, "Hamlet . . . Act V, Scene V."

Remember? Lorabeth winked back tears. How could she forget? That was the real question.

"Come along, Lorabeth. You look as pretty as can be. No need for any more primping." Aunt Laura's teasing voice jolted Lorabeth back to the present. The scene in the morning woods faded abruptly as she spun around from the mirror.

"Come on, dear," Aunt Laura urged gently. "I can see poor Blakely from here, pacing the hall, eager to claim the first dance with you."

Aunt Laura was right. As soon as the two women emerged into the hall milling with groups of gaily dressed people drifting from one parlor to the other there stood the patient Blakely, waiting for Lorabeth.

Laura watched them move toward the sound of the lively music emanating from both parlors—he, tall, fine-looking in blue satin, frothed with lace; she, small, slim, graceful, in her swinging hooped gown. *What a handsome couple they make!* she smiled to herself. And almost on top of that came the irrelevant thought, *Oh dear! Lorabeth just may break Blakely's heart.*

Now why in the world would she think such a thing, Laura asked herself, startled. Quickly she brushed away the unnerving thought and went to find her mother so that she could be comfortably settled to watch the dancing.

On the dance floor, Lorabeth found herself only half-listening to Blakely's quiet conversation as they moved through the intricate steps of the first quadrille. Her eyes unconsciously sought someone among the dancers and then, with a kind of chill, she spotted the tall figure she had been looking for—and he was with Malinda.

At the sight of them together, Lorabeth experienced a stab of resentment so violent she was shaken by its force. If it had not been clear to her before what her feelings for Cameron were, she understood now. For if Lorabeth had never known love until Cameron, she had never known jealousy until Malinda.

Quickly she offered up a prayer for forgiveness. To be fair, Malinda was enchanting. It was easy to see why any man—even Cameron—might be bewitched by her pert manner, her coquettishness, the creamy skin, flirtatious, long-lashed blue eyes.

It was mean and shallow and wicked of her to be envious, Lorabeth scolded herself sternly. She must put out of her head this morning's madness, the reckless way she had responded to Cameron's kisses. He was betrothed to Malinda, a commitment almost as binding as marriage.

Besides he was her cousin. There was no future for them.

But all her arguments and resolutions vanished in a second when the music ended and suddenly Cameron, handsome in a claret-satin coat and lace jabot, stood in front of her, bowing and requesting the honor of the next dance.

As she looked up at him, Lorabeth saw her own surge of joy mirrored in his eyes as he gazed down at her. Almost dizzy with irrational happiness, she put her hand in his and let him lead her onto the dance floor.

CHAPTER 8

THE CARRIAGE CARRYING LORABETH and Aunt Laura back to Williamsburg rumbled over rutted country roads. Grandmother had returned home the morning after the Camerons' Ball, but Noramary had prevailed upon the others to remain for a few days longer.

Preoccupied and pensive, Lorabeth stared out the window as each mile took her farther and farther from Montclair and Cameron. *A safe distance,* she thought ironically. As if any place on earth would be safe from thoughts of Cameron now! She allowed herself the luxury of thinking about him. What harm was there in that, since nothing could come of it?

He must have realized it, too. For after the Ball, he had made it a point to be away from the house much of the time Lorabeth remained at Montclair. It was as if they had made a mutual decision, an unspoken pact, that in the future they must avoid each other entirely.

The presence of almost constant company at Montclair helped to ease the pain. Malinda and her mother, for instance, made frequent visits while Lorabeth and her aunt were there. And Blakely, who was still the Camerons' house-guest, rode over every day to call on Lorabeth.

Maybe it was easier that way. Lorabeth could not imagine another intense encounter with Cameron. All she knew was they must be careful from now on. What they felt for each other might become too obvious, even to the casual observer. They must learn somehow to live with the reality of what could never be. And with the families so close, that would be the most difficult task of all.

"We must celebrate your birthday here!" Noramary had said as she kissed Lorabeth goodbye. "I've already discussed it with Aunt Betsy and she has agreed. September is such a lovely month—not so hot as summer, and not yet cold."

Cameron was nowhere in sight the morning they departed. Perhaps he had not dared to say his farewell in front of everyone, Lorabeth thought with an inner trembling.

Up to the last minute, she had been conscious of a tension—a mixed dread and longing for him to appear. But he didn't, and she got into the carriage without seeing him again.

It *is for the best,* she decided wearily, leaning her head back upon the velvet upholstery.

Although they reached Williamsburg long after dark, a light supper had been prepared to welcome the travelers home. Aunt Laura said some tea was all she wanted and, pleading a slight headache and fatigue, said good night, took her cup and went straight up to bed.

Lorabeth, however, felt very hungry and followed her grandmother into the small parlor where a table set with snowy linen held a dish of fruit, a plate of sandwiches, lemon pound cake, and a silver pot of tea.

Lorabeth chatted cheerfully about the visitors and events that had taken place at Montclair after her grandmother's return to Williamsburg. She was conscious, however, of a peculiar lack of response on Betsy's part. When she had brushed the crumbs of her second piece of cake into her napkin and wiped her fingers carefully, she looked up to see Betsy regarding her speculatively. Then her grandmother got up, settled herself in her favorite wing chair, and motioned Lorabeth to sit on the love seat facing her.

"Lorabeth, my dear, I think it is time we had a nice talk," her grandmother began gently. As she spoke she picked up an envelope from the little piecrust table beside her and tapped the edge of it against her teeth thoughtfully.

Lorabeth felt a stirring of apprehension as her grandmother fixed her with a sharp, inquiring look.

"I received a letter from your mother, my dear, and it has raised a number of questions. I am sure you must be aware of some of them." She paused significantly. "Life is full of surprises, as I surely know from my own experiences, but I must admit this comes as quite a shock."

Under her Grandmother Branwell's unrelenting gaze, Lorabeth felt her knees begin to shake. She took the place on the love seat Betsy had indicated, and clasped her hands tightly in her lap.

"In this letter your mother says you are—to quote her—a 'runaway.' Is that true? Did you leave England without her knowledge? And is there a gentleman to whom a great deal of explanation is in order?"

"Oh, Grandmother!" Lorabeth said in dismay. There was a long pause, then she blurted out, "Yes! It is all true! Oh Grandmother, I'm so sorry. I should have told you. I was going to . . . I didn't think Mama would catch up with me this soon or that a letter could arrive before I had a chance . . ." Lorabeth's voice broke.

She buried her head in both hands for a moment, then lifted it bravely. "You see without my consent, Mama arranged an engagement. Not that she needed my consent, of course, but at least, one should be fond of—or at least feel something less than aversion for—the person one is supposed to marry, shouldn't one?

"Oh, it's all such a muddle! I don't know whether or not I can explain, or if you could possibly understand—"

"Well, do try, dear, . . . and *I* shall try to understand," Betsy said, with a slight twitching of her lips.

"Ever since Father died, or even before that, I

suppose, Mama kept telling me that with my looks and my brains I should be able to—to use her words—make a fine catch. Over and over she would say how very important it was to make a good marriage."

Betsy controlled an impulse to comment in view of Winnifred's own disastrous choice. Lorabeth's next words, however, assured Betsy that her daughter had learned something in the years of her exile since her youthful escapade.

"I know it was wrong to resent her constant nagging. Mama meant it for my own good! She doesn't want me to end up as she did . . . first, the widow of a penniless n'er-do-well, then, of an impoverished schoolmaster. That is why she went to such trouble to bring me up as a lady, with all the refinement and manners and accomplishments you instilled in her.

"And poor Father—he insisted on educating me as well. He kept saying he could not let a bright mind go fallow. So I really don't fit in anywhere in England, where everything depends so much on one's family background. The only other option was becoming a governess. . . . And Mama insisted my prospects for marriage were such that I would never have to resort to caring for someone else's children."

At this point Lorabeth jumped to her feet and, unconsciously wringing her small hands, began pacing in front of her grandmother as she went on with her explanation.

"When I returned to school last fall after the summer holiday, I knew things were becoming difficult at home. The house we lived in belonged to the school and would have to be given up when the new Headmaster arrived to take over Father's position. We had been allowed to remain there only because they had not yet secured someone approved by their Board.

"I had been promised a teaching position when I completed my education, so we felt it was best for me to continue there, since I got my tuition and board by helping in the lower forms and tutoring some of the slower pupils.

"But just before the Christmas holidays, I got a letter from Mama, declaring that she believed she had made an arrangement that would benefit us both and secure our future. I could not have imagined what it was, but was pleased that Mama was not so melancholy and worried as before.

"However, what she had arranged was for me to marry—or at least to accept as a serious suitor—Mr. Horace Merriman."

Here Lorabeth paused dramatically, waiting for some reaction from her grandmother. When none was forthcoming, she went on in a trembling voice.

"I cannot tell you how unhappy this made me, Grandmother. I didn't want to marry. Certainly not someone I couldn't even remember having ever seen. But Mama said it was all but settled— that she had invited Mr. Merriman to have tea with us on my first day home. She reminded me of our situation and hoped I would take every means to make a good impression. She told me that he was a prosperous merchant with a lovely home and other property, that he had been a widower for a number of years and was eager to marry again. She presented all the reasons, all the advantages of such a marriage. But, Grandmother, I honestly think the greatest advantage was that I would be off her hands! And that's what I did, didn't I? I took myself off her hands!

"Well, to make a long tale brief . . . I came home on holiday. Such a fuss, such preparations and then—when I met Mr. Merriman . . . Well, Grandmother, he was way past forty and totally bald. His wig kept slipping and I could see the pink scalp underneath . . . and he had a paunch so that his waistcoat buttons were gaping . . . and oh, it was dreadful."

Here Lorabeth whirled about and flung out her hands despairingly. "But, Grandmother, he talked about his house, and I could see from what he said that I would have to move right in and live in that house, just as it was, with all his first wife's things, her furniture and her pictures and her china. . . . Well I just couldn't do it! I simply couldn't. And so I refused his suit. There was the most awful scene. And Mama went to bed with a sick headache, saying I was an ungrateful girl. She was still hardly speaking to me when I returned to school before the holiday was up."

Lorabeth, looking distressed, sighed deeply before continuing. "Mama barely wrote to me the next few months while I was still at school, after I wrote the note to Mr. Merriman officially refusing his proposal.

"Well, sometime later Mama took the position of housekeeper with the Fairchilds, a wealthy family of Kent. She was given her own suite of rooms, luxuriously furnished, and ran the household for Squire Fairchild, who had been a widower for years and was in ill heath. At last Mama had what she had never been able to afford. But when I came home for the summer at the end of the term, another conflict arose between us. It came in the person of Willie Fairchild, a distant relative of the Squire's and quite obnoxious—in my opinion. To make matters worse, this person, Willie Fairchild, made himself quite a nuisance. But Mama was terribly impressed by his family background. She kept reminding me of what lay ahead of me unless I was sensible and accepted him! But, Grandmother, he was foppish. I know that sounds harsh, but after all, I am by my father's own words, an intelligent person capable of a great deal of understanding and comprehension, and the thought of spending the rest of my life with such a silly person was more than I could bear.

"Mama threw a dreadful fit. She reminded me that she was still young herself, and attractive, with many admirers of her own. That she could have married again many times, but that she had to take care of me until I was safely married. She demanded I accept Willie."

Her slender shoulders seemed to slump, and Lorabeth shook her head sadly. "I returned to school in despair. I was so torn between duty to my mother and my own feelings.

"Truly, Grandmother, I believe Providence provided me an escape. I had become friends with one of the students, Dora Carrington, an orphaned heiress, who was often lonely. We spent much time together. She confided that her dead parents' lawyer had arranged for her to leave England and make her home with relatives she had never met on a sugar plantation in the West Indies. She hated the idea and did not want to go, because she was in love with a fine young man. She begged me to help her elope with him. Naturally I sympathized with her situation.

"Now, Grandmother, you may say two wrongs don't make a right, but we were both desperate! We formed a plan for our mutual benefit. Since her passage and ticket had already been bought, and the school notified of her departure, I volunteered to accompany her and see her safely on board ship. Instead, her young man met her and off they went, I pray, to live happily ever after. She had given me leave to exchange her ticket to Jamaica for passage on an American ship coming to Virginia. I wrote a letter to Mama that would reach her after the ship sailed."

Here, Lorabeth's voice broke, and the tears that had been hovering, spilled over and rolled down her cheeks unchecked.

"I know you will think I was deceitful and disobedient, to do what I did, Grandmother. And I am truly sorry to have hurt Mama or offended you. But can you understand at all how I could not bring myself to marry someone I hardly knew . . . and could never love?"

Her grandmother pursed her lips and tapped the edge of the envelope against the polished tabletop thoughtfully.

"If it's true that your mother's main ambition

is to see you married to a man of property and wealth . . . it would not matter precisely who the man was? Am I correct? Therefore, if we had someone in mind, equally well endowed, should she not be as pleased? In other words, we can— as the saying goes—catch two birds with one net, eh? Never fret, my dear. I shall take care of this. No need to worry your poor little head any longer. If your mother's price is money . . . then we shall *ransom* you!"

"*Ransom me?*" Lorabeth looked puzzled, but a flicker of hope rose within her. "How?" she asked.

"I hear, from three reliable sources—Laura, Noramary, and Jacqueline Cameron—that young Blakely Ashford is, to coin a phrase, 'sick with love' for you, dear child. A finer young man of more distinguished family would be hard to find. He would meet every requirement of your mother's and more. In fact, as his wife, you would be one of the wealthiest young women in Virginia. He stands to inherit a fortune from both parents, as well as being independently wealthy.

"As you can see, he is good-looking, nice mannered, of pleasant personality, and no breath of scandal has ever touched him. I think, as a comparative match, this Willie Fairchild might run a poor second. What say you, Lorabeth? Would you find it in your heart to look kindly on young Ashford's proposal?"

Lorabeth swallowed hard. She knew there was no place in her heart for any man since she had met and fallen hopelessly in love with Cameron. *Hopelessly.* Yes, that was the word for it.

Her grandmother, seeing her hesitation, prodded gently, "The alternative, of course, is what your mother suggests—that we put you on the next ship sailing for England . . . and into the waiting arms of Willie Fairchild," she added, with a tinge of irony.

"Oh, no Grandmother! I do want to stay in Virginia," Lorabeth protested.

"Well, then, shall I make Blakely aware that we look upon his suit favorably? By the subtlest of means . . ."

Betsy let the thought dangle tentatively as she watched her granddaughter's reaction to the idea.

Lorabeth's face in the firelight, eyes bright with tears, the red lips parted as if ready to speak or answer, touched her grandmother's heart. What a child this lovely young woman still was. A child in need of comfort and advice and help.

Heavy-hearted, Lorabeth hesitated only a minute longer, then sighed and said, "Yes, Grandmother . . . I suppose that is what I must do."

"Then leave everything to me, my dear. We shall work out the best possible solution to this problem. I shall write your mother that what we have in mind is beyond her own dreams for you."

She patted the soft cheek and spoke reassuringly. "Now run along to bed. You are worn out. And you need your beauty sleep."

Betsy Barnwell gazed after the small, slim figure of Lorabeth and shook her head slightly. Well, there was nothing to do but to figure some way out of it. Goodness knows she'd had enough experience at such things. And there was no way that she was going to let that sweet young thing go back to her grasping, ambitious mother, even if Winnie *was* her own daughter!

Lorabeth lay long awake in the canopy bed in which her mother had slept as a girl and faced, alone in the dark, the harshest reality yet encountered in her short life.

She was caught in a web not of her own making. She tried to have compassion for her mother, who, also, had had to face harsh realities alone. All her life Lorabeth had heard how Winnie had been abandoned by the irresponsible Jouquet, left alone until taken in by the Headmaster of the school where the Frenchman had taught before eloping with one of the wealthy pupils. When the Headmaster's young and delicate wife died, Winnie had married the widower, Lorabeth's father. As Lorabeth grew up, she realized theirs had not been a marriage of love, but of convenience, for there could not have been two more unlikely partners. Her gentle, bookish father; her snappish, discontented mother. Lorabeth understood how her experiences might have embittered her mother. Still, she could not allow herself to be forced by circumstances into a loveless marriage.

Blakely was kind, gentle, handsome, intelligent—everything any sensible girl could want in a husband. It would be easy to learn to love him—*if* she had never met Cameron.

To think that less than a month ago she had not even known Cameron Montrose existed. Now he filled her world. His face, his voice, the way he moved and smiled, consumed her waking thoughts and her dreams at night! Without him her world would be empty. But they both knew their love was impossible.

If she returned to England, she would likely never see him again. And that would be even worse. One was dying by inches; the other, sudden death. Lorabeth pulled the quilt over her head and wept the bitterest, loneliest tears of her lifetime.

CHAPTER 9

THE SEPTEMBER AFTERNOON WAS WARM as June in the Barnwells' back garden. Only the scarlet tinge on the gold maple leaves and the brisk breeze causing the shaggy purple asters and orange wall flowers to dance, hinted of autumn. Standing at her parlor window, Betsy observed with satisfaction the two young people strolling along the brick paths. Lorabeth, dainty in pink muslin, the lacy film of fichu outlining delicately the gentle roundness of her bosom, chatted with Blakely who was all listening attentiveness.

An indulgent smile played around Betsy's mouth. Young Ashford was certainly enamored of her charming granddaughter, she sighed happily. And what more could any young girl want in a suitor? Courteous, considerate, handsome, with manners and wealth besides. Winnie could not have arranged a better match herself, Betsy thought smugly. Yes, Blakely's ardent courtship of Lorabeth had fit perfectly into her own plans. It had been a wise decision to "ransom" Lorabeth by promising Winnie if she allowed the girl to remain in Virginia, she was sure to make an advantageous marriage. Indeed, things could not be progressing more smoothly.

Winnie, however, had not accepted defeat gracefully. Betsy recalled with some indignation the sharply worded reply from Lorabeth's mother. At the time, Betsy had simply dismissed it with a shrug, as a display of Winnie's predictable temper. She had always been a difficult child— the only one of her children to rebel openly— and had grown into an equally difficult woman. It was almost as if Winnie resented Lorabeth's opportunity to marry an American and live in Virginia! Well, she had thrown away her own chances by her youthful folly. Now she must reap what she had sown, Betsy thought grimly.

In the garden, quite unaware of the grandmotherly surveillance, Lorabeth halted for a moment to pluck some of the flowers and make them into a nosegay. Blakely said something in a low tone of voice and, as she turned toward him to hear him better, the rose-colored ribbon that bound her curls came loose and her long, silky hair fell in a cascade over her shoulders.

Blakely caught the ribbon and as Lorabeth reached for it, Blakely took her hand instead, lifted it to his lips, then held it, winding the ribbon around her third finger, left hand, as if measuring it.

They stood gazing at each other for a long moment. Betsy, witnessing the pretty little scene, turned away. In her romantic heart she felt sure Blakely was about to make the hoped-for proposal.

At supper Lorabeth seemed quietly thoughtful. Betsy kept waiting for Lorabeth's announcement, for certainly the girl knew how anxious her grandmother was to know if her well-laid plans had come to fruition. But Lorabeth seemed almost pensive.

It was her aunt who inadvertently sensed Lorabeth's unusual introspectiveness and asked gently, "Are you quite well, dear? You don't seem quite yourself this evening."

"It's been a busy summer," Betsy interjected provocatively. "So many callers, so many parties, so much visiting back and forth." She paused significantly. It was, after all, Blakely who had been the most frequent "caller," Lorabeth's faithful escort to rounds of parties and fêtes, as well as Sunday services. But Lorabeth did not take the cue. So then Betsy said briskly, "It's probably this long hot spell. You know, Laura, Lorabeth isn't used to the Virginia climate yet. She does look a bit pale. Perhaps some sage tea would help."

Lorabeth meekly submitted to the prescribed treatment—sipping the strong, spicy beverage under her aunt's concerned supervision. Only *she* knew there was nothing wrong with her strange apathy, the result of what had taken place in the garden that afternoon.

All summer she had accepted the flattering attention of this very personable young man as he pursued the approved pattern of courtship. She had grown very fond of Blakely, who was delightful company, amusing, affable, and respectfully affectionate. He had wooed her by every traditional means—with flowers, poetry, confections of all kinds, small gifts—all within the acceptable, rigid code of what a young gentleman should offer and what a young lady could receive.

Without a doubt she knew the fairly obvious ploy he had chosen, wrapping her finger with the ribbon, had implied his next gift would be a betrothal ring.

Ah, well, Lorabeth sighed. It was exactly what Grandmother had wanted, the precise solution to her prickly problem—and yet—if only she could forget Cameron Montrose, then she could, perhaps, be content.

As they left the dining room, while crossing the hall into the small parlor, Betsy could not contain her curiosity any longer. She slipped her arm through Lorabeth's and asked in a confidential tone, "So did young Ashford finally find the nerve to propose?"

Taken by surprise, not knowing her Grandmother had witnessed the intimate little tableau in the garden, Lorabeth answered, "Why, yes, Grandmother, this very afternoon. He asked if I cared enough for him to speak to his parents about an engagement before approaching you for permission."

"How splendid!" Betsy exclaimed. "The announcement could be made at your Birthday Ball at Montclair." She gave Lorabeth's arm an excited little squeeze. "Didn't I tell you, my dear, that we would 'ransom' you from that unhappy situation at home? Now there's no more cause for worry." She gave Lorabeth a reassuring pat. "Did you hear that, Laura? Lorabeth has some very interesting news. It looks like a wedding is in the offing!"

Laura gave Lorabeth a hug. "Now we can be sure you will remain in Virginia! I've so dreaded the thought of losing you on the chance that your mother would insist on your return to England. Now we can all be happy."

Happy? Lorabeth wished she could share her aunt's and grandmother's jubilance. They began chatting about what must be done about her trousseau as if the matter were already settled.

While they seated themselves and began a discussion of fabrics, choice of trim and lace, Lorabeth wandered into the music room adjoining the small parlor and sat down at the harpsichord. Her fingers ran idly over the keyboard while her mind was filled with errant thoughts of Cameron.

If it had been possible to avoid him, it might have been easier. But at every one of the summer parties, fêtes, and picnics, they had met. He was, of course, always in attendance with Malinda and she, in the company of Blakely.

"That's a nice idea, my dear. Play something light and spritely," her grandmother called.

The music soothed the aching in her heart. She had not realized, even though she knew their paths were bound to cross just as Cameron had predicted, that each time it would be like a knife thrust in her breast. If only . . .

Lorabeth had been playing for perhaps a half hour when suddenly the front door burst open and, caught by the wind, slammed sharply against the wall. Grandmother and Aunt Laura jumped, and Lorabeth abruptly stopped her playing. There in the doorway stood Cameron.

"Sorry to startle you, Auntie B.," he grinned even as his eyes roamed the room seeking Lorabeth. When they found her at the harpsichord, they feasted on her like a starving man. Then reluctantly crossed the room to focus on Betsy and to explain his unexpected appearance.

"I came into Williamsburg this morning on plantation business for my father, and things took longer to conclude than I expected. It's now too late to start back for Montclair. May I stay the night?"

Lorabeth, meanwhile, tried to still her trembling hands, quiet her pounding heart. It was as if by her thoughts of him, she had brought him here.

Cameron's eyes once again sought Lorabeth, his voice drifting off as if entranced by the picture she made, her face softly lighted by the candles in the sconces on either side of the music rack.

Betsy, who never missed a thing, saw the look and felt a twinge of apprehension. She also noticed how Lorabeth's face had flushed at his glance, acknowledging his presence with a sweet, wistful expression.

"Do go on playing, Lorabeth," he commanded. "Don't let me interrupt a concert. I'm a real connoisseur of music, am I not, Aunt Laura?"

He gave a brittle laugh. "Never could learn how to read notes, no matter how hard you tried to teach me, could I? So, Lorabeth, if you make a mistake, I'll never know the difference."

"Lorabeth plays beautifully," Aunt Laura protested.

"I'll come turn the pages for you," offered Cameron, going over to the harpsichord.

Betsy saw Lorabeth's face lifted like a flower to the sun as her tall cousin came over to stand beside her. Her perceptive eyes noted the intimate smile that passed between them, and an inner warning sounded in her mind, chilling her with its truth.

So that's the way the land lies! Well, I must do something about it, right away, before a worse disaster than Lorabeth being sent back to England occurs.

Quickly gathering her wits, she addressed Cameron directly. "Of course, dear boy, you know you're always welcome. In fact, you're just in time to hear the news. We're planning Lorabeth's birthday ball, which is, as you know, to be held at Montclair. And now we've learned that something else may be the cause of even greater celebration—Lorabeth's engagement to Blakely Ashford! What better time to announce such a happy event than at the ball?"

Betsy's sharp eyes did not fail to detect Lorabeth's sudden pallor, the slight stiffening of Cameron's shoulders. Lorabeth's hands faltered momentarily on the keys, striking a discordant note.

These reactions were almost imperceptible.

Only Betsy, her intuition sharpened by the years, would have noticed. Something had happened between them. Something strong and irrevocable, she felt sure. When? And how had it happened so quickly? But then young love was the most unreliable emotion there was. Like a will-o-the-wisp, it blew where it wandered and lighted where it would.

It was a good thing that Cameron's engagement to Malinda Draper had taken place months ago, she sighed inwardly. From what she had heard, Betsy was certain wedding preparations had already begun. Now Blakely and Lorabeth's engagement must be announced before—*before what?* Betsy demanded of herself.

Of course, engagements had been known to be broken—but not without much upheaval, gossip, even scandal, she knew too well from personal experience. In this case, it was not even to be contemplated. Whatever was between them must be nipped in the bud at once!

Cameron was the one to watch, Betsy thought shrewdly. He had a certain reckless impatience. From early childhood, as the eldest child and first son, he had never been refused anything his parents could provide him or his own beguiling nature might win him. He was also strong, adventurous, and passionate. With years he might become disciplined and cautious, like Duncan, his father. . . but not yet.

And Lorabeth, for all her gentle manner, must have a rebellious streak in her as well. Hadn't she flaunted her own mother's wishes, and run away to Virginia by herself?

110

Betsy knew, without a doubt, that this danger-ous attraction must be diverted at once. So in a while, she beckoned Lorabeth from the harpsi-chord, ordered tea brought in, and launched an elaborate discussion of the gowns they must have Madame Luisa stitch for Lorabeth's trousseau. It was a subject designed to quickly dispel a man's ardor and send him to the limits of his patience.

Stifling a yawn, Cameron pleaded weariness and an early departure for Montclair the next morning and bade them all good night, knowing his own way to the guest bedroom.

To her concealed dismay, Betsy noticed that after Cameron left the room, Lorabeth wilted visibly, the shining look on her face fading as if someone had removed a mask.

Oh dear, thought Betsy, this impossible notion may have gone further than she had imagined. The best thing would be to set an early date for Lorabeth's marriage to Blakely. Too, she might drop a careful hint to Noramary that it might be well to urge that Cameron's wedding to Malinda not be delayed indefinitely.

Marriages when they were carefully arranged, when the partners were well-suited to each other by birth, breeding and family, were for the most part the best possible situation for both man and woman. Love, actually, had little to do with it, so Betsy believed. Common goals, determination to create a good home for the children they had, provide a name with an honorable place in society—these were of utmost importance. Cer-tainly not love. That fleeting emotion had caused more trouble in the world than anyone knew.

111

Betsy sighed, folded up her embroidery, and announced she was ready to retire. Bleakly she wished she believed all those firm convictions, but too often she had seen a passionate love send all such firmly held convictions fleeing! Suddenly she felt her sixty-odd years.

CHAPTER 10

ON THE NIGHT OF HER BIRTHDAY BALL at Montclair, Lorabeth was met at the bottom of the curving stairway by her hosts, Noramary and Duncan Montrose to join them in the receiving line.

"How lovely you look, my dear." Her aunt smiled benignly, then, turning to her tall husband, asked, "Doesn't she, Duncan?"

"A vision to behold!" agreed the dignified master of Montclair.

Indeed Lorabeth did look lovely. Her gown, made especially for this occasion by the famed Williamsburg seamstress, Mme. Luisa, was dusty rose taffeta, appliqued with a trail of silken apple-blossoms extending from one shoulder across the fitted bodice and down the wide paniered skirt, draped to reveal a shirred underskirt of deep pink.

Knowing from his wife that Uncle Duncan was

a man of few words and rare compliments, Lorabeth felt warm with pleasure. To cover her sudden confusion, Lorabeth said quickly.

"And *you* look *beautiful,* Aunt Noramary."

"She *always* does!" declared Uncle Duncan, the affectionate glance he gave his tiny wife softening his rather stern expression.

At his remark, surprisingly Lorabeth saw her aunt blush and realized that even though these two had an "arranged marriage" over twenty years ago, they were deeply in love.

Perhaps that was possible, Lorabeth mused thoughtfully, as she took her place beside her aunt on the wide veranda in front of the open doors to the house. Perhaps love could follow even an arranged marriage such as Noramary's and Duncan's. Aunt Laura had told her that at the time of Winnie's elopement, Noramary and a young Williamsburg neighbor had an "understanding." But when she had been asked to become the "substitute bride" by the distraught Barnwells, she had given him up to "do her duty." Looking at Noramary now, so secure and happy in Duncan's obvious adoration, she certainly had no regrets. Maybe that was the best way. To do one's duty, do what you were called upon to do. After all, Scripture reminded: "Everything works together for good to those who love the Lord and are the called to His purpose."

I must remember that, Lorabeth admonished herself, concealing her private misery behind a bright smile and gracious manner as the guests began to arrive.

But the heartache within was a heavy burden. Cameron had been nowhere to be seen since her arrival at Montclair that afternoon. Maybe he wouldn't show up at all!

Finally, unable to suppress her burning curiosity, she inquired of her aunt. "Where is Cameron? Isn't he coming to my party?"

"Oh course, dear," Noramary assured her. "He wouldn't miss it. Early this morning he rode over to Woodlawn, the Drapers' plantation and will be returning this evening to escort Malinda to the ball."

Lorabeth tried to swallow her rush of disappointment. Cameron, coming with Malinda. But, of course! Naturally he would be escorting his fiancée.

A short time later an open carriage came to a stop in front, and Lorabeth immediately recognized Mrs. Draper, fussily swathed in netting covering an elaborate powdered coiffure. Then she saw Cameron and her heart nearly stopped. He had stepped down from the carriage to assist Mrs. Draper, then handed down Malinda, who looked like a yellow butterfly in yards of tulle.

Lorabeth watched Malinda make an imperious gesture and Cameron shook his head. Then, with a toss of her curls, she placed her hand on his arm and they mounted the steps together.

As Cameron approached, Lorabeth felt a spreading warmth. Then just as quickly she went cold all over. It was like the fever she had contracted the summer she was twelve. Her hands turned icy, her wrists weak, her legs unsteady. It was all she could do to maintain her composure as Cameron bowed before her, lifted her small, cold fingers to his lips and smiled down at her.

"Happy Birthday, Lorabeth."

His eyes moved over her upturned face slowly, almost as if they were caressing her, lingering on her mouth like a kiss. He was so close she was newly aware of his eyes, the strong line of his jaw, the way his russet hair grew back from the high, broad forehead. His nearness made her quite breathless.

"You will save me a dance?" he asked her, still smiling, though his eyes were steady and serious.

"Of course," Lorabeth replied lightly, aware of Malinda beside him, an annoyed frown puckering her smooth white brow.

"Maybe I best make sure. Let me have your dance card," Cameron suggested.

She handed him the small, tasseled card and, with a kind of reckless abandon, he scribbled his initials on three lines. When he returned it, their eyes met in a moment of complete communication, a silent affirmation of what they were both feeling.

Pointedly, Malinda slipped her hand through Cameron's arm then, smiling at Lorabeth with cloying sweetness, wished her a "Happy Birthday" and led Cameron away.

Feeling irrationally bereft, Lorabeth's eyes followed them until she caught Aunt Laura gazing at her with anxious speculation. Lorabeth hoped desperately her aunt had not been able to read her mind.

116

Within the next few minutes, distraction in the form of the arrival of Blakely and his parents, provided Lorabeth a welcome release.

"You look unbelievably beautiful!" Blakely told her adoringly as he bent over her hand. "I feel I am the most fortunate man in the world tonight."

Smiling fondly at them, Aunt Noramary whispered to Lorabeth that she was excused and to go along with Blakely to begin the dancing. Happily Blakely drew her hand through his and clasped it warmly, leading her into the large parlor that had been cleared of furniture, the floor waxed for dancing.

As he bowed and they moved gracefully into the promenade, Blakely beamed at Lorabeth. "I'm so proud and happy, dearest. I cannot wait much longer to announce my happiness to the world. Mama and my father are delighted, and will be speaking to your grandmother later this evening."

Lorabeth smiled at him vaguely. As he led her into the intricate steps of the minuet, her efforts to focus on him were dissipated by her realization that the couple dancing next to them was Malinda and Cameron.

Why, she asked herself, had God brought her and Cameron together at all, if only to keep them apart? Once more she felt an unhappy helplessness. Some of her abstraction must have been evident, for Blakely broke into her wandering thoughts reproachfully.

"You're not listening Lorabeth."

"Sorry, Blakely. What was it?" She willed her attention back to him.

"Never mind, my darling. We'll have time to slip away and be together at supper. Besides the dance is ending now, and here comes your next partner."

There were two others before Cameron, at last, appeared to claim Lorabeth for his dance. He extended his arm, his eyes grave, his mouth smiling. On the dance floor facing each other, they spoke not a word, mutely following the steps precisely to the measure of the music. But they held each other in a rapt gaze. Immersed in each other, yet very conscious they were not alone, they moved withing the pattern of the dance, touching each other only as it was choreographed. Because they dared not utter what was in their hearts, they were bonded in silence.

When the music stopped, Cameron bowed; Lorabeth curtsied. Still no word had passed between them. Only their reeling senses and pounding pulses revealed each one's inner feelings.

Even in the misty realm in which she floated, Lorabeth knew she should put all thoughts of him from her. She told herself it was Blakely she should be thinking about, not Cameron. Blakely—eminently eligible, hand-picked by her grandmother, who unquestionably adored her and was the ultimate means of her escape from her mother's plans. What useless fantasy to dream of Cameron. If it had not been for Blakely, it was very likely Lorabeth would already be packed aboard a ship to England—and Willie Fairchild!

The last dance before supper was Cameron's

and, instead of leading her onto the dance floor again, he tucked her arm through his and guided her out through the French windows onto the shadowed porch.

As soon as they were outside, Cameron's hand tightened on her wrist and he hurried her to the far side of the veranda, down the steps and into the garden. The air was heavy with the scent of late-blooming roses. A safe distance from the lights of the house, with only the faint sound of the music drifting out to them, Cameron took Lorabeth in his arms. He held her for a long moment, so tightly she could feel his heart beating against her own.

"We must talk, Lorabeth. Alone. There's no time to waste. Listen, darling"—his voice was low and husky—"after everyone has gone, wait until the grandfather clock in the hall strikes two . . . then meet me here."

"But Cameron, we can't—"

He pressed his fingers lightly over her mouth to halt the flow of protest.

"Don't say 'no,' Lorabeth. It is of utmost importance . . ."

She started to say something else, but his mouth quieted hers in a kiss so sweetly tender that she lost all thought of denying him. The moment seemed to last for an eternity in which the world spun with a dizzying joy.

Then they heard a voice calling from the porch, and they broke apart as Aunt Laura came to the edge of the veranda.

Seeing them, she said, "Lorabeth, it's time for you to open your presents, dear."

"I'll give you mine later, when you meet me," Cameron whispered as they went up the steps together.

Lorabeth stood behind her half-open bedroom door, breathlessly awaiting the deep-toned striking of the clock. One. Two.

She took a long, shaky breath. Then, carrying her pink satin slippers, one in each hand, she moved like a shadow down the stairway, across the front hall and through the drawing room. Once something creaked and she paused, looking over her shoulder to be sure no one was about before proceeding to the French doors. She carefully turned the handle and stepped out onto the veranda.

There was a slight movement near the lilac bushes, and she halted, standing absolutely still, not daring to move or breathe. Then, out of the darkness, Cameron appeared.

Without speaking, he took her hand and led her to the side of the house, through the gate and into his mother's English garden. In the pale light of the silvery new moon, the garden had a magic luminosity. Once safe inside its walls, Cameron settled Lorabeth on the bench within the little latticed arched enclosure.

His own tension transferred itself to her. Her whole body was trembling, her heart beat wildly, her hands were cold, and her breath shallow. She knew they were on the brink of danger in this secret meeting. But now she was powerless to avoid whatever might be its outcome.

Cameron drew a long breath, then spoke in a

low, urgent voice, "I love you, Lorabeth. I know I've no right to speak to you of this. I'm not free. Besides, our being related, I know, such an idea would shock the family. Wait! Hear me out." He held up his hand as if warning her not to interrupt. "Maybe it was meant to be. Maybe it was part of God's plan for both our lives. Why else would you have come halfway round the world? Why else would we have met if not for some reason—some Divine purpose?"

Lorabeth shook her head, bewildered at his impetuousness.

"Don't deny it, Lorabeth. I think you feel the same way. Don't you love me, too?" Not waiting for her answer, he rushed on. "Whatever you say, I see it in your eyes."

"Oh, Cam, don't!" she begged. "It cannot be. It is too late. You're engaged to Malinda. And— tonight—well, it is practically settled. Grand- mother agreed to Blakely's proposal and—" The tightness in her throat choked out the next words. "Besides . . . under the circumstances . . . it would never be allowed."

Cameron shook his head impatiently. "One thing at a time. All that can be worked out, I'm sure. It will just take time and *patience*, which is *not* one of my virtues." He paused with a half- smile as he added ruefully, "In fact, impatience, impulsiveness are my worst flaws. But this is too important to me. And I'll have to learn patience. Pray for it!" Again he halted, "I'm wildly impatient now to declare my love for you before the whole world!"

At this he put his arm around her waist and

gently drew her to him. He put one hand under her chin, tilted her slightly resisting chin upward, then slowly with infinite tenderness kissed her. For a timeless moment the world rocked, then became quite still. Lorabeth looked up at Cam's face, illuminated by the newly risen moon, searching hers for an answer. Her resistance melted and she lifted her lips once more for his kiss.

"Don't you *know* now, Lorabeth?" he whispered softly as he cradled her gently close. "I *do,* and *whatever* it takes—time, tact, *patience*—I will practice it, learn it, *pray* for it. It is worth whatever I have to do. Because it's you I love, and you I must have!"

In his arms she felt cherished, protected. Against her breast she could feel the heavy beat of his heart. She sighed, feeling the strength of his arms enfolding her.

If for this kiss alone, Lorabeth had traveled thousands of miles—if only for this one moment of happiness, she would gladly have traveled ten thousand more.

Slowly they drew apart and Cameron sighed. "Oh, my very dear, somehow we must sort this out. It simply has to be. I cannot imagine life without you now."

Lorabeth found her voice at last. "Cameron, you know it is impossible," she said sadly. "It was foolish for me to meet you here—"

He jumped to his feet, still clasping her hands. "I can't accept that. I won't," he declared.

Startled by his vehemence, Lorabeth put a restraining hand on his.

"Cam, listen to me. We're both promised to others. We've given our word. Too many people would be hurt and disappointed. And there's more. So much more. You don't know that Grandmother Barnwell has staked her own honor on my betrothal to Blakely. You see, when I came to Virginia I was running away."

He made a gesture as if to protest, but she hurried on.

"Yes, it's true. If I had stayed in England, I would be married now. My mother had arranged a marriage I could not tolerate. So, when I told Grandmother—Blakely was already courting me—she wrote to my mother telling her my marriage to him would be a prestigious one, better even than the one she herself had planned. So you see Grandmother and Blakely saved me, actually *ransomed* me, from a situation that was worse than you can imagine. There is no way I can go back now."

He stared at her, then shook his head in disbelief. "It doesn't matter," he said stubbornly. "I love you. I won't give you up so easily." He caught her to him so that her face was pressed against the rough lace of his jabot. "I can't lose you, Lorabeth—not *now!* I can't imagine living without you!"

"But you have—all these years."

"I didn't know what I was missing, that someone like you even existed. I thought what I was getting was all there is. That everyone's marriage is a kind of compromise—"

"Not your father and mother's," she reminded him gently.

"Yes, but they're different, special."

She tried to pull away but he only held her closer.

"It was a mistake for me to come out here," she said quietly, firmly. "We must go back in, Cam."

He held her for a moment longer, then with a sigh, released her. Fumbling in his waistcoat pocket, he drew out a small box and handed it to Lorabeth.

"Wait, at least, until I give you your birthday present."

She took it into trembling hands.

"What is it?" she asked tremulously, for it looked like a jewel case and she was afraid to see the contents.

"Open it."

She untied the ribbon and the silk cloth that wrapped it, removed the lid, and found inside a small porcelain box adorned with two delicately painted birds.

"A trinket box! How lovely!"

"No, it's a music box. It's best you don't lift the lid just now," he explained. But every time you hear its melody, it will remind you that I love you, Lorabeth. Now and forever."

"Oh, Cameron, we are deceiving ourselves if we think . . ." As she held up her hand as if to wave away any more useless argument, the moonlight picked up the sparkle of the sapphire ring on her third finger, left hand. Almost as an afterthought, she held it out to show Cameron. "Blakely gave me this tonight in front of Grandmother, Aunt Laura, and his parents. And I accepted it, Cam. There's nothing either of us can do now.''

"There must be. There *has* to be." Cameron's voice grew rough with emotion. We'll find a way.''

The moon moved across the sky from behind the sheltering trees, and the two of them were suddenly enveloped in moonlight. As if on cue, they put their arms out simultaneously and clung together, heart beating against heart, the bitter-sweetness of the moment too deep for any words. It was as if they knew they had to seize this moment before the reality of their situation crashed against them.

At last, reluctantly, they released each other.

"Believe me, my darling," Cameron repeated, "we'll find a way."

Lorabeth checked the reply she knew she should make. For now, she would just savor this precious time they had shared. Nothing would be changed by this clandestine meeting, this secret declaration of their love. Tomorrow, Cameron would still be engaged to Malinda; she, promised to Blakely. And, of course, they would always be cousins—bonded by the familial tie that sealed a lover's doom.

CHAPTER 11

LORABETH LET HERSELF BACK INTO THE HOUSE cautiously, tiptoed up the stairs along the upper hall and back into her room. She shut the door noiselessly, leaning against it for a moment as a shuddering sigh escaped her.

Slowly she turned around, then gave a horrified gasp when she saw a figure silhouetted by the moonlight. It was Aunt Laura, seated on the window seat in the recessed alcove.

At first Lorabeth could neither move nor speak.

"Aunt Laura! What are you doing here?"

"I couldn't sleep. I was overtired, overstimulated from the party. My room seemed too warm, I got up to open the window. Then I saw you— and Cameron—in the garden." Her voice faltered. Then she rose and came toward Lorabeth, holding out her arms. "Oh, my poor dear."

Something inside Lorabeth crumbled. For the

first time since her arrival in Virginia, she felt she could drop the facade she had so carefully erected. She went into her aunt's arms, and let herself be comforted.

When her sobs diminished, she dried her tears, and with some effort poured out the story of her love for Cameron, of his for her.

"It took us both completely by surprise. It was so unexpected. We felt it almost from the first, but it wasn't until tonight—"

"But tonight you accepted Blakely's ring." Aunt Laura shook her head in distress.

"I know! I know!" Lorabeth exclaimed desperately, putting up both hands to cover burning cheeks. "It was wrong. It was all wrong! But tonight, when Malinda was flaunting Cameron so, I was filled with envy—"

"Envy is a sin!" Aunt Laura said in a shocked whisper.

"Yes, I know that too, and I confess it. I envy everything about her. I envy her beauty, her manner, her lovely clothes, her wealth. Mostly I envy her—Cameron!" Lorabeth put her face in her hands.

"But he's your cousin, dear. Any romantic thoughts of Cameron—well, it's impossible, you know," Laura said with finality.

"Oh, Aunt Laura—tonight it *did* seem possible! Maybe it was the excitement of the evening the music, the gaiety. The fact that it was my birthday. Somehow it all seemed within my reach—"

"But, my dear, think of the consequences. All the lives involved in such folly. Certainly you knew better than to think anything could come of such an attachment?''

"Yes, I knew better, Aunt Laura. I've known all along. And I've tried—really I have. But knowledge and trying doesn't keep one from dreaming. . . .''

Laura put out her hand in a comforting gesture.

But Lorabeth shook her head and, straightening her slim shoulders, drew a long shaky breath.

"I knew better, but I'm afraid I couldn't help loving Cameron. Now I suppose I must pay the price.'' She turned her tear-stained face to Aunt Laura's kind searching look. "I hope—*pray*—it will never happen again. I wouldn't want to hurt anyone.''

"Then we must leave first thing in the morning,'' Aunt Laura said decisively—"before Cameron does anything rash. And you must promise, my dear, that you will not allow such a meeting to take place again. For both your sakes. You *do* promise, don't you, Lorabeth?''

Lorabeth nodded. "You're right, of course, Aunt Laura, and I promise. But it will be so hard.''

"You are strong, Lorabeth. Look at what you've done already, how much you've survived! For many reasons you must be stronger still. Perhaps even stronger than Cameron. He does not know what it is like to be denied anything. He is a fine young man with many good qualities . . . but he lacks discipline. What he wants, he *will* have. You must be the one, Lorabeth, to be wise, to do the *right* thing, the *best* thing for everyone concerned.''

Tears crowded Lorabeth's eyes, rolling down her cheeks unchecked. "Weren't you ever in love, Aunt Laura?"

There was a short silence, then her aunt patted Lorabeth's hand sympathetically. "Oh, yes, my dear. I was. Never think that I cannot understand."

"Why then did you never marry?" Lorabeth asked the question she had longed to ask.

"There was a terrible misunderstanding, never resolved. And he married someone else." She paused. "After him—well, I never found anyone else I could love."

"Maybe, for some women, it is like that," Lorabeth said solemnly. "Maybe there is only one love in a lifetime."

"But that doesn't mean you cannot have a successful marriage, Lorabeth," Aunt Laura reminded her gently. "For me, it wasn't necessary to marry. My father left me my own inheritance. But for someone like you, my dear . . ." Her voice trailed off. What she had been about to say was painfully obvious.

Promising to make all the necessary explanations and arrangements to return to Williamsburg early the next day, Aunt Laura went back to her own bedroom. Lorabeth sat for a long time at the window gazing out into the darkness, knowing that the memory of this night would haunt her forever.

Aunt Laura had spoken gently, but the harsh reality remained that Lorabeth really had no alternative. She was a woman alone in the world, with no security, no family. She was utterly defenseless. Blakely would be a good, faithful, devoted husband. The Ashfords were kind and had welcomed their son's choice graciously, even though she was coming to him without dowry or property. But Lorabeth knew the bitter truth. She did not love Blakely as she should, for her heart was already given to another man and would be his forever, no matter what the outer circumstances of her life.

Lorabeth buried her face in her hands and the tears poured down her cheeks, trickling through her fingers onto the beautiful dress. Finally, she slipped to her knees, knowing only God could help her bear what must be borne.

For what purpose had He brought her safely to America, to Virginia? Perhaps, after all, it was to make this good, solid marriage to Blakely. It could not have been to break every tradition of society and the church, to fall in love with a cousin, already engaged, whom she would never been allowed to marry even if he were free.

"Oh, dear Lord, whatever is Your will for my life, I accept it. I promise—from this day forward—to put away all foolish, vain longings for something—*someone* who does not belong to me and never can. Help me to be conformed to Your will."

Even as the pinkish-gray light of dawn crept through the window, a strange kind of peace pervaded Lorabeth's spirit. Although her heart still felt like a bruised, battered weight within her, she knew what she must do. All the lovely possibilities of the night before in the garden with Cameron vanished with the moonlight.

131

Aunt Laura was right. She and Cameron should never have declared themselves. She must return to Williamsburg before any further damage was done.

But she could not leave without some word to him—"a word well-chosen" to close the dangerous door they had opened, to release him from any rashly made promise.

Lorabeth got out of bed, found some paper in the escritoire by the window overlooking the garden where only the night before they had held each other. Biting her lip, she thought for a moment, then dipped the quill into the inkwell and began to write.

When she had finished, she folded the paper and, opening the bedroom door to see that the hallway was empty, tiptoed along the passage to Cameron's room. There she dropped the note on the floor and carefully slipped it under his door.

When Lorabeth, Grandmother and Aunt Laura were ready to leave Montclair the next morning, Cameron was nowhere in sight. It was accepted by his family that the young man came and went as he chose, so no one took special note of his absence. In her troubled heart, however, Lorabeth felt he did not dare tell her goodbye in front of the others. For that she was thankful. She could not have trusted herself, either, not to betray their forbidden bond.

Aunt Noramary had accepted Aunt Laura's excuse that they must get back to Williamsburg immediately to begin making the preparations for Lorabeth's trousseau and wedding.

"The Ashfords are anxious to set a date and, no wonder, when they will be getting such a lovely daughter-in-law." She smiled at Lorabeth indulgently. "And," she added mischievously, "I've never seen a bridegroom-to-be more ready to leave off bachelorhood than Blakely!"

Lorabeth could not help wondering what her aunt would think if she knew what had taken place in her very garden, and felt fresh shame.

Back in Williamsburg plans for the wedding proceeded with frightening rapidity. Grandmother Barnwell and Aunt Laura were busy from morning till night, making lists of all kinds. The trousseau was of paramount importance. Ashford was a proud and prominent Virginia name, and any young woman marrying into their family would be expected to have an extensive and elaborate wardrobe.

There were endless sessions with Madame Luisa. Or so it seemed to Lorabeth. The noted seamstress, ever mindful of her reputation, was a perfectionist, and every detail of her creations must be flawless, down to the last inch of trimming. She would sketch, then discard, then present a new design, explaining in detail each fold of drapery, each cut of a sleeve or bodice. The two Barnwell ladies were fascinated and wholly absorbed. But Lorabeth, used to twice-turned skirts and made-over dresses for most of her life, found the proceedings tedious.

She did not often allow herself the luxury of thinking about Cameron. But there were moments of despair when the need to see him again was insistent and demanding. What was he doing now? What was he feeling or thinking? Sometimes she felt as if their brief encounters, so intensely rich and meaningful, would serve her for a lifetime. At other times, confronted by the thought of long years without him, her courage failed her and she wept for what could never be. Over and over, she resolved steadfastly to put aside all further thoughts of him.

At those times she sought the comfort of the strengthening words of Psalms. In David's prayers for protection against his enemies, Lorabeth found enormous identification. Her love for Cameron was her enemy; the temptation, constant to throw off restraint, to give in and abandon herself to their forbidden alliance.

On her knee the battle was daily waged and won.

Although Grandmother Barnwell noted Lorabeth's wan expression, her lassitude and loss of appetite, she put it down to prewedding doldrums. All young girls suffered such symptoms, Betsy assured herself, and only reminded Lorabeth of the fine match she was making.

To complicate matters, letters from Winnie, filled with recriminations, reproach and stinging accusations, arrived almost weekly. Lorabeth was accustomed to such scoldings in person, but seeing them written in her mother's slashing handwriting made them seem even more shattering. In her letters Winnie repeated the cruel remarks she had often told Lorabeth verbally, that she was an "ungrateful, deceitful, and disobedient girl."

Grandmother barely skimmed the letters. "Humph! What mother could want more than for her daughter to marry into one of Virginia's first families? Blakely is not only one of the finest young gentlemen in the county, but one of the wealthiest. He will inherit both from his mother and father. His mother was a Sedgewick on her mother's side and a Llewellyn on her father's, and brought both wealth and property when she married Squire Ashford. You will be very well set, my dear, and why should Winnie not rejoice at that?"

Lorabeth had no answer.

"Winnie is simply having a tantrum on paper! Once she meets Blakely and his family and sees their manner of living, she'll change her tune. Then all will be forgiven and soon forgotten as far as you're concerned. So don't fret, my dear. I've told Winnie she is to come to Virginia at my expense to attend her daughter's wedding, and we shall all have a pleasant, happy reunion."

Lorabeth was not so sure, knowing how her mother harbored grudges and nurtured unforgiveness. But until it was known if Winnie was coming, no wedding date would be set.

Blakely was in constant attendance. Although this in itself was a distraction for Lorabeth, it was also an increasing source of anxiety. Was it fair to him to give him only half her heart, mind and soul? Knowing he might possess her body but never know her spirit plunged Lorabeth into periods of great distress.

Blakely, however, seemed content. Not knowing what she regretfully withheld from him, he happily escorted Lorabeth everywhere, eager to show off the "English beauty" he had won.

When she was not with Blakely, Lorabeth was most often at one of the interminable fittings. Returning from Madame Luisa's one afternoon, she found the house quiet. Betsy was napping, she discovered upon peeping into her bedroom, and Aunt Laura must be making social calls.

Fighting melancholy, Lorabeth decided to go into the music room. The harpsichord had always proven an antidote for dejected spirits. Pausing in front of the hall mirror to remove her bonnet, she became aware of another reflection. Startled, she whirled about to find Cameron standing in the doorway.

"I had to see you," he said in a low, tense voice.

"But, you shouldn't have . . ."

She stood staring at him, unable to speak or move. On one level of consciousness she longed to fly into his arms; on the other, she wished for escape. She was like a moth inexorably drawn to a flame, sensing its danger, yet willing to risk that danger.

"We *must* talk, Lorabeth."

"It's no use, Cameron."

Lorabeth had not seen him since the night of her birthday ball. The only reminder of that enchanted evening was the small music box he had given her. She had hidden it in one of the drawers of the applewood chest in her bedroom, only daring to take it out when she was by herself, lest someone hear its sweet, tinkling melody.

There was a pounding in her temples and her heart was beating uncomfortably fast. Still, she hesitated.

It was Cameron who, at last, made the decision. With a few purposeful strides he walked over to the door of the music room, thrust it open and motioned her forward.

Meekly Lorabeth followed him into the room. Quickly she moved behind the love seat, placing both hands on its back, bracing herself behind this safe barricade.

"You should not have come and I should not be receiving you alone. This is folly, Cameron."

"I've come, Lorabeth, because I've thought and thought about this and I finally had to act. You must not rush into this marriage with Blakely before we can work things out. My mother told me you are waiting to hear if Aunt Winnie is coming before setting a date. In the meantime, I will explain to Malinda and—"

"Oh, no, Cameron, you mustn't!" Lorabeth cried out, thoroughly alarmed.

"But I *must*. I don't love Malinda. I love *you!* I can't marry someone I don't love, and neither can *you!* Where is the honor in that?"

"There is no use discussing this as though there could be a future for us. You are forgetting the most important point of all—we are *first cousins!* We cannot marry. Our families would be horrified! The church would never condone—"

"Blast it all, Lorabeth! We can elope, find someone who would marry us. The Church of England isn't the only church authorized to perform a marriage ceremony!"

"You can't mean what you're saying! What about your family. . . . you're the oldest son, the heir to Montclair. You can't abandon your responsibilities, your inheritance, your duty!"

"I have two younger brothers. In a few years, either of them could learn to run the plantation— eventually take over . . ."

But into the confident tone he had used earlier had crept a note of uncertainty. Lorabeth heard it immediately and knew she had struck a sensitive area.

"Cameron, I said everything I felt in the note I wrote to you before leaving Montclair. You must accept it. There is no way for us. The best, the bravest, the kindest thing we can do for each other is to help each other bear it."

Lorabeth struggled to hold back the tears that rushed into her eyes, and clenched her hands until the nails dug into the soft flesh of her palms. She managed a wistful smile as Cameron fixed his gaze upon her.

Knowing she was near the breaking point, Lorabeth knew she must get our of his sight, away from the refuge his arms might hold for her if she yielded.

She moved from behind the love seat and started toward the door. But to reach it, she had to pass him. He effectively prevented this ma-neuver by stepping squarely into her path. He then stretched one arm across the door, and, leaning toward her, placed the other hand on her waist. He was so near she could see his eyes, the dark pupils, the stubby lashes.

He drew in his breath sharply and, with

something like a moan, gathered her to him. "Oh, my darling, how can I let you go?"

In spite of herself Lorabeth clung to him.

"I can't, I *won't* let this happen to us!" Cameron's voice was ragged. "How can we live without each other?"

Sobs tore at her throat as finally, with all the strength at her command, Lorabeth pulled herself out of his embrace. "Only with God's help, Cameron!"

With that, she turned and fled through the door, across the hall and up the steps, never once looking back at the stricken young man.

CHAPTER 12

THE FIRST PART OF OCTOBER, called "Indian Summer" by Virginians, boasted warm, sunny days and crisp evenings. Morning fires were needed in the fireplaces of all the rooms in the Barnwell house to dispel the lingering chill. On one such morning, Lorabeth sat propped up in bed watching Odelia Essie's niece, stir the ashes of last night's fire before starting a new one. Being waited on was still an unaccustomed luxury, one that Lorabeth found difficult to accept.

So she rested uneasily against the plump pillows, sipping the cup of chocolate Odelia had brought her, and tried to exercise patience. She would have to heed Odelia's warning, "to wait 'til it's good and warm 'fore you venture out of baid. Dey is frost on de groun' dis mawnin'." At least she would wait until the young maid left, Lorabeth decided.

There was an extra reason for Lorabeth's restlessness this particular morning. The day before something had happened that weighed heavily on her heart.

In the afternoon Blakely's mother had come to call on Grandmother Barnwell. The intent of her visit was soon apparent. With well-mannered curiosity she had inquired as to whether Lorabeth's mother would be attending the wedding. She did so want to give the young couple a prenuptial party. But, until she knew when the date was to be, well—Mrs. Ashford had sighed and flung out her dainty hands in a hopeless gesture.

There had been an ominous silence from England since the invitation to her daughter's wedding was dispatched to Winnie. All Grandmother could do was to cover her own irritation at Winnie's failure to reply with her usual optimism. She spoke of a Christmas wedding or, "If not then, spring is always a beautiful time for a wedding, don't you agree?"

Mrs. Ashford had left in a rather unsettled frame of mind, and Lorabeth herself felt vaguely unhappy. Only Betsy maintained her determinedly cheerful attitude. Things had proceeded according to her plans thus far, and she had no reason to believe, despite Winnie's petulance, that everything would not work out well.

After Mrs. Ashford left, Lorabeth had climbed the stairs to her room. She did not wish to have to explain her strange mood, caused by the underlying reason for her unhappiness.

When alone, she had taken from its hiding

place the music box Cam gave her. Cradling it in her hands, she lifted its lid to listen to the melody. She seated herself on the window seat and, while the merry little tune played, she looked out at the bare trees against a blue-gray sky and watched a flock of birds in a rushing V streak across it. The music box ran down, and with a sigh, Lorabeth closed the top, a forlorn emptiness filling her heart.

Just then the door opened and Odelia peeked in, looking about. Seeing that Lorabeth was alone, she advanced into the room and handed her an envelope, whispering conspiratorially. "Mr. Cam lef' it fo' you, Miss Lorabeth. Say doan tell nobody. Jes' be sure yo' got it when yo' was by yo'sef. Say I was to gib yo' answer to young Micah, and he would carry it to Mr. Cam at de Raleigh Tavern. He waiting' dere 'til yo' send him word."

Lorabeth took the envelope with hands that shook and read it hastily.

Lorabeth, I have to see you. It is of utmost importance. Where can I meet you so we may talk privately? I beg you not to refuse.—C.

She knew the right thing, the sensible thing, would be to send Micah, his messenger boy, back to the Raleigh with the word IMPOSSIBLE scribbled across the bottom of his note. Still, Lorabeth hesitated.

What now could be "of utmost importance"? Hadn't they said all that could be said, only to part at an impasse? The only honorable solution was renunciation. What could possibly come of their seeing each other again—what, but more pain? Nothing had or could change their circumstances. Not even God Himself could alter the conditions of their birth.

But the thought of being with Cam for even a short time was so overwhelming that, in the next moment, she was scribbling a note under Cam's signature: "I have an appointment at 10 tomorrow morning at Mme. Luisa's."

It was done. Guiltily she refolded the note, placed it in its envelope and handed it back to Odelia. She was sure Cam would find a way to meet her there.

Now, in the light of this clear October morning, Lorabeth regretted her rash decision. She should have resisted her longing to see Cam. Nothing but further heartache could result. But it would be pointless to try to get another message to Cameron now.

As she dressed, Lorabeth was nearly sick with guilt. She hated dishonesty in any form, yet it seemed much of her life lately had been marked by deception. She dreaded to think what her grandmother, and especially Aunt Laura, would make of what she was doing this day.

Heavy-hearted, Lorabeth started out for her appointment at Madame Luisa's, accompanied by Odelia. She had one moment of stark terror when Aunt Laura considered coming along. Then an unexpected caller arrived, and she had to stay at home.

Though the shop was only a short walk from the Barnwell house, to Lorabeth it felt as if it were a thousand miles. With each step her conscience reproached her, even while her defiant heart rejoiced at the thought of even this stolen time with Cam.

Lorabeth could not imagine on what pretext Cameron had convinced Mme. Luisa's servant to let him wait in the small sitting room where she found him when she was ushered in. She was aware of little else but her own heart's frantic beat and the joy she felt at seeing his tall figure standing by the fireplace.

In a few long strides he was at her side, took both her hands in his and pressed them to his chest.

"I was afraid you might not come," he said, his eyes sweeping over her as if memorizing every detail of her appearance. "How lovely you are. I've starved for the sight of you."

She drew her hands from his firm clasp. "I shouldn't have. . . ." She shook her head in dismay at her own foolhardiness.

Cameron ignored her protest. "Listen, my darling," he began, rushing on. "There's still time. We have two choices open to us. The truth is the most direct way. Simply go to your grandmother, my parents, tell them we are in love and that we want to be married. Of course, they will offer all sorts of objections. Malinda's pride will be hurt, but little else. Her feelings for me are of the most shallow sort, and can be just as easily bestowed on some other willing man. Auntie B. may be upset after all her manuever-ings to 'ransom' you from your mother's arrange-ments, but only temporarily. I think she would be on our side. Blakely, poor lad—but all's fair in love and war. No matter, it is far better for two engagements to be broken than for four people to marry the wrong partners and live in misery for the rest of their days!"

Lorabeth was speechless before his logic.

When she did not reply Cameron, went on, "Of course, the other choice is much simpler. We just run off together—and right now!"

She stared at him numbly, twisting her hands in anguish. She was stunned by his recklessness, his daring, his lack of regard for consequences. It had been Cameron's sense of honor that had always been the bulwark against her own weakness. And even as everything inside her melted at the look of adoration in his eyes, the confidence in his voice, she began to shake her head. His dear face blurred through the tears that filled her eyes.

Lorabeth had always heard that a person sees his whole life pass before him in a moment of crisis. She saw now her mother's face in the dreadful scenes that followed Lorabeth's rejection of each suitor; next came Grandmother Barnwell's look of disappointment upon learning the truth; then, Aunt Laura's kind but reproachful one, followed by Blakely's cheerful countenance, his trusting eyes. One by one, all the people who would be shocked, hurt, disillusioned crushed by the rash act Cameron was suggesting, flashed into her mind. The momentary exhilaration she had felt while caught up in Cam's excitement, the thought of escaping from all the pressures that weighed upon her, were swept away.

She put out one hand to touch Cam's arm and slowly shook her head. "We can't. You *know* we can't."

There was a taut pause. Cameron straightened his shoulders and snapped out his next words crisply. "All right then. It's hopeless to try to convince you."

He turned, picked up his tricorne from the table and held it in front of him. His fingers kneading the brim were the only evidence of agitation. But his voice was clipped as he spoke.

"You know what you're doing, Lorabeth, don't you? You're condemning us to a life sentence of regret. I hope you won't have cause to wish you'd decided otherwise.

"All I've ever wanted since I first met you and realized I loved you, was to protect you, care for you, see that you had everything to guarantee your happiness. In spite of everything, Lorabeth, I want you to be happy!"

At last, they looked at each other gravely—a long look filled with despair. It was as if they both knew that this moment would have to see them through a lifetime apart.

Then Cameron turned and walked out the door.

CHAPTER 13

IT TOOK EVERY OUNCE of will power Lorabeth could summon to endure the seemingly endless fitting. While Madame Luisa and her assistants fluttered about her, fussing, plucking, nipping, pinning and unpinning the length of satin and lace that was being molded to her lithe figure, Lorabeth's fists were balled tightly. When she thought she could not bear another minute, Madame Luisa stood back, her head cocked to one side, and made the final adjustment, to the awed approval of her sewing ladies.

"*Voila! C'est magnifique!*" they chorused.

Only then was Lorabeth released to leave.

Followed by Odelia, Lorabeth hurried down the paths along the road home, her head bent against a chill wind on an afternoon that had turned suddenly dreary and gray.

The minute she stepped inside the front door, Lorabeth sensed an air of foreboding. The house, normally echoing the sounds of conversation and activity at this hour of the day, was unnaturally quiet.

She stood uncertainly in the hallway, listening. Taking a few steps, she paused at the door to the parlor and saw that her grandmother and Aunt Laura were seated there.

As she looked in, her grandmother beckoned to her.

"Come, Lorabeth. We've been waiting for you."

Lorabeth moved into the arch of the doorway, glancing anxiously from one to the other. There was something in their expressions that sent a ripple of apprehension along her spine. She entered the room slowly.

Grandmother gathered an envelope and several sheets of paper from her lap and held them out to Lorabeth. She took the pages and saw the closely written lies, penned in a familiar hand.

"This letter came from your mother by this morning's post. I think you should read it."

Lorabeth, her knees suddenly shaky, sat down on the edge of the sofa and began to read,

"My dear Mama, I take pen in hand with many misgivings and yet with the fervent hope that this letter will not reach you too late. As you can imagine, with Lorabeth's hasty departure, I have suffered the same distress you must have when, as a young and foolish girl, I ran off from my good home, leaving much havoc and heartache in my wake. Only a mother's heart could understand such suffering and I have certainly been punished for my own foolhardy behavior all these years. But we learn by our mistakes and so that is why I now hasten to reply to your letter just received concerning the impending marriage between Lorabeth and Blakely Ashford.

"Heaven knows I have tried to bring Lorabeth up with a sense of duty that she sadly seems to have abandoned, preferring to display only ingratitude for all I have done for her. A marriage such as I planned for her would have saved her from the disgrace that the information I am about to give you will cause her."

At this point Lorabeth looked up from the letter in bewilderment, glancing from her grandmother to Aunt Laura for some clue. Meeting only their impassive looks, she turned back to the letter, reading on.

"In *your* letter, dear mother, you implored me to forgive and forget Lorabeth's undisciplined and deceitful behavior in leaving England without my knowledge or permission. This I shall try to do. But to let you continue under the assumption that this engagement, which you are so happy about, is, and here I quote your very words, 'the celebration of a mutually appropriate, harmonious, prideful union of two of Virginia's finest families,' would be grossly unfair. Indeed, it would be a lie of the basest kind.

"To clarify what I am about to tell you, I must reveal shameful facts that I have long kept from you to protect your precious sensitivities, and to avoid hurting you and my dear, late father, even more than when I eloped with Phillipe Jouquet twenty years ago.

"To my sorrow, I learned too late what you

tried to teach me as we were all growing up under your strict, but loving care—that 'we reap what we sow.' This I have done in full measure as my following confession will bear out.

"We had barely landed on English soil when I discovered it would be impossible for Phillipe to fulfill his promise to me—which was to marry me immediately in the first Anglican church we could find. Impossible because, he then told me to my horrified disbelief and shock, he already had a wife in France. Nothing could ever adequately describe to you, dear mother, my complete collapse at this information. Young, alone, my virtue gone, unable to return to my homeland or to my family who, for all I knew had totally disowned me, what was I to do?

"Phillipe convinced me his wife would never consent to a divorce because of her religion. He swore to me that he had never loved her, that he had been coerced into the marriage, that the woman, several years his senior, had tricked him. He had come to America, he told me, to escape an insufferable situation. He swore he loved me, that even our unsanctified union was his only 'real marriage.' All this may sound as though I am trying to justify my original error. I am only saying that it remained wrong and, as it turned out, ended in further sorrow and disgrace.

"However, try to imagine my plight—barely eighteen, alone except for this man, without family or friends, adrift in a strange country, afraid to write my parents the truth. Finally I was forced to accept my lot. Phillipe secured a position as French teacher at a boarding school about twenty miles south of London. With the position came a small cottage, and there we lived as man and wife. How was I to guess that, a little over a year later, he would do to me the same thing he had done to the unfortunate woman in France. Yes, dear mother, Phillipe 'eloped' again—this time with the wealthiest young lady at the school.

"I suppose Phillipe assumed I was a wealthy young American heiress when he persuaded me to run away with him. I believe he felt that eventually I would be 'reconciled' with my family and at least receive a 'comfortable allowance.' I could never prevail upon myself to tell you the true state of my situation, so of course, no 'allowance' was forthcoming. Phillipe, to whom the luxuries of life meant so much, soon tired of living on a school teacher's income, and when he saw the chance to use his charm on another unsuspecting victim, he did so with no remorse.

"Again, my dear mother, can you imagine my distress. Still young, although now thoroughly disillusioned, I was once more left alone, penniless, and disgraced. It was only through the kindness of the Headmaster and his wife that I was not thrown upon the mercy of a heartless fate. They took me into their home as companion-helper to the wife, who was in a delicate condition. Sad to relate, this dear lady died in childbirth, leaving a motherless infant and a bereaved husband, himself without kith or kin.

"In this time of grief, I stayed to take care of the baby, remaining as a kind of housekeeper.

For the sake of appearances, after the year of mourning, we married. He had been offered a new position as Headmaster at another school, and I accompanied him there as his wife with 'our' baby daughter. As you may now have guessed, that baby was Lorabeth. When she was christened, poor Edgar was too stricken with the loss of his beloved wife, so I took care of all the arrangements, and it was I who chose her name—Laura Elizabeth.

"If you remember, I wrote you at the time of my marriage to Edgar Whitaker, telling you of Phillipe's 'death,' then waited an appropriate length of time before telling you of 'our' baby's birth. So actually Lorabeth is nearly a year older than you think.

"I know this will all come as a painful surprise, but I could not allow the real child of a humble English schoolmaster whose lineage is undistinguished, himself the son of a village vicar, to be passed off as a member of *our* family and be married to one of an equally prestigious Virginia family.

"I am sure you will appreciate learning the truth even after so long a time, and before you are yourself implicated in the fraudulent position of presenting Lorabeth to the Ashfords as your true granddaughter.

"Under these circumstances, you will, I am sure, send Lorabeth back to England at once to avoid any scandal following the quiet cancellation of her wedding plans there. I shall try, as I have done in the past, to do my best for her. To my great wonderment, especially after all the grief she has caused, Willie Fairchild is still willing to marry her.

"I want to get this letter to you by the next ship sailing to Virginia, so I shall now close, I remain as ever,

"Yr. affectionate daughter,

"Winnifred."

The pages of the letter fluttered to the floor from Lorabeth's numbed fingers.

"Poor Mama."

Lorabeth's unexpected words caused Betsy to give her a startled glance. This was not the reaction she might have expected after such staggering news.

"Now, I understand so much," Lorabeth continued so softly she might have been talking to herself. "No wonder she was frantic for me to make a good marriage. She knew what it was like to be alone with no one to depend upon, without family or fortune." All at once Lorabeth identified with the frightened girl left abandoned in a strange country, the girl who had grown up to be her sharp-tongued, complaining mother—*step*-mother, she quickly corrected herself mentally. Even that made it more understandable. Saddled with a stubborn, willful child who was not even her own. How difficult her life must have been, Lorabeth sympathized.

"I suppose that rascal Jouquet thought our eldest daughter would have a handsome dowry. And when he discovered that dowry would naturally fall to Noramary, who took Winnie's place as Duncan Montrose's bride, it must have come as quite a blow. Two wives and not a penny between them!" Grandmother said with some irony and a hint of satisfaction. Then matter-of-factly, she continued, "The task now is to break the news to the Ashfords that their son is not actually uniting with the Barnwell family. Not that it will make a mite of difference to Blakely nor to them either, if I'm right. Nonetheless, they must be told."

Lorabeth turned her wide eyes on Betsy, with an unspoken question she was not yet ready to frame.

But will it make a difference to you? Now that you know I'm not really your granddaughter? she pondered. *I don't belong here under your roof. I don't deserve all the kindnesses, the gracious provisions, the clothes, the affection, the full-hearted acceptance I have received from you! And now, the embarrassment of going to the family-conscious Ashfords, dragging out the almost-forgotten scandal of Winnie and its aftermath, now blighting the pristine plans for a wedding of social importance!* At the thought, tears welled up, stinging her eyes.

"I think I'll go upstairs to my room for a while, Grandmother," Lorabeth said, getting to her feet. Then at the use of the now familiar name, she stopped in confusion. She lifted her hands in a pitiful gesture. "I mean—what shall I call you now?"

"Oh, for pity's sake, my dear! *Grandmother,* what else? Wouldn't it be silly to start treating each other any differently now?" Betsy demanded.

Wordlessly Lorabeth turned and left the parlor.

156

CHAPTER 14

LORABETH HAD NOT EXPECTED TO SLEEP at all that night. Exhausted from weeping, however, she had drifted off, awakening some time in the night to find the room bright with moonlight.

Slowly she raised herself from the crumpled pillows and arose from the bed where she had flung herself, fully-clothed. She loosened her stays and undressed.

Donning a soft, woolen wrapper, she went to the window seat and looked out. The garden was beautiful, bathed in a luminous glow. Then, before her eyes, the moon suddenly disappeared behind a cloud, blackening the sky. Lorabeth shivered and turned away.

The fuzziness of her deep yet troubled slumber gradually cleared, and she was again confronted with the problem she could no longer avoid. Earlier, she had escaped to her room to sob out her heart after reading the terrible letter. But there was no escape from the truth.

She was not just a "poor relation," but a penniless stranger, with no real home—not even in England! The person she had believed all these years to be her mother was only a woman who, in the interest of expediency, had taken on her care. For the first time Lorabeth understood Winnie's lack of warmth, her indifference toward her. What a burden she must have been to that sadly harassed lady!

Now, of course, she must decide what to do. She could not go on as if everything were the same, that this startling information about her birth and her real ancestry were not known.

She certainly could not stay on here, imposing on the Barnwells' hospitality, expecting them to continue treating her as a member of the family.

Whatever was to be done must be done with the least amount of fuss, the least trouble for everyone. She felt a cold knot of misery twist inside her when she thought of Grandmother Barnwell and all the planning, the parties, the clothes that had been prepared in the belief that Lorabeth was her granddaughter. Perhaps the best way would be to slip away without painful partings, without any reproaches or false promises. Yes, that was the only thing left for her to do—to get out of the Barnwells' life as quickly as possible. There would be enough explaining to do even if she were not still here to be an embarrassment to them.

Somehow she must get back to England, Lorabeth decided. There she was sure to find a position as a governess or a teacher. She had mastered all the skills and accomplishments of a real lady and the experience of teaching when she was at Briarwood. She could then begin a new life where no one knew her or of her ill-fated sojourn in Virginia. She was certainly not going to impose further on Winnie—nor would she marry Willie Fairchild! From now on, she would make it on her own—as lonely and frightening a prospect as that might be.

But how was she to obtain money for her passage on a ship? And how was she to leave without anyone knowing? All these details must be worked out, and quickly, before anyone suspected. Speed was of utmost importance, for Lorabeth knew that Grandmother and Aunt Laura would never allow her to feel the impossibility of her position, nor make her feel uncomfortable in any way. In her fondness for them, she must spare them further distress.

Lorabeth paced restlessly—across the room, over to the bed, back to the window, then to the armoire, wringing her hands. As she did so, she absent-mindedly twisted her engagement ring. Suddenly she became aware of it. She took it off, examining it closely. Blakely had had the ring specially designed. It was a lovely sapphire, mounted with two small pansies fashioned of diamonds and emerald chips. It must be returned, of course, and Blakely released from their engagement immediately.

The ring! It must be very valuable. It was a large, flawless stone—a deep, rich, fiery blue— with small diamonds in the flowers. It must be worth a great deal of money, Lorabeth speculated.

She could pawn it to get money for her passage! The thought suddenly spun into her mind. She would do that at once. Then write Blakely a letter, enclosing the receipt so he could redeem the ring. By that time, if luck were with her, she would be on board a ship sailing out of Yorktown harbor and on the high seas. If she timed it just right, everything would work out satisfactorily for everyone.

Of course, Blakely would be hurt at first. But when she explained, she felt sure he would eventually understand that it was the only way. And he would find a more socially acceptable young lady to marry before too long. Yes, it was as if she had been given a way.

Her mind raced ahead. She would take nothing with her but the clothes she had brought here. She would pack her one small trunk and leave instructions that it be sent when she had a new address. At this point the bleakness of her situation momentarily overwhelmed her, and tears of self-pity flooded her eyes.

The thought of setting out alone again into the unknown was frightening. Here she had been loved, cherished, protected, had known the comfort of a loving family for the first time in her short life. It would be hard to forsake that sweet affection and once more be buffeted by the harsh coldness of the world.

Into her mind came the Scripture that had stood her in good stead nearly a year ago when she had first crossed the ocean to come to Virginia. It would sustain her now as she left. "I will never fail thee nor forsake thee." She had to trust God to guide her in the way she should go.

Sternly, Lorabeth dried her tears, told herself she must be brave. There was too much to do, too many things to take care of; she could not fall apart now.

In order to avoid detection, she would have to take someone into her confidence. But who? The only one she could think of was Odelia. But could the young maid keep a secret? And would she be willing to help?

She would have to take that chance, Lorabeth decided. Odelia was bright, clever, quick-witted, and she had become very fond of Lorabeth. But was her loyalty to the Barnwells stronger than any temporary promise Lorabeth might be able to elicit from her? She would have to see—to think of some way to pledge Odelia to secrecy, at least until she was safely away.

As it turned out, it was easier than Lorabeth had imagined it would be. The next morning when Odelia brought her her tray of chocolate and fresh rolls, Lorabeth fixed her with a solemn look.

"Odelia, you must give me your promise that you will do exactly what I say and tell no one anything. If you do so, I will give you a fine reward."

The girl's eyes grew very large and round and her dark face took on an expression of great seriousness. "Oh yes, missy, I shure will."

That day everything held a special poignancy for Lorabeth, knowing it would be the last in the home that had sheltered her.

It was easy enough to plead a headache as an excuse to retire early. As she went up the steps to her bedroom, she paused in the curve of the landing and looked back toward the parlor, where she could see Betsy chatting with Aunt Laura as she bent over her embroidery frame. There was a cheerful fire crackling in the fireplace, sending out a mellow glow on the polished furniture, and touching the brass candlesticks, the bronze and gold flowers in the blue pottery bowl.

A lump rose in Lorabeth's throat and she closed her eyes for a moment to memorize the scene. *When I am very old,* she thought, *with only my memories to comfort me, this picture will come to me.* It would be a precious reminder of a time she had first known the meaning of home.

CHAPTER 15

THE NEXT MORNING, AS LORABETH eased her way down the back stairs of the slumbering Barnwell household, she was almost overcome by her feeling of sorrow. She valiantly blinked back her tears and went out through the kitchen door Odelia had left unlocked, hurrying through the garden to the road.

A thin veil of frost covered the ground, and drifts of fallen leaves cluttered the path she took toward the Duke of Gloucester Street and the Raleigh Tavern, where she would catch the stage to Yorktown.

She felt a certain eerie similarity in this, not unlike the morning she had crept away from Briarwood School to board the ocean vessel for Virginia. She swallowed back the feeling of desolation and loneliness that threatened to engulf her. Again, the feeling of not belonging anywhere washed over her.

As the stagecoach rumbled through the Williamsburg streets heading out of town, Lorabeth leaned her aching head against the window, bidding a silent farewell to the pretty little town that had opened its heart to her. Her eyes blurred with tears as the coach jostled over the rutted country roads, passing pastures, stone walls and white farm houses set against dark, green pines. Virginia! How beautiful it was, she thought, remembering how this same wild beauty had frightened her a little when she first came. Would she ever see it again?

Lorabeth sighed deeply, settling into the corner of the coach, drawing her woolen cape closely about her. She was experiencing the depths of loneliness, almost as painful as when her father had died. But what she now felt was different. Never had she felt a loneliness of spirit so overwhelming nor so deep.

She burrowed her hands into her velvet muff, unconsciously touching the small leather pouch inside to reassure herself. It contained all the money she had in the world—money, that in all honesty, she could not call her own, unless the recipient of a gift was the rightful owner. But what if that gift implied a promise? Ah, but at this point, she could not afford to split hairs.

To some, she knew, a betrothal ring was the outward symbol of the sacred vows of marriage, although not yet consummated. All Lorabeth could hope was that kind, compassionate Blakely would understand when he read her letter of explanation.

Somewhere she had heard the saying, "Desperate times require desperate measures." Surely her position was desperate. And even if Blakely were broken-hearted for a time, he would certainly come to agree that what she had done was for the best.

It had all gone so much more easily than Lorabeth could have imagined. In a few hours Odelia would deliver her letters—the first, to Betsy; then, the one to Blakely, in which she had enclosed the redeemable ticket for the ring.

Lorabeth's cheeks burned, remembering the humiliating experience of pawning her engagement ring. She had tried to maintain a dignified hauteur as the hump-shouldered little man with the twisted smile held his jeweler's glass up and examined her beautiful ring for an interminable length of time.

Then he had fastened a curiously, malicious gaze upon Lorabeth and, with a deprecating cackle, asked, "And why would such a pretty young lady wish to part with this lovely ring? Obviously it is a token of some sentiment."

Lorabeth had drawn herself up haughtily and stared back at him so steadily that he was forced to look away and mumble a sum he was willing to pay.

"But, surely the ring is worth twice that!" she had exclaimed indignantly. Inwardly she was trembling and uncertain, but she was convinced this seedy character was offering her much less than its true value. She made a motion as if to take the ring back and leave, when he reluctantly named a price somewhat higher. The amount was still less than Lorabeth knew it must be worth, but his offer would cover her expenses until she was aboard ship, passage paid, and with a little to tide her over once she was back in England. So in the end she accepted it.

Remembering the scene, Lorabeth shuddered, sensing again the shame she felt at trading such a tender expression of devotion of bright hope and affection for mere cash.

Lorabeth steeled herself to weakening remorse, regrets. She knew it was fatal to look back. Looking back could be her undoing. She repeated her Scripture verse to stiffen her resolve. What she was doing was the best and bravest thing—the best for *everyone*. For Blakely as well, for he was too good and fine to have a wife who did not love him truly. She must believe she had taken the right course of action. If she began to question any part of her plan, she would falter.

When the stagecoach from Williamsburg finally rattled to a stop, its few passengers, cramped and cold from the long ride, got out and hurried up the steps of the Inn just on the outskirts of Yorktown. Inside, a fire blazed on the wide hearth in the front room. The men went straight to the public room to warm themselves with a tankard of hot rum, while Lorabeth remained in front of the fire, holding out her numbed hands to its comforting warmth.

She looked around, trying not to reveal the anxiety she was experiencing. Eyeing her curiously was a stout, motherly looking woman in a ruffled cap, homespun dress, and apron.

Lorabeth knew it was not often, nor customary, for a lady to travel unaccompanied by either a gentleman or a maid. She must speak to her at once, Lorabeth decided, before she became suspicious. Gathering all the poise at her command, she approached the woman who was standing behind the high desk in the partition between the front and public room.

"Good morning, madam. I should like to have a room for perhaps a day and a night, while I arrange passage on the next ship setting sail for England." Then Lorabeth lowered her voice significantly so as not to be overheard by curious ears, and told the woman in a confidential manner. "I am recently bereaved of family and seek only privacy and solitude while I await word of the ship's departure date. I will take my meals in my room, if that could be arranged."

A look of sympathy immediately crossed the kindly florid face as she listened to the words of the pale and lovely young lady. For a moment Lorabeth, reading her expression, felt a stab of guilt. However, in a way it was true. She *had* lost her family just as surely as in any sudden tragedy that might befall a person.

Lorabeth had lifted three large silver coins from her purse, and was holding them in her palm as she spoke. The glint of silver as they clinked together brought an instant response from the innkeeper's wife.

"Of course, m'lady," she replied, bobbing a little curtsy. "We have three nice rooms in the front upstairs for special guests. As it happens, one is just turned out and ready. Come along. I'll show you." She took a ring of keys from her pocket and came out from around her slanted wood desk. "Have you any luggage, m'lady?"

"Only one small box—if you would be kind enough to have the coachman bring it in."

As she followed the woman up the narrow stairway to the second floor, Lorabeth breathed a prayer of gratitude for the ease of her venture thus far. The woman opened the door into a room, then stepped back for Lorabeth to proceed her.

The room was clean and plain, with a wide pine poster bed, a little round table, two chairs and a fireplace. There were two small windows set in dormers and the walls were of white plaster. Lorabeth stood in the middle, turning slowly around, as if inspecting it. In reality, she was mentally contrasting it with the pretty room at the Barnwells that had been hers, as well as the large, luxurious guest bedroom at Montclair. The thought of Montclair instantly brought the image of Cameron to her mind. What would he think or say when he learned she was gone?

"Will this do then, m'lady?" the woman asked, bringing Lorabeth slowly back from her painful memories.

It was impersonal, just a way-station after all, Lorabeth thought, and she nodded.

"It will do nicely, thank you. And how can I find a ship sailing within a day or two, and the name of the ship's master with whom to book passage?"

"My Tom will take care of it for you. I'll speak to him right away. And would you like tea brought up?"

"Yes, thank you, that would be lovely."

Suddenly Lorabeth felt exhausted, worn out from the last few days, the stress of the past few hours during her secret preparations and clandestine departure. Unwanted tears sprang into her eyes at the woman's kindness. She tried to turn away so as to avoid the sharp-eyed innkeeper's wife. But she was not quick enough.

The woman lingered, then said in a softer voice, "Would you be wantin' anything else then?"

"No, thank you. Just the tea," Lorabeth replied in a muffled voice.

"Right away, m'lady. Rest yourself now. I'll bring you word as soon as we can find out about your ship and passage." She went to the door then with her hand on its latch, she spoke again in her rough country brogue. "My name is Sara Hutchins, m'lady. If there's anything at all I can do, you've only to ask." With that she was gone.

Lorabeth realized that somehow she had touched the motherly heart of the woman and in a way she was grateful. But she must be careful, she warned herself. It would not be wise to attract any undue attention to herself, even if it was sympathetic.

All that long day, as Lorabeth waited for word of whether she could get passage on a ship leaving Yorktown soon, she was filled with an aching loneliness.

This loneliness was worse than any she had ever experienced. Often, when she had been away at Briarwood, she had known times of vague, empty longings—not exactly for her

169

mother nor for the shabby little house they called home. Nor was it the same kind of pain she knew after her father died and she realized she would no longer be able to see or talk to him.

This was something deeper, stronger, more painful. This was an emotion Lorabeth knew would be with her for the rest of her life. It was the longing for something she would never possess—something she had only glimpsed and known for a moment of time—the fiery sweetness of a lover's embrace, the memory of a kiss that would burn her lips forever, the void in her heart that would never be filled. It was Cameron Montrose she was lonely for, whom she would go on missing and from whom she could never really run away.

Somehow the afternoon passed. It was a gray, overcast day with occasional flurries of drifting snow. Lorabeth had heard that Virginia winters were fairly short but severe. She also knew a moment of apprehension, recalling the seamen's talk on her first trip across the Atlantic last spring, that winter crossings were treacherous.

Desperately Lorabeth prayed that there would be no problem booking passage, that she could go quickly from this Inn, board the ship, and set sail. She wanted to be on her way before there was any chance of anyone tracing her here.

She had given Odelia strict orders to report that she had a sick headache and wished to remain undisturbed all day. But Lorabeth could not be sure that Aunt Laura, in her concern, might not tiptoe into the bedroom to check on her and find the bundled pillows under the coverlet. She had told Odelia not to deliver her letters until a full twenty-four hours had passed. She did not want to risk discovery of her absence until she had a day's head start. Her hope was that, upon reading her reasons for leaving in this manner, they would all understand and accept her decision and would not attempt to bring her back.

The day darkened rapidly, and a knock at her door toward early evening brought a rosy-cheeked serving maid with a tray of supper. Lorabeth ate hungrily of the vegetable stew with chunks of meat, thick slices of rough-textured bread, sweet butter and a pot of tea. The meal did not compare with the delicacies of the Barnwells' table or the elaborate meals served at Montclair. But it was hearty and satisfying, and afterwards she undressed and climbed into the high bed.

Lorabeth did not go right to sleep in the strange surroundings, but lay wakefully wondering what was ahead of her. She could hear the noise, the laughter and voices floating up to her from the tap room of the Tavern part of the Inn. Since this room was on the front of the house, there was a continuous sound of horses hooves outside as men came to spend the evening drinking and talking with neighbors—swapping news, gossip and politics. In spite of the noise, Lorabeth gradually grew drowsy. Worn out by the travel, the waiting, and the stress of anxiety, she fell asleep.

Lorabeth awoke, shivering and cold. During the night the small fire had gone out and the quilt

171

had slipped off the bed and in the chill of the unheated room, she shuddered. Reaching for her cloak, she drew it around her and huddled back under the quilt. The gray light of early morning sifted through the small windows and Lorabeth was helpless to restrain the tears that slid down her cheeks. Somehow her situation had never seemed quite so bleak, her future quite so frightening or futile.

She dressed hurriedly, scolding herself for being weak, fighting the tears that came so easily. It was the waiting that was the hardest, she reminded herself firmly. Once you had made up your mind about something, it was best if you could go on and be done with it. Not that she could have arranged anything sooner.

Almost as if in answer to her impatient thoughts, there was a knock at the door. This time it was Mrs. Hutchins herself, bearing a tray of tea and cornbread and bringing good news.

"Tom sent a messenger into Yorktown early, m'lady, and we should have the answer back before evening. Last night he heard in the tavern that the 'Mary Deane,' a British ship, was loading the last of its cargo yesterday and should be setting sail by tomorrow at the latest. The passenger list was not full, so he understood, and you should be in good luck, if it's in a hurry you are." She paused as if to give Lorabeth an opportunity to tell the rest of her sad story.

But Lorabeth, although she appreciated the woman's good-hearted sympathy, knew the less said, the less chance of revealing her true situation. She thanked Mrs. Hutchins for the information, asking the good woman to let her know as soon as word came.

Now with the final arrangements set in motion Lorabeth was as restless as a caged wild thing. She moved uneasily around the room, stopping every so often to peer out one of the windows, as if by so doing she could hasten the message she was waiting to hear. Outside, a raw wind, was blowing, whipping the bare tree branches. The few people she saw down below, were holding on to their tricornes, wrapping their cloaks about them as they strained against the strength of the wind.

She had seen a Virginia spring in all its shimmering beauty; summer, with its lush fullness, its warm dusky evenings; and the glory of its brilliant fall. But she had never known a Virginia winter, she thought, and now would never know one. By tomorrow she would be on board ship, moving out of the harbor. When winter came, she would be on the high seas.

Late in the afternoon in began to rain. The endless day was spent in alternating desperate prayer, and the reading of spirit-soothing Psalms. Even then, Lorabeth found herself pacing the length of the small room, unconsciously wringing her hands, her stomach knotted in anxiety.

At length she stretched out on the bed, allowing herself for the first time that day to imagine what was going on in the Barnwell household. By now they had discovered she was gone. She hoped poor Odelia was not being punished for her participation in the departure. She prayed they, Grandmother and Aunt Laura, would not think her an ungrateful wretch but understand that she had wanted to leave with as little distress to everyone as possible.

Her thoughts were jolted back to the present by a rap at the door. She bolted up as the round, rosy face of the little maid peered around the door's edge. "'Scuse me, m'lady, but Mistress says to tell you there's a gentleman to see you in the keepin' room and would you please come down."

The man from the ship's captain! Lorabeth hopped off the bed, smoothing her hair quickly, adjusting her bodice and skirt. Then she took her leather pouch of money, slipped it into her inner pocket and hurried out the door.

Holding her wide skirts, she ran lightly down the narrow stairway, wondering how much of her precious money would have to be paid out for the passage. The messenger and the Innkeeper would also be expecting their share.

Downstairs in the front room, Mrs. Hutchins looked up from her tall desk where she was working on a ledger, and, with the hand holding the quill, she pointed to a door at the far end of the room.

"He's waiting in there, m'lady."

"Thank you," Lorabeth said a little breathlessly and went forward to the closed door.

The room was in shadows. The autumn darkness had come early and the candles had not yet been lighted. Lorabeth saw the cloaked figure of a tall man, his back to the door. Standing in front of the fireplace, he blocked the fire's light.

She cleared her throat and began. "Sir, I

understand you bring word of the availability of passage on the 'Mary Deane' and I—"

But he neither answered nor did she ever finish her sentence.

The man turned around and, in a startled flash of recognition, Lorabeth gave a muted cry. Her head spun dizzily and her knees buckled and she would have surely collapsed had she not been caught up in two strong arms and lifted into an ardent embrace.

"Oh, my darling," the voice whispered against her cheek. Familiar lips kissed her temple.

"Cameron! Oh, Cam, how did you know? How did you find me?" Lorabeth found her voice at last and it was a moan of anguish, and joy.

He held her tighter still. She could feel his strength flowing into her as he drew her more closely to him.

"Did you really think I would let you go?"

CHAPTER 16

THEY KISSED AGAIN WITH ALL the intensity that separation and reunion engendered. They said all the little loving, inconsequential things reunited lovers say as they clung desperately to each other.

At last Cameron wiped away Lorabeth's tears and kissed her again.

She leaned against him weakly, murmuring, "Oh, Cam, now it will be all the harder to part!"

"You're wrong, Lorabeth," he said tenderly. "We won't be parting. I'll never let you go—not now, not ever."

"But, Cam—how can that be?"

"Listen, my darling. I'll tell you how it's going to be."

Lorabeth listened, wide-eyed, as Cameron told her how Blakely had ridden out to Montclair as soon as he had received her letter breaking their engagement and enclosing the pawn ticket. Then, as kindly as he could, Cameron had told Blakely of his own love for Lorabeth, and his certainty that she loved him in return. He then told his friend that he intended to go after Lorabeth and somehow work out their problems so that they could marry.

"Blakely Ashford is a real man and a gentleman as well," Cameron told Lorabeth with genuine admiration. "I only hope I would have taken such a blow in the same honorable way had I been in his boots." Cameron shook his head. "If I've learned anything from all this, it's how to pray! I had to be brought to my knees, I suppose, to the point of accepting that I was going to lose you—if *that* was God's will for our lives. If your marrying Blakely *was* the right thing. I learned it wasn't right to 'bargain' with God nor to make your own personal happiness override honor. Thank God, I did not succumb to the temptation simply to kidnap you and impose my own desire above everything else."

Cameron stopped and smiled wryly. "I learned the hard way God's ways are not our ways, but that He 'works in mysterious ways' to bring about his purposes. Well, to go on with my story, I rode into Williamsburg and found the Barnwell household in a fine state of upheaval at their discovery of your disappearance.

"Furthermore, additional information concerning you has come to light, and we have Aunt Laura to thank for it," Cameron spoke in a decidedly firm tone of voice.

"What no one seemed to comprehend at first after receiving Aunt Winnie's letter was that if you are not Aunt B.'s real granddaughter, and no real kin to the Barnwells, then *we*—you and I—are *not* cousins!"

At this point Cameron leaned forward and kissed the lips Lorabeth had parted in astonishment, as she realized that neither had *she* fully comprehended that aspect of the shocking news of her parentage. Wordless, she listened as Cameron continued.

"Besides that bit of *very important* information, there is more. It seems, dear Lorabeth, that we are not even remotely related, as it turns out. My family has always accepted that my mother, Noramary Marsh's mother was a *half*-sister to William Barnwell, Winnie and Aunt Laura's father. Well, the truth of the matter, is they were *step*-brother and sister. William's father married a young widow with a daughter who was Noramary's mother. So there are actually no blood ties at all!" he finished with an air of triumph as though he were personally responsible for this amazing turn of events. "So, after all this, my darling, since there are no so-called 'impediments,' we can be married with the blessings of family and in the church as soon as the banns are announced."

Lorabeth simply stared at Cameron. She could find no words to express what she was feeling.

Cameron clasping both her small hands in his, threw back his head and laughed uproariously.

"You don't have to say anything. Just kiss me again."

Lorabeth happily obliged.

After a bit she opened her eyes slowly and in

their depths lurked a mischievous twinkle as she said lightly, "So, then, 'all's well that ends well,' is it?"

Cameron pretended to frown, then said ponderously, "Ah, 'so wise, so young, they say—'"

Lorabeth interrupted. "Richard III, Act 3."

Cameron struck his forehead in mock despair. "This woman I love is as bright as she is beautiful."

Lorabeth looked askance. "I don't know that one."

"I just made it up," Cameron grinned.

"It sounds as if it might be from 'The Taming of the Shrew,'" Lorabeth said thoughtfully.

"Then 'Kiss me, Kate'!" Cameron ordered.

This time Lorabeth offered no resistance. As Cameron's soft, firm mouth found hers again, she relinquished herself to the wild, sweet, soaring sensation. She had never imagined life could hold such bliss.

A MONTH LATER

AUNT LAURA ADJUSTED THE FRAGILE LACE VEIL over Lorabeth's shining hair, tucking pearl-headed pins into her piled up curls to hold it in place. Then she stepped back to survey her handiwork.

"You are simply lovely," she sighed to Lorabeth's reflection in the mirror.

Lorabeth, her dark eyes sparkling with excitement, smiled happily and, glancing over her shoulder, said to her aunt, "Thank you, Aunt Laura. My hands are shaking so, I could never have managed it myself."

"Stand up, Lorabeth, so we can see if your dress hangs properly," Aunt Laura directed, trying to regard the slim young bride critically while all the time seeing her through the misty haze of tears. Although they were happy tears, still she did not want to spoil this day for Lorabeth with any untoward show of sentiment. It was not always that such a love story ended

181

this happily, she thought remembering her own lost love.

Lorabeth stood, whirled around twice, her wide hoops lifting prettily. Her gown of creamy velvet, its deep, square-cut neckline edged with lace, tiny bows of satin extended the length of the fitted bodice to the point where the velvet skirt draped back to show an underskirt of embroidered damask. Her feet were shod in pointed white satin slippers with roses fashioned of silk on the toes.

From downstairs they could hear the sound of the quartet of musicians tuning their instruments, and, outside, the wheels of carriages on the crushed shell drive as the guests of both the Montrose and Barnwell families arrived for Lorabeth's wedding to the oldest son and heir of Montclair.

"It's almost time," Aunt Laura said in a hushed voice.

"My bouquet?" asked Lorabeth, her heart beginning a staccato beat. She had never dreamed the day would come when she would become a bride at Montclair.

"It's a very special one with special meaning. I arranged it myself," Aunt Laura told her. "Of course, I had the run of Noramary's greenhouse." she rustled to the other side of the room where she busied herself for a minute or so, then returned to hand Lorabeth a froth of starched lace with knotted satin streamers. Nestled within was a bunch of fragrant white lilies-of-the-valley, a single perfect white rose in its center.

"The lilies mean 'the return of happiness,' the rose 'single-hearted devotion'," she smiled.

For a moment Lorabeth's eyes misted. Indeed, her happiness had returned, a hundred-fold. The impossible had happened, the dream she had hardly dared to dream had come true.

Escorted by her aunt, Lorabeth went out to the upper hall, stood at the balcony encircling the downstairs entrance hall, and at the top of the stairs she paused and looked down.

There stood Cameron, handsome in a saffron velvet coat, buff-colored breeches, ruffled lace jabot and satin waistcoat, his rich, brown hair smoothed back from his brow, his face upturned toward the staircase.

As Lorabeth descended toward her bridegroom he looked up at her. All devotion, all promise, all love shone in his eager eyes. Everything she had ever hoped for in life was about to become a reality.

The music played softly in the background as, step by measured step, Lorabeth Whitaker approached him. Three steps from the bottom, he went up to meet her, holding out his hand. She put her small one in his and the look that passed between them confirmed all the vows they were about to make.